More Stories We Tell

ALSO BY WENDY MARTIN

An American Triptych:
The Lives and Work of Anne Bradstreet,
Emily Dickinson, and Adrienne Rich (1984)

ALSO EDITED BY WENDY MARTIN

The Cambridge Companion to Emily Dickinson (2000)

The Beacon Book of Essays
by Contemporary American Women (1997)

Colonial American Travel Narratives (1994)

We Are the Stories We Tell:
Best Short Fiction by North American Women Writers
Since 1945 (1990)

New Essays on "The Awakening" (1988)

The American Sisterhood:
Feminist Writing from Colonial Times
to the Present (1972)

More Stories We Tell

THE BEST CONTEMPORARY SHORT STORIES BY NORTH AMERICAN WOMEN

Edited by Wendy Martin

PANTHEON BOOKS
NEW YORK

Owing to limitations of space, all acknowledgments for
permission to reprint previously published material may
be found on the pages following author biographies.

Library of Congress Cataloging-in-Publication Data
More stories we tell : the best contemporary short stories
by North American women / edited by Wendy Martin.
p. cm.
ISBN 0-375-71450-2
1. Short stories, American—Women authors. 2. United
States—Social life and customs—Fiction. 3. Canada—Social
life and customs—Fiction. 4. Short stories, Canadian—
Women authors. 5. Women—United States—Fiction.
6. Women—Canada—Fiction. I. Martin, Wendy, 1940–

PS647.W6M67 2004

813'.01089287—dc22   2003063208

www.pantheonbooks.com

Printed in the United States of America

First Edition

2 4 6 8 9 7 5

To Elaine Showalter,
whose friendship for more than forty years has brought
inspiration as well as joy to my life.

As always, to my husband, Jed Harris,
and to my daughter, Laurel Martin-Harris,
for making it possible for me to have both love and work in
the world. Their dedication to our shared vision of family
and professional life is truly
courageous.

Contents

ᔓ

Acknowledgments

VERY SPECIAL THANKS to Jan Gravlin Roselle for her immense help in the selection of these stories; to Aija Simpson, Danielle Hinrichs, and Bonnie Millhollin-Bane for their many contributions ranging from selection of stories, to headnotes, to permissions.

Much appreciation to Tom Schmidt for reading an early version of this collection and to Beverly Gross for reading the penultimate and final versions.

Thanks to the many people who suggested stories for consideration; the following is a very partial list indeed: Lisa Colletta, Marilyn Fabe, Susan Fox, Lynn Hunt, Claire Kahane, Mardi Louisell, Gayle Greene, Victoria Nelson, Judith Richardson, Margret Schaefer, Madeleon Sprengnether, Frances Starn, Donald Stone, Sharon Traweek, and Brenda Webster.

Much gratitude, also, to members of the UC Berkeley Psychobiography group for their careful consideration of the issues and concerns that I explore in my introduction. I am indebted, as well, to my students in graduate seminars in the short story at Claremont Graduate University who, with me, patiently read through many hundreds of stories in an effort to find the ones that most fully express the complexity of contemporary women's experience.

Finally, I would like to thank Altie Karper and Ilana Kurshan, my editors at Pantheon, for their expert judgment, sustaining support, and remarkable patience.

Editor's Introduction

WHEN *We Are the Stories We Tell* was published in 1990, American women writers had emphatically come into their own. Writing in a wide range of voices, they expressed the complexities and challenges of living in the second half of the twentieth century, an age of rapid change in which the psychological, cultural, and economic expectations and possibilities for women were in extraordinary flux. Building on the extremely positive response to *We Are the Stories We Tell,* this new collection seeks to provide representative narratives that are a pleasure to read and that portray women's experiences in the final decades of the twentieth century and the beginning of the twenty-first.

Although today we take for granted that women writers command a large audience, it was not until after World War II that women from a wide range of backgrounds successfully entered the literary marketplace. The rapid urbanization of the postwar period as well as the dramatic increase in educational and employment opportunities created greater visibility for women in public life than ever before. In spite of a return to domesticity and the "feminine mystique" in the 1950s, there was a growing concern for disenfranchised groups and an increased sensitivity to hierarchical power relationships throughout the 1960s and 1970s. A heightened awareness of the social construction of gender as well as class and race, along with the invention of birth control, set the stage for new lives for women.

In addition to the impressive increase in women's educational and employment opportunities, the closing decades of the twentieth century have been marked by significant changes in family structure as well as shifting expectations about the female life cycle: More women today marry later, have fewer children, and work outside the home. Half of all first marriages now end in divorce, and the percentage of households headed by women has risen correspondingly, as has the number of single women without families. With these developments come increased autonomy and freedom of choice, along with increased responsibility. And these shifts in the lives of women have meant shifts in the literature they write as well.

The short story is the genre that perhaps registers most readily and rapidly the political and personal changes in women's lives from childhood and adolescence to adulthood, from menstruation, celibacy, sexual intimacy, pregnancy, miscarriage, abortion, childbirth, and motherhood to menopause, aging, and finally death. Its compressed form captures the kaleidoscopic richness and variety of contemporary lives in flux, revealing the pressure points in our culture. Certainly, the number of stories about divorce, about the rewards and difficulties of raising children alone or in blended families, and about episodic relationships has increased dramatically. In this volume, we see a range of women's responses to these challenges in the stories of Amy Hempel, Gish Jen, and Jamaica Kincaid, among others.

Cultural diversity has continued to be an important force in women's fiction at the turn of the twenty-first century. As with the previous collection, the stories in this volume are written by women from African, Hispanic, Asian, Native American, Jewish, and European traditions. These narratives delineate the often complex contours of women's experience, illuminating what has been occluded as well as excluded. They give meaning to the observation that the personal is political, making clear the need for continuing struggle and risk-taking as women reshape their lives.

Many writers on the margins, such as multicultural and lesbian women, challenge traditional narratives that focus on romantic love, the nuclear family, and lifelong monogamous marriage. Perhaps because these writers never had expectations or illusions of control, choice, or privilege, they seem to have summoned up an energy that is life-affirming; for them, necessity is often the mother of invention, giving rise to imaginative and engaging stories told in highly expressive and vigorous language. In the first story in this collection, "The Lesson," Toni Cade Bambara conveys this sense of positive determination when her spunky protagonist, Sylvia, declares, "Ain't nobody gonna beat me at nothin." A similar spirit can also be found in the stories of Sandra Cisneros, Louise Erdrich, Jhumpa Lahiri, ZZ Packer, and Grace Paley, which introduce new voices, new narratives, and new possibilities for interpreting experience.

Love in all of its aspects continues to figure prominently in women's writing, although many of the writers here challenge accepted romantic ideals. In this volume, Amy Bloom and Ellen Gilchrist create portraits of domesticity that offer a bulwark against life's vicissitudes, while Mary Gaitskill and Stephanie Vaughn expose the fissures and rifts of family life, including domestic violence.

Disappointment, disillusionment, and dependency, tentatively explored in *We Are the Stories We Tell,* have become major concerns in recent decades. Many writers in *More Stories We Tell* deeply question traditional ideals including a happy marriage and family life; others mourn the loss of economic and emotional support on which they depended. Female protagonists in this elegiac fiction are sometimes mired in relationships with men who are portrayed as careless and callow, and these negative narratives are often filled with loss and anger instead of confidence and hope.

Some of these stories portray extramarital affairs that parody problematic marriages by playing out the tension between dependence and autonomy against a backdrop of illicit eroticism. Ann Beattie's "The Burning House" provides an excellent example of an affair that mirrors the dissatisfaction and disillusionment with bourgeois marriage; Margaret Atwood's "Hairball" savagely attacks the smug conventions of marital propriety; and Andrea Lee's "The Birthday Present" offers an imaginative, if cynical, solution to marital infidelity. Other stories reflect the growing realization among contemporary women that men cannot save them; men are no less vulnerable, in spite of our cultural expectation that masculinity is autonomous and unflinching. The women in these stories must save themselves.

Women are increasingly learning to find meaning in their professional and public lives. Although women have always worked, only in recent decades has their work outside the home been valued. Since 1970, women have entered the public sphere in huge numbers, so much so that currently more than half of all married women with children have paying jobs. Today, most women expect to be part of the workforce. This participation in the wider world has led to increased financial power, greater self-esteem, and broader social engagement. The stories by Andrea Barrett and Lorrie Moore delineate the complex interactions between work and love as well as celebrate these new opportunities for women to take their place in public life.

As this extraordinary social flux continues to reshape American society, we can look forward to deeper explorations of new possibilities. We will see more stories about love that go beyond sentimental prescriptions; more stories in which people are partners in various undertakings rather than lifelong mates for all aspects of life; more stories celebrating love in all its variety—between mothers and children, siblings, lovers, and friends. We will also see more stories about nonromantic friendship between women and men; more stories about friendship as well as erotic love between women; more stories that value reciprocity, mutual enjoyment, humor, cooperation, and complementarity. Finally, we will see more stories about women at work, work that is challenging and deeply satisfying.

Writers of fiction write from experience, capturing life as it is actually lived in a given historical moment. Think of these stories as wrestling with the cultural restraints and social prohibitions that have been with us, sometimes for centuries—restraints and prohibitions that, however frustrating, are giving way to greater personal freedom and a broader range of choices. These stories mirror this transformation.

More
Stories
We Tell

Toni Cade Bambara

～

The Lesson

BACK IN THE DAYS when everyone was old and stupid or young and foolish and me and Sugar were the only ones just right, this lady moved on our block with nappy hair and proper speech and no makeup. And quite naturally we laughed at her, laughed the way we did at the junk man who went about his business like he was some big-time president and his sorry-ass horse his secretary. And we kinda hated her, too, hated the way we did the winos who cluttered up our parks and pissed on our handball walls and stank up our hallways and stairs so you couldn't halfway play hide-and-seek without a goddamn gas mask. Miss Moore was her name. The only woman on the block with no first name. And she was black as hell, cept for her feet, which were fish-white and spooky. And she was always planning these boring-ass things for us to do, us being my cousin, mostly, who lived on the block cause we all moved North the same time and to the same apartment then spread out gradual to breathe. And our parents would yank our heads into some kinda shape and crisp up our clothes so we'd be presentable for travel with Miss Moore, who always looked like she was going to church, though she never did. Which is just one of the things the grown-ups talked about when they talked behind her back like a dog. But when she came calling with some sachet she'd sewed up or some gingerbread she'd made or some book, why then they'd all be too embarrassed to turn her down and we'd get handed over all spruced up. She'd been to college and said it was only right that she should take responsibility for the young ones' education, and she not even related by marriage or blood. So they'd go for it. Specially Aunt Gretchen. She was the main gofer in the family. You got some ole dumb shit foolishness you want somebody to go for, you send for Aunt Gretchen. She been screwed into the go-along for so long, it's a blood-deep natural thing with her. Which is how she got saddled with me and Sugar and Junior in the first place while our mothers were in a la-de-da apartment up the block having a good ole time.

So this one day Miss Moore rounds us all up at the mailbox and it's purdee hot and she's knockin herself out about arithmetic. And school suppose to let up in summer I heard, but she don't never let up. And the starch in my pinafore scratching the shit outta me and I'm really hating this nappy-head bitch and her goddamn college degree. I'd much rather go to the pool or to the show where it's cool. So me and Sugar leaning on the mailbox being surly, which is a Miss Moore word. And Flyboy checking out what everybody brought for lunch. And Fat Butt already wasting his peanut-butter-and-jelly sandwich like the pig he is. And Junebug punchin on Q.T.'s arm for potato chips. And Rosie Giraffe shifting from one hip to the other waiting for somebody to step on her foot or ask her if she from Georgia so she can kick ass, preferably Mercedes'. And Miss Moore asking us do we know what money is, like we a bunch of retards. I mean real money, she say, like it's only poker chips or monopoly papers we lay on the grocer. So right away I'm tired of this and say so. And would much rather snatch Sugar and go to the Sunset and terrorize the West Indian kids and take their hair ribbons and their money too. And Miss Moore files that re-mark away for next week's lesson on brotherhood, I can tell. And finally I say we oughta get to the subway cause it's cooler and be-side we might meet some cute boys. Sugar done swiped her mama's lipstick, so we ready.

So we heading down the street and she's boring us silly about what things cost and what our parents make and how much goes for rent and how money ain't divided up right in this country. And then she gets to the part about we all poor and live in the slums, which I don't feature. And I'm ready to speak on that, but she steps out in the street and hails two cabs just like that. Then she hustles half the crew in with her and hands me a five-dollar bill and tells me to calculate 10 percent tip for the driver. And we're off. Me and Sugar and Junebug and Flyboy hangin out the window and hollering to everybody, putting lipstick on each other cause Flyboy a faggot anyway, and making farts with our sweaty armpits. But I'm mostly trying to figure how to spend this money. But they all fascinated with the meter ticking and Junebug starts laying bets as to how much it'll read when Flyboy can't hold his breath no more. Then Sugar lays bets as to how much it'll be when we get there. So I'm stuck. Don't nobody want to go for my plan, which is to jump out at the next light and run off to the first bar-b-que we can find. Then the driver tells us to get the hell out cause we there already. And the meter reads eighty-five cents. And I'm starting to figure out the tip and Sugar say give him a dime. And I decide he don't need it bad as I do, so later for him. But then he tries to take off with Junebug foot still in the door so we talk about his mama something ferocious. Then we check out that we on Fifth Avenue and everybody dressed up in stockings. One lady in a fur coat, hot as it is. White folks crazy.

"This is the place," Miss Moore say, presenting it to us in the voice she uses at the museum. "Let's look in the windows before we go in."

"Can we steal?" Sugar asks very serious like she's getting the ground rules squared away before she plays. "I beg your pardon," say Miss Moore, and we fall out. So she leads us around the windows of the toy store and me and Sugar screamin, "This is mine, that's mine, I gotta have that, that was made for me, I was born for that," till Big Butt drowns us out.

"Hey, I'm goin to buy that there."

"That there? You don't even know what it is, stupid."

"I do so," he say punchin on Rosie Giraffe. "It's a microscope."

"Whatcha gonna do with a microscope, fool?"

"Look at things."

"Like what, Ronald?" ask Miss Moore. And Big Butt ain't got the first notion. So here go Miss Moore gabbing about the thousands of bacteria in a drop of water and the somethinorother in a speck of blood and the million and one living things in the air around us is invisible to the naked eye. And what she say that for? Junebug go to town on that "naked" and we rolling. Then Miss Moore ask what it cost. So we all jam into the window smudgin it up and the price tag say $300. So then she ask how long'd take for Big Butt and Junebug to save up their allowances. "Too long," I said. "Yeh," adds Sugar, "outgrown it by that time." And Miss Moore say no, you never outgrow learning instruments. "Why, even medical students and interns and," blah, blah, blah. And we ready to choke Big Butt for bringing it up in the first damn place.

"This here costs four hundred eighty dollars," say Rosie Giraffe. So we pile up all over her to see what she pointin out. My eyes tell me it's a chunk of glass cracked with something heavy and different-color inks dripped into the splits, then the whole thing put into a oven or something. But for $480 it don't make sense.

"That's a paperweight made of semi-precious stones fused together under tremendous pressure," she explains slowly, with her hands doing the mining and all the factory work.

"So what's a paperweight?" asks Rosie Giraffe.

"To weigh paper with, dumbbell," say Flyboy, the wise man from the East.

"Not exactly," say Miss Moore, which is what she say when you warm or way off too. "It's to weigh paper down so it won't scatter and make your desk untidy." So right away me and Sugar curtsy to each other and then to Mercedes who is more the tidy type.

"We don't keep paper on top of the desk in my class," say Junebug, figuring Miss Moore crazy or lyin one.

"At home, then," she say. "Don't you have a calendar and a pencil case and a blotter and a letter-opener on your desk at home where you do your homework?" And she know damn well what our homes look like cause she nosys around in them every chance she gets.

"I don't even have a desk," say Junebug. "Do we?"

"No. And I don't get no homework neither," say Big Butt.

"And I don't even have a home," say Flyboy like he do at school to keep the white folks off his back and sorry for him. Send this poor kid to camp posters, is his specialty.

"I do," say Mercedes. "I have a box of stationery on my desk and a picture of my cat. My godmother bought the stationery and the desk. There's a big rose on each sheet and the envelopes smell like roses."

"Who wants to know about your smelly-ass stationery," say Rosie Giraffe fore I can get my two cents in.

"It's important to have a work area all your own so that . . ."

"Will you look at this sailboat, please," say Flyboy, cuttin her off and pointin to the thing like it was his. So once again we tumble all over each other to gaze at this magnificent thing in the toy store which is just big enough to maybe sail two kittens across the pond if you strap them to the posts tight. We all start reciting the price tag like we in assembly. "Handcrafted sailboat of fiberglass at one thousand one hundred ninety-five dollars."

"Unbelievable," I hear myself say and am really stunned. I read it again for myself just in case the group recitation put me in a trance. Same thing. For some reason this pisses me off. We look at Miss Moore and she lookin at us, waiting for I dunno what.

Who'd pay all that when you can buy a sailboat set for a quarter at Pop's, a tube of glue for a dime, and a ball of string for eight cents? "It must have a motor and a whole lot else besides," I say. "My sailboat cost me about fifty cents."

"But will it take water?" say Mercedes with her smart ass.

"Took mine to Alley Pond Park once," say Flyboy. "String broke. Lost it. Pity."

"Sailed mine in Central Park and it keeled over and sank. Had to ask my father for another dollar."

"And you got the strap," laugh Big Butt. "The jerk didn't even have a string on it. My old man wailed on his behind."

Little Q.T. was staring hard at the sailboat and you could see he wanted it bad. But he too little and somebody'd just take it from him. So what the hell. "This boat for kids, Miss Moore?"

"Parents silly to buy something like that just to get all broke up," say Rosie Giraffe.

"That much money it should last forever," I figure.

"My father'd buy it for me if I wanted it."

"Your father, my ass," say Rosie Giraffe getting a chance to finally push Mercedes.

"Must be rich people shop here," say Q.T.

"You are a very bright boy," say Flyboy. "What was your first clue?" And he rap him on the head with the back of his knuckles, since Q.T. the only one he could get away with. Though Q.T. liable to come up behind you years later and get his licks in when you half expect it.

"What I want to know is," I say to Miss Moore though I never talk to her, I wouldn't give the bitch that satisfaction, "is how much a real boat costs? I figure a thousand'd get you a yacht any day."

"Why don't you check that out," she say, "and report back to the group?" Which really pains my ass. If you gonna mess up a perfectly good swim day least you could do is have some answers. "Let's go in," she say like she got something up her sleeve. Only she don't lead the way. So me and Sugar turn the corner to where the entrance is, but when we get there I kinda hang back. Not that I'm scared, what's there to be afraid of, just a toy store. But I feel funny, shame. But what I got to be shamed about? Got as much right to go in as anybody. But somehow I can't seem to get hold of the door, so I step away for Sugar to lead. But she hangs back too. And I look at her and she looks at me and this is ridiculous. I mean, damn, I have never ever been shy about doing nothing or going nowhere. But then Mercedes steps up and then Rosie Giraffe and Big Butt crowd in behind and shove, and next thing we all stuffed into the doorway with only Mercedes squeezing past us, smoothing out her jumper and walking right down the aisle. Then the rest of us tumble in like a glued-together jigsaw done all wrong. And people lookin at us. And it's like the time me and Sugar crashed into the Catholic church on a dare. But once we got in there and everything so hushed and holy and the candles and the bowin and the handkerchiefs on all the drooping heads, I just couldn't go through with the plan. Which was for me to run up to the altar and do a tap dance while Sugar played the nose flute and messed around in the holy water. And Sugar kept givin me the elbow. Then later teased me so bad I tied her up in the shower and turned it on and locked her in. And she'd be there till this day if Aunt Gretchen hadn't finally figured I was lyin about the boarder takin a shower.

Same thing in the store. We all walkin on tiptoe and hardly touchin the games and puzzles and things. And I watched Miss Moore who is steady watchin us like she waitin for a sign. Like Mama Drewery watches the sky and sniffs the air and takes note of just how much slant is in the bird formation. Then me and Sugar bump smack into each other, so busy gazing at the toys, 'specially the sailboat. But we don't laugh and go into our fat-lady bump-stomach routine. We just stare at that price tag. Then Sugar run a finger over the whole boat. And I'm jealous and want to hit her. Maybe not her, but I sure want to punch somebody in the mouth.

"Watcha bring us here for, Miss Moore?"

"You sound angry, Sylvia. Are you mad about something?" Givin me one of them grins like she tellin a grown-up joke that never turns out to be funny. And she's lookin very closely at me like maybe she plannin to do my portrait from memory. I'm mad, but I won't give her that satisfaction. So I slouch around the store being very bored and say, "Let's go."

Me and Sugar at the back of the train watchin the tracks whizzin by large then small then gettin gobbled up in the dark. I'm thinkin about this tricky toy I saw in the store. A clown that somersaults on a bar then does chin-ups just cause you yank lightly at his leg. Cost $35. I could see me askin my mother for a $35 birthday clown. "You wanna who that costs what?" she'd say, cocking her head to the side to get a better view of the hole in my head. Thirty-five dollars could buy new bunk beds for Junior and Gretchen's boy. Thirty-five dollars and the whole household could go visit Granddaddy Nelson in the country. Thirty-five dollars would pay for the rent and the piano bill too. Who are those people that spend that much for performing clowns and $1,000 for toy sailboats? What kinda work they do and how they live and how come we ain't in on it? Where we are is who we are, Miss Moore always pointin out. But it don't necessarily have to be that way, she always adds then waits for somebody to say that poor people have to wake up and demand their share of the pie and don't none of us know what kind of pie she talkin about in the first damn place. But she ain't so smart cause I still got her four dollars from the taxi and she sure ain't gettin it. Messin up my day with this shit. Sugar nudges me in my pocket and winks.

Miss Moore lines us up in front of the mailbox where we started from, seem like years ago, and I got a headache for thinkin so hard. And we lean all over each other so we can hold up under the draggy-ass lecture she always finishes us off with at the end before we thank her for borin us to tears. But she just looks at us like she readin tea leaves. Finally she say, "Well, what did you think of F.A.O. Schwarz?"

Rosie Giraffe mumbles, "White folks crazy."

"I'd like to go there again when I get my birthday money," says Mercedes, and we shove her out the pack so she has to lean on the mailbox by herself.

"I'd like a shower. Tiring day," said Flyboy.

Then Sugar surprises me by sayin, "You know, Miss Moore, I don't think all of us here put together eat in a year what that sailboat costs." And Miss Moore lights up like somebody goosed her. "And?" she say, urging Sugar on. Only I'm standin on her foot so she don't continue.

"Imagine for a minute what kind of society it is in which some people can spend on a toy what it would cost to feed a family of six or seven. What do you think?"

"I think," say Sugar pushing me off her feet like she never done before, cause I whip her ass in a minute, "that this is not much of a democracy if you ask me. Equal chance to pursue happiness means an equal crack at the dough, don't it?" Miss Moore is besides herself and I am disgusted with Sugar's treachery. So I stand on her foot one more time to see if she'll shove me. She shuts up, and Miss Moore looks at me, sorrowfully I'm thinkin. And somethin weird is goin on, I can feel it in my chest.

"Anybody else learn anything today?" lookin dead at me. I walk away and Sugar has to run to catch up and don't even seem to notice when I shrug her arm off my shoulder.

"Well, we got four dollars anyway," she said.

"Uh hunh."

"We could go to Hascombs and get half a chocolate layer and then go to the Sunset and still have plenty money for potato chips and ice-cream sodas."

"Uh hunh."

"Race you to Hascombs," she say.

We start down the block and she gets ahead which is O.K. by me cause I'm goin to the West End and then over to the Drive to think this day through. She can run if she want to and even run faster. But ain't nobody gonna beat me at nuthin.

Ann Beattie

ᔓ

The Burning House

FREDDY FOX is in the kitchen with me. He has just washed and dried an avocado seed I don't want, and he is leaning against the wall, rolling a joint. In five minutes, I will not be able to count on him. However: he started late in the day, and he has already brought in wood for the fire, gone to the store down the road for matches, and set the table. "You mean you'd know this stuff was Limoges even if you didn't turn the plate over?" he called from the dining room. He pretended to be about to throw one of the plates into the kitchen, like a Frisbee. Sam, the dog, believed him and shot up, kicking the rug out behind him and skidding forward before he realized his error; it was like the Road Runner tricking Wile E. Coyote into going over the cliff for the millionth time. His jowls sank in disappointment.

"I see there's a full moon," Freddy says. "There's just nothing that can hold a candle to nature. The moon and the stars, the tides and the sunshine—and we just don't stop for long enough to wonder at it all. We're so engrossed in ourselves." He takes a very long drag on the joint. "We stand and stir the sauce in the pot instead of going to the window and gazing at the moon."

"You don't mean anything personal by that, I assume."

"I love the way you pour cream in a pan. I like to come up behind you and watch the sauce bubble."

"No, thank you," I say. "You're starting late in the day."

"My responsibilities have ended. You don't trust me to help
with the cooking, and I've already brought in firewood and run
an errand, and this very morning I exhausted myself by taking
Mr. Sam jogging with me, down at Putnam Park. You're sure you
won't?"

"No, thanks," I say. "Not now, anyway."

"I love it when you stand over the steam coming out of a pan
and the hairs around your forehead curl into damp little curls."

My husband, Frank Wayne, is Freddy's half brother. Frank is an
accountant. Freddy is closer to me than to Frank. Since Frank talks
to Freddy more than he talks to me, however, and since Freddy is
totally loyal, Freddy always knows more than I know. It pleases me
that he does not know how to stir sauce; he will start talking, his
mind will drift, and when next you look the sauce will be lumpy,
or boiling away.

Freddy's criticism of Frank is only implied. "What a gracious
gesture to entertain his friends on the weekend," he says.

"Male friends," I say.

"I didn't mean that you're the sort of lady who doesn't draw the
line. I most certainly did not mean that," Freddy says. "I would
even have been surprised if you had taken a toke of this deadly stuff
while you were at the stove."

"O.K.," I say, and take the joint from him. Half of it is left when
I take it. Half an inch is left after I've taken two drags and given it
back.

"More surprised still if you'd shaken the ashes into the sauce-
pan."

"You'd tell people I'd done it when they'd finished eating, and
I'd be embarrassed. You can do it, though. I wouldn't be embarrassed if it was a story you told on yourself."

"You really understand me," Freddy says. "It's moon-madness, but I have to shake just this little bit in the sauce. I have to do it."

He does it.

FRANK AND TUCKER are in the living room. Just a few minutes ago, Frank returned from getting Tucker at the train. Tucker loves to visit. To him, Fairfield County is as mysterious as Alaska. He brought with him from New York a crock of mustard, a jeroboam of champagne, cocktail napkins with a picture of a plane flying over a building on them, twenty egret feathers ("You cannot get them anymore—strictly illegal," Tucker whispered to me), and, under his black cowboy hat with the rhinestone-studded chin strap, a toy frog that hopped when wound. Tucker owns a gallery in SoHo, and Frank keeps his books. Tucker is now stretched out in the living room, visiting with Frank, and Freddy and I are both listening.

"... so everything I've been told indicates that he lives a purely Jekyll-and-Hyde existence. He's twenty years old, and I can see that since he's still living at home he might not want to flaunt his gayness. When he came into the gallery, he had his hair slicked back—just with water, I got close enough to sniff—and his mother was all but holding his hand. So fresh-scrubbed. The stories I'd heard. Anyway, when I called, his father started looking for the number where he could be reached on the Vineyard—very irritated, because I didn't know James, and if I'd just phoned James I could have found him in a flash. He's talking to himself, looking for the number, and I say, 'Oh, did he go to visit friends or—' and his father interrupts and says, 'He was going to a gay pig roast. He's been gone since Monday.' *Just like that.*"

Freddy helps me carry the food out to the table. When we are all at the table, I mention the young artist Tucker was talking about. "Frank says his paintings are really incredible," I say to Tucker.

"Makes Estes look like an Abstract Expressionist," Tucker says. "I want that boy. I really want that boy."

"You'll get him," Frank says. "You get everybody you go after."

Tucker cuts a small piece of meat. He cuts it small so that he can talk while chewing. "Do I?" he says.

Freddy is smoking at the table, gazing dazedly at the moon centered in the window. "After dinner," he says, putting the back of his hand against his forehead when he sees that I am looking at him, "we must all go to the lighthouse."

"If only *you* painted," Tucker says. "I'd want you."

"You couldn't have me," Freddy snaps. He reconsiders. "That sounded halfhearted, didn't it? Anybody who wants me can have me. This is the only place I can be on Saturday night where somebody isn't hustling me."

"Wear looser pants," Frank says to Freddy.

"This is so much better than some bar that stinks of cigarette smoke and leather. Why do I do it?" Freddy says. "Seriously—do you think I'll ever stop?"

"Let's not be serious," Tucker says.

"I keep thinking of this table as a big boat, with dishes and glasses rocking on it," Freddy says.

He takes the bone from his plate and walks out to the kitchen, dripping sauce on the floor. He walks as though he's on the deck of a wave-tossed ship. "Mr. Sam!" he calls, and the dog springs up from the living-room floor, where he had been sleeping; his toenails on the bare wood floor sound like a wheel spinning in gravel. "You don't have to beg," Freddy says. "Jesus, Sammy—I'm just giving it to you."

"I hope there's a bone involved," Tucker says, rolling his eyes to Frank. He cuts another tiny piece of meat. "I hope your brother does understand why I couldn't keep him on. He was good at what he did, but he also might say just *anything* to a customer. You have to believe me that if I hadn't been extremely embarrassed more than once I never would have let him go."

"He should have finished school," Frank says, sopping up sauce on his bread. "He'll knock around a while longer, then get tired of it and settle down to something."

"You think I died out here?" Freddy calls. "You think I can't hear you?"

"I'm not saying anything I wouldn't say to your face," Frank says.

"I'll tell you what I wouldn't say to your face," Freddy says. "You've got a swell wife and kid and dog, and you're a snob, and you take it all for granted."

Frank puts down his fork, completely exasperated. He looks at me.

"He came to work once this stoned," Tucker says. *"Comprenez-vous?"*

"YOU LIKE me because you feel sorry for me," Freddy says.

He is sitting on the concrete bench outdoors, in the area that's a garden in the springtime. It is early April now—not quite spring. It's very foggy out. It rained while we were eating, and now it has turned mild. I'm leaning against a tree, across from him, glad it's so dark and misty that I can't look down and see the damage the mud is doing to my boots.

"Who's his girlfriend?" Freddy says.

"If I told you her name, you'd tell him I told you."

"Slow down. What?"

"I won't tell you, because you'll tell him that I know."

"He knows you know."

"I don't think so."

"How did you find out?"

"He talked about her. I kept hearing her name for months, and then we went to a party at Garner's, and she was there, and when I said something about her later he said, 'Natalie who?' It was much too obvious. It gave the whole thing away."

He sighs. "I just did something very optimistic," he says. "I came out here with Mr. Sam and he dug up a rock and I put the avocado seed in the hole and packed dirt on top of it. Don't say it— I know: can't grow outside, we'll still have another snow, even if it grew, the next year's frost would kill it."

"He's embarrassed," I say. "When he's home, he avoids me. But it's rotten to avoid Mark, too. Six years old, and he calls up his friend Neal to hint that he wants to go over there. He doesn't do that when we're here alone."

Freddy picks up a stick and pokes around in the mud with it. "I'll bet Tucker's after that painter personally, not because he's the hottest thing since pancakes. That expression of his—it's always the same. Maybe Nixon really loved his mother, but with that expression who could believe him? It's a curse to have a face that won't express what you mean."

"Amy!" Tucker calls. "Telephone."

Freddy waves goodbye to me with the muddy stick. " 'I am not a crook,' " Freddy says. "Jesus Christ."

Sam bounds halfway toward the house with me, then turns and goes back to Freddy.

It's Marilyn, Neal's mother, on the phone.

"Hi," Marilyn says. "He's afraid to spend the night."

"Oh, no," I say. "He said he wouldn't be."

She lowers her voice. "We can try it out, but I think he'll start crying."

"I'll come get him."

"I can bring him home. You're having a dinner party, aren't you?"

I lower my voice. "Some party. Tucker's here. J.D. never showed up."

"Well," she says. "I'm sure that what you cooked was good."

"It's so foggy out, Marilyn. I'll come get Mark."

"He can stay. I'll be a martyr," she says, and hangs up before I can object.

Freddy comes into the house, tracking in mud. Sam lies in the kitchen, waiting for his paws to be cleaned. "Come on," Freddy says, hitting his hand against his thigh, having no idea what Sam is doing. Sam gets up and runs after him. They go into the small downstairs bathroom together. Sam loves to watch people urinate. Sometimes he sings, to harmonize with the sound of the urine going into the water. There are footprints and pawprints everywhere. Tucker is shrieking with laughter in the living room. ". . . he says, he says to the other one, 'Then, dearie, have you ever played *spin* the bottle?' " Frank's and Tucker's laughter drowns out the sound of Freddy peeing in the bathroom. I turn on the water in the kitchen sink, and it drowns out all the noise. I begin to scrape the dishes. Tucker is telling another story when I turn off the water: ". . . that it was Onassis in the Anvil, and nothing would talk him out of it. They told him Onassis was dead, and he thought they were trying to make him think he was crazy. There was nothing to do but go along with him, but, God—he was trying to goad this poor old fag into fighting about Stavros Niarchos. You know— Onassis's *enemy*. He thought it was *Onassis*. In the *Anvil*." There is a sound of a glass breaking. Frank or Tucker puts *John Coltrane Live in Seattle* on the stereo and turns the volume down low. The bathroom door opens. Sam runs into the kitchen and begins to lap water from his dish. Freddy takes his little silver case and his rolling papers out of his shirt pocket. He puts a piece of paper on the kitchen table and is about to sprinkle grass on it, but realizes just in time that the paper has absorbed water from a puddle. He balls it up with his thumb, flicks it to the floor, puts a piece of rolling paper where the table's dry and shakes a line of grass down it. "You smoke this," he says to me. "I'll do the dishes."

"We'll both smoke it. I'll wash and you can wipe."

"I forgot to tell them I put ashes in the sauce," he says.

"I wouldn't interrupt."

"At least he pays Frank ten times what any other accountant for an art gallery would make," Freddy says.

Tucker is beating his hand on the arm of the sofa as he talks, stomping his feet. ". . . so he's trying to feel him out, to see if this old guy with the dyed hair knew *Maria Callas.* Jesus! And he's so out of it he's trying to think what opera singers are called, and instead of coming up with *'diva'* he comes up with *'duenna.'* At this point, Larry Betwell went up to him and tried to calm him down, and he breaks into song—some aria or something that Maria Callas was famous for. Larry told him he was going to lose his *teeth* if he didn't get it together, and . . ."

"He spends a lot of time in gay hangouts, for not being gay," Freddy says.

I scream and jump back from the sink, hitting the glass I'm rinsing against the faucet, shattering green glass everywhere.

"What?" Freddy says. "Jesus Christ, what is it?"

Too late, I realize what it must have been that I saw: J.D. in a goat mask, the puckered pink plastic lips against the window by the kitchen sink.

"I'm sorry," J.D. says, coming through the door and nearly colliding with Frank, who has rushed into the kitchen. Tucker is right behind him.

"Oooh," Tucker says, feigning disappointment, "I thought Freddy smooched her."

"I'm sorry," J.D. says again. "I thought you'd know it was me."

The rain must have started again, because J.D. is soaking wet. He has turned the mask around so that the goat's head stares out from the back of his head. "I got lost," J.D. says. He has a farmhouse upstate. "I missed the turn. I went miles. I missed the whole dinner, didn't I?"

"What did you do wrong?" Frank asks.

"I didn't turn left onto 58. I don't know why I didn't realize my mistake, but I went *miles.* It was raining so hard I couldn't go over twenty-five miles an hour. Your driveway is all mud. You're going to have to push me out."

"There's some roast left over. And salad, if you want it," I say.

"Bring it in the living room," Frank says to J.D. Freddy is holding out a plate to him. J.D. reaches for the plate. Freddy pulls it back. J.D. reaches again, and Freddy is so stoned that he isn't quick enough this time—J.D. grabs it.

"I thought you'd know it was me," J.D. says. "I apologize." He dishes salad onto the plate. "You'll be rid of me for six months, in the morning."

"Where does your plane leave from?" Freddy says.

"Kennedy."

"Come in here!" Tucker calls. "I've got a story for you about Perry Dwyer down at the Anvil last week, when he thought he saw Aristotle Onassis."

"Who's Perry Dwyer?" J.D. says.

"That is not the point of the story, dear man. And when you're in Cassis, I want you to look up an American painter over there. Will you? He doesn't have a phone. Anyway—I've been tracking him, and I know where he is now, and I am *very* interested, if you would stress that with him, to do a show in June that will be *only* him. He doesn't answer my letters."

"Your hand is cut," J.D. says to me.

"Forget it," I say. "Go ahead."

"I'm sorry," he says. "Did I make you do that?"

"Yes, you did."

"Don't keep your finger under the water. Put pressure on it to stop the bleeding."

He puts the plate on the table. Freddy is leaning against the counter, staring at the blood swirling in the sink, and smoking the joint all by himself. I can feel the little curls on my forehead that Freddy was talking about. They feel heavy on my skin. I hate to see my own blood. I'm sweating. I let J.D. do what he does; he turns off the water and wraps his hand around my second finger, squeezing. Water runs down our wrists.

Freddy jumps to answer the phone when it rings, as though a

siren just went off behind him. He calls me to the phone, but J.D. steps in front of me, shakes his head no, and takes the dish towel and wraps it around my hand before he lets me go.

"Well," Marilyn says. "I had the best of intentions, but my battery's dead."

J.D. is standing behind me, with his hand on my shoulder.

"I'll be right over," I say. "He's not upset now, is he?"

"No, but he's dropped enough hints that he doesn't think he can make it through the night."

"O.K.," I say. "I'm sorry about all of this."

"Six years old," Marilyn says. "Wait till he grows up and gets that feeling."

I hang up.

"Let me see your hand," J.D. says.

"I don't want to look at it. Just go get me a Band-Aid, please."

He turns and goes upstairs. I unwrap the towel and look at it. It's pretty deep, but no glass is in my finger. I feel funny; the outlines of things are turning yellow. I sit in the chair by the phone. Sam comes and lies beside me and I stare at his black-and-yellow tail, beating. I reach down with my good hand and pat him, breathing deeply in time with every second pat.

"*Rothko?*" Tucker says bitterly, in the living room. "Nothing is great that can appear on greeting cards. Wyeth is that way. Would 'Christina's World' look bad on a cocktail napkin? You know it wouldn't."

I jump as the phone rings again. "Hello?" I say, wedging the phone against my shoulder with my ear, wrapping the dish towel tighter around my hand.

"Tell them it's a crank call. Tell them anything," Johnny says. "I miss you. How's Saturday night at your house?"

"All right," I say. I catch my breath.

"Everything's all right here, too. Yes indeed. Roast rack of lamb. Friend of Nicole's who's going to Key West tomorrow had too much to drink and got depressed because he thought it was raining in Key West, and I said I'd go in my study and call the National Weather Service. Hello, Weather Service. How are you?"

J.D. comes down from upstairs with two Band-Aids and stands beside me, unwrapping one. I want to say to Johnny, "I'm cut. I'm bleeding. It's no joke."

It's all right to talk in front of J.D., but I don't know who else might overhear me.

"I'd say they made the delivery about four this afternoon," I say.

"This is the church, this is the steeple. Open the door and see all the people," Johnny says. "Take care of yourself. I'll hang up and find out if it's raining in Key West."

"Late in the afternoon," I say. "Everything is fine."

"Nothing is fine," Johnny says. "Take care of yourself."

He hangs up. I put the phone down, and realize that I'm still having trouble focusing, the sight of my cut finger made me so light-headed. I don't look at the finger again as J.D. undoes the towel and wraps the Band-Aids around my finger.

"What's going on in here?" Frank says, coming into the dining room.

"I cut my finger," I say. "It's O.K."

"You did?" he says. He looks woozy—a little drunk. "Who keeps calling?"

"Marilyn. Mark changed his mind about staying all night. She was going to bring him home, but her battery's dead. You'll have to get him. Or I will."

"Who called the second time?" he says.

"The oil company. They wanted to know if we got our delivery today."

He nods. "I'll go get him, if you want," he says. He lowers his voice. "Tucker's probably going to whirl himself into a tornado for an encore," he says, nodding toward the living room. "I'll take him with me."

"Do you want me to go get him?" J.D. says.

"I don't mind getting some air," Frank says. "Thanks, though. Why don't you go in the living room and eat your dinner?"

"You forgive me?" J.D. says.

"Sure," I say. "It wasn't your fault. Where did you get that mask?"

"I found it on top of a Goodwill box in Manchester. There was also a beautiful old birdcage—solid brass."

The phone rings again. I pick it up. "Wouldn't I love to be in Key West with you," Johnny says. He makes a sound as though he's kissing me and hangs up.

"Wrong number," I say.

Frank feels in his pants pocket for the car keys.

J.D. KNOWS about Johnny. He introduced me, in the faculty lounge, where J.D. and I had gone to get a cup of coffee after I registered for classes. After being gone for nearly two years, J.D. still gets mail at the department—he said he had to stop by for the mail anyway, so he'd drive me to campus and point me toward the registrar's. J.D. taught English; now he does nothing. J.D. is glad that I've gone back to college to study art again, now that Mark is in school. I'm six credits away from an M.A. in art history. He wants me to think about myself, instead of thinking about Mark all the time. He talks as though I could roll Mark out on a string and let him fly off, high above me. J.D.'s wife and son died in a car crash. His son was Mark's age. "I wasn't prepared," J.D. said when we were driving over that day. He always says this when he talks about it. "How could you be prepared for such a thing?" I asked him. "I am now," he said. Then, realizing he was acting very hardboiled, made fun of himself. "Go on," he said, "punch me in the stomach. Hit me as hard as you can." We both knew he wasn't prepared for anything. When he couldn't find a parking place that day, his hands were wrapped around the wheel so tightly that his knuckles turned white.

Johnny came in as we were drinking coffee. J.D. was looking at his junk mail—publishers wanting him to order anthologies, ways to get free dictionaries.

"You are so lucky to be out of it," Johnny said, by way of greeting. "What do you do when you've spent two weeks on *Hamlet* and the student writes about Hamlet's good friend Horchow?"

He threw a blue book into J.D.'s lap. J.D. sailed it back.

"Johnny," he said, "this is Amy."

"Hi, Amy," Johnny said.

"You remember when Frank Wayne was in graduate school here? Amy's Frank's wife."

"Hi, Amy," Johnny said.

J.D. told me he knew it the instant Johnny walked into the room—he knew that second that he should introduce me as somebody's wife. He could have predicted it all from the way Johnny looked at me.

For a long time J.D. gloated that he had been prepared for what happened next—that Johnny and I were going to get together. It took me to disturb his pleasure in himself—me, crying hysterically on the phone last month, not knowing what to do, what move to make next.

"Don't do anything for a while. I guess that's my advice," J.D. said. "But you probably shouldn't listen to me. All I can do myself is run away, hide out. I'm not the learned professor. You know what I believe. I believe all that wicked fairy-tale crap: your heart will break, your house will burn."

Tonight, because he doesn't have a garage at his farm, J.D. has come to leave his car in the empty half of our two-car garage while he's in France. I look out the window and see his old Saab, glowing in the moonlight. J.D. has brought his favorite book, *A Vision*, to read on the plane. He says his suitcase contains only a spare pair of jeans, cigarettes, and underwear. He is going to buy a leather jacket in France, at a store where he almost bought a leather jacket two years ago.

. . .

IN OUR BEDROOM there are about twenty small glass prisms hung with fishing line from one of the exposed beams; they catch the morning light, and we stare at them like a cat eyeing catnip held above its head. Just now, it is 2 a.m. At six-thirty, they will be filled with dazzling color. At four or five, Mark will come into the bedroom and get in bed with us. Sam will wake up, stretch, and shake, and the tags on his collar will clink, and he will yawn and shake again and go downstairs, where J.D. is asleep in his sleeping bag and Tucker is asleep on the sofa, and get a drink of water from his dish. Mark has been coming into our bedroom for about a year. He gets onto the bed by climbing up on a footstool that horrified me when I first saw it—a gift from Frank's mother: a footstool that says "Today Is the First Day of the Rest of Your Life" in needlepoint. I kept it in a closet for years, but it occurred to me that it would help Mark get up onto the bed, so he would not have to make a little leap and possibly skin his shin again. Now Mark does not disturb us when he comes into the bedroom, except that it bothers me that he has reverted to sucking his thumb. Sometimes he lies in bed with his cold feet against my leg. Sometimes, small as he is, he snores.

Somebody is playing a record downstairs. It's the Velvet Underground—Lou Reed, in a dream or swoon, singing "Sunday Morning." I can barely hear the whispering and tinkling of the record. I can only follow it because I've heard it a hundred times.

I am lying in bed, waiting for Frank to get out of the bathroom. My cut finger throbs. Things are going on in the house even though I have gone to bed; water runs, the record plays. Sam is still downstairs, so there must be some action.

I have known everybody in the house for years, and as time goes by I know them all less and less. J.D. was Frank's adviser in college. Frank was his best student, and they started to see each other outside of class. They played handball. J.D. and his family came to dinner. We went there. That summer—the summer Frank decided to go to graduate school in business instead of English—J.D.'s wife and son deserted him in a more horrible way, in that car crash. J.D. has quit his job. He has been to Las Vegas, to Colorado, New Orleans, Los Angeles, Paris twice; he tapes post cards to the walls of his living room. A lot of the time, on the weekends, he shows up at our house with his sleeping bag. Sometimes he brings a girl. Lately, not. Years ago, Tucker was in Frank's therapy group in New York, and ended up hiring Frank to work as the accountant for his gallery. Tucker was in therapy at the time because he was obsessed with foreigners. Now he is also obsessed with homosexuals. He gives fashionable parties to which he invites many foreigners and homosexuals. Before the parties he does TM and yoga, and during the parties he does Seconals and isometrics. When I first met him, he was living for the summer in his sister's house in Vermont while she was in Europe, and he called us one night, in New York, in a real panic because there were wasps all over. They were "hatching," he said—big, sleepy wasps that were everywhere. We said we'd come; we drove all through the night to get to Brattleboro. It was true: there were wasps on the undersides of plates, in the plants, in the folds of curtains. Tucker was so upset that he was out behind the house, in the cold Vermont morning, wrapped like an Indian in a blanket, with only his pajamas on underneath. He was sitting in a lawn chair, hiding behind a bush, waiting for us to come.

And Freddy—"Reddy Fox," when Frank is feeling affectionate toward him. When we first met, I taught him to ice-skate and he taught me to waltz; in the summer, at Atlantic City, he'd go with me on a roller coaster that curved high over the waves. I was the one—not Frank—who would get out of bed in the middle of the night and meet him at an all-night deli and put my arm around his shoulders, the way he put his arm around my shoulders on the roller coaster, and talk quietly to him until he got over his latest anxiety attack. Now he tests me, and I retreat: this man he picked up, this man who picked him up, how it feels to have forgotten somebody's name when your hand is in the back pocket of his jeans and you're not even halfway to your apartment. Reddy Fox—admiring my new red silk blouse, stroking his fingertips down the front, and my eyes wide, because I could feel his fingers on my chest, even though I was holding the blouse in front of me on a hanger to be admired. All those moments, and all they meant was that I was fooled into thinking I knew these people because I knew the small things, the personal things.

Freddy will always be more stoned than I am, because he feels comfortable getting stoned with me, and I'll always be reminded that he's more lost. Tucker knows he can come to the house and be the center of attention; he can tell all the stories he knows, and we'll never tell the story we know about him hiding in the bushes like a frightened dog. J.D. comes back from his trips with boxes full of post cards, and I look at all of them as though they're photographs taken by him, and I know, and he knows, that what he likes about them is their flatness—the unreality of them, the unreality of what he does.

Last summer, I read *The Metamorphosis* and said to J.D., "Why did Gregor Samsa wake up a cockroach?" His answer (which he would have toyed over with his students forever) was "Because that's what people expected of him."

They make the illogical logical. I don't do anything, because I'm waiting, I'm on hold (J.D.); I stay stoned because I know it's better to be out of it (Freddy); I love art because I myself am a work of art (Tucker).

Frank is harder to understand. One night a week or so ago, I thought we were really attuned to each other, communicating by telepathic waves, and as I lay in bed about to speak I realized that the vibrations really existed: they were him, snoring.

Now he's coming into the bedroom, and I'm trying again to think what to say. Or ask. Or do.

"Be glad you're not in Key West," he says. He climbs into bed.

I raise myself up on one elbow and stare at him.

"There's a hurricane about to hit," he says.

"What?" I say. "Where did you hear that?"

"When Reddy Fox and I were putting the dishes away. We had the radio on." He doubles up his pillow, pushes it under his neck. "Boom goes everything," he says. "Bam. Crash. Poof." He looks at me. "You look shocked." He closes his eyes. Then, after a minute or two, he murmurs, "Hurricanes upset you? I'll try to think of something nice."

He is quiet for so long that I think he has fallen asleep. Then he says, "Cars that run on water. A field of flowers, none alike. A shooting star that goes slow enough for you to watch. Your life to do over again." He has been whispering in my ear, and when he takes his mouth away I shiver. He slides lower in the bed for sleep. "I'll tell you something really amazing," he says. "Tucker told me he went into a travel agency on Park Avenue last week and asked the travel agent where he should go to pan for gold, and she told him."

"Where did she tell him to go?"

"I think somewhere in Peru. The banks of some river in Peru."

"Did you decide what you're going to do after Mark's birthday?" I say.

He doesn't answer me. I touch him on the side, finally.

"It's two o'clock in the morning. Let's talk about it another time."

"You picked the house, Frank. They're your friends downstairs. I used to be what you wanted me to be."

"They're your friends, too," he says. "Don't be paranoid."

"I want to know if you're staying or going."

He takes a deep breath, lets it out, and continues to lie very still.

"Everything you've done is commendable," he says. "You did the right thing to go back to school. You tried to do the right thing by finding yourself a normal friend like Marilyn. But your whole life you've made one mistake—you've surrounded yourself with men. Let me tell you something. All men—if they're crazy, like

Tucker, if they're gay as the Queen of the May, like Reddy Fox, even if they're just six years old—I'm going to tell you something about them. Men think they're Spider Man and Buck Rogers and Superman. You know what we all feel inside that you don't feel? That we're going to the stars."

He takes my hand. "I'm looking down on all of this from space," he whispers. "I'm already gone."

Bobbie Ann Mason

Big Bertha Stories

DONALD IS HOME again, laughing and singing. He comes home from Central City, near the strip mines, only when he feels like it, like an absentee landlord checking on his property. He is always in such a good humor when he returns that Jeannette forgives him. She cooks for him—ugly, pasty things she gets with food stamps. Sometimes he brings steaks and ice cream, occasionally money. Rodney, their child, hides in the closet when he arrives, and Donald goes around the house talking loudly about the little boy named Rodney who used to live there—the one who fell into a septic tank, or the one stolen by gypsies. The stories change. Rodney usually stays in the closet until he has to pee, and then he hugs his father's knees, forgiving him, just as Jeannette does. The way Donald saunters through the door, swinging a six-pack of beer, with a big grin on his face, takes her breath away. He leans against the door facing, looking sexy in his baseball cap and his shaggy red beard and his sunglasses. He wears sunglasses to be like the Blues Brothers, but he in no way resembles either of the Blues Brothers. I should have my head examined, Jeannette thinks.

The last time Donald was home, they went to the shopping center to buy Rodney some shoes advertised on sale. They stayed at the shopping center half the afternoon, just looking around. Donald and Rodney played video games. Jeannette felt they were a normal family. Then, in the parking lot, they stopped to watch a man on a platform demonstrating snakes. Children were petting a twelve-foot python coiled around the man's shoulders. Jeannette felt faint.

"Snakes won't hurt you unless you hurt them," said Donald as Rodney stroked the snake.

"It feels like chocolate," he said.

The snake man took a tarantula from a plastic box and held it lovingly in his palm. He said, "If you drop a tarantula, it will shatter like a Christmas ornament."

"I hate this," said Jeannette.

"Let's get out of here," said Donald.

Jeannette felt her family disintegrating like a spider shattering as Donald hurried them away from the shopping center. Rodney squalled and Donald dragged him along. Jeannette wanted to stop for ice cream. She wanted them all to sit quietly together in a booth, but Donald rushed them to the car, and he drove them home in silence, his face growing grim.

"Did you have bad dreams about the snakes?" Jeannette asked Rodney the next morning at breakfast. They were eating pancakes made with generic pancake mix. Rodney slapped his fork in the pond of syrup on his pancakes. "The black racer is the farmer's friend," he said soberly, repeating a fact learned from the snake man.

"Big Bertha kept black racers," said Donald. "She trained them for the 500." Donald doesn't tell Rodney ordinary children's stories. He tells him a series of strange stories he makes up about Big Bertha. Big Bertha is what he calls the huge strip-mining machine in Muhlenberg County, but he has Rodney believing that Big Bertha is a female version of Paul Bunyan.

"Snakes don't run in the 500," said Rodney.

"This wasn't the Indy 500 or the Daytona 500—none of your well-known 500s," said Donald. "This was the Possum Trot 500, and it was a long time ago. Big Bertha started the original 500, with snakes. Black racers and blue racers mainly. Also some red-and-white-striped racers, but those are rare."

"We always ran for the hoe if we saw a black racer," Jeannette said, remembering her childhood in the country.

IN A WAY, Donald's absences are a fine arrangement, even considerate. He is sparing them his darkest moods, when he can't cope with his memories of Vietnam. Vietnam had never seemed such a meaningful fact until a couple of years ago, when he grew depressed and moody, and then he started going away to Central City. He frightened Jeannette, and she always said the wrong thing in her efforts to soothe him. If the welfare people find out he is spending occasional weekends at home, and even bringing some money, they will cut off her assistance. She applied for welfare because she can't depend on him to send money, but she knows he blames her for losing faith in him. He isn't really working regularly at the strip mines. He is mostly just hanging around there, watching the land being scraped away, trees coming down, bushes flung in the air. Sometimes he operates a steam shovel, and when he comes home his clothes are filled with the clay and it is caked on his shoes. The clay is the color of butterscotch pudding.

At first, he tried to explain to Jeannette. He said, "If we could have had tanks over there as big as Big Bertha, we wouldn't have lost the war. Strip mining is just like what we were doing over there. We were stripping off the top. The topsoil is like the culture and the people, the best part of the land and the country. America was just stripping off the top, the best. We ruined it. Here, at least the coal companies have to plant vetch and loblolly pines and all kinds of trees and bushes. If we'd done that in Vietnam, maybe we'd have left that country in better shape."

"Wasn't Vietnam a long time ago?" Jeannette asked.

She didn't want to hear about Vietnam. She thought it was unhealthy to dwell on it so much. He should live in the present. Her mother is afraid Donald will do something violent, because she once read in the newspaper that a veteran in Louisville held his little girl hostage in their apartment until he had a shootout with the police and was killed. But Jeannette can't imagine Donald doing anything so extreme. When she first met him, several years ago, at her parents' pit-barbecue luncheonette, where she was working then, he had a good job at a lumberyard and he dressed nicely. He took her out to eat at a fancy restaurant. They got plastered and ended up in a motel in Tupelo, Mississippi, on Elvis Presley Boulevard. Back then, he talked nostalgically about his year in Vietnam, about how beautiful it was, how different the people were. He could never seem to explain what he meant. "They're just different," he said.

They went riding around in a yellow 1957 Chevy convertible. He drives too fast now, but he didn't then, maybe because he was so protective of the car. It was a classic. He sold it three years ago and made a good profit. About the time he sold the Chevy, his moods began changing, his even-tempered nature shifting, like driving on a smooth interstate and then switching to a secondary road. He had headaches and bad dreams. But his nightmares seemed trivial. He dreamed of riding a train through the Rocky Mountains, of hijacking a plane to Cuba, of stringing up barbed wire around the house. He dreamed he lost a doll. He got drunk and rammed the car, the Chevy's successor, into a Civil War statue in front of the courthouse. When he got depressed over the meaninglessness of his job, Jeannette felt guilty about spending money on something nice for the house, and she tried to make him feel his job had meaning by reminding him that, after all, they had a child to think of. "I don't like his name," Donald said once. "What a stupid name. Rodney. I never did like it."

.   .   .

RODNEY HAS DREAMS about Big Bertha, echoes of his father's nightmare, like TV cartoon versions of Donald's memories of the war. But Rodney loves the stories, even though they are confusing, with lots of loose ends. The latest in the Big Bertha series is "Big Bertha and the Neutron Bomb." Last week it was "Big Bertha and the MX Missile." In the new story, Big Bertha takes a trip to California to go surfing with Big Mo, her male counterpart. On the beach, corn dogs and snow cones are free and the surfboards turn into dolphins. Everyone is having fun until the neutron bomb comes. Rodney loves the part where everyone keels over dead. Donald acts it out, collapsing on the rug. All the dolphins and the surfers keel over, everyone except Big Bertha. Big Bertha is so big she is immune to the neutron bomb.

"Those stories aren't true," Jeannette tells Rodney.

Rodney staggers and falls down on the rug, his arms and legs akimbo. He gets the giggles and can't stop. When his spasms finally subside, he says, "I told Scottie Bidwell about Big Bertha and he didn't believe me."

Donald picks Rodney up under the armpits and sets him upright. "You tell Scottie Bidwell if he saw Big Bertha he would pee in his pants on the spot, he would be so impressed."

"Are you scared of Big Bertha?"

"No, I'm not. Big Bertha is just like a wonderful woman, a big fat woman who can sing the blues. Have you ever heard Big Mama Thornton?"

"No."

"Well, Big Bertha's like her, only she's the size of a tall building. She's slow as a turtle and when she crosses the road they have to reroute traffic. She's big enough to straddle a four-lane highway. She's so tall she can see all the way to Tennessee, and when she belches, there's a tornado. She's really something. She can even fly."

"She's too big to fly," Rodney says doubtfully. He makes a face like a wadded-up washrag and Donald wrestles him to the floor again.

. . .

DONALD HAS BEEN drinking all evening, but he isn't drunk. The ice cubes melt and he pours the drink out and refills it. He keeps on talking. Jeannette cannot remember him talking so much about the war. He is telling her about an ammunitions dump. Jeannette had the vague idea that an ammo dump is a mound of shotgun shells, heaps of cartridge casings and bomb shells, or whatever is left over, a vast waste pile from the war, but Donald says that is wrong. He has spent an hour describing it in detail, so that she will understand.

He refills the glass with ice, some 7-Up, and a shot of Jim Beam. He slams doors and drawers, looking for a compass. Jeannette can't keep track of the conversation. It doesn't matter that her hair is uncombed and her lipstick eaten away. He isn't seeing her.

"I want to draw the compound for you," he says, sitting down at the table with a sheet of Rodney's tablet paper.

Donald draws the map in red and blue ballpoint, with asterisks and technical labels that mean nothing to her. He draws some circles with the compass and measures some angles. He makes a red dot on an oblique line, a path that leads to the ammo dump.

"That's where I was. Right there," he says. "There was a water buffalo that tripped a land mine and its horn just flew off and stuck in the wall of the barracks like a machete thrown backhanded." He puts a dot where the land mine was, and he doodles awhile with the red ballpoint pen, scribbling something on the edge of the map that looks like feathers. "The dump was here and I was there and over there was where we piled the sandbags. And here were the tanks." He draws tanks, a row of squares with handles—guns sticking out.

"Why are you going to so much trouble to tell me about a buffalo horn that got stuck in a wall?" she wants to know.

But Donald just looks at her as though she has asked something obvious.

"Maybe I *could* understand if you'd let me," she says cautiously.

"You could never understand." He draws another tank.

In bed, it is the same as it has been since he started going away to Central City—the way he claims his side of the bed, turning away from her. Tonight, she reaches for him and he lets her be close to him. She cries for a while and he lies there, waiting for her to finish, as though she were merely putting on makeup.

"Do you want me to tell you a Big Bertha story?" he asks playfully.

"You act like you're in love with Big Bertha."

He laughs, breathing on her. But he won't come closer.

"You don't care what I look like anymore," she says. "What am I supposed to think?"

"There's nobody else. There's not anybody but you."

Loving a giant machine is incomprehensible to Jeannette. There must be another woman, someone that large in his mind. Jeannette has seen the strip-mining machine. The top of the crane is visible beyond a rise along the parkway. The strip mining is kept just out of sight of travelers because it would give them a poor image of Kentucky.

FOR THREE WEEKS, Jeannette has been seeing a psychologist at the free mental health clinic. He's a small man from out of state. His name is Dr. Robinson, but she calls him The Rapist, because the word *therapist* can be divided into two words, *the rapist*. He doesn't think her joke is clever, and he acts as though he has heard it a thousand times before. He has a habit of saying, "Go with that feeling," the same way Bob Newhart did on his old TV show. It's probably the first lesson in the textbook, Jeannette thinks.

She told him about Donald's last days on his job at the lumberyard—how he let the stack of lumber fall deliberately and didn't know why, and about how he went away soon after that, and how the Big Bertha stories started. Dr. Robinson seems to be waiting for her to make something out of it all, but it's maddening that he won't tell her what to do. After three visits, Jeannette has grown angry with him, and now she's holding back things. She won't tell him whether Donald slept with her or not when he came home last. Let him guess, she thinks.

"Talk about yourself," he says.

"What about me?"

"You speak so vaguely about Donald that I get the feeling that you see him as somebody larger than life. I can't quite picture him. That makes me wonder what that says about you." He touches the end of his tie to his nose and sniffs it.

When Jeannette suggests that she bring Donald in, the therapist looks bored and says nothing.

"He had another nightmare when he was home last," Jeannette says. "He dreamed he was crawling through tall grass and people were after him."

"How do *you* feel about that?" The Rapist asks eagerly.

"I didn't have the nightmare," she says coldly. "Donald did. I came to you to get advice about Donald, and you're acting like I'm the one who's crazy. I'm not crazy. But I'm lonely."

JEANNETTE'S MOTHER, behind the counter of the luncheonette, looks lovingly at Rodney pushing buttons on the jukebox in the corner. "It's a shame about that youngun," she says tearfully. "That boy needs a daddy."

"What are you trying to tell me? That I should file for divorce and get Rodney a new daddy?"

Her mother looks hurt. "No, honey," she says. "You need to get Donald to seek the Lord. And you need to pray more. You haven't been going to church lately."

"Have some barbecue," Jeannette's father booms, as he comes in from the back kitchen. "And I want you to take a pound home with you. You've got a growing boy to feed."

"I want to take Rodney to church," Mama says. "I want to show him off, and it might do some good."

"People will think he's an orphan," Dad says.

"I don't care," Mama says. "I just love him to pieces and I want to take him to church. Do you care if I take him to church, Jeannette?"

"No. I don't care if you take him to church." She takes the pound of barbecue from her father. Grease splotches the brown wrapping paper. Dad has given them so much barbecue that Rodney is burned out on it and won't eat it anymore.

JEANNETTE WONDERS if she would file for divorce if she could get a job. It is a thought—for the child's sake, she thinks. But there aren't many jobs around. With the cost of a baby-sitter, it doesn't pay her to work. When Donald first went away, her mother kept Rodney and she had a good job, waitressing at a steak house, but the steak house burned down one night—a grease fire in the kitchen. After that, she couldn't find a steady job, and she was reluctant to ask her mother to keep Rodney again because of her bad hip. At the steak house, men gave her tips and left their telephone numbers on the bill when they paid. They tucked dollar bills and notes in the pockets of her apron. One note said, "I want to hold your muffins." They were real-estate developers and businessmen on important missions for the Tennessee Valley Authority. They were boisterous and they drank too much. They said they'd take her for a cruise on the *Delta Queen,* but she didn't believe them. She knew how expensive that was. They talked about their speedboats and invited her for rides on Lake Barkley, or for spins in their private planes. They always used the word *spin.* The idea made her dizzy. Once, Jeannette let an electronics salesman take her for a ride in his Cadillac, and they breezed down the wilderness road through the Land Between the Lakes. His car had automatic windows and a stereo system and lighted computer-screen numbers on the dash that told him how many miles to the gallon he was getting and other statistics. He said the numbers distracted him and he had almost had several wrecks. At the restaurant, he had been flamboyant, admired by his companions. Alone with Jeannette in the Cadillac, on The Trace, he was shy and awkward, and really not very interesting. The most interesting thing about him, Jeannette thought, was all the lighted numbers on his dashboard. The Cadillac had everything but video games. But she'd rather be riding around with Donald, no matter where they ended up.

WHILE THE SOCIAL WORKER is there, filling out her report, Jeannette listens for Donald's car. When the social worker drove up, the flutter and wheeze of her car sounded like Donald's old Chevy, and for a moment Jeannette's mind lapsed back in time. Now she listens, hoping he won't drive up. The social worker is younger than Jeannette and has been to college. Her name is Miss Bailey, and she's excessively cheerful, as though in her line of work she has seen hardships that make Jeannette's troubles seem like a trip to Hawaii.

"Is your little boy still having those bad dreams?" Miss Bailey asks, looking up from her clipboard.

Jeannette nods and looks at Rodney, who has his finger in his mouth and won't speak.

"Has the cat got your tongue?" Miss Bailey asks.

"Show her your pictures, Rodney." Jeannette explains, "He won't talk about the dreams, but he draws pictures of them."

Rodney brings his tablet of pictures and flips through them silently. Miss Bailey says, "Hmm." They are stark line drawings, remarkably steady lines for his age. "What is this one?" she asks. "Let me guess. Two scoops of ice cream?"

The picture is two huge circles, filling the page, with three tiny stick people in the corner.

"These are Big Bertha titties," says Rodney.

Miss Bailey chuckles and winks at Jeannette. "What do you like to read, hon?" she asks Rodney.

"Nothing."

"He can read," says Jeannette. "He's smart."

"Do you like to read?" Miss Bailey asks Jeannette. She glances at the pile of paperbacks on the coffee table. She is probably going to ask where Jeannette got the money for them.

"I don't read," says Jeannette. "If I read, I just go crazy."

When she told The Rapist she couldn't concentrate on anything serious, he said she read romance novels in order to escape from reality. "Reality, hell!" she had said. "Reality's my whole problem."

"IT'S TOO BAD Rodney's not here," Donald is saying. Rodney is in the closet again. "Santa Claus has to take back all these toys. Rodney would love this bicycle! And this Pac-Man game. Santa has to take back so many things he'll have to have a pickup truck!"

"You didn't bring him anything. You never bring him anything," says Jeannette.

He has brought doughnuts and dirty laundry. The clothes he is wearing are caked with clay. His beard is lighter from working out in the sun, and he looks his usual joyful self, the way he always is before his moods take over, like migraine headaches, which some people describe as storms.

Donald coaxes Rodney out of the closet with the doughnuts.

"Were you a good boy this week?"

"I don't know."

"I hear you went to the shopping center and showed out." It is not true that Rodney made a big scene. Jeannette has already explained that Rodney was upset because she wouldn't buy him an Atari. But she didn't blame him for crying. She was tired of being unable to buy him anything.

Rodney eats two doughnuts and Donald tells him a long, confusing story about Big Bertha and a rock-and-roll band. Rodney interrupts him with dozens of questions. In the story, the rock-and-roll band gives a concert in a place that turns out to be a toxic-waste dump and the contamination is spread all over the country. Big Bertha's solution to this problem is not at all clear. Jeannette stays in the kitchen, trying to think of something original to do with instant potatoes and leftover barbecue.

"We can't go on like this," she says that evening in bed. "We're just hurting each other. Something has to change."

He grins like a kid. "Coming home from Muhlenberg County is like R and R—rest and recreation. I explain that in case you think R and R means rock and roll. Or maybe rumps and rears. Or rust and rot." He laughs and draws a circle in the air with his cigarette.

"I'm not that dumb."

"When I leave, I go back to the mines." He sighs, as though the mines were some eternal burden.

Her mind skips ahead to the future: Donald locked away somewhere, coloring in a coloring book and making clay pots, her and Rodney in some other town, with another man—someone dull and not at all sexy. Summoning up her courage, she says, "I haven't been through what you've been through and maybe I don't have a right to say this, but sometimes I think you act superior because you went to Vietnam, like nobody can ever know what you know. Well, maybe not. But you've still got your legs, even if you don't know what to do with what's between them anymore." Bursting into tears of apology, she can't help adding, "You can't go on telling Rodney those awful stories. He has nightmares when you're gone."

Donald rises from bed and grabs Rodney's picture from the dresser, holding it as he might have held a hand grenade. "Kids betray you," he says, turning the picture in his hand.

"If you cared about him, you'd stay here." As he sets the picture down, she asks, "What can I do? How can I understand what's going on in your mind? Why do you go there? Strip mining's bad for the ecology and you don't have any business strip mining."

"My job is serious, Jeannette. I run that steam shovel and put the topsoil back on. I'm reclaiming the land." He keeps talking, in a gentler voice, about strip mining, the same old things she has heard before, comparing Big Bertha to a supertank. If only they had had Big Bertha in Vietnam. He says, "When they strip off the top, I keep looking for those tunnels where the Viet Cong hid. They had so many tunnels it was unbelievable. Imagine Mammoth Cave going all the way across Kentucky."

"Mammoth Cave's one of the natural wonders of the world," says Jeannette brightly. She is saying the wrong thing again.

AT THE KITCHEN table at 2 a.m., he's telling about C-5A's. A C-5A is so big it can carry troops and tanks and helicopters, but it's not big enough to hold Big Bertha. Nothing could hold Big Bertha. He rambles on, and when Jeannette shows him Rodney's drawing of the circles, Donald smiles. Dreamily, he begins talking about women's breasts and thighs—the large, round thighs and big round breasts of American women, contrasted with the frail, delicate beauty of the Orientals. It is like comparing oven broilers and banties, he says. Jeannette relaxes. A confession about another lover from long ago is not so hard to take. He seems stuck on the breasts and thighs of American women—insisting that she understand how small and delicate the Orientals are, but then he abruptly returns to tanks and helicopters.

"A Bell Huey Cobra—my God, what a beautiful machine. So efficient!" Donald takes the food processor blade from the drawer where Jeannette keeps it. He says, "A rotor blade from a chopper could just slice anything to bits."

"Don't do that," Jeannette says.

He is trying to spin the blade on the counter, like a top. "Here's what would happen when a chopper blade hits a power line—not many of those over there!—or a tree. Not many trees, either, come to think of it, after all the Agent Orange." He drops the blade and it glances off the open drawer and falls to the floor, spiking the vinyl.

At first, Jeannette thinks the screams are hers, but they are his. She watches him cry. She has never seen anyone cry so hard, like an intense summer thundershower. All she knows to do is shove Kleenex at him. Finally, he is able to say, "You thought I was going to hurt you. That's why I'm crying."

"Go ahead and cry," Jeannette says, holding him close.

"Don't go away."

"I'm right here. I'm not going anywhere."

IN THE NIGHT, she still listens, knowing his monologue is being burned like a tattoo into her brain. She will never forget it. His voice grows soft and he plays with a ballpoint pen, jabbing holes in a paper towel. Bullet holes, she thinks. His beard is like a bird's nest, woven with dark corn silks.

"This is just a story," he says. "Don't mean nothing. Just relax." She is sitting on the hard edge of the kitchen chair, her toes cold on the floor, waiting. His tears have dried up and left a slight catch in his voice.

"We were in a big camp near a village. It was pretty routine and kind of soft there for a while. Now and then we'd go into Da Nang and whoop it up. We had been in the jungle for several months, so the two months at this village was a sort of rest—an R and R almost. Don't shiver. This is just a little story. Don't mean nothing! This is nothing, compared to what I could tell you. Just listen. We lost our fear. At night there would be some incoming and we'd see these tracers in the sky, like shooting stars up close, but it was all pretty minor and we didn't take it seriously, after what we'd been through. In the village I knew this Vietnamese family—a woman and her two daughters. They sold Cokes and beer to GIs. The oldest daughter was named Phan. She could speak a little English. She was really smart. I used to go see them in their hooch in the afternoons—in the siesta time of day. It was so hot there. Phan was beautiful, like the country. The village was ratty, but the country was pretty. And she was beautiful, just like she had grown up out of the jungle, like one of those flowers that bloomed high up in the trees and freaked us out sometimes, thinking it was a sniper. She was so gentle, with these eyes shaped like peach pits, and she was no bigger than a child of maybe thirteen or fourteen. I felt funny about her size at first, but later it didn't matter. It was just some wonderful feature about her, like a woman's hair, or her breasts."

He stops and listens, the way they used to listen for crying sounds when Rodney was a baby. He says, "She'd take those big banana leaves and fan me while I lay there in the heat."

"I didn't know they had bananas over there."

"There's a lot you don't know! Listen! Phan was twenty-three, and her brothers were off fighting. I never even asked which side they were fighting on." He laughs. "She got a kick out of the word *fan*. I told her that *fan* was the same word as her name. She thought I meant her name was banana. In Vietnamese the same word can have a dozen different meanings, depending on your tone of voice. I bet you didn't know that, did you?"

"No. What happened to her?"

"I don't know."

"Is that the end of the story?"

"I don't know." Donald pauses, then goes on talking about the village, the girl, the banana leaves, talking in a monotone that is making Jeannette's flesh crawl. He could be the news radio from the next room.

"You must have really liked that place. Do you wish you could go back there to find out what happened to her?"

"It's not there anymore," he says. "It blew up."

Donald abruptly goes to the bathroom. She hears the water running, the pipes in the basement shaking.

"It was so pretty," he says when he returns. He rubs his elbow absentmindedly. "That jungle was the most beautiful place in the world. You'd have thought you were in paradise. But we blew it sky-high."

In her arms, he is shaking, like the pipes in the basement, which are still vibrating. Then the pipes let go, after a long shudder, but he continues to tremble.

THEY ARE DRIVING to the Veterans Hospital. It was Donald's idea. She didn't have to persuade him. When she made up the bed that morning—with a finality that shocked her, as though she knew they wouldn't be in it again together—he told her it would be like R and R. Rest was what he needed. Neither of them had slept at all during the night. Jeannette felt she had to stay awake, to listen for more.

"Talk about strip mining," she says now. "That's what they'll do to your head. They'll dig out all those ugly memories, I hope. We don't need them around here." She pats his knee.

It is a cloudless day, not the setting for this sober journey. She drives and Donald goes along obediently, with the resignation of an old man being taken to a rest home. They are driving through southern Illinois, known as Little Egypt, for some obscure reason Jeannette has never understood. Donald still talks, but very quietly, without urgency. When he points out the scenery, Jeannette thinks of the early days of their marriage, when they would take a drive like this and laugh hysterically. Now Jeannette points out funny things they see. The Little Egypt Hot Dog World, Pharaoh Cleaners, Pyramid Body Shop. She is scarcely aware that she is driving, and when she sees a sign, LITTLE EGYPT STARLITE CLUB, she is confused for a moment, wondering where she has been transported.

As they part, he asks, "What will you tell Rodney if I don't come back? What if they keep me here indefinitely?"

"You're coming back. I'm telling him you're coming back soon."

"Tell him I went off with Big Bertha. Tell him she's taking me on a sea cruise, to the South Seas."

"No. You can tell him that yourself."

He starts singing "Sea Cruise." He grins at her and pokes her in the ribs.

"You're coming back," she says.

DONALD WRITES from the VA Hospital, saying that he is making progress. They are running tests, and he meets in a therapy group in which all the veterans trade memories. Jeannette is no longer on welfare because she now has a job waitressing at Fred's Family Restaurant. She waits on families, waits for Donald to come home so they can come here and eat together like a family. The fathers look at her with downcast eyes, and the children throw food. While Donald is gone, she rearranges the furniture. She reads some books from the library. She does a lot of thinking. It occurs to her that even though she loved him, she has thought of Donald primarily as a husband, a provider, someone whose name she shared, the father of her child, someone like the fathers who come to the Wednesday night all-you-can-eat fish fry. She hasn't thought of him as himself. She wasn't brought up that way, to examine someone's soul. When it comes to something deep inside, nobody will take it out and examine it, the way they will look at clothing in a store for flaws in the manufacturing. She tries to explain all this to The Rapist, and he says she's looking better, got sparkle in her eyes. "Big deal," says Jeannette. "Is that all you can say?"

She takes Rodney to the shopping center, their favorite thing to do together, even though Rodney always begs to buy something. They go to Penney's perfume counter. There, she usually hits a sample bottle of cologne—Chantilly or Charlie or something strong. Today she hits two or three and comes out of Penney's smelling like a flower garden.

"You stink!" Rodney cries, wrinkling his nose like a rabbit.

"Big Bertha smells like this, only a thousand times worse, she's so big," says Jeannette impulsively. "Didn't Daddy tell you that?"

"Daddy's a messenger from the devil."

This is an idea he must have gotten from church. Her parents have been taking him every Sunday. When Jeannette tries to reassure him about his father, Rodney is skeptical. "He gets that funny look on his face like he can see through me," the child says.

"Something's missing," Jeannette says, with a rush of optimism, a feeling of recognition. "Something happened to him once and took out the part that shows how much he cares about us."

"The way we had the cat fixed?"

"I guess. Something like that." The appropriateness of his remark stuns her, as though, in a way, her child has understood Donald all along. Rodney's pictures have been more peaceful lately, pictures of skinny trees and airplanes flying low. This morning he drew pictures of tall grass, with creatures hiding in it. The grass is tilted at an angle, as though a light breeze is blowing through it.

With her paycheck, Jeannette buys Rodney a present, a miniature trampoline they have seen advertised on television. It is called Mr. Bouncer. Rodney is thrilled about the trampoline, and he jumps on it until his face is red. Jeannette discovers that she enjoys it, too. She puts it out on the grass, and they take turns jumping. She has an image of herself on the trampoline, her sailor collar flapping, at the moment when Donald returns and sees her flying. One day a neighbor driving by slows down and calls out to Jeannette as she is bouncing on the trampoline, "You'll tear your insides loose!" Jeannette starts thinking about that, and the idea is so horrifying she stops jumping so much. That night, she has a nightmare about the trampoline. In her dream, she is jumping on soft moss, and then it turns into a springy pile of dead bodies.

Amy Hempel

✤

Beg, Sl Tog, Inc, Cont, Rep

THE MOHAIR WAS scratchy, the stria too bulky, but the homespun tweed was right for a small frame. I bought slate-blue skeins softened with flecks of pink, and size-10 needles for a sweater that was warm but light. The pattern I chose was a two-tone V-neck with an optional six-stitch cable up the front. Pullovers mess the hair, but I did not want to buttonhole the first time out.

From a needlework book, I learned to cast on. In the test piece, I got the gauge and correct tension. Knit and purl came naturally, as though my fingers had been rubbed in spiderwebs at birth. The sliding of the needles was as rhythmic as water.

Learning to knit was the obvious thing. The separation of tangled threads, the working-together of raveled ends into something tangible and whole—this *mending* was as confounding as the groom who drives into a stop sign on the way to his wedding. Because symptoms mean just what they are. What about the woman whose empty hand won't close because she cannot grasp that her child is gone?

"WOULD YOU get me a Dr Pep, gal, and would you turn up the a-c?"

I put down my knitting. In the kitchen I found some sugar-free, and took it, with ice, to Dale Anne. It was August. Air-conditioning lifted her hair as she pressed the button on the Niagara bed. Dr. Diamond insisted she have it the last month. She was also renting a swivel TV table and a vibrating chaise—the Niagara adjustable home.

When the angle was right, she popped a Vitamin E and rubbed the oil where the stretch marks would be.

I could be doing this, too. But I had had the procedure instead. That was after the father had asked me, Was I sure? To his credit, he meant—sure that I *was,* not sure was it he. He said he had never made a girl pregnant before. He said that he had never even made a girl late.

I moved in with Dale Anne to help her near the end. Her husband is often away—in a clinic or in a lab. He studies the mind. He is not a doctor yet, but we call him one by way of encouragement.

I had picked up a hank of yarn and was winding it into a ball when the air-conditioner choked to a stop.

Dale Anne sighed. "I will *cook* in this robe. Would you get me that flowered top in the second drawer?"

While I looked for the top, Dale Anne twisted her hair and held it tight against her head. She took one of my double-pointed six-inch needles and wove it in and out of her hair, securing the twist against her scalp. With the hair off her face, she looked wholesome and very young—"the person you would most like to go camping with if you couldn't have sex," is how she put it.

I turned my back while Dale Anne changed. She was as modest as I was. If the house caught fire one night, we would both die struggling to hook brassieres beneath our gowns.

I went back to my chair, and as I did, a sensational cramp snapped me over until I was nearly on the floor.

"Easy, gal—what's the trouble?" Dale Anne started out of bed to come see.

I said it sometimes happens since the procedure, and Dale Anne said, "Let's not talk about that for at *least* ten years."

I could not think of what to say to that. But I didn't have to. The front door opened, earlier than it usually did. It was Dr. Diamond, home from the world of spooks and ghosts and loony bins and Ouija boards. I knew that a lack of concern for others was a hallmark of mental illness, so I straightened up and said, after he'd kissed his pregnant wife, "You look hot, Dr. Diamond. Can I get you a drink?"

I BUY my materials at a place in the residential section. The owner's name is Ingrid. She is a large Norwegian woman who spells needles "kneedles." She wears sample knits she makes up for the class demonstrations. The vest she wore the day before will be hanging in the window.

There are always four or five women at Ingrid's round oak table, knitting through a stretch they would not risk alone.

Often I go there when I don't need a thing. In the small back room that is stacked high with pattern books, I can sift for hours. I scan the instructions abbreviated like musical notation: *K10, sl 1, K2 tog, psso, sl 1, K10 to end.* I feel I could *sing* these instructions. It is compression of language into code; your ability to decipher it makes you privy to the secrets shared by Ingrid and the women at the round oak table.

In the other room, Ingrid tells a customer she used to knit two hundred stitches a minute.

I scan the French and English catalogues, noting the longer length of coat. There is so much to absorb on each visit.

Mary had a little lamb, I am humming when I leave the shop. *Its feet were—its fleece was white as wool.*

. . .

DALE ANNE wanted a nap, so Dr. Diamond and I went out for margaritas. At La Rondalla, the colored lights on the Virgin tell you every day is Christmas. The food arrives on manhole covers and mariachis fill the bar. Dr. Diamond said that in Guadalajara there is a mariachi college that turns out mariachis by the classful. But I could tell that these were not graduates of even mariachi high school.

I shooed the serenaders away, but Dr. Diamond said they meant well.

Dr. Diamond likes for people to mean well. He could be president of the Well-Meaning Club. He has had a buoyant feeling of fate since he learned Freud died the day he was born.

He was the person to talk to, all right, so I brought up the stomach pains I was having for no bodily reason that I could think of.

"You know how I think," he said. "What is it you can't stomach?"

I knew what he was asking.

"Have you thought about how you will feel when Dale Anne has the baby?" he asked.

With my eyes, I wove strands of tinsel over the Blessed Virgin. That was the great thing about knitting, I thought—everything was fiber, the world a world of natural resource.

"I thought I would burn that bridge when I come to it," I said, and when he didn't say anything to that, I said, "I guess I will think that there is a mother who *kept* hers."

"*One* of hers might be more accurate," Dr. Diamond said.

I ARRIVED at the yarn shop as Ingrid turned over the *Closed* sign to *Open*. I had come to buy Shetland wool for a Fair Isle sweater. I felt nothing would engage my full attention more than a pattern of ancient Scottish symbols and alternate bands of delicate design. Every stitch in every color is related to the one above, below, and to either side.

I chose the natural colors of Shetland sheep—the chalky brown of the Moorit, the blackish brown of the black sheep, fawn, gray, and pinky beige from a mixture of Moorit and white. I held the wool to my nose, but Ingrid said it was fifty years since the women of Fair Isle dressed the yarn with fish oil.

She said the yarn came from Sheep Rock, the best pasture on Fair Isle. It is a ten-acre plot that is four hundred feet up a cliff, Ingrid said. "Think what a man has to go through to harvest the wool."

I was willing to feel an obligation to the yarn, and to the hardy Scots who supplied it. There was heritage there, and I could keep it alive with my hands.

DALE ANNE patted capers into a mound of raw beef, and spread some onto toast. It was not a pretty sight. She offered some to me, and I said not a chance. I told her Johnny Carson is someone else who won't go near that. I said, "Johnny says he won't eat steak tartare because he has seen things hurt worse than that get better."

"Johnny was never pregnant," Dale Anne said.

WHEN THE contractions began, I left a message with the hospital and with Dr. Diamond's lab. I turned off the air-conditioner and called for a cab.

"Look at you," Dale Anne said.

I told her I couldn't help it. I get rational when I panic.

The taxi came in minutes.

"Hold on," the driver said. "I know every bump in these roads, and I've never been able to miss one of them."

Dale Anne tried to squeeze my wrist, but her touch was weightless, as porous as wet silk.

"When this is over . . ." Dale Anne said.

. . .

WHEN THE BABY was born, I did not go far. I sublet a place on the other side of town. I filled it with patterns and needles and yarn. It was what I did in the day. On a good day, I made a front and two sleeves. On a bad day, I ripped out stitches from neck to hem. For variety, I made socks. The best ones I made had beer steins on the sides, and the tops spilled over with white angora foam.

I did not like to work with sound in the room, not even the sound of a fan. Music slowed me down, and there was a great deal to do. I planned to knit myself a mailbox and a car, perhaps even a dog and a lead to walk him.

I BLOCKED the finished pieces and folded them in drawers.

Dr. Diamond urged me to exercise. He called from time to time, looking in. He said exercise would set me straight, and why not have some fun with it? Why not, for example, tap-dancing lessons?

I told him it would be embarrassing because the rest of the class would be doing it right. And with all the knitting, there wasn't time to dance.

Dale Anne did not look in. She had a pretty good reason not to.

The day I went to see her in the hospital, I stopped at the nursery first. I saw the baby lying facedown. He wore yellow duck-print flannels. I saw that he was there—and then I went straight home.

That night the dreams began. A giant lizard ate people from the feet upwards, swallowing the argyles on the first bite, then drifting into obscurity like a ranger of forgotten death. I woke up remembering and, like a chameleon, assumed every shade of blame.

Asleep at night, I went to an elegant ball. In the center of the dance floor was a giant aquarium. Hundreds of goldfish swam inside. At a sign from the bandleader, the tank was overturned. Until someone tried to dance on the fish, the floor was aswirl with gold glory.

DR. DIAMOND told a story about the young daughter of a friend. The little girl had found a frog in the yard. The frog appeared to be dead, so her parents let her prepare a burial site—a little hole surrounded by pebbles. But at the moment of the lowering, the frog, which had only been stunned, kicked its legs and came to.

"Kill him!" the girl had shrieked.

I BEGAN to take walks in the park. In the park, I saw a dog try to eat his own shadow, and another dog—I am sure of it—was herding a stand of elms. I stopped telling people how handsome their dogs were; too many times what they said was, "You want him?"

When the weather got nicer, I stayed home to sit for hours.

I had accidents. Then I had bigger ones. But the part that hurt was never the part that got hurt.

The dreams came back and back until they were just—again. I wished that things would stay out of sight the way they did in mountain lakes. In one that I know, the water is so cold, gas can't form to bring a corpse to the surface. Although you would not want to think about the bottom of the lake, what you can say about it is—the dead stay down.

Around that time I talked to Dr. Diamond.

The point that he wanted to make was this: that conception was not like walking in front of traffic. No matter how badly timed, it was, he said, an affirmation of life.

"You have to believe me here," he said. "Do you see that this is true? Do you know this about yourself?"

"I do and I don't," I said.

"You do and you *do,*" he said.

I remembered when another doctor made the news. A young

retarded boy had found his father's gun, and while the family slept, he shot them all in bed. The police asked the boy what he had done. But the boy went mute. He told them nothing. Then they called in the doctor.

"We know *you* didn't do it," the doctor said to the boy, "but tell me, did the *gun* do it?"

And yes, the boy was eager to tell him just what that gun had done.

I wanted the same out, and Dr. Diamond wouldn't let me have it.

"Dr. Diamond," I said, "I am giving up."

"Now you are ready to begin," he said.

I thought of Andean alpaca because that was what I planned to work up next. The feel of that yarn was not the only wonder—there was also the name of it: Alpaquita Superfina.

Dr. Diamond was right.

I was ready to begin.

Beg, sl tog, inc, cont, rep.

Begin, slip together, increase, continue, repeat.

Dr. Diamond answered the door. He said Dale Anne had run to the store. He was leaving, too, flying to a conference back East. The baby was asleep, he said, I should make myself at home.

I left my bag of knitting in the hall and went into Dale Anne's kitchen. It had been a year. I could have looked in on the baby. Instead, I washed the dishes that were soaking in the sink. The scouring pad was steel wool waiting for knitting needles.

The kitchen was filled with specialized utensils. When Dale Anne couldn't sleep she watched TV, and that's where the stuff was advertised. She had a thing to core tomatoes—it was called a Tomato Shark—and a metal spaghetti wheel for measuring out spaghetti. She had plastic melon-ballers and a push-in device that turned ordinary cake into ladyfingers.

I found pasta primavera in the refrigerator. My fingers wanted to knit the cold linguini, laying precisely cabled strands across the oily red peppers and beans.

Dale Anne opened the door.

"*Look* out, gal," she said, and dropped a shopping bag on the counter.

I watched her unload ice cream, potato chips, carbonated drinks, and cake.

"It's been a long time since I walked into a market and expressed myself," she said.

She turned to toss me a carton of cigarettes.

"Wait for me in the bedroom," she said. "*West Side Story* is on."

I went in and looked at the color set. I heard the blender crushing ice in the kitchen. I adjusted the contrast, then Dale Anne handed me an enormous peach daiquiri. The goddamn thing had a tide factor.

Dale Anne left the room long enough to bring in the take-out chicken. She upended the bag on a plate and picked out a leg and a wing.

"I like my dinner in a bag and my life in a box," she said, nodding toward the TV.

We watched the end of the movie, then part of a lame detective program. Dale Anne said the show *owed* Nielsen four points, and reached for the *TV Guide*.

"Eleven-thirty," she read. "*The Texas Whiplash Massacre:* Unexpected stop signs were their weapon."

"Give me that," I said.

DALE ANNE said there was supposed to be a comet. She said we could probably see it if we watched from the living room. Just to be sure, we pushed the couch up close to the window. With the lights off, we could see everything without it seeing us. Although both of us had quit, we smoked at either end of the couch.

"Save my place," Dale Anne said.

She had the baby in her arms when she came back in. I looked at the sleeping child and thought, Mercy, Land Sakes, Lordy Me. As though I had aged fifty years. For just a moment then I wanted nothing that I had and everything I did not.

"He told his first joke today," Dale Anne said.

"What do you mean he told a joke?" I said. "I didn't think they could talk."

"Well, he didn't really *tell* a joke—he poured his orange juice over his head, and when I started after him, he said, 'Raining?'"

"'Raining?' That's what he said? The kid is a genius," I told Dale Anne. "What Art Linkletter could do with this kid."

Dale Anne laid him down in the middle of the couch, and we watched him or watched the sky.

"WHAT A GYP," Dale Anne said at dawn.

There had not been a comet. But I did not feel cheated, or even tired. She walked me to the door.

The knitting bag was still in the hall.

"Open it later," I said. "It's a sweater for him."

But Dale Anne had to see it then.

She said the blue one matched his eyes and the camel one matched his hair. The red would make him glow, she said, and then she said, "Help me out."

Cables had become too easy; three more sweaters had pictures knitted in. They buttoned up the front. Dale Anne held up a parade of yellow ducks.

There were the Fair Isles, too—one in the pattern called Tree of Life, another in the pattern called Hearts.

It was an excess of sweaters—a kind of precaution, a rehearsal against disaster.

Dale Anne looked at the two sweaters still in the bag.

"Are you really okay?" she said.

. . .

THE WORST OF IT is over now, and I can't say that I am glad. Lose that sense of loss—you have gone and lost something else. But the body moves toward health. The mind, too, in steps. One step at a time. Ask a mother who has just lost a child, How many children do you have? "Four," she will say, "—three," and years later, "Three," she will say, "—four."

It's the little steps that help. Weather, breakfast, crossing with the light—sometimes it is all the pleasure I can bear to sleep, and know that on a rack in the bath, damp wool is pinned to dry.

Dale Anne thinks she would like to learn to knit. She measures the baby's crib and I take her over to Ingrid's. Ingrid steers her away from the baby pastels, even though they are machine-washable. Use a pure wool, Ingrid says. Use wool in a grown-up shade. And don't boast of your achievements or you'll be making things for the neighborhood.

On Fair Isle there are only five women left who knit. There is not enough lichen left growing on the island for them to dye their yarn. But knitting machines can't produce their designs, and they keep on, these women, working the undyed colors of the sheep.

I wait for Dale Anne in the room with the patterns. The songs in these books are like lullabies to me.

K tog rem st. Knit together remaining stitches.

Cast off loosely.

Ellen Gilchrist

🜲

Light Can Be Both Wave and Particle

LIN TAN SING was standing on the bridge overlooking Puget Sound, watching the seagulls (white against the blue sky) caught in the high conflicting winds. He was trying to empty his mind, even of pleasant memories like his talk with Miss Whittington on the train.

Just Lin Tan, he was thinking. Just sunrise, just sea. Sometimes I go about in pity for myself, and all the while, a great wind is bearing me across the sky. He sighed. Lin Tan was very wise for his age. It was a burden he must bear and he was always thinking of ways to keep it from showing, so that other people would not seem small or slow-witted by comparison. All men have burdens, he decided. Only mine is greater burden. I am like great tanker making waves in harbor, about to swamp somebody. This is bad thinking for early morning. I am on vacation now, must enjoy myself. He sighed again. The sun was moving up above the smokestacks on the horizon. The first day of his vacation was ending and the second was about to begin.

A girl stepped out onto the bridge and stood very still with her hands in the pockets of her raincoat. She was looking at him. Just beautiful girl, Lin Tan thought. Just karma. Twin fetuses inside Miss Whittington and now this girl comes like a goddess from the sea.

"Are you lost?" he said. "Have you lost your way?"

"No," she answered. "I just wanted to see the place where my cousin committed suicide. Isn't that morbid?"

"Curiosity is normal mode of being," he said. "I am Lin Tan Sing of San Francisco, California, and China. I am candidate for doctor of medicine at University of California in San Francisco. Third-year student. I am honored to make your acquaintance on lucky second day of my vacation."

"I'm Margaret McElvoy of Fayetteville, Arkansas. Look down there." She leaned far out over the rail. "My God, how could anybody jump into that."

"Water is not responsible for man's unhappiness."

"Well, I guess you're right about that. My father says religion is."

"What!"

"Oh, nothing. I didn't mean to say that." She straightened her shoulders, leaned down and looked again into the deep salty bay. Now the sun threw lines of brilliant dusty rose across the water. On a pillar of the middle span someone had written "Pussy" with a can of spray paint. Margaret giggled.

"Please continue," Lin Tan said. He thought she was thinking of the dark ridiculous shadows of religion.

"Oh, it's nothing. My father thinks he can find out what got us in all this trouble. He thinks we're in trouble." She turned and really looked at him, took him in. He was tall for an Oriental, almost as tall as her brothers, and he was very handsome with strong shoulders and a wide strong face. His eyes were wise, dark and still, and Margaret completely forgot she wasn't supposed to talk to strangers. Something funny might be going on, she thought, like kismet or chemistry or magnetism or destiny and so forth.

"Great paradox of religion must be explored by man," Lin Tan said. "In its many guises it has brought us where we are today, I agree with your father. We must judge its worth and its excesses. I am Buddhist, of Mayany Timbro sect. I am more scientist than Buddhist however."

"I'm nothing. My mother's Catholic and my father's a poet. Well, the sun's coming up and the gulls are feeding." Margaret pushed her bangs back with her hand. She smiled into Lin Tan's eyes. She wasn't doing anything on purpose. She was just standing there letting him fall in love with her.

"I am very hungry after night on supertrain called Starlight Express. It would be great honor for me if you would accompany me to breakfast. I am alone in Seattle on first morning of my vacation and need someone to ask about problem I have just encountered."

"Oh, what is that?"

"I am working part-time in women's clinic in Berkeley, near to campus of University of California. I am in charge of test results from amniocentesis, do you know what that is?"

"Sure."

"Some months ago I made analysis of amniotic fluid from one Miss Nora Jane Whittington of Berkeley. Was auspicious day in my life as I had been given honor by university for my work in fetal biology. So I remember date. Also, this test was unusual as it revealed twin female fetuses with AB positive blood, very special kind of blood, very rare. Often found in people whose ancestors came from British Isles, especially Scotland and Wales. So I wrote out the report and later I found I had made a mistake on it. I made a notation that the blood type is that of universal donor. I should have written universal recipient. Now, last night, in coincidence of first order, if you believe theory of random events and accidents, last night on the train I meet this Miss Whittington, now seven and a half months pregnant and in the course of our conversation she tells me how happy she is that her daughters will be able to give blood to whole world if needed. She has in her pocketbook a copy of the report, with this false notation signed with my name. I am not in habit of making even slightest mistake. Now I must decide whether to tell my superiors at the lab and spoil my record of unblemished work."

"Could anyone be hurt by this?"

"No."

"Then let it lay. Let sleeping dogs lie, that's what my mother says."

"Very wise, very profound saying."

"Well, I'm a teacher. I'm supposed to know things. I teach first grade." She pushed the hood back from her hair. A cascade of golden curls fell across the shoulders of her raincoat. Her eyes were beautiful, large and violet colored and clear. "I was on my way to school when I stopped by here."

"I will walk you there." His throat constricted. His voice was growing deeper. He heard it as if from a great distance. Just love, he was thinking. Just divine madness.

"Well, why not." She looked out across the water, thinking of her cousin, dead as he could be. "I don't pick men up usually, but I'm a linguist. I can't miss a chance like this. I already speak French and Russian and Italian and some Greek. No Chinese, so far. What's your name?" She began walking down from the bridge. Lin Tan was beside her. The fog was lifting. The sun rising above the waters of Puget Sound. The dawn of a clear day.

"My name is Lin Tan Sing. Here, I give you my card." He pulled a card out of his pocket, a white card embossed in red. Down the center ran a curved red line. To remind him in case he should forget.

"I have to go to the launderette and get some clothes I left in the dryer," she said. "Then we'll go and get some breakfast."

SOON THEY WERE sitting in a small restaurant by the quay. They were at a table by a window. The window had old-fashioned panes and white lace curtains. A glass vase held wildflowers. A waiter appeared and took their orders.

"So this is the Tao on your card," she said. "I read a lot of Zen literature. And I try meditating but it always fails. My dad says the Western mind is no good for meditation. He writes books of philosophy. He's wonderful. I bet you'd love him if you met him."

"I would be honored to do so. I have wondered where the poets of United States were living. Where is he now? This father of yours?"

"In Arkansas. Do you have any idea where that is?"

"No. I am ashamed to say I do not understand geography of United States yet. I have been very busy since I arrived and have had no time to travel."

"It's a small state on the Mississippi River. We have wild forests and trees and chicken farms, the richest man in the world lives there, and we have minerals and coal. In the Delta we grow cotton and sometimes rice." She was enchanted by the foreignness of his manner. This is just my luck, she was thinking, to run into a Chinese doctor and get to find out all about China on my way to school.

"Oh, this is strange coincidence," he was saying. "In province where I come from, we are also growing cotton. Yes, I have heard of this Mississippi Delta cotton. Yours is very beautiful but no longer picked by hand, is it not true?"

"Yours is?"

"Oh, yes. I have picked it myself when I was a small boy. The staple is torn by machine. The cloth will not be perfect. Perhaps I could invent a better cotton picking machine. I have often thought I should have been an inventor instead of a scientist but my mother died when I was thirteen so I have lived to save lives of others. I had meant it as an act of revenge against disease, now see it as finding harmony for life in its myriad forms. So you know the Tao?"

"I know of it. I don't know how to do it yet." The light of morning was shining on her face. Just face, he thought. Just light of sun. Just Tao. "It is the middle way, the way of balance and of harmony." He picked up a napkin, took a pen from his pocket and drew a diagonal line down the center of it. "This is the life we are living, now, at this moment, which is all we ever have. This is where we are. It is all that is and contains everybody." He looked at her. She was listening. She understood.

"I want to see you a lot," she said. "I want us to be friends." Her voice was as beautiful as the song of birds, more beautiful than temple bells. Her voice was light made manifest. Now Lin Tan's throat was thick with desire. He suffered it. There was nothing in the world as beautiful as her face, her voice, her hands, the smell of her dress. She took a small blue flower from the bouquet on the table and twisted it between her fingers. She looked at him. She returned his look. This was the moment men live for. This was philosophy and reason. Shiva, Beatrice, the dance of birth and death. If I enter into this moment, Lin Tan knew, I will be changed forever. If I refuse this moment then I will go about the world as an old man goes, with no hope, no songs to sing, no longing or desire, no miracles of sunlight. So I will allow this to happen to me. As if a man can refuse his destiny. As if the choice were mine. Let it come to me.

He closed his eyes for a second. Wait, his other mind insisted. Get up and leave. Get back on the train and ride back down the coast and enter the train station at San Francisco. Go to the lab. Work overtime on vacation. Catch up on all work of lab. Take money and increase holdings of gold coins in lockbox at Wells Fargo Bank of San Francisco, California. Spend vacation time at home. Go with friends to the beach, there is no destiny that holds me in this chair. Here is where I could prove free will, could test hypotheses. If not for all mankind, at least in my case.

"I would like very much if you would have dinner with me when you finish teaching for the day," he said. "I will be finding the greatest restaurant in all Seattle while you bestow gift of knowledge on young minds. I will tell you about my home and language and you will tell me of Romance languages and Arkansas."

"There's a Japanese movie at the Aristophanes. It's by Kurosawa. We could get a sandwich somewhere and go to the movie. I don't need to go to great restaurants." The waitress had appeared with their waffles and orange juice. "To think I started out this morning to go see where somebody committed suicide." She raised her orange juice. "This table reminds me of a painting I saw last year at the Metropolitan Museum of Art in New York City. It was by Manet. It was just incredible. I almost died. A painting of a bar with a barmaid. This sad-eyed blond barmaid standing behind a bar filled with glasses and bottles of colored liquid. The light was all over everything and her face was shining out from all that. It was real primal. My father loves paintings. We couldn't afford the real thing, but there were always wonderful prints and posters all over our house, even on the ceiling. This waffle is perfect. Go on and eat yours."

She took a bite of golden waffle soaked in syrup, then wiped her mouth daintily, with a napkin. A queen is inside of this girl, Lin Tan thought. She is a princess. He laughed with delight at everything she had said, at the light on the table, the syrup soaking into the waffle, the largess, bounty, divinity of the day.

"We will go and see what the barbaric Japanese have done with your film," he said. "Or anything that will seem nice to you."

"What time is it getting to be?" she answered. "I've got to hurry up. I'm going to be late to school."

THEY NEVER MADE IT to the movie. They walked for miles after dinner talking in all the languages they knew and telling their stories. She talked of the origins of language, how she wished to study man's speech and was teaching six-year-olds so she could investigate their minds as they learned to read and write. As they formed the letters and grew bold and turned the letters into words.

He told her of physics, of quantum mechanics and particle physics, the quark and chaos, a vision of reality as a swirling mass of energy bound into forms that are always changing. The greatest mystery is time, he insisted. Energy is held for a moment in form, then flung back into chaos, re-formed, captured again, undone, done and undone, an endless dance which we glimpse when we hear music. "Man is the inventor of time," he said. "Only man has need of it."

"You don't care if it is meaningless?"

"Is even more beautiful that way. I think I am falling in love with you, Margaret."

"I was afraid you would say that." She stopped by a stone wall and allowed him to take her hands. "It excites me, the way you talk. But we have to be careful. I could just be getting you mixed up with my dad. He talks like that all the time. It's sort of made me older than a lot of people. It has made me older." She pulled her hands away. "I don't want to fall in love with someone just because he talks like my father. Even if you are Chinese. I mean, he is Scotch-Irish. His father was all Irish. We have a lot of Irish blood."

"The blood of poets."

"How did you know that?"

"Because I read your literature."

"Well, I'm not going to bed with you tonight."

"Oh, no." Lin Tan bowed his head. "I was not expecting you to. I will take you home now. In the morning I will come and propose marriage. But not until I know you better." He laughed a great hearty laugh, a laugh he had forgotten he possessed. It was the best laugh he had ever laughed in the United States. He leaned back against the wall and laughed for several minutes and Margaret McElvoy laughed with him.

"This is the strangest night I ever spent in my life," she said. "Come on, let's go home."

SHE TOOK HIM to visit her school. On the fourth day of his vacation Lin Tan found himself lecturing on Chinese education to a combined first- and second-grade class. He told them everything he knew about grade school in rural China, then showed them a dance Chinese children learn to help them remember their multiplication tables. He had gone to Seattle's Chinatown and borrowed a traditional Chinese teacher's costume to wear to the school. Margaret sat in the back of the class and watched the muscles of his back as they moved his arm up and down on the blackboard. The soft blue cloth of his jacket rippled as his muscles moved his hand, and Lin Tan knew she was watching him and kept his body as graceful and supple as a dancer's as he taught. That night she went to bed with him.

"This might be too soon," he said, when she suggested it.

"It's too soon but I haven't done it with anybody in a year, so that makes up for it."

Then, in a rented room in a small hotel, with a lamp burning on the table and the sounds of Seattle outside the windows, they offered their bodies to each other, as children would, with giggles and embarrassment and seriousness, with shame and passion and a very large amount of silliness they searched each other out and made love, not very well at first, then better. "Here is where my knowledge of anatomy and obstetrics should come in handy," Lin Tan said. "Here is where the doctor comes in."

"I used to play doctor with my cousin, but we always got caught. We would put baby oil on each other because her mother was always having babies and we'd get it on the sheets, then they would catch us and take us off to the living room and tell us not to do it. You should have seen my mother's face when she'd be telling me not to. The smell of baby oil would be everywhere. She was a girl but we were only four so I don't think that means I'm a lesbian, do you?"

"What would you do with the baby oil?" They were lying side by side on the bed, talking without looking at each other.

"We would put it on and then stick this toy thermometer in each other. I guess that really was dangerous, wasn't it? Maybe that's what made them so mad." She sat up on one elbow and looked at him. "I wonder if it was made of glass. We could have killed each other sticking glass up our vaginas."

"Perhaps made of wood," Lin Tan said. "Many toys are made of wood."

"We could have gotten splinters. No wonder they got so mad, but I think they were really mad because we had found out about sex. They were so protective. They still are, to tell the truth."

"What would you say to one another when you would stick this thermometer into your hollow places? Did you say, 'I will diagnose you now'?"

"We said, 'This will make you feel better.' " She started giggling and Lin Tan laughed his great lost belly laugh again and they rolled back into each other's arms.

"Will you stay the night with me," he asked, "or shall I take you to your home?"

"I'll stay. When I do this I always do it right. My dad told us not to sleep with anybody unless we liked them enough to spend the night."

"And what else?"

"To call up the next day and talk about it. I mean, say something. Because it's pretty important, you know. It's not nothing, making love to another person."

"What did your mother say?"

"She said not to do it until you get married. She says it's for making babies, not some game."

"I would like to meet these parents of yours. I would like to talk with them."

"Well, if things keep going like this I guess you'll get to." She touched his hand. She was falling asleep. She left the waking universe and entered the world of sleep. Once we were always asleep, Lin Tan remembered. Slowly man has awakened. Oh, let the awakening proceed. Let us rouse to clarity and not blow up the world where Margaret sleeps. He stilled his mind then with a mantra of wind and water and slipped down into the ancient mystery of sleep himself.

In the morning they woke very early and talked for a while. Then Margaret dressed and Lin Tan walked her down to the car. "It is very awkward to leave someone after making love," he said. "It is very hard to know what to say."

"I know," she answered. "Well, say you'd like to see me again. That's the main thing anyone wants to hear."

"Oh, I want to see you many more times."

"Then come over tonight. Can you remember the way?"

"I will be there," Lin Tan answered. He helped her into the car and stood watching as she drove away. He shook his head. It amazed him that Americans worried about him finding his way from one place to another when the country was filled with maps and street signs. At the place where her car had been, several pigeons flew down from a roof and began to peck at the sidewalk. Lin took that for a sign and went back into the hotel and sat in meditation for an hour, remembering the shape of the universe and the breathtaking order of the species. He imagined the spirit of Margaret and the forms of her ancestors back a hundred generations. Then he imagined Margaret in the womb and spoke to her in a dream on the day she was conceived. Then he dressed and walked around the city of Seattle, Washington, all day long, bestowing blessings in his mind and being blessed.

As soon as Margaret got home from school that afternoon she sat down at her desk and wrote the first of what her family would later refer to as the Chinese Letters.

> Dear Mom and Dad, Jane and Teddy and Len,
>   I have met THE MAN. I'm not kidding you. This one is too much. I don't know where to begin. In the first place I met him on the exact place *on the bridge where Sherman jumped off. He*

was standing there when I got there. He is Chinese. Dad, don't go crazy. Listen to this. He is the smartest person I have ever met in my life except for you. He reminds me a lot of Professor Levine. I mean he has the same kind of penetrating black eyes that just bore into you and like you so much you feel like you have known him always. He is twenty-five. He's a medical student (third year) at the University of California at San Francisco and has a job besides. He runs a diagnostic lab and he is going to graduate with high high honors, then go back to China to help his people. Please don't worry about this. I had to tell you, but not if I get a lot of phone calls at seven in the morning telling me what to do. Momma, thank you for sending the sweater and the blouses. They will come in handy with the laundry problems. Love and kisses. I love you,

Margaret

She sat back, read over what she had written, drew a few trees on the leftover paper on the bottom, addressed and stamped an envelope and stuck the letter in. Then she left her apartment and went down to the mailbox to mail the letter. While she was gone Lin Tan tried to call four times. Each time he left a message on her answering machine. The last time he left a poem.

Miracle of seven redbirds
On snow-covered bamboo
What brings them here on such a day?

Miracle of a tall woman
Watching beside me
She bends her head my way.

"By the poet Wang Wei from Qixion County in Shaanxi. I am counting the moments until I am with you again."

.   .   .

THAT NIGHT HE STAYED at her home. A small apartment overlooking the bay. A balcony was on the back. They sat with their feet on the railings and he told her about his work. "Then I will see into the heart of life, the very heart of the beginning of life, and, for my specialty, I am studying the beginning and formation of the human brain. At a moment soon after conception one cell of the zygote splits off and decides to become brain. After that moment, that cell and all its progeny become the brain stem and the brain, the miraculous brain of man. This happens, oh, a million times a minute. Everywhere on earth new people are being created. Inside women this miracle is going on and inside miracle, second miracle of brain formation is happening. Oh, problem is how to feed and care for them. There is so much work, it must be done. Must be done. It is very presumptuous to wish to do such important work but so my dreams are. Dreams often come true. If something is not within human grasp we cannot conceive of it. Think of Thomas Edison with his dream of electricity. Light up the world. Yes, and my friend, Randal Yung of Pisgah, New Jersey, only this very week, has captured atoms in a prison of laser beams and is watching them grow. They are growing because he is watching. Is called the Bose-Einstein condensation and was only a theory until this week. I have been invited to go and view this experiment. Would you care to fly to New Jersey sometime to see miracle of captured atoms?"

"You know the guy in New Jersey who did that?" She had been taking a roasted chicken from the oven to baste it. Now she closed the oven door and walked over to the table where he was sitting. "You know that guy?"

"He is a friend of mine from boyhood. From village next to mine. His Chinese name is difficult to pronounce in English so he has taken the name of Randal. We were sent to the advanced school together from our province. He is very advanced about everything, is very smart, is great scientist. Randal wishes to live in the stars. He is a beautiful man. All the girls are ready to die for him."

"And we could go up there and really look at this?"

"Yes, we could."

"Then we have to go. My God, this is the chance of a lifetime. I can get a substitute to teach for me. I'll tell them where I'm going. Oh, God, my father will have a fit when he finds out. He adores physicists. He says they are doing things they don't even understand. My God." She threw her hair back from her face. A pot of green beans was boiling over on the stove. Lin Tan got up and took the pot holder from her and saved their dinner.

LATER, THEY MADE LOVE again. This time it was better than it was the first time since they were no longer afraid of each other.

It is a strange thing to make love to a member of another race. Exciting and strange, curious and amazing. The amazing thing is that nothing unusual happens. The foreign person doesn't turn into a demon or begin to speak in pagan incantations or turn out to be automatically unsound. They just get in bed and make love with the same old set of moves and pleasures that have stood all the races in good stead for many centuries. This is me with this beautiful goddess, Lin Tan was saying to himself now, as he watched Margaret pulling a pink satin petticoat over her head. Just Lin Tan. Just Margaret. Just fantastic sexual activity of species. Oh, if she will only love me I will solve riddle of cancer and also learn to operate on fetal heart.

"What are you thinking about?" she said. The petticoat was across her legs.

"I am thinking of the fetal heart. Sometime the valves develop in bad sequence. If the mother has been smoking or not eating properly or very nervous and worried. You must come sometime to my lab and see the sonograms. Very beautiful to watch babies like fish swimming." He was quiet. When he raised his head there were tears in his eyes. "Sometimes, by the time they are in our laboratories, they are not happy swimmers. Sometimes they are in trouble. Last week, we thought we had triplets on the screen. Much excitement. It was two little boys fighting to live. They had transfused each other through the common umbilical cord. So tragic. The mother was struggling and in pain. We delivered them by cesarean section and did all that was possible but they were gone by the time we got them to the incubator. Poor little mother. Thinking of this makes me wonder what has been happening with Miss Whittington." He got up. He was wearing a terry cloth robe that had belonged to one of Margaret's brothers. He walked over to where he had left his clothes and found his billfold and searched in it for the phone number Miss Whittington had given him on the train. "She should not have been traveling so late in her pregnancy. I should have left the train to see that she made it safely to a place of rest, but if I had done that I would not have been standing on bridge when you came out of fog bank. Like a goddess."

"You are crying over a stranger."

"All the world is one reality. Each man or woman is exerting many influences every moment of day. This is the night I meant to show you my great Zen lovemaking I read about today in a book while you were in school. Instead, I tell you this sad story." He stood by the bedpost holding his billfold, the drapes of the terry robe falling open across his chest and stomach. Margaret crawled across the bed and pulled him into her arms. She stretched him out on the bed and began to count his ribs. "I never had this much fun knowing anybody," she said. "I can't believe you left a poem on my phone."

"I must find a more romantic poem for you. I will translate modern Chinese poetry for you so you can know my country through its poets."

"You are going back there to live?"

"I am not certain yet." He closed his eyes. She will think me ignoble, he decided, if I tell her that I wish to stay in the United States and make money. She is daughter of poet, very romantic upbringing. "I wish to go heal my people," he added. "I wish to be noble physician so that Margaret McElroy will think I am a wonderful man and care for me."

"I do," she said. "What do you think I'm doing here?"

"Would you go with me to live in China?"

"I don't know," she answered. "I've never been there."

HER FATHER CALLED at seven the next morning. "What's going on?"

"Nothing's going on. I only met him a week ago."

"Your mother's worried. Here, talk to her."

"Margaret."

"Yes."

"Don't do anything foolish."

"I'm not writing to you anymore if you call me up this early."

"Come home and bring this Chinese doctor with you. Your father wants to meet him."

"He's on his vacation. He doesn't want to come to Fayetteville, Arkansas." She looked across the bed at Lin Tan. He was nodding his head up and down. His mouth was saying, Yes, I will. Yes, I do. "He wants to," Margaret added. "He's here."

"In your apartment? At seven o'clock in the morning?"

"It's nineteen eighty-six, Mother. Look, I'm hanging up. I'll call you later."

"We'll pay for the plane ticket. Get down here this weekend, Margaret Anne."

"Mother, I have company now. I'll call you later."

"Your father and I want you to come home this weekend. You can bring your friend with you. I don't know what you are doing out there, Margaret. If you don't come here, we are coming out there."

"I'll try. Wait a minute." She put her hand over the receiver and turned to Lin Tan. "You want to go visit them? Momma works for a travel agency. She'll send us some tickets. You want to go?"

"I would be honored to go meet your mother and father. But I can pay for my own airplane ticket."

"We'll come. Send me some tickets. Oh, okay. We'll do that. I'll call you tomorrow." She hung up and turned back to Lin Tan. "Well here we go. Now you'll see the real me, I guess. My parents are wonderful but they boss us all around like crazy. You sure you want to do this?"

"Of course. It will be great honor and also allow me to see interior of United States. But I must pay for my own airplane fare."

"Don't worry about that. It's her perks, you know, she gets a certain number of tickets free. She gets mad if we won't use them. Well, I guess we're going then, aren't we? Imagine you meeting my dad. Just imagine." She moved closer to him and it was several hours before they finished their other plans.

TWO THOUSAND MILES away Big Ted McElvoy was sitting at his desk trying to write a poem. He had been reading *The Seven Pillars of Zen.* The poem was subtly but not greatly influenced by that reading.

> *Hostages to fortune, what does that mean?*
> *A man should bow his head and watch his children*
> *Disappear? Has* given *hostages, a conscious act? . . .*

He studied the lines, tore the page from the tablet, laid it on a stack. He went back to the tablet, drew several parallelograms, then four isosceles triangles, then a cone. He got out a compass, measured the angles of the triangles, then laid the compass down and picked up the phone. He called a close friend who was a doctor and asked him to come by on his way home from work.

"I'm writing a poem about daughters. You might want to see it. Where's Drew?"

"She's still in Tulsa. She changed jobs. So what's up? I take it you heard from Margaret. How is she?"

"She's out in Seattle seeing some Chinese doctor she met on a bridge. It's too hard, Ken. It's too goddamn hard to do."

"She'll be okay."

"I don't know. I don't know about letting them go off to goddamn cities and start screwing anybody they meet on a bridge. Well, she's bringing him here Saturday. Jane sent them tickets."

"I'd like to meet this Chinese doctor."

"Damn right. That's why I'm calling. Come give me a printout. She says he plays chess. Come Saturday night."

"Sure, and Ted, I'll be over as soon as I finish up here."

"Good. Hurry up."

THE BEAUTIFUL and awesome scene when Margaret and Lin Tan arrived in Fayetteville, Arkansas. The progress of the car that carried them from the airport to the house where she was born. The embraces at the baggage claim, father and daughter, mother and daughter, mother and Lin Tan. They drove home through the campus of the University of Arkansas. The oaks and maples were golden and red and the Ozarks were a dark dusty blue on the horizon. The marching band was practicing in the Greek amphitheater. "Sweet Georgia Brown" filled the brisk fall air. Big Ted steered the old Buick slowly past the buildings that housed his life's work. Twenty-seven years of English students had floundered beneath the gaze and searing intelligence of Big Ted. But he was not teaching now. His face was straight ahead. His hands were on the wheel. His mind was concentrated on one thing and one thing only. To get to know this Chinese man before he pronounced judgment on him. He had been up since dawn reading the late poems of William Butler Yeats to fortify himself.

"Where were you raised?" he asked. "Tell me where you come from.

"My father owns small plot of land. He was doctor for our section for many years. Not member of party but looked on with favor by party. I am the oldest son. I was chosen to come here and learn Western medicine. There are many medicines and tools here that we need." Lin Tan paused. He folded his hands together. "I will graduate with highest honors. Perhaps at head of class. At least in number-two spot."

"How do you know Randal Yung?"

"Is cousin and boyhood friend from school. Same age as me."

"Have you talked to him since he did it?"

"Oh, yes. Several times."

"What did he see?"

"Atoms swimming in thick honey of light. Very confused activity. Random and unpredictable. Entropy setting in. Disequilibrium. Atoms are moving very slowly now. Like death of organism, he says."

"We'll talk when we get home." Big Ted shook his head, as if to say, Don't talk about this in front of the women. In the back seat Jane McElvoy gave her daughter a look and Margaret McElvoy returned the look.

They pulled into the driveway of the house. A frame house painted blue with white trim. An old-fashioned screened-in porch with two porch swings ran across the front of the house. Gardens with chrysanthemums blooming bordered the porch and the sidewalk leading from the driveway. A silver maple in full fall color commanded the yard. A sleepy old fox terrier guarded the stairs. "This is it," Margaret said. "This is where I live."

"Come on in," Big Ted said to Lin Tan. "We'll talk in my office."

THEY BROUGHT the suitcases inside and put them on the beds in the downstairs bedrooms, then the two men walked down a hall and out the back door to a small building beside a vegetable garden. "Office," it said on the door, and Big Ted formally and with graciousness escorted Lin Tan into his place of business. Held the door open for him, then waved him to the place of honor in a brown leather chair beside a desk. The office had been made from an old double garage. The walls of the room were lined with books, poems in glass frames, posters from museums. Propped against the books were other poems, framed and glued to pieces of cardboard or attached to the spines of books by paper clips. This is part of one of the poems Lin Tan could read from where he was sitting.

> *They flee from me, that sometime did me seek*
> *With naked foot, stalking in my chamber.*
> *I have seen them gentle, tame, and meek,*
> *That now are wild, and do not remember*
> *That sometime they put themselves in danger*
> *To take bread at my hand; and now they range,*
> *Busily seeking with a continual change,*
>
>   *Thanked be fortune it hath been otherwise,*
> *Twenty times better; but once in special,*
> *In thin array, after a pleasant guise,*
> *When her loose gown from her shoulders did fall,*
> *And she me caught in her arms long and small,*
> *Therewith all sweetly did me kiss,*
> *And softly said, "Dear heart, how like you this?"* . . .

"So you are going back to China when you finish your degree?" Big Ted said.

"No, first I have to do my residency."

"Where will that be?"

"I am not certain yet. Perhaps on East Coast or in Seattle."

"If you're one or two you ought to have your choice."

"Perhaps. They have not written to me yet."

"Then what? After you finish your residency?"

"It will take several years. I wish to operate on fetal heart. Also, to pursue studies of child development."

"You've got that pretty well knocked in your culture. Why study it here?"

"I might remain in this country. Perhaps mental aspects of child rearing are key to all health, or perhaps all is genes, chromosome charts of children with lymphomas are very interesting. Perhaps we can teach body of child to heal itself. If mothers can be taught to carry babies in their arms for one year after birth. But this is all theory of mine."

"No, it's common sense. Difficult to teach in the United States in nineteen eighty-six." Big Ted sighed. He looked across the desk at the young man. The energy flowed from Lin Tan's body, made an aura around him. It was going to be okay. I did good, Big Ted thought. Goddammit, I raised a girl with a brain in her head, hitting on all cylinders the morning she plucked this one from the sea. So, we'll let go. Let her go. Lose her. Maybe never see her again. Goddammit, she could wind up in a rice field or a prison. No, not with this man. He could take care of her.

Big Ted sighed again. He reached into a drawer of the desk and took out a bottle of whiskey and two small glasses. "You want a drink of whiskey?"

"You are worried about something? Tell me what you are thinking."

"I'm thinking you'll take my daughter to a communist country and I can't protect her there. Convince me I'm wrong."

"I might not return to my country. I have done a wrong thing. I have allowed her to think I am hero who would give up opportunity to stay in the United States and be a wealthy man to go back and serve my people. It was unworthy subterfuge." Lin Tan looked Big Ted straight in the eye. Outside someone was knocking on the door. "Lin Tan." It was Margaret's voice. "Come to the phone. It's a man at Johns Hopkins calling you. It's the dean of Johns Hopkins."

"There goes your noble subterfuge," Big Ted said. "Go and answer it."

THEY WERE offering Lin Tan the moon and he said yes, he would be glad to come and take it. Later that night he asked Margaret very formally to be his wife and she accepted and Big Ted and Jane got on the phone and started calling their friends.

"Do WE still have to sleep in separate rooms now that we're engaged?" Margaret asked her mother, later, when the two of them were down in her mother's room. "I mean, is it all right if I go in Teddy's room and sleep with him?"

"Oh, my darling, please don't ask that. I'm not ready for that."

"We're going to be married, Mother. Think how strange it must be for him, being here in this country, with us. I mean, after all."

"If you want to sleep with him go on and marry him then. We could have a wedding. You could get married while you're here." Her mother sank back against the pillows of the bed. It was a huge four-poster bed made from cypress logged on her grandfather's land. It had been a wedding gift from her parents, a quarter of a century ago, in another place, another time. Margaret's mother had been the most beautiful girl in that world. She was beautiful still, serene and sure, elegant and kind. Margaret hugged the bedpost. She was always a child in this room. All her life she had come in and hugged this bedpost while she asked questions and made pleas and waited for answers. Never once in her life had she been treated unfairly or unkindly in this room. So she looked upon the world as a place that could be expected to be kind and to be fair.

"It's too late to get married tonight," she said. "May we sleep with each other if we're going to get married tomorrow?"

"I don't want to discuss this any further," her mother said. She picked up a magazine and pretended to read it. "We'll talk about it tomorrow."

MARGARET WENT to her bedroom and bathed and put on her best nightgown and unbraided her hair and brushed it. She put perfume on her wrists and knees and behind her ears. She opened the door to her brother's old room which adjoined her own. She gathered all of her old fashion magazines from around the room and sat down crosslegged on the bed and began to read. It was ten-fifteen.

OUTSIDE IN THE OFFICE Lin Tan and Big Ted were talking context. "It's got to be seen in the scheme of things," Big Ted was saying. "Bateson's got a nice little book on it. Trying, for God's sake, to make them comprehend they are part of nature. Poor babies. They've lost that in our cities. Poor goddamn babies. Makes me want to cry." He filled a glass with ice from a cooler, added two small jiggers of whiskey, and signaled Lin Tan to hand his over for a refill.

There was a knock on the door. Big Ted got up, opened it, let his friend Kenneth Felder in. "This is Doctor Felder, Lin Tan. He's our heart man around here. His daddy did it before him. This is Lin Tan, Ken. He got the big fellowship at Johns Hopkins handed him today. You two have plenty to talk about." He took Ken Felder's coat, motioned him to a red leather chair beside the brown one.

"So how do you like it here?" Ken said. "Have you figured out where you are yet?"

"Oh, yes, we studied a map on the airplane flying here. Margaret is very good guide. This country is larger than can be imagined from maps. We flew over mountains of the west. Very beautiful country. Here in your home is very beautiful also."

"Your own country's doing good. My wife and I were there last summer. We were impressed with the schools. She's a teacher like Ted here. She had Margaret. She had all these kids. Well, we're all glad to have you here."

"They want to get married," Big Ted said. "Margaret's down there with Jane making plans. And I don't mind." He raised his glass in Lin Tan's direction. "The global village. Jesus, imagine the kids. And tomorrow we're going up to New Jersey to look at his buddy's atoms before they condense any further. You want to go along? It's Saturday. Call and see if you can get a plane ticket."

"Oh, yes," Lin Tan said. "Please go with us. My friend, Randal, is very lonesome for someone he knows to come and share triumph with him. He has been surrounded by reporters for many days now. We would be honored if you would go along."

"I can't do that," Ken said. "Well, Johns Hopkins. That's fine, Lin Tan. Really fine. You must have worked hard."

"Very hard. Also, very lucky. There are many fine students in class with me." He glanced at his watch. He sipped his whiskey. He stretched out his legs from the brown chair until they met Doctor Felder's legs, sticking out from the red one. Just Chinese man being enveloped by the culture of the West, he decided. Just one more adventure on the road of life.

"I brought the portable chess board out," Big Ted said. "If you're ready, we can play."

Stephanie Vaughn

ふ

Able, Baker, Charlie, Dog

WHEN I WAS twelve years old, my father was tall and awesome. I can see him walking across the parade ground behind our quarters. The wind blew snow into the folds of his coat and made the hem swoop around his legs. He did not lower his head, he did not jam his hands into the pockets. He was coming home along a diagonal that would cut the parade ground into perfect triangles, and he was not going to be stopped by any snowstorm. I stood at the kitchen door and watched him through a hole I had rubbed in the steamy glass.

My grandmother and mother fidgeted with pans of food that had been kept warm too long. It was one o'clock on Saturday and he had been expected home at noon.

"You want to know what this chicken looks like?" said my grandmother. "It looks like it died last year."

My mother looked into the pan but didn't say anything.

My grandmother believed my mother should have married a minister, not an Army officer. Once my mother had gone out with a minister, and now he was on the radio every Sunday in Ohio. My grandmother thought my father had misrepresented himself as a religious man. There was a story my mother told about their first date. They went to a restaurant and my father told her that he was going to have twelve sons and name them Peter, James, John, et cetera. "And I thought, Twelve sons!" said my mother. "Boy, do I pity your poor wife." My mother had two miscarriages and then she had me. My father named me Gemma, which my grandmother believed was not even a Christian name.

"You want to know what this squash looks like?" said my grandmother.

"It'll be fine," said my mother.

Just then the wind gusted on the parade ground, and my father veered to the left. He stopped and looked up. How is it possible you have caught me off guard, he seemed to ask. Exactly where have I miscalculated the velocities, how have I misjudged the vectors?

"It looks like somebody peed in it," my grandmother said.

"KEEP YOUR VOICE low," my father told me that day as we ate the ruined squash and chicken. "Keep your voice low and you can win any point."

We were living in Fort Niagara, a little Army post at the juncture of the Niagara River and Lake Ontario. We had been there through the fall and into the winter, as my father, who was second in command, waited for his next promotion. It began to snow in October. The arctic winds swept across the lake from Canada and shook the windows of our house. Snow drifted across the parade ground, and floes of ice piled up against each other in the river, so that if a person were courageous enough, or foolhardy enough, and also lucky, he could walk the mile across the river to Canada.

"And always speak in sentences," he told me. "You have developed a junior-high habit of speaking in fragments. Learn to come to a full stop when you complete an idea. Use semicolons and periods in your speech."

My mother put down her fork and knife. Her hands were so thin and light they seemed to pass through the table as she dropped them in her lap. "Zachary, perhaps we could save some of the lecture for dessert?" she said.

My grandmother leaned back into her own heaviness. "The poor kid never gets to eat a hot meal," she said. She was referring to the rule that said I could not cut my food or eat while I was speaking or being spoken to. My father used mealtimes to lecture on the mechanics of life, the how-tos of a civilized world. Normally I was receptive to his advice, but that day I was angry with him.

"You know, Dad," I said, "I don't think my friends are going to notice a missing semicolon."

I thought he would give me a fierce look, but instead he winked. "And don't say 'you know,' " he said.

He never said "you know," never spoke in fragments, never slurred his speech, even years later when he had just put away a fifth of scotch and was trying to describe the Eskimo custom of chewing up the meat before it was given to the elders, who had no teeth. He spoke with such calculation and precision that his sentences hung over us like high vaulted ceilings, or rolled across the table like ornaments sculptured from stone. It was a huge cathedral of a voice, full of volume and complexity.

HE TAUGHT ME the alphabet. Able, Baker, Charlie, Dog. It was the alphabet the military used to keep *b*'s separate from *v*'s and *i*'s separate from *y*'s. He liked the music of it, the way it sounded on his fine voice. I was four years old and my grandmother had not come to live with us yet. We were stationed in Manila, and living in a house the Army had built on squat stilts to protect us from the insects. There was a typhoon sweeping inland, and we could hear the hoarse sound of metal scraping across the Army's paved street. It was the corrugated roof of the house next door.

"Don't you think it's time we went under the house?" my mother said. She was sitting on a duffel bag that contained our tarps and food rations. The house had a loose plank in the living-room floor, so that if the roof blew away, or the walls caved in, we could escape through the opening and sit in the low space between the reinforced floor and the ground until the military rescue bus came.

My father looked at me and said, "Able, Baker, Charlie, Dog. Can you say it, Gemma?"

I looked up at the dark slope of our own metal roof.

"Can you say it?"

"Able, Baker, Charlie, Dog," I said.

The metal rumbled on the road outside. My mother lifted the plank.

"We will be all right," he said. "Easy, Fox, George, How."

"Anybody want to join me?" said my mother.

"Easy."

"Rachel, please put that plank back."

"Easy, Fox, George, How," I said.

My mother replaced the plank and sat on the floor beside me. The storm grew louder, the rain fell against the roof like handfuls of gravel.

"Item, Jig, King." My father's voice grew lower, fuller. We sat under the sound of it and felt safe. "Love, Mike, Nan."

But then we heard another sound—something that went *whap-whap*, softly, between the gusts of rain. We tilted our heads toward the shuttered windows.

"Well," said my father, standing up to stretch. "I think we are losing a board or two off the side of the house."

"Where are you going?" said my mother. "Just where do you think you're going?"

He put on his rain slicker and went into the next room. When he returned, he was carrying a bucket of nails and a hammer. "Obviously," he said, "I am going fishing."

WE MOVED BACK to the States when I was six, and he taught me how to play Parcheesi, checkers, chess, cribbage, dominoes, and twenty questions. "When you lose," he told me, "don't cry. When you win, don't gloat."

He taught me how to plant tomatoes and load a shotgun shell. He showed me how to gut a dove, turning it inside out as the Europeans do, using the flexible breastbone for a pivot. He read a great many books and never forgot a fact or a technical description. He explained the principles of crop rotation and the flying buttress. He discussed the Defenestration of Prague.

When I was in elementary school, he was sent abroad twice on year-long tours—once to Turkey and once to Greenland, both strategic outposts for America's Early Warning System. I wanted to, but I could not write him letters. His came to me every week, but without the rhythms of his voice the words seemed pale and flat, like the transparent shapes of cells under a microscope. He did not write about his work, because his work was secret. He did not send advice, because that he left to my mother and grandmother in his absence. He wrote about small things—the smooth white rocks he found on a mountainside in Turkey, the first fresh egg he ate in Greenland. When I reread the letters after he died, I was struck by their grace and invention. But when I read them as a child, I looked through the words—"eggs . . . shipment . . . frozen"—and there was nothing on the other side but the great vacuum of his missing voice.

"I can't think of anything to say," I told my mother the first time she urged me to write to him. He had already been in Turkey for three months. She stood behind me at the heavy library table and smoothed my hair, touched my shoulders. "Tell him about your tap lessons," she said. "Tell him about ballet."

"Dear Dad," I wrote. "I am taking tap lessons. I am also taking ballet." I tried to imagine what he looked like. I tried to put a face before my face, but it was gray and featureless, like the face of a statue worn flat by wind and rain. "And I hope you have a Happy Birthday next month," I concluded, hoping to evade the necessity of writing him again in three weeks.

. . .

THE AUTUMN I turned twelve, we moved to Fort Niagara, which was the administrative base for the missile sites strung along the Canadian border between Lake Erie and Lake Ontario. It was a handsome post, full of oak trees, brick buildings, and history. The French had taken the land from the Indians and built the original fort. The British took the fort from the French, and the Americans took it from the British. My father recounted the battles for us as we drove there along the wide sweep of the Niagara River, past apple orchards and thick pastures. My grandmother sat in the back seat and made a note of each red convertible that passed. I was supposed to be counting the white ones. When we drove through the gate and saw the post for the first time—the expanses of clipped grass, the tall trees, the row of Colonial houses overlooking the river—my grandmother put down her tablet and said, "This is some post." She looked at my father admiringly, the first indication she had ever given that he might be a good match for my mother after all. She asked to be taken to the far end of the post, where the Old Fort was. It sat on a point of land at the juncture of the lake and river, and looked appropriately warlike, with its moat and tiny gun windows, but it was surprisingly small—a simple square of yellow stone, a modest French chateau. "Is this all there is?" I said as my grandmother and I posed for pictures on the drawbridge near two soldiers dressed in Revolutionary War costumes. It was hard to imagine that chunks of a vast continent had been won and lost within the confines of a fortress hardly bigger than Sleeping Beauty's castle at Disneyland. Later, as we drove back along the river, my father said in his aphoristic way, "Sometimes the biggest battles are the smallest ones."

The week after we settled in our quarters, we made the obligatory trip to the Falls. It was a sultry day—Indian summer—and our eyes began to water as we neared the chemical factories that surrounded the city of Niagara Falls. We stopped for iced tea and my father explained how the glaciers had formed the escarpment through which the Falls had cut a deep gorge. *Escarpment*—that was the term he used, instead of *cliff*. It skidded along the roof of his mouth and entered the conversation with a soft explosion.

We went to the Niagara Falls Museum and examined the containers people had used successfully to go over the Falls early in the century, when there was a thousand-dollar prize given to survivors. Two were wooden barrels strapped with metal bands. One was a giant rubber ball reinforced with a steel cage. A fourth was a long steel capsule. On the walls were photographs of each survivor and plaques explaining who had been injured and how. The steel capsule was used by a man who had broken every bone in his body. The plaque said that he was in the hospital for twenty-three weeks and then took his capsule around the world on a speaking tour. One day when he was in New Zealand, he slipped on an orange peel, broke his leg, and died of complications.

We went next to Goat Island and stood on the open bank to watch the leap and dive of the white water. My mother held her handbag close to her breasts. She had a habit of always holding things this way—a stack of dinner plates, the dish towel, some mail she had brought in from the porch; she hunched over slightly, so that her body seemed at once to be protective and protected. "I don't like the river," she said. "I think it wants to hypnotize you." My father put his hands in his pockets to show how at ease he was, and my grandmother went off to buy an ice-cream cone.

At the observation point, we stood at a metal fence and looked into the frothing water at the bottom of the gorge. We watched bits and pieces of rainbows appear and vanish in the sunlight that was refracted off the water through the mist. My father pointed to a black shape in the rapids above the Horseshoe Falls. "That's a river barge," he said. He lowered his voice so that he could be heard under the roar of the water. "A long time ago, there were two men standing on that barge waiting to see whether in the next moment of their lives they would go over."

He told us the story of the barge then—how it had broken loose from a tug near Buffalo and floated downriver, gathering speed. The two men tore at the air, waved and shouted to people on shore, but the barge entered the rapids. They bumped around over the rocks, and the white water rose in the air. One man—"He was the thinking man," said my father—thought they might be able to wedge the barge among the rocks if they allowed the hull to fill with water. They came closer to the Falls—four hundred yards, three hundred—before the barge jerked broadside and stopped. They were there all afternoon and night, listening to the sound of the water pounding into the boulders at the bottom of the gorge. The next morning they were rescued, and one of the men, the thinking man, told the newspapers that he had spent the night playing poker in his head. He played all the hands, and he bluffed himself. He drew to inside straights. If the barge had torn loose from the rocks in the night, he was going to go over the Falls saying, "Five-card draw, jacks or better to open." The other man sat on the barge, his arms clasped around his knees, and watched the mist blow back from the edge of the Falls in the moonlight. He could not speak.

"The scream of the water entered his body," said my father. He paused to let us think about that.

"Well, what does that mean?" my grandmother said at last.

My father rested his arms on the fence and gazed pleasantly at the Falls. "He went insane."

The river fascinated me. I often stood between the yellow curtains of my bedroom and looked down upon it and thought about how deep and swift it was, how black under the glittering surface. The newspaper carried stories about people who jumped over the Falls, fourteen miles upriver from our house. I thought of their bodies pushed along the soft silt of the bottom, tumbling silently, huddled in upon themselves like fetuses—jilted brides, unemployed factory workers, old people who did not want to go to rest homes, teenagers who got bad grades, young women who fell in love with married men. They floated invisibly past my bedroom window, out into the lake.

THAT WINTER, I thought I was going to die. I thought I had cancer of the breasts. My mother had explained to me about menstruation, she had given me a book about the reproductive systems of men and women, but she had not told me about breasts and how they begin as invisible lumps that become tender and sore.

I thought the soreness had begun in a phys. ed. class one day in December when I was hit in the chest with a basketball. I didn't worry about it, and it went away by New Year's. In January, I found a pamphlet at the bus stop. I was stamping my feet in the cold, looking down at my boots, when I saw the headline—CANCER: SEVEN WARNING SIGNALS. When I got home, I went into the bathroom and undressed. I examined myself for enlarged moles and small wounds that wouldn't heal. I was systematic. I sat on the edge of the tub with the pamphlet by my side and began with my toenails, looking under the tips of them. I felt my soles, arches, ankles. I worked my way up my body and then I felt the soreness again, around both nipples. At dinner that night I didn't say anything all through the meal. In bed I slept on my back, with my arms stiff against my sides.

The next Saturday was the day my father came home late for lunch. The squash sat on the back of the stove and turned to ocher soup. The chicken fell away from the bones. After lunch he went into the living room and drank scotch and read a book. When I came down for supper, he was still sitting there, and he told my mother he would eat later. My grandmother, my mother, and I ate silently at the kitchen table. I took a long bath. I scrubbed my chest hard.

I went straight to my bedroom, and after a while my mother came upstairs and said, "What's wrong?"

I didn't say anything.

She stood in front of me with her hands clasped in front of her. She seemed to lean toward her own hands. "But you've been acting, you know"—and here she laughed self-consciously, as she used the forbidden phrase—"you know, you've been acting different. You were so quiet today."

I went to my chest of drawers and took the pamphlet out from under a stack of folded underpants and gave it to her.

"What's this?" she said.

"I think I have Number Four," I said.

She must have known immediately what the problem was, but she didn't smile. She asked me to raise my nightgown and she examined my chest, pressing firmly, as if she were a doctor. I told her about the soreness. "Here?" she said. "And here? What about here, too?" She told me I was beginning to "develop." I knew what she meant, but I wanted her to be precise.

"You're getting breasts," she said.

"But I don't *see* anything."

"You will."

"You never told me it would hurt."

"Oh, dear. I just forgot. When you're grown up you just forget what it was like."

I asked her whether, just to be safe, I could see a doctor. She said that of course I could, and I felt better, as if I had had a disease and already been cured. As she was leaving the room, I said, "Do you think I need a bra?" She smiled. I went to sleep watching the snow fall past the window. I had my hands cupped over my new breasts.

WHEN I AWOKE, I did not recognize the window. The snow had stopped and moonlight slanted through the glass. I could not make out the words, but I heard my father's voice filling up the house. I tiptoed down the back staircase that led to the kitchen and stood in the slice of shadow near the doorjamb. My grandmother was telling my mother to pack her bags. He was a degenerate, she said—she had always seen that in him. My mother said, "Why, Zachary, why are you doing this?"

"Just go pack your bags," my grandmother said. "I'll get the child."

My father said conversationally, tensely, "Do I have to break your arms?"

I leaned into the light. He was holding on to a bottle of scotch with one hand, and my mother was trying to pull it away with both of hers. He jerked his arm back and forth, so that she was drawn into a little dance, back and forth across the linoleum in front of him.

"The Lord knows the way of righteousness," said my grandmother.

"Please," said my mother. "Please, please."

"And the way of the ungodly shall perish," said my grandmother.

"Whose house is this?" said my father. His voice exploded. He snapped his arm back, trying to take the bottle from my mother in one powerful gesture. It smashed against the wall, and I stepped into the kitchen. The white light from the ceiling fixture burned across the smooth surfaces of the refrigerator, the stove, the white Formica countertops. It was as if an atom had been smashed somewhere and a wave of radiation was rolling through the kitchen. I looked him in the eye and waited for him to speak. I sensed my mother and grandmother on either side of me, in petrified postures. At last, he said, "Well." His voice cracked. The word split in two. "Wel-el." He said it again. His face took on a flatness.

"I am going back to bed," I said. I went up the narrow steps, and he followed me. My mother and grandmother came along behind, whispering. He tucked in the covers, and sat on the edge of the bed, watching me. My mother and grandmother stood stiff against the door. "I am sorry I woke you up," he said finally, and his voice was deep and soothing. The two women watched him go down the hall, and when I heard his steps on the front staircase I rolled over and put my face in the pillow. I heard them turn off the lights and say good-night to me. I heard them go to their bedrooms. I lay there for a long time, listening for a sound downstairs, and then it came—the sound of the front door closing.

I went downstairs and put on my hat, coat, boots. I followed his footsteps in the snow, down the front walk, and across the road to the riverbank. He did not seem surprised to see me next to him. We stood side by side, hands in our pockets, breathing frost into the air. The river was filled from shore to shore with white heaps of ice, which cast blue shadows in the moonlight.

"This is the edge of America," he said, in a tone that seemed to answer a question I had just asked. There was a creak and crunch of ice as two floes below us scraped each other and jammed against the bank.

"You knew all week, didn't you? Your mother and your grandmother didn't know, but I knew that you could be counted on to know."

I hadn't known until just then, but I guessed the unspeakable thing—that his career was falling apart—and I knew. I nodded. Years later, my mother told me what she had learned about the incident, not from him but from another Army wife. He had called a general a son of a bitch. That was all. I never knew what the issue was or whether he had been right or wrong. Whether the defense of the United States of America had been at stake, or merely the pot in a card game. I didn't even know whether he had called the general a son of a bitch to his face or simply been overheard in an unguarded moment. I only knew that he had been given a 7 instead of a 9 on his Efficiency Report and then passed over for promotion. But that night I nodded, not knowing the cause but knowing the consequences, as we stood on the riverbank above the moonlit ice. "I am looking at that thin beautiful line of Canada," he said. "I think I will go for a walk."

"No," I said. I said it again. "No." I wanted to remember later that I had told him not to go.

"How long do you think it would take to go over and back?" he said.

"Two hours."

He rocked back and forth in his boots, looked up at the moon, then down at the river. I did not say anything.

He started down the bank, sideways, taking long, graceful sliding steps, which threw little puffs of snow in the air. He took his hands from his pockets and hopped from the bank to the ice. He tested his weight against the weight of the ice, flexing his knees. I watched him walk a few yards from the shore and then I saw him rise in the air, his long legs scissoring the moonlight, as he crossed from the edge of one floe to the next. He turned and waved to me, one hand making a slow arc.

I could have said anything. I could have said "Come back" or "I love you." Instead, I called after him, "Be sure and write!" The last thing I heard, long after I had lost sight of him far out on the river, was the sound of his laugh splitting the cold air.

IN THE SPRING he resigned his commission and we went back to Ohio. He used his savings to invest in a chain of hardware stores with my uncle. My uncle arranged the contracts with builders and plumbers, and supervised the employees. My father controlled the inventory and handled the books. He had been a logistics officer, and all the skills he might have used in supervising the movement of land, air, and sea cargoes, or in calculating the disposition of several billion dollars' worth of military supplies, were instead brought to bear on the deployment of nuts and bolts, plumbers' joints and nipples, No. 2 pine, Con-Tact paper, acrylic paint, caulking guns, and rubber dishpans. He learned a new vocabulary—traffic builders, margins, end-cap displays, perfboard merchandisers, seasonal impulse items—and spoke it with the ostentation and faint amusement of a man who has just mastered a foreign language.

"But what I really want to know, Mr. Jenkins," I heard him tell a man on the telephone one day, "is why you think the Triple Gripper Vegetable Ripper would make a good loss-leader item in mid-winter." He had been in the hardlines industry, as it was called, for six months, and I was making my first visit to his office, and then only because my mother had sent me there on the pretext of taking him a midmorning snack during a busy Saturday. I was reluctant to confront him in his civilian role, afraid I would find him somehow diminished. In fact, although he looked incongruous among the reds, yellows, and blues that the previous owner had used to decorate the office, he sounded much like the man who had taught me to speak in complete sentences.

"Mr. Jenkins, I am not asking for a discourse on coleslaw."

When he hung up, he winked at me and said, "Your father is about to become the emperor of the building-and-housewares trade in Killbuck, Ohio."

I nodded and took a seat in a red-and-blue chair.

Then he looked at his hands spread upon the spotless ink blotter and said, "Of course, you know that I do not give a damn about the Triple Gripper Vegetable Ripper."

I had skipped a grade and entered high school. I saw less and less of him, because I ate dinner early so that I could go to play rehearsals, basketball games, dances. In the evenings he sat in a green chair and smoked cigarettes, drank scotch, read books—the same kinds of books, year after year. They were all about Eskimos and Arctic explorations—an interest he had developed during his tour in Greenland. Sometimes, when I came in late and was in the kitchen making a snack, I watched him through the doorway. Often he looked away from the book and gazed toward the window. He would strike a match and let it burn to his thumb and fingertip, then wave it out. He would raise the glass but not drink from it. I think he must have imagined himself to be in the Arctic during those moments, a warrior tracking across the ice for bear or seal. Sometimes he was waiting for me to join him. He wanted to tell me about the techniques the Eskimos had developed for survival, the way they stitched up skins to make them watertight vessels. He became obsessive on the subject of meat. The Eskimo diet was nearly all protein. "Eat meat," he said. Two professors at Columbia had tested the value of the Eskimo diet by eating nothing but caribou for a year and claimed they were healthier at the end of the experiment than they had been before.

Later, when I went to college, he developed the habit of calling me long distance when my mother and grandmother had gone to bed and he was alone downstairs with a drink. "Are you getting enough protein?" he asked me once at three in the morning. It was against dorm rules to put through calls after midnight except in cases of emergency, but his deep, commanding voice was so authoritative ("This is Gemma Jackson's father, and I must speak with her immediately") that it was for some time believed on my corridor that the people in my family were either accident-prone or suffering from long terminal illnesses.

HE DIED the summer I received my master's degree. I had accepted a teaching position at a high school in Chicago, and I went home for a month before school began. He was overweight and short of breath. He drank too much, smoked too many cigarettes. The doctor told him to stop, my mother told him, my grandmother told him.

My grandmother was upstairs watching television and my mother and I were sitting on the front porch. He was asleep in the green chair, with a book in his lap. I left the porch to go to the kitchen to make a sandwich, and as I passed by the chair I heard him say, "Ahhhh. Ahhhhh." I saw his fist rise to his chest. I saw his eyes open and dilate in the lamplight. I knelt beside him.

"Are you okay?" I said. "Are you dreaming?"

We buried him in a small cemetery near the farm where he was born. In the eulogy he was remembered for having survived the first wave of the invasion of Normandy. He was admired for having been the proprietor of a chain of excellent hardware stores.

"He didn't have to do this," my mother said after the funeral. "He did this to himself."

"He was a good man," said my grandmother. "He put a nice roof over our heads. He sent us to Europe twice."

Afterward I went alone to the cemetery. I knelt beside the heaps of wilting flowers—mostly roses and gladiolus, and one wreath of red, white, and blue carnations. Above me, the maple pods spun through the sunlight like wings, and in the distance the corn trumpeted green across the hillsides. I touched the loose black soil at the edge of the flowers. Able, Baker, Charlie, Dog. I could remember the beginning of the alphabet, up through Mike and Nan. I could remember the end. X-ray, Yoke, Zebra. I was his eldest child, and he taught me what he knew. I wept then, but not because he had gone back to Ohio to read about the Eskimos and sell the artifacts of civilized life to homeowners and builders. I wept because when I was twelve years old I had stood on a snowy riverbank as he became a shadow on the ice, and waited to see whether he would slip between the cracking floes into the water.

Margaret Atwood

✌

Hairball

ON THE THIRTEENTH of November, day of unluck, month of the dead, Kat went into the Toronto General Hospital for an operation. It was for an ovarian cyst, a large one.

Many women had them, the doctor told her. Nobody knew why. There wasn't any way of finding out whether the thing was malignant, whether it contained, already, the spores of death. Not before they went in. He spoke of "going in" the way she'd heard old veterans in TV documentaries speak of assaults on enemy territory. There was the same tensing of the jaw, the same fierce gritting of the teeth, the same grim enjoyment. Except that what he would be going into was her body. Counting down, waiting for the anesthetic, Kat too gritted her teeth fiercely. She was terrified, but also she was curious. Curiosity has got her through a lot.

She'd made the doctor promise to save the thing for her, whatever it was, so she could have a look. She was intensely interested in her own body, in anything it might choose to do or produce; although when flaky Dania, who did layout at the magazine, told her this growth was a message to her from her body and she ought to sleep with an amethyst under her pillow to calm her vibrations, Kat told her to stuff it.

The cyst turned out to be a benign tumor. Kat liked that use of *benign,* as if the thing had a soul and wished her well. It was big as a grapefruit, the doctor said. "Big as a coconut," said Kat. Other people had grapefruits. "Coconut" was better. It conveyed the hardness of it, and the hairiness, too.

The hair in it was red—long strands of it wound round and round inside, like a ball of wet wool gone berserk or like the guck you pulled out of a clogged bathroom-sink drain. There were little bones in it too, or fragments of bone; bird bones, the bones of a sparrow crushed by a car. There was a scattering of nails, toe or finger. There were five perfectly formed teeth.

"Is this abnormal?" Kat asked the doctor, who smiled. Now that he had gone in and come out again, unscathed, he was less clenched.

"Abnormal? No," he said carefully, as if breaking the news to a mother about a freakish accident to her newborn. "Let's just say it's fairly common." Kat was a little disappointed. She would have preferred uniqueness.

She asked for a bottle of formaldehyde, and put the cut-open tumor into it. It was hers, it was benign, it did not deserve to be thrown away. She took it back to her apartment and stuck it on the mantelpiece. She named it Hairball. It isn't that different from having a stuffed bear's head or a preserved ex-pet or anything else with fur and teeth looming over your fireplace; or she pretends it isn't. Anyway, it certainly makes an impression.

Ger doesn't like it. Despite his supposed yen for the new and outré, he is a squeamish man. The first time he comes around (sneaks around, creeps around) after the operation, he tells Kat to throw Hairball out. He calls it "disgusting." Kat refuses point-blank, and says she'd rather have Hairball in a bottle on her mantelpiece than the soppy dead flowers he's brought her, which will anyway rot a lot sooner than Hairball will. As a mantelpiece ornament, Hairball is far superior. Ger says Kat has a tendency to push things to extremes, to go over the edge, merely from a juvenile desire to shock, which is hardly a substitute for wit. One of these days, he says, she will go way too far. Too far for him, is what he means.

"That's why you hired me, isn't it?" she says. "Because I go way too far." But he's in one of his analyzing moods. He can see these tendencies of hers reflected in her work on the magazine, he says. All that leather and those grotesque and tortured-looking poses are heading down a track he and others are not at all sure they should continue to follow. Does she see what he means, does she take his point? It's a point that's been made before. She shakes her head slightly, says nothing. She knows how that translates: there have been complaints from the advertisers. *Too bizarre, too kinky.* Tough.

"Want to see my scar?" she says. "Don't make me laugh, though, you'll crack it open." Stuff like that makes him dizzy; anything with a hint of blood, anything gynecological. He almost threw up in the delivery room when his wife had a baby two years ago. He'd told her that with pride. Kat thinks about sticking a cigarette into the side of her mouth, as in a black-and-white movie of the forties. She thinks about blowing the smoke into his face.

Her insolence used to excite him, during their arguments. Then there would be a grab of her upper arms, a smoldering, violent kiss. He kisses her as if he thinks someone else is watching him, judging the image they make together. Kissing the latest thing, hard and shiny, purple-mouthed, crop-headed; kissing a girl, a woman, a girl, in a little crotch-hugger skirt and skin-tight leggings. He likes mirrors.

But he isn't excited now. And she can't decoy him into bed; she isn't ready for that yet, she isn't healed. He has a drink, which he doesn't finish, holds her hand as an afterthought, gives her a couple of avuncular pats on the off-white outsized alpaca shoulder, leaves too quickly.

"Goodbye, Gerald," she says. She pronounces the name with mockery. It's a negation of him, an abolishment of him, like ripping a medal off his chest. It's a warning.

He'd been Gerald when they first met. It was she who transformed him, first to Gerry, then to Ger. (Rhymed with *flair*, rhymed with *dare*.) She made him get rid of those sucky pursed-mouth ties, told him what shoes to wear, got him to buy a loose-cut Italian suit, redid his hair. A lot of his current tastes—in food, in drink, in recreational drugs, in women's entertainment underwear—were once hers. In his new phase, with his new, hard, stripped-down name ending on the sharpened note of *r*, he is her creation.

As she is her own. During her childhood she was a romanticized Katherine, dressed by her misty-eyed, fussy mother in dresses that looked like ruffled pillowcases. By high school she'd shed the frills and emerged as a bouncy, round-faced Kathy, with gleaming freshly washed hair and enviable teeth, eager to please and no more interesting than a health-food ad. At university she was Kath, blunt and no-bullshit in her Take-Back-the-Night jeans and checked shirt and her bricklayer-style striped-denim peaked hat. When she ran away to England, she sliced herself down to Kat. It was economical, street-feline, and pointed as a nail. It was also unusual. In England you had to do something to get their attention, especially if you weren't English. Safe in this incarnation, she Ramboed through the eighties.

It was the name, she still thinks, that got her the interview and then the job. The job with an avant-garde magazine, the kind that was printed on matte stock in black and white, with overexposed close-ups of women with hair blowing over their eyes, one nostril prominent: *the razor's edge,* it was called. Haircuts as art, some real art, film reviews, a little stardust, wardrobes of ideas that were clothes and of clothes that were ideas—the metaphysical shoulder pad. She learned her trade well, hands-on. She learned what worked.

She made her way up the ladder, from layout to design, then to the supervision of whole spreads, and then whole issues. It wasn't easy, but it was worth it. She had become a creator; she created total looks. After a while she could walk down the street in Soho or stand in the lobby at openings and witness her handiwork incarnate, strolling around in outfits she'd put together, spouting her warmed-over pronouncements. It was like being God, only God had never got around to off-the-rack lines.

By that time her face had lost its roundness, though the teeth of course remained: there was something to be said for North American dentistry. She'd shaved off most of her hair, worked on the drop-dead stare, perfected a certain turn of the neck that conveyed an aloof inner authority. What you had to make them believe was that you knew something they didn't know yet. What you also had to make them believe was that they too could know this thing, this thing that would give them eminence and power and sexual allure, that would attract envy to them—but for a price. The price of the magazine. What they could never get through their heads was that it was done entirely with cameras. Frozen light, frozen time. Given the angle, she could make any woman look ugly. Any man as well. She could make anyone look beautiful, or at least interesting. It was all photography, it was all iconography. It was all in the choosing eye. This was the thing that could never be bought, no matter how much of your pitiful monthly wage you blew on snakeskin.

Despite the status, *the razor's edge* was fairly low-paying. Kat herself could not afford many of the things she contextualized so well. The grottiness and expense of London began to get to her; she got tired of gorging on the canapés at literary launches in order to scrimp on groceries, tired of the fuggy smell of cigarettes ground into the red-and-maroon carpeting of pubs, tired of the pipes bursting every time it froze in winter, and of the Clarissas and Melissas and Penelopes at the magazine rabbiting on about how they had been literally, absolutely, totally freezing all night, and how it literally, absolutely, totally, usually never got that cold. It always got that cold. The pipes always burst. Nobody thought of putting in real pipes, ones that would not burst next time. Burst pipes were an English tradition, like so many others.

Like, for instance, English men. Charm the knickers off you with their mellow vowels and frivolous verbiage, and then, once they'd got them off, panic and run. Or else stay and whinge. The English called it *whinging* instead of whining. It was better, really. Like a creaking hinge. It was a traditional compliment to be whinged at by an Englishman. It was his way of saying he trusted you, he was conferring upon you the privilege of getting to know the real him. The inner, whinging him. That was how they thought of women, secretly: whinge receptacles. Kat could play it, but that didn't mean she liked it.

She had an advantage over the English women, though: she was of no class. She had no class. She was in a class of her own. She could roll around among the English men, all different kinds of them, secure in the knowledge that she was not being measured against the class yardsticks and accent-detectors they carried around in their back pockets, was not subject to the petty snobberies and resentments that lent such richness to their inner lives. The flip side of this freedom was that she was beyond the pale. She was a colonial—how fresh, how vital, how anonymous, how finally of no consequence. Like a hole in the wall, she could be told all secrets and then be abandoned with no guilt.

She was too smart, of course. The English men were very competitive; they liked to win. Several times it hurt. Twice she had abortions, because the men in question were not up for the alternative. She learned to say that she didn't want children anyway, that if she longed for a rug-rat she would buy a gerbil. Her life began to seem long. Her adrenaline was running out. Soon she would be thirty, and all she could see ahead was more of the same.

THIS WAS how things were when Gerald turned up. "You're terrific," he said, and she was ready to hear it, even from him, even though *terrific* was a word that had probably gone out with fifties crew-cuts. She was ready for his voice by that time too: the flat, metallic nasal tone of the Great Lakes, with its clear hard *r*'s and its absence of theatricality. Dull normal. The speech of her people. It came to her suddenly that she was an exile.

Gerald was scouting, Gerald was recruiting. He'd heard about her, looked at her work, sought her out. One of the big companies back in Toronto was launching a new fashion-oriented magazine, he said: upmarket, international in its coverage, of course, but with some Canadian fashion in it too, and with lists of stores where the items portrayed could actually be bought. In that respect they felt they'd have it all over the competition, those American magazines that assumed you could only get Gucci in New York or Los Angeles. Heck, times had changed, you could get it in Edmonton! You could get it in Winnipeg!

Kat had been away too long. There was Canadian fashion now? The English quip would be to say that "Canadian fashion" was an oxymoron. She refrained from making it, lit a cigarette with her cyanide-green Covent Garden–boutique leather-covered lighter (as featured in the May issue of *the razor's edge*), looked Gerald in the eye. "London is a lot to give up," she said levelly. She glanced around the see-me-here Mayfair restaurant where they were finishing lunch, a restaurant she'd chosen because she'd known he was paying. She'd never spend that kind of money on food otherwise. "Where would I eat?"

Gerald assured her that Toronto was now the restaurant capital of Canada. He himself would be happy to be her guide. There was a great Chinatown, there was world-class Italian. Then he paused, took a breath. "I've been meaning to ask you," he said. "About the name. Is that Kat as in Krazy?" He thought this was suggestive. She'd heard it before.

"No," she said. "It's Kat as in KitKat. That's a chocolate bar. Melts in your mouth." She gave him her stare, quirked her mouth, just a twitch.

Gerald became flustered, but he pushed on. They wanted her, they needed her, they loved her, he said in essence. Someone with her fresh, innovative approach and her experience would be worth a lot of money to them, relatively speaking. But there were rewards other than the money. She would be in on the initial concept, she would have a formative influence, she would have a free hand. He named a sum that made her gasp, inaudibly of course. By now she knew better than to betray desire.

SO SHE MADE the journey back, did her three months of culture shock, tried the world-class Italian and the great Chinese, and seduced Gerald at the first opportunity, right in his junior vice-presidential office. It was the first time Gerald had been seduced in such a location, or perhaps ever. Even though it was after hours, the danger frenzied him. It was the idea of it. The daring. The image of Kat kneeling on the broadloom, in a legendary bra that until now he'd seen only in the lingerie ads of the Sunday *New York Times,* unzipping him in full view of the silver-framed engagement portrait of his wife that complemented the impossible ball-point pen set on his desk. At that time he was so straight he felt compelled to take off his wedding ring and place it carefully in the ashtray first. The next day he brought her a box of David Wood Food Shop chocolate truffles. They were the best, he told her, anxious that she should recognize their quality. She found the gesture banal, but also sweet. The banality, the sweetness, the hunger to impress: that was Gerald.

Gerald was the kind of man she wouldn't have bothered with in London. He was not funny, he was not knowledgeable, he had little verbal charm. But he was eager, he was tractable, he was blank paper. Although he was eight years older than she was, he seemed much younger. She took pleasure from his furtive, boyish delight in his own wickedness. And he was so grateful. "I can hardly believe this is happening," he said, more frequently than was necessary and usually in bed.

His wife, whom Kat encountered (and still encounters) at many tedious company events, helped to explain his gratitude. The wife was a priss. Her name was Cheryl. Her hair looked as if she still used big rollers and embalm-your-hairdo spray; her mind was room-by-room Laura Ashley wallpaper: tiny, unopened pastel buds arranged in straight rows. She probably put on rubber gloves to make love, and checked it off on a list afterwards. One more messy household chore. She looked at Kat as if she'd like to spritz her with air deodorizer. Kat revenged herself by picturing Cheryl's bathrooms: hand towels embroidered with lilies, fuzzy covers on the toilet seats.

The magazine itself got off to a rocky start. Although Kat had lots of lovely money to play with, and although it was a challenge to be working in color, she did not have the free hand Gerald had promised her. She had to contend with the company board of directors, who were all men, who were all accountants or indistinguishable from them, who were cautious and slow as moles.

"It's simple," Kat told them. "You bombard them with images of what they ought to be, and you make them feel grotty for being the way they are. You're working with the gap between reality and perception. That's why you have to hit them with something new, something they've never seen before, something they aren't. Nothing sells like anxiety."

The board, on the other hand, felt that the readership should simply be offered more of what they already had. More fur, more sumptuous leather, more cashmere. More established names. The board had no sense of improvisation, no wish to take risks; no sporting instincts, no desire to put one over on the readers just for the hell of it. "Fashion is like hunting," Kat told them, hoping to appeal to their male hormones, if any. "It's playful, it's intense, it's predatory. It's blood and guts. It's erotic." But to them it was about good taste. They wanted Dress-for-Success. Kat wanted scattergun ambush.

Everything became a compromise. Kat had wanted to call the magazine *All the Rage,* but the board was put off by the vibrations of anger in the word "rage." They thought it was too feminist, of all things. "It's a *forties* sound," Kat said. "Forties is *back.* Don't you get it?" But they didn't. They wanted to call it *Or.* French for *gold,* and blatant enough in its values, but without any base note, as Kat told them. They sawed off at *Felice,* which had qualities each side wanted. It was vaguely French-sounding, it meant "happy" (so much less threatening than rage), and, although you couldn't expect the others to notice, for Kat it had a feline bouquet which counteracted the laciness. She had it done in hot-pink lipstick-scrawl, which helped some. She could live with it, but it had not been her first love.

This battle has been fought and refought over every innovation in design, every new angle Kat has tried to bring in, every innocuous bit of semi-kink. There was a big row over a spread that did lingerie, half pulled off and with broken glass perfume bottles strewn on the floor. There was an uproar over the two nouveau-stockinged legs, one tied to a chair with a third, different-colored stocking. They had not understood the man's three-hundred-dollar leather gloves positioned ambiguously around a neck.

And so it has gone on, for five years.

AFTER GERALD has left, Kat paces her living room. Pace, pace. Her stitches pull. She's not looking forward to her solitary dinner of microwaved leftovers. She's not sure now why she came back here, to this flat burg beside the polluted inland sea. Was it Ger? Ludicrous thought but no longer out of the question. Is he the reason she stays, despite her growing impatience with him?

He's no longer fully rewarding. They've learned each other too well, they take short-cuts now; their time together has shrunk from whole stolen rolling and sensuous afternoons to a few hours snatched between work and dinnertime. She no longer knows what she wants from him. She tells herself she's worth more, she should branch out; but she doesn't see other men, she can't, somehow. She's tried once or twice but it didn't work. Sometimes she goes out to dinner or a flick with one of the gay designers. She likes the gossip.

Maybe she misses London. She feels caged, in this country, in this city, in this room. She could start with the room, she could open a window. It's too stuffy in here. There's an undertone of formaldehyde, from Hairball's bottle. The flowers she got for the operation are mostly wilted, all except Gerald's from today. Come to think of it, why didn't he send her any at the hospital? Did he forget, or was it a message?

"Hairball," she says, "I wish you could talk. I could have a more intelligent conversation with you than with most of the losers in this turkey farm." Hairball's baby teeth glint in the light; it looks as if it's about to speak.

Kat feels her own forehead. She wonders if she's running a temperature. Something ominous is going on, behind her back. There haven't been enough phone calls from the magazine; they've been able to muddle on without her, which is bad news. Reigning queens should never go on vacation, or have operations either. Uneasy lies the head. She has a sixth sense about these things, she's been involved in enough palace coups to know the signs, she has sensitive antennae for the footfalls of impending treachery.

The next morning she pulls herself together, downs an espresso from her mini-machine, picks out an aggressive touch-me-if-you-dare suede outfit in armor gray, and drags herself to the office, although she isn't due in till next week. Surprise, surprise. Whispering knots break up in the corridors, greet her with false welcome as she limps past. She settles herself at her minimalist desk, checks her mail. Her head is pounding, her stitches hurt. Ger gets wind of her arrival; he wants to see her a.s.a.p., and not for lunch.

He awaits her in his newly done wheat-on-white office, with the eighteenth-century desk they chose together, the Victorian inkstand, the framed blow-ups from the magazine, the hands in maroon leather, wrists manacled with pearls, the Hermès scarf twisted into a blindfold, the model's mouth blossoming lusciously beneath it. Some of her best stuff. He's beautifully done up, in a lick-my-neck silk shirt open at the throat, an eat-your-heart-out Italian silk-and-wool loose-knit sweater. Oh, cool insouciance. Oh, eyebrow language. He's a money man who lusted after art, and now he's got some, now he is some. Body art. Her art. She's done her job well; he's finally sexy.

He's smooth as lacquer. "I didn't want to break this to you until next week," he says. He breaks it to her. It's the board of directors. They think she's too bizarre, they think she goes way too far. Nothing he could do about it, although naturally he tried.

Naturally. Betrayal. The monster has turned on its own mad scientist. "I gave you life!" she wants to scream at him.

She isn't in good shape. She can hardly stand. She stands, despite his offer of a chair. She sees now what she's wanted, what she's been missing. Gerald is what she's been missing—the stable, unfashionable, previous, tight-assed Gerald. Not Ger, not the one she's made in her own image. The other one, before he got ruined. The Gerald with a house and a small child and a picture of his wife in a silver frame on his desk. She wants to be in that silver frame. She wants the child. She's been robbed.

"And who is my lucky replacement?" she says. She needs a cigarette, but does not want to reveal her shaking hands.

"Actually, it's me," he says, trying for modesty.

This is too absurd. Gerald couldn't edit a phone book. "You?" she says faintly. She has the good sense not to laugh.

"I've always wanted to get out of the money end of things here," he says, "into the creative area. I knew you'd understand, since it can't be you at any rate. I knew you'd prefer someone who could, well, sort of build on your foundations." Pompous asshole. She looks at his neck. She longs for him, hates herself for it, and is powerless.

The room wavers. He slides towards her across the wheat-colored broadloom, takes her by the gray suede upper arms. "I'll write you a good reference," he says. "Don't worry about that. Of course, we can still see one another. I'd miss our afternoons."

"Of course," she says. He kisses her, a voluptuous kiss, or it would look like one to a third party, and she lets him. *In a pig's ear.*

She makes it home in a taxi. The driver is rude to her and gets away with it; she doesn't have the energy. In her mailbox is an engraved invitation: Ger and Cheryl are having a drinks party, tomorrow evening. Postmarked five days ago. Cheryl is behind the times.

Kat undresses, runs a shallow bath. There's not much to drink around here, there's nothing to sniff or smoke. What an oversight; she's stuck with herself. There are other jobs. There are other men, or that's the theory. Still, something's been ripped out of her. How could this have happened to her? When knives were slated for backs, she'd always done the stabbing. Any headed her way she's seen coming in time, and thwarted. Maybe she's losing her edge.

She stares into the bathroom mirror, assesses her face in the misted glass. A face of the eighties, a mask face, a bottom-line face; push the weak to the wall and grab what you can. But now it's the nineties. Is she out of style, so soon? She's only thirty-five, and she's already losing track of what people ten years younger are thinking. That could be fatal. As time goes by she'll have to race faster and faster to keep up, and for what? Part of the life she should have had is just a gap, it isn't there, it's nothing. What can be salvaged from it, what can be redone, what can be done at all?

When she climbs out of the tub after her sponge bath, she almost falls. She has a fever, no doubt about it. Inside her something is leaking, or else festering; she can hear it, like a dripping tap. A running sore, a sore from running so hard. She should go to the Emergency ward at some hospital, get herself shot up with antibiotics. Instead she lurches into the living room, takes Hairball down from the mantelpiece in its bottle, places it on the coffee table. She sits cross-legged, listens. Filaments wave. She can hear a kind of buzz, like bees at work.

She'd asked the doctor if it could have started as a child, a fertilized egg that escaped somehow and got into the wrong place. No, said the doctor. Some people thought this kind of tumor was present in seedling form from birth, or before it. It might be the woman's undeveloped twin. What they really were was unknown. They had many kinds of tissue, though. Even brain tissue. Though of course all of these tissues lack structure.

Still, sitting here on the rug looking in at it, she pictures it as a child. It has come out of her, after all. It is flesh of her flesh. Her child with Gerald, her thwarted child, not allowed to grow normally. Her warped child, taking its revenge.

"Hairball," she says. "You're so ugly. Only a mother could love you." She feels sorry for it. She feels loss. Tears run down her face. Crying is not something she does, not normally, not lately.

Hairball speaks to her, without words. It is irreducible, it has the texture of reality, it is not an image. What it tells her is everything she's never wanted to hear about herself. This is new knowledge, dark and precious and necessary. It cuts.

She shakes her head. What are you doing, sitting on the floor and talking to a hairball? You are sick, she tells herself. Take a Tylenol and go to bed.

THE NEXT DAY she feels a little better. Dania from layout calls her and makes dovelike, sympathetic coos at her, and wants to drop by during lunch hour to take a look at her aura. Kat tells her to come off it. Dania gets huffy, and says that Kat's losing her job is a price for immoral behavior in a previous life. Kat tells her to stuff it; anyway, she's done enough immoral behavior in this life to account for the whole thing. "Why are you so full of hate?" asks Dania. She doesn't say it like a point she's making, she sounds truly baffled.

"I don't know," says Kat. It's a straight answer.

After she hangs up she paces the floor. She's crackling inside, like hot fat under the broiler. What she's thinking about is Cheryl, bustling about her cozy house, preparing for the party. Cheryl fiddles with her freeze-framed hair, positions an overloaded vase of flowers, fusses about the caterers. Gerald comes in, kisses her lightly on the cheek. A connubial scene. His conscience is nicely washed. The witch is dead, his foot is on the body, the trophy; he's had his dirty fling, he's ready now for the rest of his life.

Kat takes a taxi to the David Wood Food Shop and buys two dozen chocolate truffles. She has them put into an oversized box, then into an oversized bag with the store logo on it. Then she goes home and takes Hairball out of its bottle. She drains it in the kitchen strainer and pats it damp-dry, tenderly, with paper towels. She sprinkles it with powdered cocoa, which forms a brown pasty crust. It still smells like formaldehyde, so she wraps it in Saran Wrap and then in tinfoil, and then in pink tissue paper, which she ties with a mauve bow. She places it in the David Wood box in a bed of shredded tissue, with the truffles nestled around. She closes the box, tapes it, puts it into the bag, stuffs several sheets of pink paper on top. It's her gift, valuable and dangerous. It's her messenger, but the message it will deliver is its own. It will tell the truth, to who-ever asks. It's right that Gerald should have it; after all, it's his child too.

She prints on the card, "Gerald, Sorry I couldn't be with you. This is all the rage. Love, K."

When evening has fallen and the party must be in full swing, she calls a delivery taxi. Cheryl will not distrust anything that ar-rives in such an expensive bag. She will open it in public, in front of everyone. There will be distress, there will be questions. Secrets will be unearthed. There will be pain. After that, everything will go way too far.

She is not well; her heart is pounding, space is wavering once more. But outside the window it's snowing, the soft, damp, wind-less flakes of her childhood. She puts on her coat and goes out, foolishly. She intends to walk just to the corner, but when she reaches the corner she goes on. The snow melts against her face like small fingers touching. She has done an outrageous thing, but she doesn't feel guilty. She feels light and peaceful and filled with charity, and temporarily without a name.

Amy Bloom

჻

Silver Water

M Y S I S T E R ' S V O I C E was like mountain water in a silver pitcher;
the clear blue beauty of it cools you and lifts you up beyond your
heat, beyond your body. After we went to see *La Traviata,* when she
was fourteen and I was twelve, she elbowed me in the parking lot
and said, "Check this out." And she opened her mouth unnaturally
wide and her voice came out, so crystalline and bright that all the
departing operagoers stood frozen by their cars, unable to take out
their keys or open their doors until she had finished, and then they
cheered like hell.

That's what I like to remember, and that's the story I told to all
of her therapists. I wanted them to know her, to know that who
they saw was not all there was to see. That before her constant tinkling of commercials and fast-food jingles there had been Puccini
and Mozart and hymns so sweet and mighty you expected Jesus to
come down off his cross and clap. That before there was a mountain of Thorazined fat, swaying down the halls in nylon maternity
tops and sweatpants, there had been the prettiest girl in Arrandale
Elementary School, the belle of Landmark Junior High. Maybe
there were other pretty girls, but I didn't see them. To me, Rose,
my beautiful blond defender, my guide to Tampax and my mother's
moods, was perfect.

She had her first psychotic break when she was fifteen. She had been coming home moody and tearful, then quietly beaming, then she stopped coming home. She would go out into the woods behind our house and not come in until my mother went after her at dusk, and stepped gently into the briars and saplings and pulled her out, blank-faced, her pale blue sweater covered with crumbled leaves, her white jeans smeared with dirt. After three weeks of this, my mother, who is a musician and widely regarded as eccentric, said to my father, who is a psychiatrist and a kind, sad man, "She's going off."

"What is that, your professional opinion?" He picked up the newspaper and put it down again, sighing. "I'm sorry, I didn't mean to snap at you. I know something's bothering her. Have you talked to her?"

"What's there to say? David, she's going crazy. She doesn't need a heart-to-heart talk with Mom, she needs a hospital."

They went back and forth, and my father sat down with Rose for a few hours, and she sat there licking the hairs on her forearm, first one way, then the other. My mother stood in the hallway, dry-eyed and pale, watching the two of them. She had already packed, and when three of my father's friends dropped by to offer free consultations and recommendations, my mother and Rose's suitcase were already in the car. My mother hugged me and told me that they would be back that night, but not with Rose. She also said, divining my worst fear, "It won't happen to you, honey. Some people go crazy and some people never do. You never will." She smiled and stroked my hair. "Not even when you want to."

Rose was in hospitals, great and small, for the next ten years. She had lots of terrible therapists and a few good ones. One place had no pictures on the walls, no windows, and the patients all wore slippers with the hospital crest on them. My mother didn't even bother to go to Admissions. She turned Rose around and the two of them marched out, my father walking behind them, apologizing to his colleagues. My mother ignored the psychiatrists, the social workers, and the nurses, and played Handel and Bessie Smith for the patients on whatever was available. At some places, she had a Steinway donated by a grateful, or optimistic, family; at others, she banged out "Gimme a Pigfoot and a Bottle of Beer" on an old, scarred box that hadn't been tuned since there'd been English-speaking physicians on the grounds. My father talked in serious, appreciative tones to the administrators and unit chiefs and tried to be friendly with whoever was managing Rose's case. We all hated the family therapists.

The worst family therapist we ever had sat in a pale green room with us, visibly taking stock of my mother's ethereal beauty and her faded blue t-shirt and girl-sized jeans, my father's rumpled suit and stained tie, and my own unreadable seventeen-year-old fashion statement. Rose was beyond fashion that year, in one of her danc-ing teddybear smocks and extra-extra-large Celtics sweatpants. Mr. Walker read Rose's file in front of us and then watched in alarm as Rose began crooning, beautifully, and slowly massaging her breasts. My mother and I laughed, and even my father started to smile. This was Rose's usual opening salvo for new therapists.

Mr. Walker said, "I wonder why it is that everyone is so enter-tained by Rose behaving inappropriately."

Rose burped, and then we all laughed. This was the seventh family therapist we had seen, and none of them had lasted very long. Mr. Walker, unfortunately, was determined to do right by us.

"What do you think of Rose's behavior, Violet?" They did this sometimes. In their manual it must say, If you think the parents are too weird, try talking to the sister.

"I don't know. Maybe she's trying to get you to stop talking about her in the third person."

"Nicely put," my mother said.

"Indeed," my father said.

"Fuckin' A," Rose said.

"Well, this is something that the whole family agrees upon," Mr. Walker said, trying to act as if he understood or even liked us.

"That was not a successful intervention, Ferret Face." Rose tended to function better when she was angry. He did look like a blond ferret, and we all laughed again. Even my father, who tried to give these people a chance, out of some sense of collegiality, had given it up.

After fourteen minutes, Mr. Walker decided that our time was up and walked out, leaving us grinning at each other. Rose was still nuts, but at least we'd all had a little fun.

The day we met our best family therapist started out almost as badly. We scared off a resident and then scared off her supervisor, who sent us Dr. Thorne. Three hundred pounds of Texas chili, cornbread, and Lone Star beer, finished off with big black cowboy boots and a small string tie around the area of his neck.

"O frabjous day, it's Big Nut." Rose was in heaven and stopped massaging her breasts immediately.

"Hey, Little Nut." You have to understand how big a man would have to be to call my sister "little." He christened us all, right away. "And it's the good Doctor Nut, and Madame Hickory Nut, 'cause they are the hardest damn nuts to crack, and over here in the overalls and not much else is No One's Nut"—a name that summed up both my sanity and my loneliness. We all relaxed.

Dr. Thorne was good for us. Rose moved into a halfway house whose director loved Big Nut so much that she kept Rose even when Rose went through a period of having sex with everyone who passed her door. She was in a fever for a while, trying to still the voices by fucking her brains out.

Big Nut said, "Darlin', I can't. I cannot make love to every beautiful woman I meet, and furthermore, I can't do that and be your therapist too. It's a great shame, but I think you might be able to find a really nice guy, someone who treats you just as sweet and kind as I would if I were lucky enough to be your beau. I don't want you to settle for less." And she stopped propositioning the crack addicts and the alcoholics and the guys at the shelter. We loved Dr. Thorne.

My father went back to seeing rich neurotics and helped out one day a week at Dr. Thorne's Walk-In Clinic. My mother finished a recording of Mozart concerti and played at fund-raisers for Rose's halfway house. I went back to college and found a wonderful linebacker from Texas to sleep with. In the dark, I would make him call me "darlin'." Rose took her meds, lost about fifty pounds, and began singing at the A.M.E. Zion Church, down the street from the halfway house.

At first they didn't know what do to with this big blond lady, dressed funny and hovering wistfully in the doorway during their rehearsals, but she gave them a few bars of "Precious Lord" and the choir director felt God's hand and saw that with the help of His sweet child Rose, the Prospect Street Choir was going all the way to the Gospel Olympics.

Amidst a sea of beige, umber, cinnamon, and espresso faces, there was Rose, bigger, blonder, and pinker than any two white women could be. And Rose and the choir's contralto, Addie Robicheaux, laid out their gold and silver voices and wove them together in strands as fine as silk, as strong as steel. And we wept as Rose and Addie, in their billowing garnet robes, swayed together, clasping hands until the last perfect note floated up to God, and then they smiled down at us.

Rose would still go off from time to time and the voices would tell her to do bad things, but Dr. Thorne or Addie or my mother could usually bring her back. After five good years, Big Nut died. Stuffing his face with a chili dog, sitting in his unair-conditioned office in the middle of July, he had one big, Texas-sized aneurysm and died.

Rose held on tight for seven days; she took her meds, went to choir practice, and rearranged her room about a hundred times. His funeral was like a Lourdes for the mentally ill. If you were psychotic, borderline, bad-off neurotic, or just very hard to get along with, you were there. People shaking so bad from years of heavy meds that they fell out of the pews. People holding hands, crying, moaning, talking to themselves. The crazy people and the not-so-crazy people were all huddled together, like puppies at the pound.

Rose stopped taking her meds, and the halfway house wouldn't keep her after she pitched another patient down the stairs. My father called the insurance company and found out that Rose's new, improved psychiatric coverage wouldn't begin for forty-five days. I put all of her stuff in a garbage bag, and we walked out of the halfway house, Rose winking at the poor drooling boy on the couch.

"This is going to be difficult—not all bad, but difficult—for the whole family, and I thought we should discuss everybody's expectations. I know I have some concerns." My father had convened a family meeting as soon as Rose finished putting each one of her thirty stuffed bears in its own special place.

"No meds," Rose said, her eyes lowered, her stubby fingers, those fingers that had braided my hair and painted tulips on my cheeks, pulling hard on the hem of her dirty smock.

My father looked in despair at my mother.

"Rosie, do you want to drive the new car?" my mother asked.

Rose's face lit up. "I'd love to drive that car. I'd drive to California, I'd go see the bears at the San Diego Zoo. I would take you, Violet, but you always hated the zoo. Remember how she cried at the Bronx Zoo when she found out that the animals didn't get to go home at closing?" Rose put her damp hand on mine and squeezed it sympathetically. "Poor Vi."

"If you take your medication, after a while you'll be able to drive the car. That's the deal. Meds, car." My mother sounded accommodating but unenthusiastic, careful not to heat up Rose's paranoia.

"You got yourself a deal, darlin'."

I was living about an hour away then, teaching English during the day, writing poetry at night. I went home every few days for dinner. I called every night.

My father said, quietly, "It's very hard. We're doing all right, I think. Rose has been walking in the mornings with your mother, and she watches a lot of TV. She won't go to the day hospital, and she won't go back to the choir. Her friend Mrs. Robicheaux came by a couple of times. What a sweet woman. Rose wouldn't even talk to her. She just sat there, staring at the wall and humming. We're not doing all that well, actually, but I guess we're getting by. I'm sorry, sweetheart, I don't mean to depress you."

My mother said, emphatically, "We're doing fine. We've got our routine and we stick to it and we're fine. You don't need to come home so often, you know. Wait 'til Sunday, just come for the day. Lead your life, Vi. She's leading hers."

I stayed away all week, afraid to pick up my phone, grateful to my mother for her harsh calm and her reticence, the qualities that had enraged me throughout my childhood.

I came on Sunday, in the early afternoon, to help my father garden, something we had always enjoyed together. We weeded and staked tomatoes and killed aphids while my mother and Rose were down at the lake. I didn't even go into the house until four, when I needed a glass of water.

Someone had broken the piano bench into five neatly stacked pieces and placed them where the piano bench usually was.

"We were having such a nice time, I couldn't bear to bring it up," my father said, standing in the doorway, carefully keeping his gardening boots out of the kitchen.

"What did Mommy say?"

"She said, 'Better the bench than the piano.' And your sister lay down on the floor and just wept. Then your mother took her down to the lake. This can't go on, Vi. We have twenty-seven days left, your mother gets no sleep because Rose doesn't sleep, and if I could just pay twenty-seven thousand dollars to keep her in the hospital until the insurance takes over, I'd do it."

"All right. Do it. Pay the money and take her back to Hartley-Rees. It was the prettiest place, and she liked the art therapy there."

"I would if I could. The policy states that she must be

symptom-free for at least forty-five days before her coverage begins. Symptom-free means no hospitalization."

"Jesus, Daddy, how could you get that kind of policy? She hasn't been symptom-free for forty-five minutes."

"It's the only one I could get for long-term psychiatric." He put his hand over his mouth, to block whatever he was about to say, and went back out to the garden. I couldn't see if he was crying.

He stayed outside and I stayed inside until Rose and my mother came home from the lake. Rose's soggy sweatpants were rolled up to her knees, and she had a bucketful of shells and seaweed, which my mother persuaded her to leave on the back porch. My mother kissed me lightly and told Rose to go up to her room and change out of her wet pants.

Rose's eyes grew very wide. "Never. I will never . . ." She knelt down and began banging her head on the kitchen floor with rhythmic intensity, throwing all her weight behind each attack. My mother put her arms around Rose's waist and tried to hold her back. Rose shook her off, not even looking around to see what was slowing her down. My mother lay up against the refrigerator.

"Violet, please . . ."

I threw myself onto the kitchen floor, becoming the spot that Rose was smacking her head against. She stopped a fraction of an inch short of my stomach.

"Oh, Vi, Mommy, I'm sorry. I'm sorry, don't hate me." She staggered to her feet and ran wailing to her room.

My mother got up and washed her face brusquely, rubbing it dry with a dishcloth. My father heard the wailing and came running in, slipping his long bare feet out of his rubber boots.

"Galen, Galen, let me see." He held her head and looked closely for bruises on her pale, small face. "What happened?" My mother looked at me. "Violet, what happened? Where's Rose?"

"Rose got upset, and when she went running upstairs she pushed Mommy out of the way." I've only told three lies in my life, and that was my second.

"She must feel terrible, pushing you, of all people. It would have to be you, but I know she didn't want it to be." He made my mother a cup of tea, and all the love he had for her, despite her silent rages and her vague stares, came pouring through the teapot, warming her cup, filling her small, long-fingered hands. She rested her head against his hip, and I looked away.

"Let's make dinner, then I'll call her. Or you call her, David, maybe she'd rather see your face first."

Dinner was filled with all of our starts and stops and Rose's desperate efforts to control herself. She could barely eat and hummed the McDonald's theme song over and over again, pausing only to spill her juice down the front of her smock and begin weeping. My father looked at my mother and handed Rose his napkin. She dabbed at herself listlessly, but the tears stopped.

"I want to go to bed. I want to go to bed and be in my head. I want to go to bed and be in my bed and in my head and just wear red. For red is the color that my baby wore and once more, it's true, yes, it is, it's true. Please don't wear red tonight, oh, oh, please don't wear red tonight, for red is the color—"

"Okay, okay, Rose. It's okay. I'll go upstairs with you and you can get ready for bed. Then Mommy will come up and say good night too. It's okay, Rose." My father reached out his hand and Rose grasped it, and they walked out of the dining room together, his long arm around her middle.

My mother sat at the table for a moment, her face in her hands, and then she began clearing the plates. We cleared without talking, my mother humming Schubert's "Schlummerlied," a lullaby about the woods and the river calling to the child to go to sleep. She sang it to us every night when we were small.

My father came into the kitchen and signaled to my mother. They went upstairs and came back down together a few minutes later.

"She's asleep," they said, and we went to sit on the porch and listen to the crickets. I don't remember the rest of the evening, but

I remember it as quietly sad, and I remember the rare sight of my parents holding hands, sitting on the picnic table, watching the sunset.

I woke up at three o'clock in the morning, feeling the cool night air through my sheet. I went down the hall for a blanket and looked into Rose's room, for no reason. She wasn't there. I put on my jeans and a sweater and went downstairs. I could feel her absence. I went outside and saw her wide, draggy footprints darkening the wet grass into the woods.

"Rosie," I called, too softly, not wanting to wake my parents, not wanting to startle Rose. "Rosie, it's me. Are you here? Are you all right?"

I almost fell over her. Huge and white in the moonlight, her flowered smock bleached in the light and shadow, her sweatpants now completely wet. Her head was flung back, her white, white neck exposed like a lost Greek column.

"Rosie, Rosie—" Her breathing was very slow, and her lips were not as pink as they usually were. Her eyelids fluttered.

"Closing time," she whispered. I believe that's what she said.

I sat with her, uncovering the bottle of white pills by her hand, and watched the stars fade.

When the stars were invisible and the sun was warming the air, I went back to the house. My mother was standing on the porch, wrapped in a blanket, watching me. Every step I took overwhelmed me; I could picture my mother slapping me, shooting me for letting her favorite die.

"Warrior queens," she said, wrapping her thin strong arms around me. "I raised warrior queens." She kissed me fiercely and went into the woods by herself.

Later in the morning she woke my father, who could not go into the woods, and still later she called the police and the funeral parlor. She hung up the phone, lay down, and didn't get back out of bed until the day of the funeral. My father fed us both and called the people who needed to be called and picked out Rose's coffin by himself.

My mother played the piano and Addie sang her pure gold notes and I closed my eyes and saw my sister, fourteen years old, lion's mane thrown back and eyes tightly closed against the glare of the parking lot lights. That sweet sound held us tight, flowing around us, eddying through our hearts, rising, still rising.

Sandra Cisneros

ๅ

Never Marry a Mexican

NEVER MARRY a Mexican, my ma said once and always. She said this because of my father. She said this though she was Mexican too. But she was born here in the U.S., and he was born there, and it's *not* the same, you know.

I'll *never* marry. Not any man. I've known men too intimately. I've witnessed their infidelities, and I've helped them to it. Unzipped and unhooked and agreed to clandestine maneuvers. I've been accomplice, committed premeditated crimes. I'm guilty of having caused deliberate pain to other women. I'm vindictive and cruel, and I'm capable of anything.

I admit, there was a time when all I wanted was to belong to a man. To wear that gold band on my left hand and be worn on his arm like an expensive jewel brilliant in the light of day. Not the sneaking around I did in different bars that all looked the same, red carpets with a black grillwork design, flocked wallpaper, wooden wagon-wheel light fixtures with hurricane lampshades a sick amber color like the drinking glasses you get for free at gas stations.

Dark bars, dark restaurants then. And if not—my apartment, with his toothbrush firmly planted in the toothbrush holder like a flag on the North Pole. The bed so big because he never stayed the whole night. Of course not.

Borrowed. That's how I've had my men. Just the cream skimmed off the top. Just the sweetest part of the fruit, without the bitter skin that daily living with a spouse can rend. They've come to me when they wanted the sweet meat then.

So, no. I've never married and never will. Not because I couldn't, but because I'm too romantic for marriage. Marriage has failed me, you could say. Not a man exists who hasn't disappointed me, whom I could trust to love the way I've loved. It's because I believe too much in marriage that I don't. Better to not marry than live a lie.

Mexican men, forget it. For a long time the men clearing off the tables or chopping meat behind the butcher counter or driving the bus I rode to school every day, those weren't men. Not men I considered as potential lovers. Mexican, Puerto Rican, Cuban, Chilean, Colombian, Panamanian, Salvadorean, Bolivian, Honduran, Argentine, Dominican, Venezuelan, Guatemalan, Ecuadorean, Nicaraguan, Peruvian, Costa Rican, Paraguayan, Uruguayan, I don't care. I never saw them. My mother did this to me.

I guess she did it to spare me and Ximena the pain she went through. Having married a Mexican man at seventeen. Having had to put up with all the grief a Mexican family can put on a girl because she was from *el otro lado,* the other side, and my father had married down by marrying her. If he had married a white woman from *el otro lado,* that would've been different. That would've been marrying up, even if the white girl was poor. But what could be more ridiculous than a Mexican girl who couldn't even speak Spanish, who didn't know enough to set a separate plate for each course at dinner, nor how to fold cloth napkins, nor how to set the silverware.

In my ma's house the plates were always stacked in the center of the table, the knives and forks and spoons standing in a jar, help yourself. All the dishes chipped or cracked and nothing matched. And no tablecloth, ever. And newspapers set on the table whenever my grandpa sliced watermelons, and how embarrassed she would be when her boyfriend, my father, would come over and there were newspapers all over the kitchen floor and table. And my grandpa, big hardworking Mexican man, saying Come, come and eat, and slicing a big wedge of those dark green watermelons, a big slice, he wasn't stingy with food. Never, even during the Depression. Come, come and eat, to whoever came knocking on the back door. Hobos sitting at the dinner table and the children staring and staring. Because my grandfather always made sure they never went without. Flour and rice, by the barrel and by the sack. Potatoes. Big bags of pinto beans. And watermelons, bought three or four at a time, rolled under his bed and brought out when you least expected. My grandpa had survived three wars, one Mexican, two American, and he knew what living without meant. He knew.

My father, on the other hand, did not. True, when he first came to this country he had worked shelling clams, washing dishes, planting hedges, sat on the back of the bus in Little Rock and had the bus driver shout, You—sit up here, and my father had shrugged sheepishly and said, No speak English.

But he was no economic refugee, no immigrant fleeing a war. My father ran away from home because he was afraid of facing his father after his first-year grades at the university proved he'd spent more time fooling around than studying. He left behind a house in Mexico City that was neither poor nor rich, but thought itself better than both. A boy who would get off a bus when he saw a girl he knew board if he didn't have the money to pay her fare. That was the world my father left behind.

I imagine my father in his *fanfarrón* clothes, because that's what he was, a *fanfarrón*. That's what my mother thought the moment she turned around to the voice that was asking her to dance. A big show-off, she'd say years later. Nothing but a big show-off. But she never said why she married him. My father in his shark-blue suits with the starched handkerchief in the breast pocket, his felt fedora, his tweed topcoat with the big shoulders, and heavy British wing tips with the pin-hole design on the heel and toe. Clothes that cost a lot. Expensive. That's what my father's things said. *Calidad*. Quality.

My father must've found the U.S. Mexicans very strange, so foreign from what he knew at home in Mexico City where the servant served watermelon on a plate with silverware and a cloth napkin, or mangos with their own special prongs. Not like this, eating with your legs wide open in the yard, or in the kitchen hunkered over newspapers. *Come, come and eat.* No, never like this.

HOW I MAKE my living depends. Sometimes I work as a translator. Sometimes I get paid by the word and sometimes by the hour, depending on the job. I do this in the day, and at night I paint. I'd do anything in the day just so I can keep on painting.

I work as a substitute teacher, too, for the San Antonio Independent School District. And that's worse than translating those travel brochures with their tiny print, believe me. I can't stand kids. Not any age. But it pays the rent.

Any way you look at it, what I do to make a living is a form of prostitution. People say, "A painter? How nice," and want to invite me to their parties, have me decorate the lawn like an exotic orchid for hire. But do they buy art?

I'm amphibious. I'm a person who doesn't belong to any class. The rich like to have me around because they envy my creativity; they know they can't buy *that*. The poor don't mind if I live in their neighborhood because they know I'm poor like they are, even if my education and the way I dress keeps us worlds apart. I don't belong to any class. Not to the poor, whose neighborhood I share. Not to the rich, who come to my exhibitions and buy my work. Not to the middle class from which my sister Ximena and I fled.

When I was young, when I first left home and rented that apartment with my sister and her kids right after her husband left, I thought it would be glamorous to be an artist. I wanted to be like

Frida or Tina. I was ready to suffer with my camera and my paint brushes in that awful apartment we rented for $150 each because it had high ceilings and those wonderful glass skylights that convinced us we had to have it. Never mind there was no sink in the bathroom, and a tub that looked like a sarcophagus, and floorboards that didn't meet, and a hallway to scare away the dead. But fourteen-foot ceilings was enough for us to write a check for the deposit right then and there. We thought it all romantic. You know the place, the one on Zarzamora on top of the barber shop with the Casasola prints of the Mexican Revolution. Neon BIRRIA TEPATITLÁN sign round the corner, two goats knocking their heads together, and all those Mexican bakeries, Las Brisas for *huevos rancheros* and *carnitas* and *barbacoa* on Sundays, and fresh fruit milk shakes, and mango *paletas,* and more signs in Spanish than in English. We thought it was great, great. The barrio looked cute in the daytime, like Sesame Street. Kids hopscotching on the sidewalk, blessed little boogers. And hardware stores that still sold ostrich-feather dusters, and whole families marching out of Our Lady of Guadalupe Church on Sundays, girls in their swirly-whirly dresses and patent-leather shoes, boys in their dress Stacys and shiny shirts.

But nights, that was nothing like what we knew up on the north side. Pistols going off like the wild, wild West, and me and Ximena and the kids huddled in one bed with the lights off listening to it all, saying, Go to sleep, babies, it's just firecrackers. But we knew better. Ximena would say, Clemencia, maybe we should go home. And I'd say, Shit! Because she knew as well as I did there was no home to go home to. Not with our mother. Not with that man she married. After Daddy died, it was like we didn't matter. Like Ma was so busy feeling sorry for herself, I don't know. I'm not like Ximena. I still haven't worked it out after all this time, even though our mother's dead now. My half brothers living in that house that should've been ours, me and Ximena's. But that's—how do you say it?—water under the damn? I can't ever get the sayings right even though I was born in this country. We didn't say shit like that in our house.

Once Daddy was gone, it was like my ma didn't exist, like if she died, too. I used to have a little finch, twisted one of its tiny red legs between the bars of the cage once, who knows how. The leg just dried up and fell off. My bird lived a long time without it, just a little red stump of a leg. He was fine, really. My mother's memory is like that, like if something already dead dried up and fell off, and I stopped missing where she used to be. Like if I never had a mother. And I'm not ashamed to say it either. When she married that white man, and he and his boys moved into my father's house, it was as if she stopped being my mother. Like I never even had one.

Ma always sick and too busy worrying about her own life, she would've sold us to the Devil if she could. "Because I married so young, *mi'ja,*" she'd say. "Because your father, he was so much older than me, and I never had a chance to be young. Honey, try to understand . . ." Then I'd stop listening.

That man she met at work, Owen Lambert, the foreman at the photo-finishing plant, who she was seeing even while my father was sick. Even then. That's what I can't forgive.

When my father was coughing up blood and phlegm in the hospital, half his face frozen, and his tongue so fat he couldn't talk, he looked so small with all those tubes and plastic sacks dangling around him. But what I remember most is the smell, like death was already sitting on his chest. And I remember the doctor scraping the phlegm out of my father's mouth with a white washcloth, and my daddy gagging and I wanted to yell, Stop, you stop that, he's my daddy. Goddamn you. Make him live. Daddy, don't. Not yet, not yet, not yet. And how I couldn't hold myself up, I couldn't hold myself up. Like if they'd beaten me, or pulled my insides out through my nostrils, like if they'd stuffed me with cinnamon and cloves, and I just stood there dry-eyed next to Ximena and my mother, Ximena between us because I wouldn't let her stand next to me. Everyone repeating over and over the Ave Marías and Padre Nuestros. The priest sprinkling holy water, *mundo sin fin, amén.*

DREW, REMEMBER when you used to call me your Malinalli? It was a joke, a private game between us, because you looked like a Cortez with that beard of yours. My skin dark against yours. Beautiful, you said. You said I was beautiful, and when you said it, Drew, I was.

My Malinalli, Malinche, my courtesan, you said, and yanked my head back by the braid. Calling me that name in between little gulps of breath and the raw kisses you gave, laughing from that black beard of yours.

Before daybreak, you'd be gone, same as always, before I even knew it. And it was as if I'd imagined you, only the teeth marks on my belly and nipples proving me wrong.

Your skin pale, but your hair blacker than a pirate's. Malinalli, you called me, remember? *Mi doradita.* I liked when you spoke to me in my language. I could love myself and think myself worth loving.

Your son. Does he know how much I had to do with his birth? I was the one who convinced you to let him be born. Did you tell him, while his mother lay on her back laboring his birth, I lay in his mother's bed making love to you.

You're nothing without me. I created you from spit and red dust. And I can snuff you between my finger and thumb if I want to. Blow you to kingdom come. You're just a smudge of paint I chose to birth on canvas. And when I made you over, you were no longer a part of her, you were all mine. The landscape of your body taut as a drum. The heart beneath that hide thrumming and thrumming. Not an inch did I give back.

I paint and repaint you the way I see fit, even now. After all these years. Did you know that? Little fool. You think I went hobbling along with my life, whimpering and whining like some twangy country-and-western when you went back to her. But I've been waiting. Making the world look at you from my eyes. And if that's not power, what is?

Nights I light all the candles in the house, the ones to La Virgen de Guadalupe, the ones to El Niño Fidencio, Don Pedrito Jaramillo, Santo Niño de Atocha, Nuestra Señora de San Juan de los Lagos, and especially, Santa Lucía, with her beautiful eyes on a plate.

Your eyes are beautiful, you said. You said they were the darkest eyes you'd ever seen and kissed each one as if they were capable of miracles. And after you left, I wanted to scoop them out with a spoon, place them on a plate under these blue blue skies, food for the blackbirds.

The boy, your son. The one with the face of that redheaded woman who is your wife. The boy red-freckled like fish food floating on the skin of water. That boy.

I've been waiting patient as a spider all these years, since I was nineteen and he was just an idea hovering in his mother's head, and I'm the one that gave him permission and made it happen, see.

Because your father wanted to leave your mother and live with me. Your mother whining for a child, at least *that*. And he kept saying, Later, we'll see, later. But all along it was me he wanted to be with, it was me, he said.

I want to tell you this evenings when you come to see me. When you're full of talk about what kind of clothes you're going to buy, and what you used to be like when you started high school and what you're like now that you're almost finished. And how everyone knows you as a rocker, and your band, and your new red guitar that you just got because your mother gave you a choice, a guitar or a car, but you don't need a car, do you, because I drive you everywhere. You could be my son if you weren't so light-skinned.

This happened. A long time ago. Before you were born. When you were a moth inside your mother's heart, I was your father's student, yes, just like you're mine now. And your father painted and painted me, because he said, I was his *doradita,* all golden and sun-baked, and that's the kind of woman he likes best, the ones brown as river sand, yes. And he took me under his wing and in his bed, this man, this teacher, your father. I was honored that he'd done me the favor. I was that young.

All I know is I was sleeping with your father the night you were born. In the same bed where you were conceived. I was sleeping with your father and didn't give a damn about that woman, your mother. If she was a brown woman like me, I might've had a harder time living with myself, but since she's not, I don't care. I was there first, always. I've always been there, in the mirror, under his skin, in the blood, before you were born. And he's been here in my heart before I even knew him. Understand? He's always been here. Always. Dissolving like a hibiscus flower, exploding like a rope into dust. I don't care what's right anymore. I don't care about his wife. She's not *my* sister.

And it's not the last time I've slept with a man the night his wife is birthing a baby. Why do I do that, I wonder? Sleep with a man when his wife is giving life, being suckled by a thing with its eyes still shut. Why do that? It's always given me a bit of crazy joy to be able to kill those women like that, without their knowing it. To know I've had their husbands when they were anchored in blue hospital rooms, their guts yanked inside out, the baby sucking their breasts while their husband sucked mine. All this while their ass stitches were still hurting.

ONCE, DRUNK on margaritas, I telephoned your father at four in the morning, woke the bitch up. Hello, she chirped. I want to talk to Drew. Just a moment, she said in her most polite drawing-room English. Just a moment. I laughed about that for weeks. What a stupid ass to pass the phone over to the lug asleep beside her. Excuse me, honey, it's for you. When Drew mumbled hello I was laughing so hard I could hardly talk. Drew? That dumb bitch of a wife of yours, I said, and that's all I could manage. That stupid stupid stupid. No Mexican woman would react like that. Excuse me, honey. It cracked me up.

HE'S GOT the same kind of skin, the boy. All the blue veins pale and clear just like his mama. Skin like roses in December. Pretty boy. Little clone. Little cells split into you and you and you. Tell me, baby, which part of you is your mother. I try to imagine her lips, her jaw, her long long legs that wrapped themselves around this father who took me to his bed.

THIS HAPPENED. I'm asleep. Or pretend to be. You're watching me, Drew. I feel your weight when you sit on the corner of the bed, dressed and ready to go, but now you're just watching me sleep. Nothing. Not a word. Not a kiss. Just sitting. You're taking me in, under inspection. What do you think already?

I haven't stopped dreaming you. Did you know that? Do you think it's strange? I never tell, though. I keep it to myself like I do all the thoughts I think of you.

After all these years.

I don't want you looking at me. I don't want you taking me in while I'm asleep. I'll open my eyes and frighten you away.

There. What did I tell you? *Drew? What is it?* Nothing. I knew you'd say that.

Let's not talk. We're no good at it. With you I'm useless with words. As if somehow I had to learn to speak all over again, as if the words I needed haven't been invented yet. We're cowards. Come back to bed. At least there I feel I have you for a little. For a moment. For a catch of the breath. You let go. You ache and tug. You rip my skin.

You're almost not a man without your clothes. How do I explain it? You're so much a child in my bed. Nothing but a big boy who needs to be held. I won't let anyone hurt you. My pirate. My slender boy of a man.

After all these years.

I didn't imagine it, did I? A Ganges, an eye of the storm. For a little. When we forgot ourselves, you tugged me, I leapt inside you and split you like an apple. Opened for the other to look and not give back. Something wrenched itself loose. Your body doesn't lie. It's not silent like you.

You're nude as a pearl. You've lost your train of smoke. You're tender as rain. If I'd put you in my mouth you'd dissolve like snow.

You were ashamed to be so naked. Pulled back. But I saw you for what you are, when you opened yourself for me. When you were careless and let yourself through. I caught that catch of the breath. I'm not crazy.

When you slept, you tugged me toward you. You sought me in the dark. I didn't sleep. Every cell, every follicle, every nerve, alert. Watching you sigh and roll and turn and hug me closer to you. I didn't sleep. I was taking *you* in that time.

YOUR MOTHER? Only once. Years after your father and I stopped seeing each other. At an art exhibition. A show on the photographs of Eugène Atget. Those images, I could look at them for hours. I'd taken a group of students with me.

It was your father I saw first. And in that instant I felt as if everyone in the room, all the sepia-toned photographs, my students, the men in business suits, the high-heeled women, the security guards, everyone, could see me for what I was. I had to scurry out, lead my kids to another gallery, but some things destiny has cut out for you.

He caught up with us in the coat-check area, arm in arm with a redheaded Barbie doll in a fur coat. One of those scary Dallas types, hair yanked into a ponytail, big shiny face like the women behind the cosmetic counters at Neiman's. That's what I remember. She must've been with him all along, only I swear I never saw her until that second.

You could tell from a slight hesitancy, only slight because he's too suave to hesitate, that he was nervous. Then he's walking toward me, and I didn't know what to do, just stood there dazed like those animals crossing the road at night when the headlights stun them.

And I don't know why, but all of a sudden I looked at my shoes and felt ashamed at how old they looked. And he comes up to me, my love, your father, in that way of his with that grin that makes me want to beat him, makes me want to make love to him, and he says in the most sincere voice you ever heard, "Ah, Clemencia! *This* is Megan." No introduction could've been meaner. *This* is Megan. Just like that.

I grinned like an idiot and held out my paw—"Hello, Megan"—and smiled too much the way you do when you can't stand someone. Then I got the hell out of there, chattering like a monkey all the ride back with my kids. When I got home I had to lie down with a cold washcloth on my forehead and the TV on. All I could hear throbbing under the washcloth in that deep part behind my eyes: *This* is Megan.

And that's how I fell asleep, with the TV on and every light in the house burning. When I woke up it was something like three in the morning. I shut the lights and TV and went to get some aspirin, and the cats, who'd been asleep with me on the couch, got up too and followed me into the bathroom as if they knew what's what. And then they followed me into bed, where they aren't allowed, but this time I just let them, fleas and all.

THIS HAPPENED, too. I swear I'm not making this up. It's all true. It was the last time I was going to be with your father. We had agreed. All for the best. Surely I could see that, couldn't I? My own

good. A good sport. A young girl like me. Hadn't I understood . . .
responsibilities. Besides, he could *never* marry *me*. You didn't
think. . . ? *Never marry a Mexican. Never marry a Mexican* . . . No, of
course not. I see. I see.

We had the house to ourselves for a few days, who knows how.
You and your mother had gone somewhere. Was it Christmas? I
don't remember.

I remember the leaded-glass lamp with the milk glass above the
dining-room table. I made a mental inventory of everything. The
Egyptian lotus design on the hinges of the doors. The narrow, dark
hall where your father and I had made love once. The four-clawed
tub where he had washed my hair and rinsed it with a tin bowl.
This window. That counter. The bedroom with its light in the
morning, incredibly soft, like the light from a polished dime.

The house was immaculate, as always, not a stray hair anywhere, not a flake of dandruff or a crumpled towel. Even the roses
on the dining-room table held their breath. A kind of airless cleanliness that always made me want to sneeze.

Why was I so curious about this woman he lived with? Every
time I went to the bathroom, I found myself opening the medicine
cabinet, looking at all the things that were hers. Her Estée Lauder
lipsticks. Corals and pinks, of course. Her nail polishes—mauve
was as brave as she could wear. Her cotton balls and blond hairpins.
A pair of bone-colored sheepskin slippers, as clean as the day she'd
bought them. On the door hook—a white robe with a MADE IN
ITALY label, and a silky nightshirt with pearl buttons. I touched the
fabrics. *Calidad.* Quality.

I don't know how to explain what I did next. While your father
was busy in the kitchen, I went over to where I'd left my backpack,
and took out a bag of gummy bears I'd bought. And while he was
banging pots, I went around the house and left a trail of them in
places I was sure *she* would find them. One in her lucite makeup
organizer. One stuffed inside each bottle of nail polish. I untwisted
the expensive lipsticks to their full length and smushed a bear on

the top before recapping them. I even put a gummy bear in her diaphragm case in the very center of that luminescent rubber moon.

Why bother? Drew could take the blame. Or he could say it was the cleaning woman's Mexican voodoo. I knew that, too. It didn't matter. I got a strange satisfaction wandering about the house leaving them in places only she would look.

And just as Drew was shouting, "Dinner!" I saw it on the desk. One of those wooden babushka dolls Drew had brought her from his trip to Russia. I know. He'd bought one just like it for me.

I just did what I did, uncapped the doll inside a doll inside a doll, until I got to the very center, the tiniest baby inside all the others, and this I replaced with a gummy bear. And then I put the dolls back, just like I'd found them, one inside the other, inside the other. Except for the baby, which I put inside my pocket. All through dinner I kept reaching in the pocket of my jean jacket. When I touched it, it made me feel good.

On the way home, on the bridge over the *arroyo* on Guadalupe Street, I stopped the car, switched on the emergency blinkers, got out, and dropped the wooden toy into that muddy creek where winos piss and rats swim. The Barbie doll's toy stewing there in that muck. It gave me a feeling like nothing before and since.

Then I drove home and slept like the dead.

THESE MORNINGS, I fix coffee for me, milk for the boy. I think of that woman, and I can't see a trace of my lover in this boy, as if she conceived him by immaculate conception.

I sleep with this boy, their son. To make the boy love me the way I love his father. To make him want me, hunger, twist in his sleep, as if he'd swallowed glass. I put him in my mouth. Here, little piece of my *corazón*. Boy with hard thighs and just a bit of down and a small hard downy ass like his father's, and that back like a valentine. Come here, *mi cariñito*. Come to *mamita*. Here's a bit of toast.

I can tell from the way he looks at me, I have him in my power. Come, sparrow. I have the patience of eternity. Come to *mamita*. My stupid little bird. I don't move. I don't startle him. I let him nibble. All, all for you. Rub his belly. Stroke him. Before I snap my teeth.

WHAT IS IT inside me that makes me so crazy at 2 a.m.? I can't blame it on alcohol in my blood when there isn't any. It's something worse. Something that poisons the blood and tips me when the night swells and I feel as if the whole sky were leaning against my brain.

And if I killed someone on a night like this? And if it was *me* I killed instead, I'd be guilty of getting in the line of crossfire, innocent bystander, isn't it a shame. I'd be walking with my head full of images and my back to the guilty. Suicide? I couldn't say. I didn't see it.

Except it's not me who I want to kill. When the gravity of the planets is just right, it all tilts and upsets the visible balance. And that's when it wants to out from my eyes. That's when I get on the telephone, dangerous as a terrorist. There's nothing to do but let it come.

So. What do you think? Are you convinced now I'm as crazy as a tulip or a taxi? As vagrant as a cloud?

Sometimes the sky is so big and I feel so little at night. That's the problem with being cloud. The sky is so terribly big. Why is it worse at night, when I have such an urge to communicate and no language with which to form the words? Only colors. Pictures. And you know what I have to say isn't always pleasant.

Oh, love, there. I've gone and done it. What good is it? Good or bad, I've done what I had to do and needed to. And you've answered the phone, and startled me away like a bird. And now you're probably swearing under your breath and going back to sleep, with that wife beside you, warm, radiating her own heat, alive under the flannel and down and smelling a bit like milk and hand cream, and that smell familiar and dear to you, oh.

Human beings pass me on the street, and I want to reach out and strum them as if they were guitars. Sometimes all humanity strikes me as lovely. I just want to reach out and stroke someone, and say There, there, it's all right, honey. There, there, there.

Joyce Carol Oates

࿒

Love, Forever

HE WAS CRAZY about her he insisted and he certainly behaved that way when they were together, and alone. Did he! But he wasn't crazy about her three kids. Don't get me wrong he said it isn't anything personal, your kids are sweet kids, real nice, and Sherri's gonna be a real knockout, but I'm just not the type, y'know?—my wife and I split over that, she wanted kids and I didn't, she found a guy who did and that's okay with me, y'know?—that's just how it is with some guys.

She was gazing hurt and eyes brimming with tears deep into his eyes. But said, softly, I know.

And she didn't hold it against him, how could she. Telling her straight out how it was with him, no lies or subterfuge. Not like some guys. (Not like her ex-husband.) Just laying his cards down, calm and clear and no excuses, so you could see what's what and were spared making an asshole of yourself. So, she appreciated that. She cried a little, but she appreciated that. Framing his face in her hands like an actress gazing into those blue eyes like sapphires whispering another time, I know, and solemnly she'd kissed his lips and he'd remember it, that kiss: that kiss he could not guess was a pledge.

Oh, I know!—but I love you anyway forever.

. . .

THE ENTIRE DAY, the sun was hidden behind clouds, one of those gauzy gray days you feel like screaming but she was calm, she was in control. Six-year-old Tommy ran inside when the school bus let him off all excited saying the bus driver had almost hit a buck in the fog and she smiled and kissed him and walked past as if she hadn't heard. She's been smiling all day. It wasn't practice, it was her natural self: as, in high school, she'd smiled all the time. She was waiting for a phone call, she'd left a message on the answering service of one of the girls she used to work with, when she was working, and when the call came she had something planned to say she'd memorized, a strange man prowling the woods behind the trailer, a man with a beard, or maybe without a beard, probably a hunter, she hadn't wanted to stare out at him and wasn't worried really but she'd mention it, then talk of something else. Not too much detail—that gave you away. From TV you learned that.

She called *him,* too: knowing he wouldn't be home.

Just to hear his voice on the answering tape. Just his voice, sometimes—that was enough.

And hanging up, quietly. No message.

She had the gun ready. She didn't believe in firearms but it was a .22 Ruger pistol a guy had given her for protection, when she'd moved out here alone with the kids. She knew the precise spot in the river to toss it where nobody would find it in a million million years. She put on gloves, old rubber dishwashing gloves she'd be throwing away, too. She was wearing a warm sweatshirt, long sleeves. It was eleven p.m. and the kids were sleeping, a dark night with no moon and everything quiet back in the woods. She hadn't even had the TV on. Tommy, who was so excitable, naturally had to be first. She went into his room where he was sleeping open-mouthed in bed, she crouched over him holding the pistol calmly, she whispered, Sweetie? as she'd planned to wake him so he'd be looking up, maybe sitting up, and when he opened his eyes she pulled the trigger. Jesus, what a noise!—she hadn't counted on so much noise. Her ears ringing.

Tommy died at once, she believed. A bullet point-blank through his chest, thus no suffering. She'd planned that.

Next was Sherri, four years old. Pale blond hair like her mommy's, and her mommy's button nose. Sherri slept in Mommy's bedroom where the baby was also, in his crib, and the gunshot noise had been so loud Sherri was naturally awake, out of bed, screaming, Mommy? Mommy?—and she ran inside, trying to stay calm, swallowing, but her voice rising shrill, It's okay, honey! Mommy's here, it's okay! And she fired at the little girl, it wasn't exactly clear what happened but there was one bullet in the chest yet more screaming, and a second bullet in the chest and still more screaming, and now she was maybe losing it just a little, panting, stooping over the fallen writhing child to press the barrel against the top of the child's head and to squeeze the trigger again.

And the baby. Baby Seth. Seven months old. In his crib, in the corner of the room—that wasn't going to be hard! Baby Seth had wakened of course in all the commotion but hadn't begun yet to cry. It was that kind of baby—a little slow.

AT THE REAR entrance to the hospital she ran inside screaming for help. Somebody shot my kids! A man, a man shot my kids! And they came out at once, no wasting time, five, six, maybe seven of them, and saw Tommy sprawled in the front seat of the Olds, and pulled him out to carry inside to try to save his life, and the baby, the baby was in the front seat, too, My God there's a baby—one of the orderlies, a big black guy, yelled, like he couldn't believe it, and she stood there watching, this little smile on her face, *bemused*— how they were all running around, not smooth and coordinated the way you'd expect, taking the kids inside to save their lives when, couldn't they tell?—these kids were dead.

Actually, in fact, Tommy was not dead, but dying: he'd die, officially, that's to say when they couldn't resuscitate him, and his heart had stopped forever, at four a.m. of the next day.

The baby *was* dead.

It had been a listless baby, conceived not in love but spite.

So much commotion at the rear of the emergency unit of the hospital, everybody gaping, like lights had come on brighter like on TV, and maybe in fact they had, and she was standing there by the automatic doors, watching, in her blood-soaked clothes, her new jeans fitting her tight as if she'd been poured into them, and her Led Zeppelin sweatshirt, and the spike-heeled cowhide glamour boots—she was blinking, smiling just faintly, as if all she was doing *was* watching, calm, and curious to see how it would go, as the medical crew would testify at her trial. Where she should have been—what? Screaming, sobbing like a madwoman, running back and forth, trying to touch her kids?—was that what another mother would do, in this situation? Or was she, you could argue this, in shock?

But, no, she was reported to have called out, following them into the hospital, Nothing but the best for these kids! And she'd sounded scolding, but sly. Her eyes making the rounds of the waiting room where everybody's eyes were sure on *her.*

But then, my God, it came to her like a blow: little Sherri was still in the car! Out there, in the car!

Nobody'd seen Sherri. She must have slipped off the backseat during the wild skidding ride nine miles to town, lying on the floor hidden from view and the goddamn careless medical crew hadn't even noticed. So, she was excited now, she had to yell to get their attention, grabbing one of the nurses by the arm, digging her nails in hard, Hey, my little girl!—don't forget *her.*

The look on their faces. Almost, you'd have to laugh.

It *was* weird, though, and she'd never understand it—forgetting Sherri like that. Sherri was the one Mommy had always loved best.

Jamaica Kincaid

⤳

Song of Roland

HIS MOUTH WAS like an island in the sea that was his face; I am sure he had ears and nose and eyes and all the rest, but I could see only his mouth, which I knew could do all the things that a mouth usually does, such as eat food, purse in approval or disapproval, smile, twist in thought; inside were his teeth and behind them was his tongue. Why did I see him that way, how did I come to see him that way? It was a mystery to me that he had been alive all along and that I had not known of his existence and I was perfectly fine—I went to sleep at night and I could wake up in the morning and greet the day with indifference if it suited me, I could comb my hair and scratch myself and I was still perfectly fine—and he was alive, sometimes living in a house next to mine, sometimes living in a house far away, and his existence was ordinary and perfect and parallel to mine, but I did not know of it, even though sometimes he was close enough to me for me to notice that he smelt of cargo he had been unloading; he was a stevedore.

His mouth really did look like an island, lying in a twig-brown sea, stretching out from east to west, widest near the centre, with tiny, sharp creases, its colour a shade lighter than that of the twig-brown sea in which it lay, the place where the two lips met disappearing into the pinkest of pinks, and even though I must have held his mouth in mine a thousand times, it was always new to me. He must have smiled at me, though I don't really know, but I don't like to think that I would love someone who hadn't first smiled at me. It had been raining, a heavy downpour, and I took shelter under the gallery of a dry-goods store along with some other people. The rain was an inconvenience, for it was not necessary; there had already been too much of it, and it was no longer only outside, overflowing in the gutters, but inside also, roofs were leaking and then falling in. I was standing under the gallery and had sunk deep within myself, enjoying completely the despair I felt at being myself. I was wearing a dress; I had combed my hair that morning; I had washed myself that morning. I was looking at nothing in particular when I saw his mouth. He was speaking to someone else, but he was looking at me. The someone else he was speaking to was a woman. His mouth then was not like an island at rest in a sea but like a small patch of ground viewed from high above and set in motion by a force not readily seen.

When he saw me looking at him, he opened his mouth wider, and that must have been the smile. I saw then that he had a large gap between his two front teeth, which probably meant that he could not be trusted, but I did not care. My dress was damp, my shoes were wet, my hair was wet, my skin was cold, all around me were people standing in small amounts of water and mud, shivering, but I started to perspire from an effort I wasn't aware I was making; I started to perspire because I felt hot, and I started to perspire because I felt happy. I wore my hair then in two plaits and the ends of them rested just below my collar-bone; all the moisture in my hair collected and ran down my two plaits, as if they were two gutters, and the water seeped through my dress just below the collar-bone and continued to run down my chest, only stopping at the place where the tips of my breasts met the fabric, revealing, plain as a new print, my nipples. He was looking at me and talking to someone else, and his mouth grew wide and narrow, small and large, and I wanted him to notice me, but there was so much noise:

all the people standing in the gallery, sheltering themselves from the strong rain, had something they wanted to say, something not about the weather (that was by now beyond comment) but about their lives, their disappointments most likely, for joy is so short-lived there isn't enough time to dwell on its occurrence. The noise, which started as a hum, grew to a loud din, and the loud din had an unpleasant taste of metal and vinegar, but I knew his mouth could take it away if only I could get to it; so I called out my own name, and I knew he heard me immediately, but he wouldn't stop speaking to the woman he was talking to, so I had to call out my name again and again until he stopped, and by that time my name was like a chain around him, as the sight of his mouth was like a chain around me. And when our eyes met, we laughed, because we were happy, but it was frightening, for that gaze asked everything: who would betray whom, who would be captive, who would be captor, who would give and who would take, what would I do. And when our eyes met and we laughed at the same time, I said, 'I love you, I love you,' and he said, 'I know.' He did not say it out of vanity, he did not say it out of conceit, he only said it because it was true.

HIS NAME was Roland. He was not a hero, he did not even have a country; he was from an island, a small island that was between a sea and an ocean, and a small island is not a country. And he did not have a history; he was a small event in somebody else's history, but he was a man. I could see him better than he could see himself, and that was because he was who he was and I was myself but also because I was taller than he was. He was unpolished, but he carried himself as if he were precious. His hands were large and thick, and for no reason that I could see he would spread them out in front of him and they looked as if they were the missing parts from a powerful piece of machinery; his legs were straight from hip to knee and then from the knee they bent at an angle as if he had been at sea too long or had never learnt to walk properly to begin with.

The hair on his legs was tightly curled as if the hairs were pieces of thread rolled between the thumb and the forefinger in preparation for sewing, and so was the hair on his arms, the hair in his underarms, and the hair on his chest; the hair in those places was black and grew sparsely; the hair on his head and the hair between his legs was black and tightly curled also, but it grew in such abundance that it was impossible for me to move my hands through it. Sitting, standing, walking, or lying down, he carried himself as if he were something precious, but not out of vanity, for it was true, he was something precious; yet when he was lying on top of me he looked down at me as if I were the only woman in the world, the only woman he had ever looked at in that way—but that was not true, a man only does that when it is not true. When he first lay on top of me I was so ashamed of how much pleasure I felt that I bit my bottom lip hard—but I did not bleed, not from biting my lip, not then. His skin was smooth and warm in places I had not kissed him; in the places I had kissed him his skin was cold and coarse, and the pores were open and raised.

Did the world become a beautiful place? The rainy season eventually went away, the sunny season came, and it was too hot; the riverbed grew dry, the mouth of the river became shallow, the heat eventually became as wearying as the rain, and I would have wished it away if I had not become occupied with this other sensation, a sensation I had no single word for. I could feel myself full of happiness, but it was a kind of happiness I had never experienced before, and my happiness would spill out of me and run all the way down a long, long road and then the road would come to an end and I would feel empty and sad, for what could come after this? How would it end?

Not everything has an end, even though the beginning changes. The first time we were in a bed together we were lying on a thin board that was covered with old cloth, and this small detail, evidence of our poverty—people in our position, a stevedore and a doctor's servant, could not afford a proper mattress—was a major contribution to my satisfaction, for it allowed me to brace myself and match him breath for breath. But how can it be that a man who can carry large sacks filled with sugar or bales of cotton on his back from dawn to dusk exhausts himself within five minutes inside a woman? I did not then and I do not now know the answer to that. He kissed me. He fell asleep. I bathed my face then between his legs; he smelt of curry and onions, for those were the things he had been unloading all day; other times when I bathed my face between his legs—for I did it often, I liked doing it—he would smell of sugar, or flour, or the large, cheap bolts of cotton from which he would steal a few yards to give me to make a dress.

WHAT IS the everyday? What is the ordinary? One day, as I was walking towards the government dispensary to collect some supplies—one of my duties as a servant to a man who was in love with me beyond anything he could help and so had long since stopped trying, a man I ignored except when I wanted him to please me—I met Roland's wife, face to face, for the first time. She stood in front of me like a sentry—stern, dignified, guarding the noble idea, if not noble ideal, that was her husband. She did not block the sun, it was shining on my right; on my left was a large black cloud; it was raining way in the distance; there was no rainbow on the horizon. We stood on the narrow strip of concrete that was the sidewalk. One section of a wooden fence that was supposed to shield a yard from passers-by on the street bulged out and was broken, and a few tugs from any careless party would end its usefulness; in that yard a primrose bush bloomed unnaturally, its leaves too large, its flowers showy, and weeds were everywhere, they had prospered in all the wet. We were not alone. A man walked past us with a cutlass in his knapsack and a mistreated dog two steps behind him; a woman walked by with a large basket of food on her head; some children were walking home from school, and they were not walking together; a man was leaning out a window, spitting, he used snuff. I was wearing a pair of modestly high heels, red, not a colour to wear to work in the middle of the day, but that was just the way I had been feeling, red with a passion, like that hibiscus that was growing under the window of the man who kept spitting from the snuff. And Roland's wife called me a whore, a slut, a pig, a snake, a viper, a rat, a low-life, a parasite, and an evil woman. I could see that her mouth formed a familiar hug around these words—poor thing, she had been used to saying them. I was not surprised. I could not have loved Roland the way I did if he had not loved other women. And I was not surprised; I had noticed immediately the space between his teeth. I was not surprised that she knew about me; a man cannot keep a secret, a man always wants all the women he knows to know each other.

I believe I said this: 'I love Roland; when he is with me I want him to love me; when he is not with me I think of him loving me. I do not love you. I love Roland.' This is what I wanted to say, and this is what I believe I said. She slapped me across the face; her hand was wide and thick like an oar; she, too, was used to doing hard work. Her hand met the side of my face: my jawbone, the skin below my eye and under my chin, a small portion of my nose, the lobe of my ear. I was then a young woman in the early twenties, my skin was supple, smooth, the pores invisible to the naked eye. It was completely without bitterness that I thought as I looked at her face, a face I had so little interest in that it would tire me to describe it, Why is the state of marriage so desirable that all women are afraid to be caught outside it? And why does this woman, who has never seen me before, to whom I have never made any promise, to whom I owe nothing, hate me so much? She expected me to return her blow but, instead, I said, again completely without bitterness, 'I consider it beneath me to fight over a man.'

I was wearing a dress of light-blue Irish linen. I could not afford to buy such material, because it came from a real country, not a false country like mine; a shipment of this material in blue, in pink, in lime green, and in beige had come from Ireland, I suppose, and

Roland had given me yards of each shade from the bolts. I was wearing my blue Irish-linen dress that day, and it was demure enough—a pleated skirt that ended beneath my knees, a belt at my waist, sleeves that buttoned at my wrists, a high neckline that covered my collar-bone—but underneath my dress I wore absolutely nothing, no undergarments of any kind, only my stockings, given to me by Roland and taken from yet another shipment of dry goods, each one held up by two pieces of elastic that I had sewn together to make a garter. My declaration of what I considered beneath me must have enraged Roland's wife, for she grabbed my blue dress at the collar and gave it a huge tug; it rent in two from my neck to my waist. My breasts lay softly on my chest, like two small pieces of unrisen dough, unmoved by the anger of this woman; not so by the touch of her husband's mouth, for he would remove my dress, by first patiently undoing all the buttons and then pulling down the bodice, and then he would take one breast in his mouth, and it would grow to a size much bigger than his mouth could hold, and he would let it go and turn to the other one; the saliva evaporating from the skin on that breast was an altogether different sensation from the sensation of my other breast in his mouth, and I would divide myself in two, for I could not decide which sensation I wanted to take dominance over the other. For an hour he would kiss me in this way and then exhaust himself on top of me in five minutes. I loved him so. In the dark I couldn't see him clearly, only an outline, a solid shadow; when I saw him in the daytime he was fully dressed. His wife, as she rent my dress, a dress made of material she knew very well, for she had a dress made of the same material, told me his history; it was not a long one, it was not a sad one, no one had died in it, no land had been laid waste, no birthright had been stolen; she had a list, and it was full of names, but they were not the names of countries.

What was the colour of her wedding day? When she first saw him was she overwhelmed with desire? The impulse to possess is alive in every heart, and some people choose vast plains, some people choose high mountains, some people choose wide seas, and some people choose husbands; I chose to possess myself. I resembled a tree, a tall tree with long, strong branches; I looked delicate, but any man I held in my arms knew that I was strong; my hair was long and thick and deeply waved naturally, and I wore it braided and pinned up, because when I wore it loosely around my shoulders it caused excitement in other people—some of them men, some of them women, some of them it pleased, some of them it did not. The way I walked depended on who I thought would see me and what effect I wanted my walk to have on them. My face was beautiful, I found it so.

And yet I was standing before a woman who found herself unable to keep her life's booty in its protective sack, a woman whose voice no longer came from her throat but from deep within her stomach, a woman whose hatred was misplaced. I looked down at our feet, hers and mine, and I expected to see my short life flash before me; instead, I saw that her feet were without shoes. She did have a pair of shoes, though, which I had seen: they were white, they were plain, a round toe and flat laces, they took shoe polish well, she wore them only on Sundays and to church. I had many pairs of shoes, in colours meant to attract attention and dazzle the eye; they were uncomfortable, I wore them every day, I never went to church at all.

MY STRONG ARMS reached around to caress Roland, who was lying on my back naked; I was naked also. I knew his wife's name, but I did not say it; he knew his wife's name, too, but he did not say it. I did not know the long list of names that were not countries that his wife had committed to memory. He himself did not know the long list of names; he had not committed this list to memory. This was not from deceit, and it was not from carelessness. He was someone so used to a large fortune that he took it for granted; he did not have a bank-book, he did not have a ledger, he had a fortune—but still he had not lost interest in acquiring more. Feeling my womb contract, I crossed the room, still naked; small drops of blood spilt from inside me, evidence of my refusal to accept his silent offering. And Roland looked at me, his face expressing confusion. Why did I not bear his children? He could feel the times that I was fertile, and yet each month blood flowed away from me, and each month I expressed confidence at its imminent arrival and departure, and always I was overjoyed at the accuracy of my prediction. When I saw him like that, on his face a look that was a mixture—confusion, dumbfoundedness, defeat—I felt much sorrow for him, for his life was reduced to a list of names that were not countries, and to the number of times he brought the monthly flow of blood to a halt; his life was reduced to women, some of them beautiful, wearing dresses made from yards of cloth he had surreptitiously removed from the bowels of the ships where he worked as a stevedore.

At that time I loved him beyond words; I loved him when he was standing in front of me and I loved him when he was out of my sight. I was still a young woman. No small impressions, the size of a child's forefinger, had yet appeared on the soft parts of my body; my legs were long and hard, as if they had been made to take me a long distance; my arms were long and strong, as if prepared for carrying heavy loads; I was not beautiful, but if I could have been in love with myself I would have been. I was in love with Roland. He was a man. But who was he really? He did not sail the seas, he did not cross the oceans, he only worked in the bottom of vessels that had done so; no mountains were named for him, no valleys, no nothing. But still he was a man, and he wanted something beyond ordinary satisfaction—beyond one wife, one love, and one room with walls made of mud and roof of cane leaves, beyond the small plot of land where the same trees bear the same fruit year following year—for it would all end only in death, for though no history yet written had embraced him, though he could not identify the small uprisings within himself, though he would deny the small uprisings within himself, a strange calm would sometimes come over him, a cold stillness, and since he could find no words for it, he was momentarily blinded with shame.

One night Roland and I were sitting on the steps of the jetty, our backs facing the small world we were from, the world of sharp, dangerous curves in the road, of steep mountains of recent volcanic formations covered in a green so humble no one had ever longed for them, of three hundred and sixty-five small streams that would never meet up to form a majestic roar, of clouds that were nothing but large vessels holding endless days of water, of people who had never been regarded as people at all; we looked into the night, its blackness did not come as a surprise, a moon full of dead white light travelled across the surface of a glittering black sky; I was wearing a dress made from another piece of cloth he had given me, another piece of cloth taken from the bowels of a ship without permission, and there was a false pocket in the skirt, a pocket that did not have a bottom, and Roland placed his hand inside the pocket, reaching all the way down to touch inside of me; I looked at his face, his mouth I could see and it stretched across his face like an island and like an island, too, it held secrets and was dangerous and could swallow things whole that were much larger than itself; I looked out towards the horizon, which I could not see but knew was there all the same, and this was also true of the end of my love for Roland.

Andrea Barrett

ॐ

The Littoral Zone

WHEN THEY MET, fifteen years ago, Jonathan had a job teaching botany at a small college near Albany, and Ruby was teaching invertebrate zoology at a college in the Berkshires. Both of them, along with an ornithologist, an ichthyologist, and an oceanographer, had agreed to spend three weeks of their summer break at a marine biology research station on an island off the New Hampshire coast. They had spouses, children, mortgages, bills; they went, they later told each other, because the pay was too good to refuse. Two-thirds of the way through the course, they agreed that the pay was not enough.

How they reached that first agreement is a story they've repeated to each other again and again and told, separately, to their closest friends. Ruby thinks they had this conversation on the second Friday of the course, after Frank Kenary's slide show on the abyssal fish and before Carol Dagliesh's lecture on the courting behavior of herring gulls. Jonathan maintains that they had it earlier—that Wednesday, maybe, when they were still recovering from Gunnar Erickson's trawling expedition. The days before they became so aware of each other have blurred in their minds, but they agree that their first real conversation took place on the afternoon devoted to the littoral zone.

The tide was all the way out. The students were clumped on the rocky, pitted apron between the water and the ledges, peering into the tidal pools and listing the species they found. Gunnar was in the equipment room, repairing one of the sampling claws. Frank was setting up dissections in the tiny lab; Carol had gone back to the mainland on the supply boat, hoping to replace the camera one of the students had dropped. And so the two of them, Jonathan and Ruby, were left alone for a little while.

They both remember the granite ledge where they sat, and the raucous quarrels of the nesting gulls. They agree that Ruby was scratching furiously at her calves and that Jonathan said, "Take it easy, okay? You'll draw blood."

Her calves were slim and tan, Jonathan remembers. Covered with blotches and scrapes.

I folded my fingers, Ruby remembers. Then I blushed. My throat felt sunburned.

Ruby said, "I know, it's so embarrassing. But all this salt on my poison ivy—God, what I wouldn't give for a bath! They never told me there wouldn't be any *water* here. . . ."

Jonathan gestured at the ocean surrounding them and then they started laughing. *Hysteria,* they have told each other since. They were so tired by then, twelve days into the course, and so dirty and overworked and strained by pretending to the students that these things didn't matter, that neither of them could understand that they were also lonely. Their shared laughter felt like pure relief.

"No water?" Jonathan said. "I haven't been dry since we got here. My clothes are damp, my sneakers are damp, my hair never dries. . . ."

His hair was beautiful, Ruby remembers. Thick, a little too long. Part blond and part brown.

"I know," she said. "But you know what I mean. I didn't realize they'd have to bring our drinking water over on a boat."

"Or that they'd expect us to wash in the ocean," Jonathan said.

Her forearms were dusted with salt, he remembers. The down along them sparkled in the sun.

"And those cots," Ruby said. "Does yours have a sag in it like a hammock?"

"Like a slingshot," Jonathan said.

For half an hour they sat on their ledge and compared their bubbling patches of poison ivy and the barnacle wounds that scored their hands and feet. Nothing healed out here, they told each other. Everything got infected. When one of the students called, "Look what I found!" Jonathan rose and held his hand out to Ruby. She took it easily and hauled herself up and they walked down to the water together. Jonathan's hand was thick and blunt-fingered, with nails bitten down so far that the skin around them was raw. Odd, Ruby remembers thinking. Those bitten stumps attached to such a good-looking man.

THEY HAVE always agreed that the worst moment, for each of them, was when they stepped from the boat to the dock on the final day of the course and saw their families waiting in the parking lot. Jonathan's wife had their four-year-old daughter balanced on her shoulders. Their two older children were leaning perilously over the guardrails and shrieking at the sight of him. Jessie had turned nine in Jonathan's absence, and Jonathan can't think of her eager face without remembering the starfish he brought as his sole, guilty gift.

Ruby's husband had parked their car just a few yards from Jonathan's family. Her sons were wearing baseball caps, and what Ruby remembers is the way the yellow linings lit their faces. For a minute she saw the children squealing near her sons as faceless, inconsequential; Jonathan later told her that her children had been similarly blurred for him. Then Jonathan said, "That's my family, there," and Ruby said, "That's mine, right next to yours," and all the faces leapt into focus for both of them.

Nothing that was to come—not the days in court, nor the days they moved, nor the losses of jobs and homes—would ever seem so awful to them as that moment when they first saw their families standing there, unaware and hopeful. Deceitfully, treacherously, Ruby and Jonathan separated and walked to the people awaiting them. They didn't introduce each other to their spouses. They didn't look at each other—although, they later admitted, they cast covert looks at each other's families. They thought they were invisible, that no one could see what had happened between them. They thought their families would not remember how they had stepped off the boat and stood, for an instant, together.

On that boat, sitting dumb and miserable in the litter of nets and equipment, they had each pretended to be resigned to going home. Each foresaw (or so they later told each other) the hysterical phone calls and the frenzied, secret meetings. Neither foresaw how much the sight of each other's family would hurt. "Sweetie," Jonathan remembers Ruby's husband saying. "You've lost so much weight." Ruby remembers staring over her husband's shoulder and watching Jessie butt her head like a dog under Jonathan's hand.

FOR THE FIRST twelve days on the island, Jonathan and Ruby were so busy that they hardly noticed each other. For the next few days, after their conversation on the ledge, they sat near each other during faculty lectures and student presentations. These were held in the library, a ramshackle building separated from the bunkhouse and the dining hall by a stretch of wild roses and poison ivy.

Jonathan had talked about algae in there, holding up samples of *Fucus* and *Hildenbrandtia*. Ruby had talked about the littoral zone, that space between high and low watermarks where organisms struggled to adapt to the daily rhythm of immersion and exposure. They had drawn on the blackboard in colored chalk while the students, itchy and hot and tired, scratched their arms and legs and feigned attention.

Neither of them, they admitted much later, had focused fully on the other's lecture. "It was *before*," Ruby has said ruefully. "I didn't know that I was going to want to have listened." And Jonathan has laughed and confessed that he was studying the shells and skulls on the walls while Ruby was drawing on the board.

The library was exceedingly hot, they agreed, and the chairs remarkably uncomfortable; the only good spot was the sofa in front of the fireplace. That was the spot they commandeered on the evening after their first conversation, when dinner led to a walk and then the walk led them into the library a few minutes before the scheduled lecture.

Erika Moorhead, Ruby remembers. Talking about the tensile strength of byssus threads.

Walter Schank, Jonathan remembers. Something to do with hydrozoans.

They both remember feeling comfortable for the first time since their arrival. And for the next few days—three by Ruby's accounting; four by Jonathan's—one of them came early for every lecture and saved a seat on the sofa for the other.

They giggled at Frank Kenary's slides, which he'd arranged like a creepy fashion show: abyssal fish sporting varied blobs of luminescent flesh. When Gunnar talked for two hours about subduction zones and the calcium carbonate cycle, they amused themselves exchanging doodles. They can't remember, now, whether Gunnar's endless lecture came before Carol Dagliesh's filmstrip on the herring gulls, or which of the students tipped over the dissecting scope and sent the dish of copepods to their deaths. But both of them remember those days and nights as being almost purely happy. They swam in that odd, indefinite zone where they were more than friends, not yet lovers, still able to deny to themselves that they were headed where they were headed.

.   .   .

RUBY MADE the first phone call, a week after they left the island. At eleven o'clock on a Sunday night, she told her husband she'd left something in her office that she needed to prepare the next day's class. She drove to campus, unlocked her door, picked up the phone and called Jonathan at his house. One of his children—Jessie, she thinks—answered the phone. Ruby remembers how, even through the turmoil of her emotions, she'd been shocked at the idea of a child staying up so late.

There was a horrible moment while Jessie went to find her father; another when Jonathan, hearing Ruby's voice, said, "Wait, hang on, I'll just be a minute," and then negotiated Jessie into bed. Ruby waited, dreading his anger, knowing she'd been wrong to call him at home. But Jonathan, when he finally returned, said, "Ruby. You got my letter."

"What letter?" she asked. He wrote to tell me good-bye, she remembers thinking.

"My *letter*," he said. "I wrote you, I have to see you. I can't stand this."

Ruby released the breath she hadn't known she was holding.

"You didn't get it?" he said. "You just called?" It wasn't only me, he remembers thinking. She feels it too.

"I had to hear your voice," she said.

Ruby called, but Jonathan wrote. And so when Jonathan's youngest daughter, Cora, later fell in love and confided in Ruby, and then asked her, "Was it like this with you two? Who started it—you or Dad?" all Ruby could say was, "It happened to both of us."

SOMETIMES, WHEN RUBY and Jonathan sit on the patio looking out at the hills above Palmyra, they will turn and see their children watching them through the kitchen window. Before the children went off to college, the house bulged with them on weekends and holidays and seemed empty in between; Jonathan's wife had custody of Jessie and Gordon and Cora, and Ruby's husband took her sons, Mickey and Ryan, when he remarried. Now that the children are old enough to come and go as they please, the house is silent almost all the time.

Jessie is twenty-four, and Gordon is twenty-two; Mickey is twenty-one, and Cora and Ryan are both nineteen. When they visit Jonathan and Ruby they spend an unhealthy amount of time talking about their past. In their conversations they seem to split their lives into three epochs: the years when what they think of as their real families were whole; the years right after Jonathan and Ruby met, when their parents were coming and going, fighting and making up, separating and divorcing; and the years since Jonathan and Ruby's marriage, when they were forced into a reconstituted family. Which epoch they decide to explore depends on who's visiting and who's getting along with whom.

"But we were happy," Mickey may say to Ruby, if he and Ryan are visiting and Jonathan's children are absent. "We were, we were fine."

"It wasn't like you and Mom ever fought," Cora may say to Jonathan, if Ruby's sons aren't around. "You could have worked it out if you'd tried."

When they are all together, they tend to avoid the first two epochs and to talk about their first strained weekends and holidays together. They've learned to tolerate each other, despite their forced introductions; Cora and Ryan, whose birthdays are less than three months apart, seem especially close. Ruby and Jonathan know that much of what draws their youngest children together is shared speculation about what happened on that island.

They look old to their children, they know. Both of them are nearing fifty. Jonathan has grown quite heavy and has lost much of his hair; Ruby's fine-boned figure has gone gaunt and stringy. They know their children can't imagine them young and strong and wrung by passion. The children can't think—can't stand to think—

about what happened on the island, but they can't stop themselves from asking questions.

"Did you have other girlfriends?" Cora asks Jonathan. "Were you so unhappy with Mom?"

"Did you know him before?" Ryan asks Ruby. "Did you go there to be with him?"

"We met there," Jonathan and Ruby say. "We had never seen each other before. We fell in love." That is all they will say, they never give details, they say "yes" or "no" to the easy questions and evade the hard ones. They worry that even the little they offer may be too much.

JONATHAN AND RUBY tell each other the stories of their talk by the tidal pool, their walks and meals, the sagging sofa, the moment in the parking lot, and the evening Ruby made her call. They tell these to console themselves when their children chide them for when, alone in the house, they sit quietly near each other and struggle to conceal their disappointments.

Of course they have expected some of these. Mickey and Gordon have both had trouble in school, and Jessie has grown much too close to her mother; neither Jonathan nor Ruby has found jobs as good as the ones they lost, and their new home in Palmyra still doesn't feel quite like home. But all they have lost in order to be together would seem bearable had they continued to feel the way they felt on the island.

They're sensible people, and very well-mannered; they remind themselves that they were young then and are middle-aged now, and that their fierce attraction would naturally ebb with time. Neither likes to think about how much of the thrill of their early days together came from the obstacles they had to overcome. Some days, when Ruby pulls into the driveway still thinking about her last class and catches sight of Jonathan out in the garden, she can't believe the heavyset figure pruning shrubs so meticulously is the man for whom she fought such battles. Jonathan, who often wakes very early, sometimes stares at Ruby's sleeping face and thinks how much more gracefully his ex-wife is aging.

They never reproach each other. When the tension builds in the house and the silence becomes overwhelming, one or the other will say, "Do you remember . . . ?" and then launch into one of the myths on which they have founded their lives. But there is one story they never tell each other, because they can't bear to talk about what they have lost. This is the one about the evening that has shaped their life together.

Jonathan's hand on Ruby's back, Ruby's hand on Jonathan's thigh, a shirt unbuttoned, a belt undone. They never mention this moment, or the moments that followed it, because that would mean discussing who seduced whom, and any resolution of that would mean assigning blame. Guilt they can handle; they've been living with guilt for fifteen years. But blame? It would be more than either of them could bear, to know the exact moment when one of them precipitated all that has happened to them. The most either of them has ever said is, "How could we have known?"

But the night in the library is what they both think about, when they lie silently next to each other and listen to the wind. It must be summer for them to think about it; the children must be with their other parents and the rain must be falling on the cedar shingles overhead. A candle must be burning on the mantel above the bed and the maple branches outside their window must be tossing against each other. Then they think of the story they know so well and never say out loud.

There was a huge storm three nights before they left the island, the tail end of a hurricane passing farther out to sea. The cedar trees creaked and swayed in the wind beyond the library windows. The students had staggered off to bed, after the visitor from Woods Hole had finished his lecture on the explorations of the *Alvin* in the Cayman Trough, and Frank and Gunnar and Carol had shrouded themselves in their rain gear and left as well, sheltering the visitor between them. Ruby sat at one end of the long table, preparing bottles of fixative for their expedition the following morning, and Jonathan lay on the sofa writing notes. The boat was leaving just after dawn and they knew they ought to go to bed.

The wind picked up outside, sweeping the branches against the walls. The windows rattled. Jonathan shivered and said, "Do you suppose we could get a fire going in that old fireplace?"

"I bet we could," said Ruby, which gave both of them the pretext they needed to crouch side by side on the cracked tiles, brushing elbows as they opened the flue and crumpled paper and laid kindling in the form of a grid. The logs Jonathan found near the lobster traps were dry and the fire caught quickly.

Who found the green candle in the drawer below the microscope? Who lit the candle and turned off the lights? And who found the remains of the jug of wine that Frank had brought in honor of the visitor? They sat there side by side, poking at the burning logs and pretending they weren't doing what they were doing. The wind pushed through the window they'd opened a crack, and the tan window shade lifted and then fell back against the frame. The noise was soothing at first; later it seemed irritating.

Jonathan, whose fingernails were bitten to the quick, admired the long nail on Ruby's right little finger and then said, half-seriously, how much he'd love to bite a nail like that. When Ruby held her hand to his mouth he took the nail between his teeth and nibbled through the white tip, which days in the water had softened. Ruby slipped her other hand inside his shirt and ran it up his back. Jonathan ran his mouth up her arm and down her neck.

They started in front of the fire and worked their way across the floor, breaking a glass, knocking the table askew. Ruby rubbed her back raw against the rug and Jonathan scraped his knees, and twice they paused and laughed at their wild excesses. They moved across the floor from east to west and later from west to east, and between those two journeys, during the time when they heaped their clothes and the sofa cushions into a nest in front of the fire, they talked.

This was not the kind of conversation they'd had during walks and meals since that first time on the rocks: who they were, where they'd come from, how they'd made it here. This was the talk where they instinctively edited out the daily pleasures of their lives on the mainland and spliced together the hard times, the dark times, until they'd constructed versions of themselves that could make sense of what they'd just done.

For months after this, as they lay in stolen, secret rooms between houses and divorces and jobs and lives, Jonathan would tell Ruby that he swallowed her nail. The nail dissolved in his stomach, he'd say. It passed into his villi and out to his blood and then flowed to bone and muscle and nerve, where the molecules that had once been part of her became part of him. Ruby, who always seemed to know more acutely than Jonathan that they'd have to leave whatever room this was in an hour or a day, would argue with him.

"Nails are keratin," she'd tell him. "Like hooves and hair. Like wool. We can't digest wool."

"Moths can," Jonathan would tell her. "Moths eat sweaters."

"Moths have a special enzyme in their saliva," Ruby would say. This was true, she knew it for a fact. She'd been so taken by Jonathan's tale that she'd gone to the library to check out the details and discovered he was wrong.

But Jonathan didn't care what the biochemists said. He held her against his chest and said, "I have an enzyme for you."

That night, after the fire burned out, they slept for a couple of hours. Ruby woke first and watched Jonathan sleep for a while. He slept like a child, with his knees bent toward his chest and his hands clasped between his thighs. Ruby picked up the tipped-over chair and swept the fragments of broken glass onto a sheet of paper. Then she woke Jonathan and they tiptoed back to the rooms where they were supposed to be.

Mary Gaitskill

༄

Tiny, Smiling Daddy

THE PHONE RANG five times before he got up to answer it. It was his friend Norm. They greeted each other and then Norm, his voice strangely weighted, said, "I saw the issue of *Self* with Kitty in it."

He waited for an explanation. None came so he said, "What? Issue of *Self*? What's *Self*?"

"Good grief, Stew, I thought for sure you'd of seen it. Now I feel awkward."

"So do I. Do you want to tell me what this is about?"

"My daughter's got a subscription to this magazine, *Self*. And they printed an article that Kitty wrote about fathers and daughters talking to each other, and she well, she wrote about you. Laurel showed it to me."

"My God."

"It's ridiculous that I'm the one to tell you. I just thought—"
"It was bad?"

"No. No, she didn't say anything bad. I just didn't understand the whole idea of it. And I wondered what you thought."

He got off the phone and walked back into the living room, shocked. His daughter Kitty was living in South Carolina working in a record store and making pots, vases, and statuettes which she sold on commission. She had never written anything that he knew of, yet she'd apparently published an article in a national magazine about him without telling him. He lifted his arms and put them on the windowsill; the air from the open window cooled his under-arms. Outside, the Starlings' tiny dog marched officiously up and down the pavement, looking for someone to bark at. Maybe she had written an article about how wonderful he was, and she was too shy to show him right away. This was doubtful. Kitty was quiet but she wasn't shy. She was untactful and she could be aggressive. Uncertainty only made her doubly aggressive.

He turned the edge of one nostril over with his thumb and nervously stroked his nose-hairs with one finger. He knew it was a nasty habit but it soothed him. When Kitty was a little girl he would do it to make her laugh: "Well," he'd say, "do you think it's time we played with the hairs in our nose?" And she would giggle, holding her hands against her face, eyes sparkling over her knuckles.

Then she was fourteen, and as scornful and rejecting as any girl he had ever thrown a spitball at when he was that age. They didn't get along so well anymore. Once, they were sitting in the rec room watching TV, he on the couch, she on the footstool. There was a Charlie Chan movie on TV, but he was mostly watching her back and her long, thick brown hair, which she had just washed and was brushing. She dropped her head forward from the neck to let the hair fall between her spread legs, and began slowly stroking it with a pink nylon brush.

"Say, don't you think it's time we played with the hairs in our nose?"

No reaction from bent back and hair.

"Who wants to play with the hairs in their nose?"

Nothing.

"Hairs in the nose, hairs in the nose," he sang.

She bolted violently up from the stool. "You are so gross you disgust me!" She stormed from the room, shoulders in a tailored jacket of indignation.

Sometimes he said it just to see her exasperation, to feel the adorable, futile outrage of her violated girl delicacy.

He wished that his wife would come home with the car so that he could drive to the store and buy a copy of *Self.* His car was being repaired and he could not walk to the little cluster of stores and parking lots that constituted "town" in this heat. It would take a good twenty minutes and he would be completely worn out when he got there. He would find the magazine and stand there in the drugstore and read it and if it was something bad, he might not have the strength to walk back.

He went into the kitchen, opened a beer and brought it into the living room. His wife had been gone for over an hour, and God knows how much longer she would be. She could spend literally all day driving around the county doing nothing but buying a jar of honey or a bag of apples. Of course, he could call Kitty, but he'd probably just get her answering machine, and besides he didn't want to talk to her before he understood the situation. He felt helplessness move through his body like a swimmer feels a large sea creature pass beneath him. How could she have done this to him? She knew how he dreaded exposure of any kind, she knew the way he guarded himself against strangers, the way he carefully drew all the curtains when twilight approached so that no one could see them walking through the house. She knew how ashamed he had been when, at sixteen, she had announced that she was lesbian.

The Starling dog was now across the street, yapping at the heels of a bow-legged old lady in a blue dress who was trying to walk down the street. "Dammit," he said. He left the window and got the afternoon opera station on the radio. They were in the final act of *La Bohème.*

He did not remember precisely when it had happened, but Kitty, his beautiful, happy little girl, turned into a glum, weird teenager that other kids picked on. She got skinny and ugly. Her blue eyes, which had been so sensitive and bright, turned filmy, as if the real Kitty had retreated so far from the surface that her eyes existed to shield rather than reflect her. It was as if she deliberately held her beauty away from them, only showing glimpses of it during unavoidable lapses, like the time she sat before the TV, daydreaming and lazily brushing her hair. At moments like this, her dormant charm broke his heart. It also annoyed him. What did she have to retreat from? They had both loved her. When she was little, and she couldn't sleep at night, Marsha would sit with her in bed for hours. She praised her stories and her drawings as if she were a genius. When Kitty was seven, she and her mother had special times, during which they went off together and talked about whatever Kitty wanted to talk about.

He tried to compare the sullen, morbid Kitty of sixteen with the slender, self-possessed twenty-eight-year-old lesbian who wrote articles for *Self.* He pictured himself in court, waving a copy of *Self* before a shocked jury. The case would be taken up by the press. He saw the headlines: Dad Sues Mag—Dyke Daughter Reveals . . . reveals what? What had Kitty found to say about him that was of interest to the entire country that she didn't want him to know about?

Anger overrode his helplessness. Kitty could be vicious. He hadn't seen her vicious side in years, but he knew it was there. He remembered the time he'd stood behind the half-open front door when fifteen-year-old Kitty sat hunched on the front steps with one of her few friends, a homely blond who wore white lipstick and a white leather jacket. He had come to the door to view the weather and say something to the girls, but they were muttering so intently that curiosity got the better of him, and he hung back a moment to listen. "Well, at least your mom's smart," said Kitty. "My mom's not only a bitch, she's stupid."

This after the lullabies and special times! It wasn't just an isolated incident either; every time he'd come home from work, his wife had something bad to say about Kitty. She hadn't set the table until she had been asked four times. She'd gone to Lois's house instead of coming straight home like she'd been told to do. She'd worn a dress to school that was short enough to show the tops of her panty hose.

By the time Kitty came to dinner, looking as if she'd been doing slave labor all day, he would be mad at her. He couldn't help it. Here was his wife doing her damnedest to raise a family and cook dinner and here was this awful kid looking ugly, acting mean and not setting the table. It seemed unreasonable that she should turn out so badly after taking up so much time. Her afflicted expression made him angry too. What had anybody ever done to her?

HE SAT forward and gently gnawed the insides of his mouth as he listened to the dying girl in *La Bohème*. He saw his wife's car pull into the driveway. He walked to the back door, almost wringing his hands, and waited for her to come through the door. When she did, he snatched the grocery bag from her arms and said, "Give me the keys." She stood open-mouthed in the stairwell, looking at him with idiotic consternation. "Give me the keys!"

"What is it, Stew? What's happened?"

"I'll tell you when I get back."

He got in the car and became part of it, this panting, mobile case propelling him through the incredibly complex and fast-moving world of other people, their houses, their children, their dogs, their lives. He wasn't usually so aware of this unpleasant sense of disconnection between him and everyone else, but he had the feeling that it had been there all along, underneath what he thought of most of the time. It was ironic that it should rear up so visibly at a time when there was in fact a mundane yet invasive and horribly real connection between him and everyone else in Wayne County: the hundreds of copies of *Self* magazine sitting in countless drugstores, bookstores, groceries, and libraries. It was as if there was a tentacle plugged into the side of the car, linking him with the random humans who picked up the magazine, possibly his very neighbors. He stopped at a crowded intersection, feeling like an ant in an enemy swarm.

Kitty had projected herself out of the house and into this swarm very early, ostensibly because life with him and Marsha had been so awful. Well, it had been awful, but because of Kitty, not them. As if it wasn't enough to be sullen and dull, she turned into a lesbian. Kids followed her down the street jeering at her. Somebody dropped her books in a toilet. She got into a fistfight. Their neighbors gave them looks. This reaction seemed only to steel Kitty's grip on her new identity; it made her romanticize herself like the kid she was. She wrote poems about heroic women warriors, she brought home strange books and magazines which, among other things, seemed to glorify prostitutes. Marsha looked for them and threw them away. Kitty screamed at her, the tendons leaping out on her slender neck. He hit Kitty, Marsha tried to stop him and he yelled at her. Kitty leapt between them, as if to defend her mother. He grabbed her and shook her but he could not shake the conviction off her face.

Most of the time though, they continued as always, eating dinner together, watching TV, making jokes. That was the worst thing; he would look at Kitty and see his daughter, now familiar in her withdrawn sullenness, and feel comfort and affection. Then he would remember that she was a lesbian and a morass of complication and wrongness would come down between them, making it impossible for him to see her. Then she would be just Kitty again. He hated it.

She ran away at sixteen and the police found her in the apartment of an eighteen-year-old body builder named Dolores who had a naked woman tattooed on her sinister bicep. Marsha made them put her in a mental hospital so psychiatrists could observe her, but he hated the psychiatrists—mean, supercilious sons of bitches who delighted in the trick question—so he took her back out. She finished school and they told her if she wanted to leave it was all right with them. She didn't waste any time getting out of the house.

She moved into an apartment near Detroit with a girl named George and took a job at a home for retarded kids. She would appear for visits with a huge bag of laundry every few weeks. She was thin and neurotically muscular, her body having the look of a fighting dog on a leash. She wore her hair like a boy's and wore black sunglasses, black leather half-gloves and leather belts. The only remnant of her beauty was her erect martial carriage and her efficient movements; she walked through a room like the commander of a guerrilla force. She would sit at the dining room table with Marsha, drinking tea and having a laconic verbal conversation, her body speaking its precise martial language while the washing machine droned from the utility room and he wandered in and out trying to make sense of what she said. Sometimes she would stay into the evening to eat dinner and watch *All in the Family*. Then Marsha would send her home with a jar of homemade tapioca pudding or a bag of apples and oranges.

One day instead of a visit they got a letter postmarked San Francisco. She had left George, she said. She listed strange details about her current environment and was vague about how she was supporting herself. He had nightmares about Kitty, with her brave, proudly muscular little body, lost among big fleshy women who danced naked in go-go bars and took drugs with needles, terrible women who his confused romantic daughter invested with oppressed heroism and intensely female glamour. He got up at night and stumbled into the bathroom for stomach medicine, the familiar darkness of the house heavy with menacing images that pressed about him, images that he saw reflected in his own expression when he turned on the bathroom light over the mirror.

Then one year she came home for Christmas. She came into the house with her luggage and a shopping bag of gifts for them and he saw that she was beautiful again. It was a beauty that both offended and titillated his senses. Her short spiky hair was streaked with purple, her dainty mouth was lipsticked, her nose and ears were pierced with amethyst and dangling silver. Her face had opened in thousands of petals. Her eyes shone with quick perception as she put down her bag and he knew that she had seen him see her beauty. She moved towards him with fluid hips, she embraced him for the first time in years. He felt her live, lithe body against him and his heart pulsed a message of blood and love. "Merry Christmas, Daddy," she said.

Her voice was husky and coarse, it reeked of knowledge and confidence. Her T-shirt said "Chicks With Balls." She was twenty-two years old.

She stayed for a week, discharging her strange jangling beauty into the house and changing the molecules of its air. She talked about the girls she shared an apartment with, her job at a coffee shop, how Californians were different from Michiganders. She talked about her friends: Lorraine, who was so pretty men fell off their bicycles as they twisted their bodies for a better look at her; Judy, a martial arts expert; and Meredith, who was raising a child with her husband, Angela. She talked of poetry readings, ceramics classes, celebrations of spring.

He realized, as he watched her, that she was now doing things that were as bad as or worse than the things that had made him angry at her five years before, yet they didn't quarrel. It seemed that a large white space existed between him and her, and that it was impossible to enter this space or to argue across it. Besides, she might never come back if he yelled at her.

Instead, he watched her, puzzling at the metamorphosis she had undergone. First she had been a beautiful, happy child turned homely, snotty, miserable adolescent. From there she had become a martinet girl with the eyes of a stifled pervert. Now she was a vibrant imp living, it seemed, in a world constructed of topsy-turvy junk pasted with rhinestones. Where had these three different people come from? Not even Marsha, who had spent so much time with her as a child, could trace the genesis of the new Kitty from the old one. Sometimes he bitterly reflected that he and Marsha weren't even real parents anymore, but bereft old people rattling around in a house, connected not to a real child who was going to college, or who at least had some kind of understandable life, but a changeling who was the product of only their most obscure quirks, a being who came from recesses that neither of them suspected they'd had.

THERE WERE ONLY a few cars in the parking lot. He wheeled through it with pointless deliberation before parking near the drugstore. He spent irritating seconds searching for *Self* until he realized that its airbrushed cover girl was grinning right at him. He stormed the table of contents, then headed for the back of the magazine. "Speak Easy" was written sideways across the top of the appointed page in round turquoise letters. At the bottom was his daughter's name in a little box. "Kitty Thorne is a ceramic artist living in South Carolina." His hands were trembling.

It was hard for him to rationally ingest the beginning paragraphs which seemed, incredibly, to be about a phone conversation they'd had some time ago about the emptiness and selfishness of people who have sex but don't get married and have children. A few phrases that stood out clearly: ". . . my father may love me but he doesn't love the way I live." ". . . even more complicated because I'm gay." "Because it still hurts me."

For reasons he didn't understand, he felt a nervous smile tremble under his skin. He suppressed it.

"This hurt has its roots deep in our relationship, starting, I think, when I was a teenager."

He had a horrible sensation of being in public so he paid for the thing and took it out to the car with him. He slowly drove to another spot in the lot, as far away from the drugstore as possible, picked up the magazine, and began again. She described "the terrible difficulties" between him and her. She recounted, briefly and with hieroglyphic politeness, the fighting, the running away, the return, the tacit reconciliation.

"There is an emotional distance that we have both accepted and chosen to work around, hoping the occasional contact—love, anger, something—will get through."

He put the magazine down and looked out the window. It was near dusk; most of the stores in the little mall were closed. There were only two other cars in the parking lot, and a big, slow, frowning woman with two grocery bags was getting ready to drive one away. He was parked before a weedy piece of land at the edge of the parking lot. In it were rough, picky weeds spread out like big green tarantulas, young yellow dandelions, frail old dandelions, and bunches of tough blue chickweed. Even in his distress he vaguely appreciated the beauty of the blue weeds against the cool white and grey sky. For a moment the sound of insects comforted him. Images of Kitty passed through his memory with terrible speed: her nine-year-old forehead bent over her dish of ice cream, her tiny nightgowned form ran up the stairs, her ringed hand brushed her face, the keys on her belt jiggled as she walked her slow blue-jeaned walk away from the house. Gone, all gone.

The article went on to describe how Kitty hung up the phone feeling frustrated and then listed all the things she could've said to him to let him know how hurt she was, paving the way for "real communication," all in ghastly talk-show language. He was unable to put these words together with the Kitty he had last seen lounging around the house. She was twenty-eight now and she no longer dyed her hair or wore jewels in her nose. Her demeanor was serious, bookish, almost old-maidish. Once he'd overheard her talking to Marsha and heard her say, "So then this Italian girl gives me the once-over and says to Joanne, 'You 'ang around with too many Wasp.' And I said, 'I'm not a Wasp, I'm white trash.' "

"Speak for yourself," he'd said.

"If the worst occurred and my father was unable to respond to me in kind, I still would have done a good thing. I would have acknowledged my own needs and created the possibility to connect with what therapists call 'the good parent' in myself."

Well, if that was the kind of thing she was going to say to him, he was relieved she hadn't said it. But if she hadn't said it to him, why was she saying it to the rest of the country?

He turned on the radio. It sang: "Try to remember, and if you remember, then follow, follow." He turned it off. He closed his eyes. When he was nine or ten an uncle of his had told him, "Everybody makes his own world. You see what you want to see and hear what you want to hear. You can do it right now. If you blink ten times and then close your eyes real tight, you can see anything you want to see in front of you." He'd tried it rather halfheartedly and hadn't seen anything but the vague suggestion of a yellowish-white ball moving creepily through the dark. At the time, he'd thought it was perhaps because he hadn't tried hard enough.

He had told Kitty to do the same thing, or something like it, when she was eight or nine. They were on the back porch sitting in striped lawn chairs holding hands and watching the fireflies turn off and on.

She closed her eyes for a long time. Then very seriously, she said, "I see big balls of color, like shaggy flowers. They're pink and red and turquoise. I see an island with palm trees and pink rocks. There's dolphins and mermaids swimming in the water around it." He'd been almost awed by her belief in this impossible vision. Then he was sad because she would never see what she wanted to see.

His memory floated back to his boyhood; he was walking down the middle of the street at dusk, sweating lightly after a basketball game. There were crickets and the muted barks of dogs and the low, affirming mumble of people on their front porches. He felt securely held by the warm light and its sounds, he felt an exquisite blend of happiness and sorrow that life could contain this perfect moment, and sadness that he would soon arrive home, walk into bright light and be on his way into the next day, with its loud noise and alarming possibility. He resolved to hold this evening walk in his mind forever, to imprint all the sensations that occurred to him as he walked by the Oatlanders' house in a permanent place, so that he could always take it out and look at it. He dimly recalled feeling that if he could successfully do that, he could stop time and hold it.

HE KNEW he had to go home soon. He didn't want to talk about the article with Marsha, but the idea of sitting in the house with her and not talking about it was hard to bear. He imagined the conversation grinding into being, a future conversation with Kitty gestating within it. The conversation was a vast, complex machine like those that occasionally appeared in his dreams; if he could only pull the switch everything would be all right, but he felt too stupefied by the weight and complexity of the thing to do so. Besides, in this case, everything might not be all right. He put the magazine under his seat and started the car.

Marsha was in her armchair reading. She looked up and the expression on her face seemed like the result of internal conflict as complicated and strong as his own, but cross-pulled in different directions, uncomprehending of him and what he knew. In his mind he withdrew from her so quickly that for a moment the familiar room was fraught with the inexplicable horror of a banal nightmare. Then the ordinariness of the scene threw the extraordinary event of the day into relief and he felt so angry and bewildered he could've howled.

"Everything all right, Stew?" asked Marsha.

"No, nothing is all right. I'm a tired old man in a shitty world I don't want to be in. I go out there, it's like walking on knives. Everything is an attack, the ugliness, the cheapness, the rudeness, everything." He sensed her withdrawing from him into her own world of disgruntlement, her lips drawn together in that look of exasperated perseverance she'd gotten from her mother. Like Kitty, like everyone, she was leaving him. "I don't have a real daughter and I don't have a real wife who's here with me because she's too busy running around on some—"

"We've been through this before. We agreed I could—"

"That was different! That was when we had two cars!" His voice tore through his throat in a jagged whiplash and came out a cracked half-scream. "I don't have a car, remember? That means I'm stranded, all alone for hours and Norm Pisarro can just call me up and casually tell me that my lesbian daughter has just betrayed me in a national magazine and what do I think about that?" He wanted to punch the wall until his hand was bloody. He wanted Kitty to see the blood. Marsha's expression broke into soft open-mouthed consternation. The helplessness of it made his anger seem huge and terrible, then impotent and helpless itself. He sat down on the couch and instead of anger felt pain.

"What did Kitty do? What happened? What does Norm have—"

"She wrote an article in *Self* magazine about being a lesbian and her problems and something to do with me. I don't know, I could barely read the crap."

Marsha looked down at her nails.

He looked at her and saw the aged beauty of her ivory skin, sagging under the weight of her years and her cockeyed bifocals, the emotional receptivity of her face, the dark down on her upper lip, the childish pearl buttons of her sweater, only the top button done.

"I'm surprised at Norm, that he would call you like that."

"Oh, who the hell knows what he thought." His heart was soothed and slowed by her words, even if they didn't address its real unhappiness.

"Here," she said, "let me rub your shoulders."

He allowed her to approach him and they sat sideways on the couch, his weight balanced on the edge by his awkwardly planted legs, she sitting primly on one hip with her legs tightly crossed.

The discomfort of the position negated the practical value of the massage, but he welcomed her touch. Marsha had strong, intelligent hands that spoke to his muscles of deep safety and love and delight of physical life. In her effort, she leaned close and her sweatered breast touched him, releasing his tension almost against his will. Through half-closed eyes he observed her sneakers on the floor—he could not quite get over this phenomenon of adult women wearing what had been boys' shoes—in the dim light, one toe atop the other as though cuddling, their laces in pretty disorganization.

Poor Kitty. It hadn't really been so bad that she hadn't set the table on time. He couldn't remember why he and Marsha had been so angry over the table. Unless it was Kitty's coldness, her always turning away, her sarcastic voice. But she was a teenager and that's what teenagers did. Well, it was too bad, but it couldn't be helped now.

He thought of his father. That was too bad too, and nobody was writing articles about that. There had been a distance between them too, so great and so absolute that the word "distance" seemed inadequate to describe it. But that was probably because he had only known his father when he was a very young child; if his father had lived longer, perhaps they would've become closer. He could recall his father's face clearly only at the breakfast table, where it appeared silent and still except for lip and jaw motions, comforting in its constancy. His father ate his oatmeal with one hand working the spoon, one elbow on the table, eyes down, sometimes his other hand holding a cold rag to his head, which always hurt with what seemed to be a noble pain, willingly taken on with his duties as a husband and father. He had loved to stare at the big face with its deep lines and long earlobes, its thin lips and loose, loopily chewing jaws. Its almost godlike stillness and expressionlessness filled him with admiration and reassurance, until one day, his father slowly looked up from his cereal, met his eyes and said, "Stop staring at me, you little shit."

In the other memories, his father was a large, heavy body with a vague oblong face. He saw him sleeping in the armchair in the living room, his large, hairy-knuckled hands grazing the floor. He saw him walking up the front walk with the quick, clipped steps that he always used coming home from work, the straight-backed choppy gait that gave the big body an awesome mechanicalness. His shirt was wet under the arms, his head down, the eyes abstracted but alert, as though keeping careful watch on the outside world in case something nasty came at him, while he attended to the more important business inside.

"The good parent in yourself."

What did the well-meaning idiots who thought of these phrases mean by them? When a father dies, he is gone, there is no tiny, smiling daddy who appears, waving happily, in a secret pocket in your chest. Some kinds of loss are absolute. And no amount of self-realization or self-expression will change that.

As if she heard him, Marsha urgently pressed her weight into her hands and applied all her strength to relaxing his muscles. Her sweat and scented deodorant filtered through her sweater, which added its muted woolliness to her smell. "All righty!" She rubbed his shoulders and briskly patted him. He reached back and touched her hand in thanks.

Across from where they sat had once been a red chair, and in it had once sat Kitty, gripping her face in her hand, her expression mottled by tears. "And if you ever try to come back here I'm going to spit in your face. I don't care if I'm on my deathbed, I'll still have the energy to spit in your face," he had said.

Marsha's hands lingered on him for a moment. Then she moved and sat away from him on the couch.

Gish Jen

๛

Who's Irish?

In China, people say mixed children are supposed to be smart, and definitely my granddaughter Sophie is smart. But Sophie is wild, Sophie is not like my daughter Natalie, or like me. I am work hard my whole life, and fierce besides. My husband always used to say he is afraid of me, and in our restaurant, busboys and cooks all afraid of me too. Even the gang members come for protection money, they try to talk to my husband. When I am there, they stay away. If they come by mistake, they pretend they are come to eat. They hide behind the menu, they order a lot of food. They talk about their mothers. Oh, my mother have some arthritis, need to take herbal medicine, they say. Oh, my mother getting old, her hair all white now.

I say, Your mother's hair used to be white, but since she dye it, it become black again. Why don't you go home once in a while and take a look? I tell them, Confucius say a filial son knows what color his mother's hair is.

My daughter is fierce too, she is vice president in the bank now. Her new house is big enough for everybody to have their own room, including me. But Sophie take after Natalie's husband's family, their name is Shea. Irish. I always thought Irish people are like Chinese people, work so hard on the railroad, but now I know why the Chinese beat the Irish. Of course, not all Irish are like the Shea family, of course not. My daughter tell me I should not say Irish this, Irish that.

How do you like it when people say the Chinese this, the Chinese that, she say.

You know, the British call the Irish heathen, just like they call the Chinese, she say.

You think the Opium War was bad, how would you like to live right next door to the British, she say.

And that is that. My daughter have a funny habit when she win an argument, she take a sip of something and look away, so the other person is not embarrassed. So I am not embarrassed. I do not call anybody anything either. I just happen to mention about the Shea family, an interesting fact: four brothers in the family, and not one of them work. The mother, Bess, have a job before she got sick, she was executive secretary in a big company. She is handle everything for a big shot, you would be surprised how complicated her job is, not just type this, type that. Now she is a nice woman with a clean house. But her boys, every one of them is on welfare, or so-called severance pay, or so-called disability pay. Something. They say they cannot find work, this is not the economy of the fifties, but I say, Even the black people doing better these days, some of them live so fancy, you'd be surprised. Why the Shea family have so much trouble? They are white people, they speak English. When I come to this country, I have no money and do not speak English. But my husband and I own our restaurant before he die. Free and clear, no mortgage. Of course, I understand I am just lucky, come from a country where the food is popular all over the world. I understand it is not the Shea family's fault they come from a country where everything is boiled. Still, I say.

She's right, we should broaden our horizons, say one brother, Jim, at Thanksgiving. Forget about the car business. Think about egg rolls.

Pad thai, say another brother, Mike. I'm going to make my fortune in pad thai. It's going to be the new pizza.

I say, You people too picky about what you sell. Selling egg rolls not good enough for you, but at least my husband and I can say, We made it. What can you say? Tell me. What can you say?

Everybody chew their tough turkey.

I especially cannot understand my daughter's husband John, who has no job but cannot take care of Sophie either. Because he is a man, he say, and that's the end of the sentence.

Plain boiled food, plain boiled thinking. Even his name is plain boiled: John. Maybe because I grew up with black bean sauce and hoisin sauce and garlic sauce, I always feel something is missing when my son-in-law talk.

But, okay: so my son-in-law can be man, I am baby-sitter. Six hours a day, same as the old sitter, crazy Amy, who quit. This is not so easy, now that I am sixty-eight, Chinese age almost seventy. Still, I try. In China, daughter take care of mother. Here it is the other way around. Mother help daughter, mother ask, Anything else I can do? Otherwise daughter complain mother is not supportive. I tell daughter, We do not have this word in Chinese, *supportive*. But my daughter too busy to listen, she has to go to meeting, she has to write memo while her husband go to the gym to be a man. My daughter say otherwise he will be depressed. Seems like all his life he has this trouble, depression.

No one wants to hire someone who is depressed, she say. It is important for him to keep his spirits up.

Beautiful wife, beautiful daughter, beautiful house, oven can clean itself automatically. No money left over, because only one income, but lucky enough, got the baby-sitter for free. If John lived in China, he would be very happy. But he is not happy. Even at the gym things go wrong. One day, he pull a muscle. Another day, weight room too crowded. Always something.

Until finally, hooray, he has a job. Then he feel pressure.

I need to concentrate, he say. I need to focus.

He is going to work for insurance company. Salesman job. A paycheck, he say, and at least he will wear clothes instead of gym shorts. My daughter buy him some special candy bars from the health-food store. They say THINK! on them, and are supposed to help John think.

John is a good-looking boy, you have to say that, especially now that he shave so you can see his face.

I am an old man in a young man's game, say John.

I will need a new suit, say John.

This time I am not going to shoot myself in the foot, say John.

Good, I say.

She means to be supportive, my daughter say. Don't start the send her back to China thing, because we can't.

SOPHIE IS THREE years old American age, but already I see her nice Chinese side swallowed up by her wild Shea side. She looks like mostly Chinese. Beautiful black hair, beautiful black eyes. Nose perfect size, not so flat looks like something fell down, not so large looks like some big deal got stuck in wrong face. Everything just right, only her skin is a brown surprise to John's family. So brown, they say. Even John say it. She never goes in the sun, still she is that color, he say. Brown. They say, Nothing the matter with brown. They are just surprised. So brown. Nattie is not that brown, they say. They say, It seems like Sophie should be a color in between Nattie and John. Seems funny, a girl named Sophie Shea be brown. But she is brown, maybe her name should be Sophie Brown. She never go in the sun, still she is that color, they say. Nothing the matter with brown. They are just surprised.

The Shea family talk is like this sometimes, going around and around like a Christmas-tree train.

Maybe John is not her father, I say one day, to stop the train. And sure enough, train wreck. None of the brothers ever say the word *brown* to me again.

Instead, John's mother, Bess, say, I hope you are not offended. She say, I did my best on those boys. But raising four boys with no father is no picnic.

You have a beautiful family, I say.

I'm getting old, she say.

You deserve a rest, I say. Too many boys make you old.

I never had a daughter, she say. You have a daughter.

I have a daughter, I say. Chinese people don't think a daughter is so great, but you're right. I have a daughter.

I was never against the marriage, you know, she say. I never thought John was marrying down. I always thought Nattie was just as good as white.

I was never against the marriage either, I say. I just wonder if they look at the whole problem.

Of course you pointed out the problem, you are a mother, she say. And now we both have a granddaughter. A little brown granddaughter, she is so precious to me.

I laugh. A little brown granddaughter, I say. To tell you the truth, I don't know how she came out so brown.

We laugh some more. These days Bess need a walker to walk. She take so many pills, she need two glasses of water to get them all down. Her favorite TV show is about bloopers, and she love her bird feeder. All day long, she can watch that bird feeder, like a cat.

I can't wait for her to grow up, Bess say. I could use some female company.

Too many boys, I say.

Boys are fine, she say. But they do surround you after a while.

You should take a break, come live with us, I say. Lots of girls at our house.

Be careful what you offer, say Bess with a wink. Where I come from, people mean for you to move in when they say a thing like that.

· · ·

NOTHING THE MATTER with Sophie's outside, that's the truth. It is inside that she is like not any Chinese girl I ever see. We go to the park, and this is what she does. She stand up in the stroller. She take off all her clothes and throw them in the fountain.

Sophie! I say. Stop!

But she just laugh like a crazy person. Before I take over as baby-sitter, Sophie has that crazy-person sitter, Amy the guitar player. My daughter thought this Amy very creative—another word we do not talk about in China. In China, we talk about whether we have difficulty or no difficulty. We talk about whether life is bitter or not bitter. In America, all day long, people talk about creative. Never mind that I cannot even look at this Amy, with her shirt so short that her belly button showing. This Amy think Sophie should love her body. So when Sophie take off her diaper, Amy laugh. When Sophie run around naked, Amy say she wouldn't want to wear a diaper either. When Sophie go *shu-shu* in her lap, Amy laugh and say there are no germs in pee. When Sophie take off her shoes, Amy say bare feet is best, even the pediatrician say so. That is why Sophie now walk around with no shoes like a beggar child. Also why Sophie love to take off her clothes.

Turn around! say the boys in the park. Let's see that ass!

Of course, Sophie does not understand. Sophie clap her hands, I am the only one to say, No! This is not a game.

It has nothing to do with John's family, my daughter say. Amy was too permissive, that's all.

But I think if Sophie was not wild inside, she would not take off her shoes and clothes to begin with.

You never take off your clothes when you were little, I say. All my Chinese friends had babies, I never saw one of them act wild like that.

Look, my daughter say. I have a big presentation tomorrow.

John and my daughter agree Sophie is a problem, but they don't know what to do.

You spank her, she'll stop, I say another day.

But they say, Oh no.

In America, parents not supposed to spank the child.

It gives them low self-esteem, my daughter say. And that leads to problems later, as I happen to know.

My daughter never have big presentation the next day when the subject of spanking come up.

I don't want you to touch Sophie, she say. No spanking, period.

Don't tell me what to do, I say.

I'm not telling you what to do, say my daughter. I'm telling you how I feel.

I am not your servant, I say. Don't you dare talk to me like that.

My daughter have another funny habit when she lose an argument. She spread out all her fingers and look at them, as if she like to make sure they are still there.

My daughter is fierce like me, but she and John think it is better to explain to Sophie that clothes are a good idea. This is not so hard in the cold weather. In the warm weather, it is very hard.

Use your words, my daughter say. That's what we tell Sophie. How about if you set a good example.

As if good example mean anything to Sophie. I am so fierce, the gang members who used to come to the restaurant all afraid of me, but Sophie is not afraid.

I say, Sophie, if you take off your clothes, no snack.

I say, Sophie, if you take off your clothes, no lunch.

I say, Sophie, if you take off your clothes, no park.

Pretty soon we are stay home all day, and by the end of six hours she still did not have one thing to eat. You never saw a child stubborn like that.

I'm hungry! she cry when my daughter come home.

What's the matter, doesn't your grandmother feed you? My daughter laugh.

No! Sophie say. She doesn't feed me anything!

My daughter laugh again. Here you go, she say.

She say to John, Sophie must be growing.

Growing like a weed, I say.

Still Sophie take off her clothes, until one day I spank her. Not too hard, but she cry and cry, and when I tell her if she doesn't put her clothes back on I'll spank her again, she put her clothes back on. Then I tell her she is good girl, and give her some food to eat. The next day we go to the park and, like a nice Chinese girl, she does not take off her clothes.

She stop taking off her clothes, I report. Finally!

How did you do it? my daughter ask.

After twenty-eight years experience with you, I guess I learn something, I say.

It must have been a phase, John say, and his voice is suddenly like an expert.

His voice is like an expert about everything these days, now that he carry a leather briefcase, and wear shiny shoes, and can go shopping for a new car. On the company, he say. The company will pay for it, but he will be able to drive it whenever he want.

A free car, he say. How do you like that.

It's good to see you in the saddle again, my daughter say. Some of your family patterns are scary.

At least I don't drink, he say. He say, And I'm not the only one with scary family patterns.

That's for sure, say my daughter.

EVERYONE IS happy. Even I am happy, because there is more trouble with Sophie, but now I think I can help her Chinese side fight against her wild side. I teach her to eat food with fork or spoon or chopsticks, she cannot just grab into the middle of a bowl of noodles. I teach her not to play with garbage cans. Sometimes I spank her, but not too often, and not too hard.

Still, there are problems. Sophie like to climb everything. If there is a railing, she is never next to it. Always she is on top of it. Also, Sophie like to hit the mommies of her friends. She learn this from her playground best friend, Sinbad, who is four. Sinbad wear army clothes every day and like to ambush his mommy. He is the one who dug a big hole under the play structure, a foxhole he call it, all by himself. Very hardworking. Now he wait in the foxhole with a shovel full of wet sand. When his mommy come, he throw it right at her.

Oh, it's all right, his mommy say. You can't get rid of war games, it's part of their imaginative play. All the boys go through it.

Also, he like to kick his mommy, and one day he tell Sophie to kick his mommy too.

I wish this story is not true.

Kick her, kick her! Sinbad say.

Sophie kick her. A little kick, as if she just so happened was swinging her little leg and didn't realize that big mommy leg was in the way. Still I spank Sophie and make Sophie say sorry, and what does the mommy say?

Really, it's all right, she say. It didn't hurt.

After that, Sophie learn she can attack mommies in the playground, and some will say, Stop, but others will say, Oh, she didn't mean it, especially if they realize Sophie will be punished.

THIS IS HOW, one day, bigger trouble come. The bigger trouble start when Sophie hide in the foxhole with that shovel full of sand. She wait, and when I come look for her, she throw it at me. All over my nice clean clothes.

Did you ever see a Chinese girl act this way?

Sophie! I say. Come out of there, say you're sorry.

But she does not come out. Instead, she laugh. Naaah, naah-na, naaa-naaa, she say.

I am not exaggerate: millions of children in China, not one act like this.

Sophie! I say. Now! Come out now!

But she know she is in big trouble. She know if she come out, what will happen next. So she does not come out. I am sixty-eight, Chinese age almost seventy, how can I crawl under there to catch her? Impossible. So I yell, yell, yell, and what happen? Nothing. A Chinese mother would help, but American mothers, they look at you, they shake their head, they go home. And, of course, a Chinese child would give up, but not Sophie.

I hate you! she yell. I hate you, Meanie!

Meanie is my new name these days.

Long time this goes on, long long time. The foxhole is deep, you cannot see too much, you don't know where is the bottom. You cannot hear too much either. If she does not yell, you cannot even know she is still there or not. After a while, getting cold out, getting dark out. No one left in the playground, only us.

Sophie, I say. How did you become stubborn like this? I am go home without you now.

I try to use a stick, chase her out of there, and once or twice I hit her, but still she does not come out. So finally I leave. I go outside the gate.

Bye-bye! I say. I'm go home now.

But still she does not come out and does not come out. Now it is dinnertime, the sky is black. I think I should maybe go get help, but how can I leave a little girl by herself in the playground? A bad man could come. A rat could come. I go back in to see what is happen to Sophie. What if she have a shovel and is making a tunnel to escape?

Sophie! I say.

No answer.

Sophie!

I don't know if she is alive. I don't know if she is fall asleep down there. If she is crying, I cannot hear her.

So I take the stick and poke.

Sophie! I say. I promise I no hit you. If you come out, I give you a lollipop.

No answer. By now I worried. What to do, what to do, what to do? I poke some more, even harder, so that I am poking and poking when my daughter and John suddenly appear.

What are you doing? What is going on? say my daughter.

Put down that stick! say my daughter.

You are crazy! say my daughter.

John wiggle under the structure, into the foxhole, to rescue Sophie.

She fell asleep, say John the expert. She's okay. That is one big hole.

Now Sophie is crying and crying.

Sophia, my daughter say, hugging her. Are you okay, peanut? Are you okay?

She's just scared, say John.

Are you okay? I say too. I don't know what happen, I say.

She's okay, say John. He is not like my daughter, full of questions. He is full of answers until we get home and can see by the lamplight.

Will you look at her? he yell then. What the hell happened?

Bruises all over her brown skin, and a swollen-up eye.

You are crazy! say my daughter. Look at what you did! You are crazy!

I try very hard, I say.

How could you use a stick? I told you to use your words!

She is hard to handle, I say.

She's three years old! You cannot use a stick! say my daughter.

She is not like any Chinese girl I ever saw, I say.

I brush some sand off my clothes. Sophie's clothes are dirty too, but at least she has her clothes on.

Has she done this before? ask my daughter. Has she hit you before?

She hits me all the time, Sophie say, eating ice cream.

Your family, say John.

Believe me, say my daughter.

. . .

A DAUGHTER I have, a beautiful daughter. I took care of her when she could not hold her head up. I took care of her before she could argue with me, when she was a little girl with two pigtails, one of them always crooked. I took care of her when we have to escape from China, I took care of her when suddenly we live in a country with cars everywhere, if you are not careful your little girl get run over. When my husband die, I promise him I will keep the family together, even though it was just two of us, hardly a family at all.

But now my daughter take me around to look at apartments. After all, I can cook, I can clean, there's no reason I cannot live by myself, all I need is a telephone. Of course, she is sorry. Sometimes she cry, I am the one to say everything will be okay. She say she have no choice, she doesn't want to end up divorced. I say divorce is terrible, I don't know who invented this terrible idea. Instead of live with a telephone, though, surprise, I come to live with Bess. Imagine that. Bess make an offer and, sure enough, where she come from, people mean for you to move in when they say things like that. A crazy idea, go to live with someone else's family, but she like to have some female company, not like my daughter, who does not believe in company. These days when my daughter visit, she does not bring Sophie. Bess say we should give Nattie time, we will see Sophie again soon. But seems like my daughter have more presentation than ever before, every time she come she have to leave.

I have a family to support, she say, and her voice is heavy, as if soaking wet. I have a young daughter and a depressed husband and no one to turn to.

When she say no one to turn to, she mean me.

These days my beautiful daughter is so tired she can just sit there in a chair and fall asleep. John lost his job again, already, but still they rather hire a baby-sitter than ask me to help, even they can't afford it. Of course, the new baby-sitter is much younger, can run around. I don't know if Sophie these days is wild or not wild.

She call me Meanie, but she like to kiss me too, sometimes. I remember that every time I see a child on TV. Sophie like to grab my hair, a fistful in each hand, and then kiss me smack on the nose. I never see any other child kiss that way.

The satellite TV has so many channels, more channels than I can count, including a Chinese channel from the Mainland and a Chinese channel from Taiwan, but most of the time I watch bloopers with Bess. Also, I watch the bird feeder—so many, many kinds of birds come. The Shea sons hang around all the time, asking when will I go home, but Bess tell them, Get lost.

She's a permanent resident, say Bess. She isn't going anywhere.

Then she wink at me, and switch the channel with the remote control.

Of course, I shouldn't say Irish this, Irish that, especially now I am become honorary Irish myself, according to Bess. Me! Who's Irish? I say, and she laugh. All the same, if I could mention one thing about some of the Irish, not all of them of course, I like to mention this: Their talk just stick. I don't know how Bess Shea learn to use her words, but sometimes I hear what she say a long time later. *Permanent resident. Not going anywhere.* Over and over I hear it, the voice of Bess.

Lorrie Moore

ॐ

Dance in America

I TELL THEM dance begins when a moment of hurt combines with a moment of boredom. I tell them it's the body's reaching, bringing air to itself. I tell them that it's the heart's triumph, the victory speech of the feet, the refinement of animal lunge and flight, the purest metaphor of tribe and self. It's life flipping death the bird.

I make this stuff up. But then I feel the stray voltage of my rented charisma, hear the jerry-rigged authority in my voice, and I, too, believe. I'm convinced. The troupe dismantled, the choreography commissions dwindling, my body harder to make limber, to make go, I have come here for two weeks—to Pennsylvania Dutch country, as a "Dancer in the Schools." I visit classes, at colleges and elementary schools, spreading Dance's holy word. My head fills with my own yack. What interior life has accrued in me is depleted fast, emptied out my mouth, as I stand before audiences, answering their fearful, forbidding *German* questions about art and my "whorish dances" (the thrusted hip, the sudden bump and grind before an *attitude*). They ask why everything I make seems so "feministic."

"I think the word is *feministical*," I say. I've grown tired. I burned down my life for a few good pieces, and now this.

With only one night left, I've fled the Quality Inn. (CREAMED CHICKEN ON WAFFLE $3.95 reads the sign out front. How could I leave?) The karaoke in the cocktail lounge has kept me up, all those tipsy and bellowing voices just back from the men's room and urged to the front of the lounge to sing "Sexual Healing" or "Alfie." I've accepted an invitation to stay with my old friend Cal, who teaches anthropology at Burkwell, one of the myriad local colleges. He and his wife own a former frat house they've never bothered to renovate. "It was the only way we could live in a house this big," he says. "Besides, we're perversely fascinated by the wreckage." It is Fastnacht, the lip of Lent, the night when the locals make hot fried dough and eat it in honor of Christ. We are outside, before dinner, walking Cal's dog, Chappers, in the cold.

"The house *is* amazing to look at," I say. "It's beat-up in such an intricate way. Like a Rauschenberg. Like one of those beautiful wind-tattered billboards one sees in the California desert." I'm determined to be agreeable; the house, truth be told, is a shock. Maple seedlings have sprouted up through the dining room floorboards, from where a tree outside has pushed into the foundation. Squirrels the size of collies scrabble in the walls. Paint is chipping everywhere, in scales and blisters and flaps; in the cracked plaster beneath are written the names of women who, in 1972, 1973, and 1974, spent the night during Spring Rush weekend. The kitchen ceiling reads "Sigma power!" and "Wank me with a spoon."

But I haven't seen Cal in twelve years, not since he left for Belgium on a Fulbright, so I must be nice. He seems different to me: shorter, older, cleaner, despite the house. In a burst of candor, he has already confessed that those long years ago, out of friendship for me, he'd been exaggerating his interest in dance. "I didn't get it," he admitted. "I kept trying to figure out the *story*. I'd look at the purple guy who hadn't moved in a while, and I'd think, So what's the issue with *him*?"

Now Chappers tugs at his leash. "Yeah, the house." Cal sighs.

"We did once have a painter give us an estimate, but we were put off by the names of the paints: Myth, Vesper, Snickerdoodle. I didn't want anything called Snickerdoodle in my house."

"What *is* a Snickerdoodle?"

"I think they're hunted in Madagascar."

I leap to join him, to play. "Or eaten in Vienna," I say.

"Or worshiped in L.A." I laugh again for him, and then we watch as Chappers sniffs at the roots of an oak.

"But a myth or a vesper—they're always good," I add.

"Crucial," he says. "But we didn't need paint for that."

Cal's son, Eugene, is seven and has cystic fibrosis. Eugene's whole life is a race with medical research. "It's not that I'm not for the arts," says Cal. "*You're* here; money for the arts brought you here. That's wonderful. It's wonderful to see you after all these years. It's wonderful to fund the arts. *It's* wonderful; you're wonderful. The arts are so nice and wonderful. But really: I say, let's give all the money, every last fucking dime, to science."

Something chokes up in him. There can be optimism in the increments, the bits, the chapters; but I haven't seen him in twelve years and he has had to tell me the whole story, straight from the beginning, and it's the whole story that's just so sad.

"We both carried the gene but never knew," he says. "That's the way it works. The odds are one in twenty, times one in twenty, and then after that, still only one in four. One in sixteen hundred, total. Bingo! We should move to Vegas."

When I first knew Cal, we were in New York, just out of graduate school; he was single, and anxious, and struck me as someone who would never actually marry and have a family, or if he did, would marry someone decorative, someone slight. But now, twelve years later, his silver-haired wife, Simone, is nothing like that: she is big and fierce and original, joined with him in grief and courage. She storms out of PTA meetings. She glues little sequins to her shoes. English is her third language; she was once a French diplomat to Belgium and to Japan. "I miss the caviar" is all she'll say of it. "I miss the caviar so much." Now, in Pennsylvania Dutchland, she paints satirical oils of long-armed handless people. "The locals," she explains in her French accent, giggling. "But I can't paint hands." She and Eugene have made a studio from one of the wrecked rooms upstairs.

"How is Simone through all this?" I ask.

"She's better than I am," he says. "She had a sister who died young. She expects unhappiness."

"But isn't there hope?" I ask, stuck for words.

Already, Cal says, Eugene has degenerated, grown worse, too much liquid in his lungs. "Stickiness," he calls it. "If he were three, instead of seven, there'd be *more* hope. The researchers are making some strides; they really are."

"He's a great kid," I say. Across the street, there are old Colonial houses with candles lit in each window; it is a Pennsylvania Dutch custom, or left over from Desert Storm, depending on whom you ask.

Cal stops and turns toward me, and the dog comes up and nuzzles him. "It's not just that Eugene's great," he says. "It's not just the precocity or that he's the only child I'll ever have. It's also that he's such a good person. He accepts things. He's very good at understanding everything."

I cannot imagine anything in my life that contains such sorrow as this, such anticipation of missing someone. Cal falls silent, the dog trots before us, and I place my hand lightly in the middle of Cal's back as we walk like that through the cold, empty streets. Up in the sky, Venus and the thinnest paring of sickle moon, like a cup and saucer, like a nose and mouth, have made the Turkish flag in the sky. "Look at that," I say to Cal as we traipse after the dog, the leash taut as a stick.

"Wow," Cal says. "The Turkish flag."

·   ·   ·

"YOU'RE BACK, you're back!" Eugene shouts from inside, dashing toward the front door as we step up onto the front porch with Chappers. Eugene is in his pajamas already, his body skinny and hunched. His glasses are thick, magnifying, and his eyes, puffed and swimming, seem not to miss a thing. He slides into the front entryway, in his stocking feet, and lands on the floor. He smiles up at me, all charm, like a kid with a crush. He has painted his face with Merthiolate and hopes we'll find that funny.

"Eugene, you look beautiful!" I say.

"No I don't!" he says. "I look *witty.*"

"Where's your mother?" asks Cal, unleashing the dog.

"In the kitchen. Dad, Mom says you have to go up to the attic and bring down one of the pans for dinner." He gets up and chases after Chappers, to tackle him and bring him back.

"We have a couple pots up there to catch leaks," Cal explains, taking off his coat. "But then we end up needing the pots for cooking, so we fetch them back."

"Do you need some help?" I don't know whether I should be with Simone in the kitchen, Cal in the attic, or Eugene on the floor.

"Oh, no. You stay here with Eugene," he says.

"Yeah. Stay here with me." Eugene races back from the dog and grabs my leg. The dog barks excitedly.

"You can show Eugene your video," Cal suggests as he leaves the room.

"Show me your dance video," he says to me in a singsong. "Show me, show me."

"Do we have time?"

"We have fifteen minutes," he says with great authority. I go upstairs and dig it out of my bag, then come back down. We plug it into the VCR and nestle on the couch together. He huddles close, cold in the drafty house, and I extend my long sweater around him like a shawl. I try to explain a few things, in a grown-up way, how this dance came to be, how movement, repeated, breaks through all resistance into a kind of stratosphere: from recalcitrance to ecstasy; from shoe to bird. The tape is one made earlier in the week. It is a demonstration with fourth graders. They each had to invent a character, then design a mask. They came up with various creatures: Miss Ninja Peacock. Mr. Bicycle Spoke Head. Evil Snowman. Saber-toothed Mom: "Half-girl-half-man-half-cat." Then I arranged the kids in a phalanx and led them, with their masks on, in an improvised dance to Kenny Loggins's "This Is It."

He watches, rapt. His brown hair hangs in strings in his face, and he chews on it. "There's Tommy Crowell," he says. He knows the fourth graders as if they were royalty. When it is over, he looks up at me, smiling, but businesslike. His gaze behind his glasses is brilliant and direct. "That was really a wonderful dance," he says. He sounds like an agent.

"Do you really think so?"

"Absolutely," he says. "It's colorful and has lots of fun, interesting steps."

"Will you be my agent?" I ask.

He scowls, unsure. "I don't know. Is the agent the person who drives the car?"

"Dinner's ready!" Simone calls from two rooms away, the "Wank me with a spoon" room.

"Coming!" shouts Eugene, and he leaps off the couch and slides into the dining room, falling sideways into her chair. *"Whoo,"* he says, out of breath. "I almost didn't make it."

"Here," says Cal. He places a goblet of pills at Eugene's place setting.

Eugene makes a face, but in the chair, he gets up on his knees, leans forward, glass of water in one hand, and begins the arduous activity of taking all the pills.

I sit in the chair opposite him and place my napkin in my lap.

.   .   .

SIMONE HAS MADE a soup with hard-boiled eggs in it (a regional recipe, she explains), as well as Peking duck, which is ropy and sweet. Cal keeps passing around the basket of bread, anxiously, talking about how modern man has only been around for 45,000 years and probably the bread hasn't changed much since then.

"Forty-five thousand years?" says Simone. "That's all? That can't be. I feel like we've been *married* for that long."

There are people who talk with their hands. Then there are people who talk with their arms. Then there are people who talk with their arms over their head. These are the ones I like best. Simone is one of those.

"Nope, that's it," says Cal, chewing. "Forty-five thousand. Though for about two hundred thousand years before that, early man was going through all kinds of anatomical changes to get where we are today. It was a *very* exciting time." He pauses, a little breathlessly. "I wish I could have been there."

"Ha!" exclaims Simone.

"Think of the parties," I say.

"Right," says Simone. " 'Joe, how've you been? Your head's so *big* now, and, well, what is this crazy thing you're doing with your thumb?' A lot like the parties in Soda Springs, Idaho."

"Simone used to be married to someone in Soda Springs, Idaho," Cal says to me.

"You're kidding!" I say.

"Oh, it was very brief," she says. "He was ridiculous. I got rid of him after about six months. Supposedly, he went off and killed himself." She smiles at me impishly.

"Who killed himself?" asks Eugene. He has swallowed all the pills but one.

"Mommy's first husband," says Cal.

"Why did he kill himself?" Eugene is staring at the middle of the table, trying to think about this.

"Eugene, you've lived with your mother for seven years now,

and you don't know why someone close to her would want to kill himself?" Simone and Cal look straight across at each other and laugh brightly.

Eugene smiles in an abbreviated and vague way. He understands this is his parents' joke, but he doesn't like or get it. He is bothered they have turned his serious inquiry into a casual laugh. He wants information! But now, instead, he just digs into the duck, poking and looking.

Simone asks about the school visits. What am I finding? Are people nice to me? What is my life like back home? Am I married?

"I'm not married," I say.

"But you and Patrick are still together, aren't you?" Cal says in a concerned way.

"Uh, no. We broke up."

"You broke up?" Cal puts his fork down.

"Yes," I say, sighing.

"Gee, I thought you guys would never break up!" he says in a genuinely flabbergasted tone.

"Really?" I find this reassuring somehow, that my relationship at least looked good from the outside, at least to someone.

"Well, not *really*," admits Cal. "Actually, I thought you guys would break up long ago."

"Oh," I say.

"So *you* could marry her?" says the amazing Eugene to his father, and we all laugh loudly, pour more wine into glasses, and hide our faces in them.

"The thing to remember about love affairs," says Simone, "is that they are all like having raccoons in your chimney."

"Oh, not the raccoon story," groans Cal.

"Yes! The raccoons!" cries Eugene.

I'm sawing at my duck.

"We have raccoons sometimes in our chimney," explains Simone.

"Hmmm," I say, not surprised.

"And once we tried to smoke them out. We lit a fire, knowing they were there, but we hoped that the smoke would cause them to scurry out the top and never come back. Instead, they caught on fire and came crashing down into our living room, all charred and in flames and running madly around until they dropped dead." Simone swallows some wine. "Love affairs are like that," she says. "They all are like that."

I'm confused. I glance up at the light, an old brass octopus of a chandelier. All I can think of is how Patrick said, when he left, fed up with my "selfishness," that if I were worried about staying on alone at the lake house, with its squirrels and call girl–style lamps, I should just rent the place out—perhaps to a nice lesbian couple like myself.

But Eugene, across from me, nods enthusiastically, looks pleased. He's heard the raccoon story before and likes it. Once again, it's been told right, with flames and gore.

Now there is salad, which we pick and tear at like crows. Afterward, we gaze upon the bowl of fruit at the center of the table, lazily pick a few grapes off their stems. We sip hot tea that Cal brings in from the kitchen. We sip until it's cool, and then until it's gone. Already the time is ten o'clock.

"Dance time, dance time!" says Eugene when we're through. Every night, before bed, they all go out into the living room and dance until Eugene is tired and falls asleep on the sofa. Then they carry him upstairs and tuck him in.

He comes over to my chair and takes my hand, leads me out into the living room.

"What music shall we dance to?" I ask.

"You choose," he says, and leads me to the shelf where they keep their compact discs. Perhaps there is some Stravinsky. Perhaps *Petrouchka,* with its rousing salute to Shrovetide.

"Will you come see me tomorrow when you visit the fourth graders?" he asks as I'm looking through the selection. Too much Joan Baez. Too much Mahler. "I'm in room one oh four," he says.

"When you visit the fourth graders, you can just stop by my class-room and wave to me from the door. I sit between the bulletin board and the window."

"Sure!" I say, not knowing that, in a rush, I will forget, and that I'll be on the plane home already, leafing through some inane airline magazine, before I remember that I forgot to do it. "Look," I say, finding a Kenny Loggins disc. It has the song he heard earlier, the one from the video. "Let's play this."

"Goody," he says. "Mom! Dad! Come on!"

"All right, Eugenie-boy," says Cal, coming in from the dining room. Simone is behind him.

"I'm Mercury, I'm Neptune, now I'm Pluto so far away," says Eugene, dashing around the room, making up his own dance.

"They're doing the planets in school," says Simone.

"Yes," says Eugene. "We're doing the planets!"

"And which planet," I ask him, "do you think is the most interesting?" Mars, with its canals? Saturn, with its rings?

Eugene stands still, looks at me thoughtfully, solemnly. "Earth, of course," he says.

Cal laughs. "Well, that's the right answer!"

"This is it!" sings Kenny Loggins. "This is it!" We make a phalanx and march, strut, slide to the music. We crouch, move backward, then burst forward again. We're aiming to create the mildewy, resinous sweat smell of dance, the parsed, repeated movement. Cal and Simone are into it. They jiggle and link arms. "This is it!" In the middle of the song, Eugene suddenly sits down to rest on the sofa, watching the grown-ups. Like the best dancers and audiences in the world, he is determined not to cough until the end.

"Come here, honey," I say, going to him. I am thinking not only of my own body here, that unbeguilable, broken basket, that stiff meringue. I am not, Patrick, thinking only of myself, my lost troupe, my empty bed. I am thinking of the dancing body's magnificent and ostentatious scorn. This is how we offer ourselves, enter heaven, enter speaking: we say with motion, in space, This is what life's done so far down here; this is all and what and everything it's managed—this body, these bodies, that body—so what do you think, Heaven? What do you fucking think?

"Stand next to me," I say, and Eugene does, looking up at me with his orange warrior face. We step in place: knees up, knees down. Knees up, knees down. Dip-glide-slide. Dip-glide-slide. "This is it!" "This is it!" Then we go wild and fling our limbs to the sky.

Lynn Freed

༈

Ma, a Memoir

HE'D GOT AWAY. Only as far as the hospital, but still she'd been left behind. Once, she would have got into her Fiat and revved and revved and gone off in a puff of blue smoke to find him, to catch him out in the arms of another woman, perhaps. Sixty years of marriage had only heated the furious war between them.

Every day, she waited impatiently for me to take her to the hospital.

"I have a bone to pick with you," she said when I arrived.

"What bone?" I asked.

"I've forgotten."

He didn't want to see her. When she came shuffling in, he pretended to be asleep.

"Say hello, Dad," I whispered.

"Hello," he said. He was very weak, a dark, gaunt, beautiful old man, not ready to die.

She settled into the armchair and sat there quite still, staring out through her milky eyes at nothing.

"See, Ma," I said. "Dad says hello."

"Well, why doesn't he *speak up*? I can hear everybody else. Why can't I hear *him*?" She reached over and placed a hand on his arm. "Come home, Harold," she said. "You know you're putting it on."

"Will *you* tell her!" he rasped at me. "Will you tell that bloody woman that I've got cancer?"

"Ma," I said. "Dad's got cancer. Don't be cruel."

"*Me* cruel! *Me* cruel! *You're* the one mentioning—that thing!" She clawed at the arms of the chair and pushed herself forward. "Here! Help me up. And then take me home, please. Right now."

I took her out for a drive in the Fiat the next day, up the coast to our favorite beach hotel for lunch.

"This way, Marmalade," I said, shepherding her down the steps one at a time.

"This way, Strawberry Jam," said the Indian waiter. "This way, Honeybunch."

She laughed, she giggled. "Go on, order crayfish," she suggested. "Why don't you order prawns? You love prawns, don't you?"

Driving back, I described the wild horses on the sea, the people selling beadwork on the beachfront. We were both happy for a moment.

"Hey ho!" she cried. "How old are you?"

"Forty-nine."

"How old am I?"

"Eighty-seven."

"Really? How can I be that much older than you?"

"Because you're my mother, Ma."

"Ha! Ha! That's a good one!"

"Beats cockfighting," said my father, smiling a bit when I repeated the conversation to him the next day. Every morning and evening, I went alone to see him. I put on the Bruch G Minor and closed his door. The pneumonia was almost gone; he could go home to die if we could arrange it.

"Dad," I said. "Do you want to go home? I can try to deal with Ma."

But he pretended not to hear. A large tear rolled down his cheek as the second movement began. "I'd like some smoked salmon," he whispered.

At home, my mother sat staring at the bookshelf, with a glass of Scotch in her hand. "I did love him so," she said, "and he seemed to love me. But what happened I don't know."

"Ma, he's sick. He's in the hospital."

She blew her nose furiously and wiped her eyes. "Don't you think two people could be happy again?"

"I think they could."

THE NEXT DAY, when I came to fetch her she was waiting at the front door. "Has he died?" she asked.

"No."

"Well, thank God for that. Wearing a hat?"

"No."

"Then nor shall I."

She was the one who was meant to die first. Once she had over-heard him saying to a widow, just engaged to be married, "Couldn't you have waited for me?"

"That husband of mine," she said now. "He was really very good to me.

"Your husband is my father, Ma," I said.

"Rubbish!" she snapped. "He's *my* father."

THE DAY AFTER she claimed him as her father, he died. When I came to tell her, she was waiting, as usual, to be taken to the hospital. "Ready?" she said. "I've been waiting for hours."

"Ma," I said. "Dad died. He just died." I sat down.

She covered her eyes with a hand and breathed deeply. Finally, she said, "It's unbearable. I cannot bear it. Don't expect me to bear it."

"I don't expect you to bear it, Ma. I can't bear it either."

She looked up as if she'd just met me at a bus stop. "It's full of emptiness, this place," she said.

AFTER THE FUNERAL, she sat in my sister's house like a refugee. The family came in one by one, veterans of the cemetery, to offer condolences. A florist delivered an arrangement of flowers. I brought it in to show her. She had always loved flowers. In our old house, she and Pillay, the gardener, had conspired together every week on which beds to plant with what, where to deploy the bulbs and seedlings he stole from the Botanic Gardens.

"Look, Ma," I said. "You got some lovely flowers."

"Really? How nice."

"Here, I'll read you the card. 'Dear Anne, We were so sad to hear of the loss of your darling Harold. We are all thinking of you with love at this time. Meg, John, and Nigel.'"

She stared out at nowhere. "Gentiles," she said.

A FEW DAYS later, I stole her away from shivah and took her to the Botanic Gardens for tea. "How long have I known you?" she asked.

"A long time."

"That's what it feels like."

She began to weep. "I don't know why I'm crying," she said. She groped in her bag for a tissue and then blew her nose loudly.

"I know why."

"My father died," she said.

"Perhaps it's time to count your blessings, Ma."

She looked up sharply. "That's a lot of rubbish and you know it!"

"It'll be lonely without Dad to fight with."

"And to love," she said. "Same thing."

"Ma, I'm worried. You're behaving magnificently, and it doesn't suit you."

She beamed. She reached out for a scone. I put it into her hand. "Now, why don't I have a daughter like you?" she asked.

Jhumpa Lahiri

ॐ

A Temporary Matter

THE NOTICE INFORMED them that it was a temporary matter: for
five days their electricity would be cut off for one hour, beginning
at eight p.m. A line had gone down in the last snowstorm, and the
repairmen were going to take advantage of the milder evenings to
set it right. The work would affect only the houses on the quiet
tree-lined street, within walking distance of a row of brick-faced
stores and a trolley stop, where Shoba and Shukumar had lived for
three years.

"It's good of them to warn us," Shoba conceded after reading
the notice aloud, more for her own benefit than Shukumar's. She
let the strap of her leather satchel, plump with files, slip from her
shoulders, and left it in the hallway as she walked into the kitchen.
She wore a navy blue poplin raincoat over gray sweatpants and
white sneakers, looking, at thirty-three, like the type of woman
she'd once claimed she would never resemble.

She'd come from the gym. Her cranberry lipstick was visible
only on the outer reaches of her mouth, and her eyeliner had left
charcoal patches beneath her lower lashes. She used to look this
way sometimes, Shukumar thought, on mornings after a party or a
night at a bar, when she'd been too lazy to wash her face, too eager
to collapse into his arms. She dropped a sheaf of mail on the table

without a glance. Her eyes were still fixed on the notice in her other hand. "But they should do this sort of thing during the day."

"When I'm here, you mean," Shukumar said. He put a glass lid on a pot of lamb, adjusting it so only the slightest bit of steam could escape. Since January he'd been working at home, trying to complete the final chapters of his dissertation on agrarian revolts in India. "When do the repairs start?"

"It says March nineteenth. Is today the nineteenth?" Shoba walked over to the framed corkboard that hung on the wall by the fridge, bare except for a calendar of William Morris wallpaper patterns. She looked at it as if for the first time, studying the wallpaper pattern carefully on the top half before allowing her eyes to fall to the numbered grid on the bottom. A friend had sent the calendar in the mail as a Christmas gift, even though Shoba and Shukumar hadn't celebrated Christmas that year.

"Today then," Shoba announced. "You have a dentist appointment next Friday, by the way."

He ran his tongue over the tops of his teeth; he'd forgotten to brush them that morning. It wasn't the first time. He hadn't left the house at all that day, or the day before. The more Shoba stayed out, the more she began putting in extra hours at work and taking on additional projects, the more he wanted to stay in, not even leaving to get the mail, or to buy fruit or wine at the stores by the trolley stop.

Six months ago, in September, Shukumar was at an academic conference in Baltimore when Shoba went into labor, three weeks before her due date. He hadn't wanted to go to the conference, but she had insisted; it was important to make contacts, and he would be entering the job market next year. She told him that she had his number at the hotel, and a copy of his schedule and flight numbers, and she had arranged with her friend Gillian for a ride to the hospital in the event of an emergency. When the cab pulled away that morning for the airport, Shoba stood waving good-bye in her robe, with one arm resting on the mound of her belly as if it were a perfectly natural part of her body.

Each time he thought of that moment, the last moment he saw Shoba pregnant, it was the cab he remembered most, a station wagon, painted red with blue lettering. It was cavernous compared to their own car. Although Shukumar was six feet tall, with hands too big ever to rest comfortably in the pockets of his jeans, he felt dwarfed in the back seat. As the cab sped down Beacon Street, he imagined a day when he and Shoba might need to buy a station wagon of their own, to cart their children back and forth from music lessons and dentist appointments. He imagined himself gripping the wheel, as Shoba turned around to hand the children juice boxes. Once, these images of parenthood had troubled Shukumar, adding to his anxiety that he was still a student at thirty-five. But that early autumn morning, the trees still heavy with bronze leaves, he welcomed the image for the first time.

A member of the staff had found him somehow among the identical convention rooms and handed him a stiff square of stationery. It was only a telephone number, but Shukumar knew it was the hospital. When he returned to Boston it was over. The baby had been born dead. Shoba was lying on a bed, asleep, in a private room so small there was barely enough space to stand beside her, in a wing of the hospital they hadn't been to on the tour for expectant parents. Her placenta had weakened and she'd had a cesarean, though not quickly enough. The doctor explained that these things happen. He smiled in the kindest way it was possible to smile at people known only professionally. Shoba would be back on her feet in a few weeks. There was nothing to indicate that she would not be able to have children in the future.

These days Shoba was always gone by the time Shukumar woke up. He would open his eyes and see the long black hairs she shed on her pillow and think of her, dressed, sipping her third cup of coffee already, in her office downtown, where she searched for typographical errors in textbooks and marked them, in a code she had once explained to him, with an assortment of colored pencils. She would do the same for his dissertation, she promised, when it was ready. He envied her the specificity of her task, so unlike the elusive nature of his. He was a mediocre student who had a facility for absorbing details without curiosity. Until September he had been diligent if not dedicated, summarizing chapters, outlining arguments on pads of yellow lined paper. But now he would lie in their bed until he grew bored, gazing at his side of the closet which Shoba always left partly open, at the row of the tweed jackets and corduroy trousers he would not have to choose from to teach his classes that semester. After the baby died it was too late to withdraw from his teaching duties. But his adviser had arranged things so that he had the spring semester to himself. Shukumar was in his sixth year of graduate school. "That and the summer should give you a good push," his adviser had said. "You should be able to wrap things up by next September."

But nothing was pushing Shukumar. Instead he thought of how he and Shoba had become experts at avoiding each other in their three-bedroom house, spending as much time on separate floors as possible. He thought of how he no longer looked forward to weekends, when she sat for hours on the sofa with her colored pencils and her files, so that he feared that putting on a record in his own house might be rude. He thought of how long it had been since she looked into his eyes and smiled, or whispered his name on those rare occasions they still reached for each other's bodies before sleeping.

In the beginning he had believed that it would pass, that he and Shoba would get through it all somehow. She was only thirty-three. She was strong, on her feet again. But it wasn't a consolation. It was often nearly lunchtime when Shukumar would finally pull himself out of bed and head downstairs to the coffeepot, pouring out the extra bit Shoba left for him, along with an empty mug, on the countertop.

. . .

SHUKUMAR GATHERED onion skins in his hands and let them drop into the garbage pail, on top of the ribbons of fat he'd trimmed from the lamb. He ran the water in the sink, soaking the knife and the cutting board, and rubbed a lemon half along his fingertips to get rid of the garlic smell, a trick he'd learned from Shoba. It was seven-thirty. Through the window he saw the sky, like soft black pitch. Uneven banks of snow still lined the sidewalks, though it was warm enough for people to walk about without hats or gloves. Nearly three feet had fallen in the last storm, so that for a week people had to walk single file, in narrow trenches. For a week that was Shukumar's excuse for not leaving the house. But now the trenches were widening, and water drained steadily into grates in the pavement.

"The lamb won't be done by eight," Shukumar said. "We may have to eat in the dark."

"We can light candles," Shoba suggested. She unclipped her hair, coiled neatly at her nape during the days, and pried the sneakers from her feet without untying them. "I'm going to shower before the lights go," she said, heading for the staircase. "I'll be down."

Shukumar moved her satchel and her sneakers to the side of the fridge. She wasn't this way before. She used to put her coat on a hanger, her sneakers in the closet, and she paid bills as soon as they came. But now she treated the house as if it were a hotel. The fact that the yellow chintz armchair in the living room clashed with the blue-and-maroon Turkish carpet no longer bothered her. On the enclosed porch at the back of the house, a crisp white bag still sat on the wicker chaise, filled with lace she had once planned to turn into curtains.

While Shoba showered, Shukumar went into the downstairs bathroom and found a new toothbrush in its box beneath the sink. The cheap, stiff bristles hurt his gums, and he spit some blood into the basin. The spare brush was one of many stored in a metal basket. Shoba had bought them once when they were on sale, in the event that a visitor decided, at the last minute, to spend the night.

It was typical of her. She was the type to prepare for surprises, good and bad. If she found a skirt or a purse she liked she bought two. She kept the bonuses from her job in a separate bank account in her name. It hadn't bothered him. His own mother had fallen to pieces when his father died, abandoning the house he grew up in and moving back to Calcutta, leaving Shukumar to settle it all. He liked that Shoba was different. It astonished him, her capacity to think ahead. When she used to do the shopping, the pantry was always stocked with extra bottles of olive and corn oil, depending on whether they were cooking Italian or Indian. There were endless boxes of pasta in all shapes and colors, zippered sacks of basmati rice, whole sides of lambs and goats from the Muslim butchers at Haymarket, chopped up and frozen in endless plastic bags. Every other Saturday they wound through the maze of stalls Shukumar eventually knew by heart. He watched in disbelief as she bought more food, trailing behind her with canvas bags as she pushed through the crowd, arguing under the morning sun with boys too young to shave but already missing teeth, who twisted up brown paper bags of artichokes, plums, gingerroot, and yams, and dropped them on their scales, and tossed them to Shoba one by one. She didn't mind being jostled, even when she was pregnant. She was tall, and broad-shouldered, with hips that her obstetrician assured her were made for childbearing. During the drive back home, as the car curved along the Charles, they invariably marveled at how much food they'd bought.

It never went to waste. When friends dropped by, Shoba would throw together meals that appeared to have taken half a day to prepare, from things she had frozen and bottled, not cheap things in tins but peppers she had marinated herself with rosemary, and chutneys that she cooked on Sundays, stirring boiling pots of tomatoes and prunes. Her labeled mason jars lined the shelves of the kitchen, in endless sealed pyramids, enough, they'd agreed, to last for their grandchildren to taste. They'd eaten it all by now. Shukumar had been going through their supplies steadily, preparing meals for the two of them, measuring out cupfuls of rice, defrosting bags of meat day after day. He combed through her cookbooks every afternoon, following her penciled instructions to use two teaspoons of ground coriander seeds instead of one, or red lentils instead of yellow. Each of the recipes was dated, telling the first time they had eaten the dish together. April 2, cauliflower with fennel. January 14, chicken with almonds and sultanas. He had no memory of eating those meals, and yet there they were, recorded in her neat proofreader's hand. Shukumar enjoyed cooking now. It was the one thing that made him feel productive. If it weren't for him, he knew, Shoba would eat a bowl of cereal for her dinner.

Tonight, with no lights, they would have to eat together. For months now they'd served themselves from the stove, and he'd taken his plate into his study, letting the meal grow cold on his desk before shoving it into his mouth without pause, while Shoba took her plate to the living room and watched game shows, or proofread files with her arsenal of colored pencils at hand.

At some point in the evening she visited him. When he heard her approach he would put away his novel and begin typing sentences. She would rest her hands on his shoulders and stare with him into the blue glow of the computer screen. "Don't work too hard," she would say after a minute or two, and head off to bed. It was the one time in the day she sought him out, and yet he'd come to dread it. He knew it was something she forced herself to do. She would look around the walls of the room, which they had decorated together last summer with a border of marching ducks and rabbits playing trumpets and drums. By the end of August there was a cherry crib under the window, a white changing table with mint-green knobs, and a rocking chair with checkered cushions. Shukumar had disassembled it all before bringing Shoba back from the hospital, scraping off the rabbits and ducks with a spatula. For some reason the room did not haunt him the way it haunted Shoba. In January, when he stopped working at his carrel in the library, he set up his desk there deliberately, partly because the room soothed him, and partly because it was a place Shoba avoided.

SHUKUMAR RETURNED to the kitchen and began to open drawers. He tried to locate a candle among the scissors, the eggbeaters and whisks, the mortar and pestle she'd bought in a bazaar in Calcutta, and used to pound garlic cloves and cardamom pods, back when she used to cook. He found a flashlight, but no batteries, and a half-empty box of birthday candles. Shoba had thrown him a surprise birthday party last May. One hundred and twenty people had crammed into the house—all the friends and the friends of friends they now systematically avoided. Bottles of vinho verde had nested in a bed of ice in the bathtub. Shoba was in her fifth month, drinking ginger ale from a martini glass. She had made a vanilla cream cake with custard and spun sugar. All night she kept Shukumar's long fingers linked with hers as they walked among the guests at the party.

Since September their only guest had been Shoba's mother. She came from Arizona and stayed with them for two months after Shoba returned from the hospital. She cooked dinner every night, drove herself to the supermarket, washed their clothes, put them away. She was a religious woman. She set up a small shrine, a framed picture of a lavender-faced goddess and a plate of marigold petals, on the bedside table in the guest room, and prayed twice a day for healthy grandchildren in the future. She was polite to Shukumar without being friendly. She folded his sweaters with an expertise she had learned from her job in a department store. She replaced a missing button on his winter coat and knit him a beige and brown scarf, presenting it to him without the least bit of ceremony, as if he had only dropped it and hadn't noticed. She never talked to him about Shoba; once, when he mentioned the baby's death, she looked up from her knitting, and said, "But you weren't even there."

It struck him as odd that there were no real candles in the house. That Shoba hadn't prepared for such an ordinary emergency. He looked now for something to put the birthday candles in and settled on the soil of a potted ivy that normally sat on the windowsill over the sink. Even though the plant was inches from the tap, the soil was so dry that he had to water it first before the candles would stand straight. He pushed aside the things on the kitchen table, the piles of mail, the unread library books. He remembered their first meals there, when they were so thrilled to be married, to be living together in the same house at last, that they would just reach for each other foolishly, more eager to make love than to eat. He put down two embroidered place mats, a wedding gift from an uncle in Lucknow, and set out the plates and wineglasses they usually saved for guests. He put the ivy in the middle, the white-edged, star-shaped leaves girded by ten little candles. He switched on the digital clock radio and tuned it to a jazz station.

"What's all this?" Shoba said when she came downstairs. Her hair was wrapped in a thick white towel. She undid the towel and draped it over a chair, allowing her hair, damp and dark, to fall across her back. As she walked absently toward the stove she took out a few tangles with her fingers. She wore a clean pair of sweatpants, a T-shirt, an old flannel robe. Her stomach was flat again, her waist narrow before the flare of her hips, the belt of the robe tied in a floppy knot.

It was nearly eight. Shukumar put the rice on the table and the lentils from the night before into the microwave oven, punching the numbers on the timer.

"You made *rogan josh*," Shoba observed, looking through the glass lid at the bright paprika stew.

Shukumar took out a piece of lamb, pinching it quickly between his fingers so as not to scald himself. He prodded a larger piece with a serving spoon to make sure the meat slipped easily from the bone. "It's ready," he announced.

The microwave had just beeped when the lights went out, and the music disappeared.

"Perfect timing," Shoba said.

"All I could find were birthday candles." He lit up the ivy, keeping the rest of the candles and a book of matches by his plate.

"It doesn't matter," she said, running a finger along the stem of her wineglass. "It looks lovely."

In the dimness, he knew how she sat, a bit forward in her chair, ankles crossed against the lowest rung, left elbow on the table. During his search for the candles, Shukumar had found a bottle of wine in a crate he had thought was empty. He clamped the bottle between his knees while he turned in the corkscrew. He worried about spilling, and so he picked up the glasses and held them close to his lap while he filled them. They served themselves, stirring the rice with their forks, squinting as they extracted bay leaves and cloves from the stew. Every few minutes Shukumar lit a few more birthday candles and drove them into the soil of the pot.

"It's like India," Shoba said, watching him tend his makeshift candelabra. "Sometimes the current disappears for hours at a stretch. I once had to attend an entire rice ceremony in the dark. The baby just cried and cried. It must have been so hot."

Their baby had never cried, Shukumar considered. Their baby would never have a rice ceremony, even though Shoba had already made the guest list, and decided on which of her three brothers she was going to ask to feed the child its first taste of solid food, at six months if it was a boy, seven if it was a girl.

"Are you hot?" he asked her. He pushed the blazing ivy pot to the other end of the table, closer to the piles of books and mail, making it even more difficult for them to see each other. He was suddenly irritated that he couldn't go upstairs and sit in front of the computer.

"No. It's delicious," she said, tapping her plate with her fork. "It really is."

He refilled the wine in her glass. She thanked him.

They weren't like this before. Now he had to struggle to say something that interested her, something that made her look up from her plate, or from her proofreading files. Eventually he gave up trying to amuse her. He learned not to mind the silences.

"I remember during power failures at my grandmother's house, we all had to say something," Shoba continued. He could barely see her face, but from her tone he knew her eyes were narrowed, as if trying to focus on a distant object. It was a habit of hers.

"Like what?"

"I don't know. A little poem. A joke. A fact about the world. For some reason my relatives always wanted me to tell them the names of my friends in America. I don't know why the information was so interesting to them. The last time I saw my aunt she asked after four girls I went to elementary school with in Tucson. I barely remember them now."

Shukumar hadn't spent as much time in India as Shoba had. His parents, who settled in New Hampshire, used to go back without him. The first time he'd gone as an infant he'd nearly died of amoebic dysentery. His father, a nervous type, was afraid to take him again, in case something were to happen, and left him with his aunt and uncle in Concord. As a teenager he preferred sailing camp or scooping ice cream during the summers to going to Calcutta. It wasn't until after his father died, in his last year of college, that the country began to interest him, and he studied its history from course books as if it were any other subject. He wished now that he had his own childhood story of India.

"Let's do that," she said suddenly.

"Do what?"

"Say something to each other in the dark."

"Like what? I don't know any jokes."

"No, no jokes." She thought for a minute. "How about telling each other something we've never told before."

"I used to play this game in high school," Shukumar recalled. "When I got drunk."

"You're thinking of truth or dare. This is different. Okay, I'll start." She took a sip of wine. "The first time I was alone in your apartment, I looked in your address book to see if you'd written me in. I think we'd known each other two weeks."

"Where was I?"

"You went to answer the telephone in the other room. It was your mother, and I figured it would be a long call. I wanted to know if you'd promoted me from the margins of your newspaper."

"Had I?"

"No. But I didn't give up on you. Now it's your turn."

He couldn't think of anything, but Shoba was waiting for him to speak. She hadn't appeared so determined in months. What was there left to say to her? He thought back to their first meeting, four years earlier at a lecture hall in Cambridge, where a group of Bengali poets were giving a recital. They'd ended up side by side, on folding wooden chairs. Shukumar was soon bored; he was unable to decipher the literary diction, and couldn't join the rest of the audience as they sighed and nodded solemnly after certain phrases. Peering at the newspaper folded in his lap, he studied the temperatures of cities around the world. Ninety-one degrees in Singapore yesterday, fifty-one in Stockholm. When he turned his head to the left, he saw a woman next to him making a grocery list on the back of a folder, and was startled to find that she was beautiful.

"Okay," he said, remembering. "The first time we went out to dinner, to the Portuguese place, I forgot to tip the waiter. I went back the next morning, found out his name, left money with the manager."

"You went all the way back to Somerville just to tip a waiter?"

"I took a cab."

"Why did you forget to tip the waiter?"

The birthday candles had burned out, but he pictured her face clearly in the dark, the wide tilting eyes, the full grape-toned lips, the fall at age two from her high chair still visible as a comma on her chin. Each day, Shukumar noticed, her beauty, which had once overwhelmed him, seemed to fade. The cosmetics that had seemed superfluous were necessary now, not to improve her but to define her somehow.

"By the end of the meal I had a funny feeling that I might marry you," he said, admitting it to himself as well as to her for the first time. "It must have distracted me."

THE NEXT NIGHT Shoba came home earlier than usual. There was lamb left over from the evening before, and Shukumar heated it up so that they were able to eat by seven. He'd gone out that day, through the melting snow, and bought a packet of taper candles from the corner store, and batteries to fit the flashlight. He had the candles ready on the countertop, standing in brass holders shaped like lotuses, but they ate under the glow of the copper-shaded ceiling lamp that hung over the table.

When they had finished eating, Shukumar was surprised to see that Shoba was stacking her plate on top of his, and then carrying them over to the sink. He had assumed she would retreat to the living room, behind her barricade of files.

"Don't worry about the dishes," he said, taking them from her hands.

"It seems silly not to," she replied, pouring a drop of detergent onto a sponge. "It's nearly eight o'clock."

His heart quickened. All day Shukumar had looked forward to the lights going out. He thought about what Shoba had said the night before, about looking in his address book. It felt good to remember her as she was then, how bold yet nervous she'd been when they first met, how hopeful. They stood side by side at the sink, their reflections fitting together in the frame of the window.

It made him shy, the way he felt the first time they stood together in a mirror. He couldn't recall the last time they'd been photographed. They had stopped attending parties, went nowhere together. The film in his camera still contained pictures of Shoba, in the yard, when she was pregnant.

After finishing the dishes, they leaned against the counter, drying their hands on either end of a towel. At eight o'clock the house went black. Shukumar lit the wicks of the candles, impressed by their long, steady flames.

"Let's sit outside," Shoba said. "I think it's warm still."

They each took a candle and sat down on the steps. It seemed strange to be sitting outside with patches of snow still on the ground. But everyone was out of their houses tonight, the air fresh enough to make people restless. Screen doors opened and closed. A small parade of neighbors passed by with flashlights.

"We're going to the bookstore to browse," a silver-haired man called out. He was walking with his wife, a thin woman in a windbreaker, and holding a dog on a leash. They were the Bradfords, and they had tucked a sympathy card into Shoba and Shukumar's mailbox back in September. "I hear they've got their power."

"They'd better," Shukumar said. "Or you'll be browsing in the dark."

The woman laughed, slipping her arm through the crook of her husband's elbow. "Want to join us?"

"No thanks," Shoba and Shukumar called out together. It surprised Shukumar that his words matched hers.

He wondered what Shoba would tell him in the dark. The worst possibilities had already run through his head. That she'd had an affair. That she didn't respect him for being thirty-five and still a student. That she blamed him for being in Baltimore the way her mother did. But he knew those things weren't true. She'd been faithful, as had he. She believed in him. It was she who had insisted he go to Baltimore. What didn't they know about each other? He knew she curled her fingers tightly when she slept, that her body twitched during bad dreams. He knew it was honeydew she favored over cantaloupe. He knew that when they returned from the hospital the first thing she did when she walked into the house was pick out objects of theirs and toss them into a pile in the hallway: books from the shelves, plants from the windowsills, paintings from walls, photos from tables, pots and pans that hung from the hooks over the stove. Shukumar had stepped out of her way, watching as she moved methodically from room to room. When she was satisfied, she stood there staring at the pile she'd made, her lips drawn back in such distaste that Shukumar had thought she would spit. Then she'd started to cry.

He began to feel cold as he sat there on the steps. He felt that he needed her to talk first, in order to reciprocate.

"That time when your mother came to visit us," she said finally. "When I said one night that I had to stay late at work, I went out with Gillian and had a martini."

He looked at her profile, the slender nose, the slightly masculine set of her jaw. He remembered that night well; eating with his mother, tired from teaching two classes back to back, wishing Shoba were there to say more of the right things because he came up with only the wrong ones. It had been twelve years since his father had died, and his mother had come to spend two weeks with him and Shoba, so they could honor his father's memory together. Each night his mother cooked something his father had liked, but she was too upset to eat the dishes herself, and her eyes would well up as Shoba stroked her hand. "It's so touching," Shoba had said to him at the time. Now he pictured Shoba with Gillian, in a bar with striped velvet sofas, the one they used to go to after the movies, making sure she got her extra olive, asking Gillian for a cigarette. He imagined her complaining, and Gillian sympathizing about visits from in-laws. It was Gillian who had driven Shoba to the hospital.

"Your turn," she said, stopping his thoughts.

At the end of their street Shukumar heard sounds of a drill and the electricians shouting over it. He looked at the darkened facades of the houses lining the street. Candles glowed in the windows of one. In spite of the warmth, smoke rose from the chimney.

"I cheated on my Oriental Civilization exam in college," he said. "It was my last semester, my last set of exams. My father had died a few months before. I could see the blue book of the guy next to me. He was an American guy, a maniac. He knew Urdu and Sanskrit. I couldn't remember if the verse we had to identify was an example of a *ghazal* or not. I looked at his answer and copied it down."

It had happened over fifteen years ago. He felt relief now, having told her.

She turned to him, looking not at his face, but at his shoes—old moccasins he wore as if they were slippers, the leather at the back permanently flattened. He wondered if it bothered her, what he'd said. She took his hand and pressed it. "You didn't have to tell me why you did it," she said, moving closer to him.

They sat together until nine o'clock, when the lights came on. They heard some people across the street clapping from their porch, and televisions being turned on. The Bradfords walked back down the street, eating ice-cream cones and waving. Shoba and Shukumar waved back. Then they stood up, his hand still in hers, and went inside.

SOMEHOW, WITHOUT SAYING anything, it had turned into this. Into an exchange of confessions—the little ways they'd hurt or disappointed each other, and themselves. The following day Shukumar thought for hours about what to say to her. He was torn between admitting that he once ripped out a photo of a woman in one of the fashion magazines she used to subscribe to and carried it in his books for a week, or saying that he really hadn't lost the sweater-vest she bought him for their third wedding anniversary but had exchanged it for cash at Filene's, and that he had gotten drunk alone in the middle of the day at a hotel bar. For their first anniversary, Shoba had cooked a ten-course dinner just for him. The vest depressed him. "My wife gave me a sweater-vest for our anniversary," he complained to the bartender, his head heavy with cognac. "What do you expect?" the bartender had replied. "You're married."

As for the picture of the woman, he didn't know why he'd ripped it out. She wasn't as pretty as Shoba. She wore a white sequined dress, and had a sullen face and lean, mannish legs. Her bare arms were raised, her fists around her head, as if she were about to punch herself in the ears. It was an advertisement for stockings. Shoba had been pregnant at the time, her stomach suddenly immense, to the point where Shukumar no longer wanted to touch her. The first time he saw the picture he was lying in bed next to her, watching her as she read. When he noticed the magazine in the recycling pile he found the woman and tore out the page as carefully as he could. For about a week he allowed himself a glimpse each day. He felt an intense desire for the woman, but it was a desire that turned to disgust after a minute or two. It was the closest he'd come to infidelity.

He told Shoba about the sweater on the third night, the picture on the fourth. She said nothing as he spoke, expressed no protest or reproach. She simply listened, and then she took his hand, pressing it as she had before. On the third night, she told him that once after a lecture they'd attended, she let him speak to the chairman of his department without telling him that he had a dab of pâté on his chin. She'd been irritated with him for some reason, and so she'd let him go on and on, about securing his fellowship for the following semester, without putting a finger to her own chin as a signal. The fourth night, she said that she never liked the one poem he'd ever published in his life, in a literary magazine in Utah. He'd written the poem after meeting Shoba. She added that she found the poem sentimental.

Something happened when the house was dark. They were able to talk to each other again. The third night after supper they'd sat together on the sofa, and once it was dark he began kissing her awkwardly on her forehead and her face, and though it was dark he closed his eyes, and knew that she did, too. The fourth night they walked carefully upstairs, to bed, feeling together for the final step with their feet before the landing, and making love with a desperation they had forgotten. She wept without sound, and whispered his name, and traced his eyebrows with her finger in the dark. As he made love to her he wondered what he would say to her the next night, and what she would say, the thought of it exciting him. "Hold me," he said, "hold me in your arms." By the time the lights came back on downstairs, they'd fallen asleep.

THE MORNING of the fifth night Shukumar found another notice from the electric company in the mailbox. The line had been repaired ahead of schedule, it said. He was disappointed. He had planned on making shrimp *malai* for Shoba, but when he arrived at the store he didn't feel like cooking anymore. It wasn't the same, he thought, knowing that the lights wouldn't go out. In the store the shrimp looked gray and thin. The coconut milk tin was dusty and overpriced. Still, he bought them, along with a beeswax candle and two bottles of wine.

She came home at seven-thirty. "I suppose this is the end of our game," he said when he saw her reading the notice.

She looked at him. "You can still light candles if you want." She hadn't been to the gym tonight. She wore a suit beneath the raincoat. Her makeup had been retouched recently.

When she went upstairs to change, Shukumar poured himself some wine and put on a record, a Thelonius Monk album he knew she liked.

When she came downstairs they ate together. She didn't thank him or compliment him. They simply ate in a darkened room, in the glow of a beeswax candle. They had survived a difficult time. They finished off the shrimp. They finished off the first bottle of wine and moved on to the second. They sat together until the candle had nearly burned away. She shifted in her chair, and Shukumar thought that she was about to say something. But instead she blew out the candle, stood up, turned on the light switch, and sat down again.

"Shouldn't we keep the lights off?" Shukumar asked.

She set her plate aside and clasped her hands on the table. "I want you to see my face when I tell you this," she said gently.

His heart began to pound. The day she told him she was pregnant, she had used the very same words, saying them in the same gentle way, turning off the basketball game he'd been watching on television. He hadn't been prepared then. Now he was.

Only he didn't want her to be pregnant again. He didn't want to have to pretend to be happy.

"I've been looking for an apartment and I've found one," she said, narrowing her eyes on something, it seemed, behind his left shoulder. It was nobody's fault, she continued. They'd been through enough. She needed some time alone. She had money saved up for a security deposit. The apartment was on Beacon Hill, so she could walk to work. She had signed the lease that night before coming home.

She wouldn't look at him, but he stared at her. It was obvious that she'd rehearsed the lines. All this time she'd been looking for an apartment, testing the water pressure, asking a Realtor if heat and hot water were included in the rent. It sickened Shukumar, knowing that she had spent these past evenings preparing for a life without him. He was relieved and yet he was sickened. This was what she'd been trying to tell him for the past four evenings. This was the point of her game.

Now it was his turn to speak. There was something he'd sworn he would never tell her, and for six months he had done his best to block it from his mind. Before the ultrasound she had asked the doctor not to tell her the sex of their child, and Shukumar had agreed. She had wanted it to be a surprise.

Later, those few times they talked about what had happened, she said at least they'd been spared that knowledge. In a way she almost took pride in her decision, for it enabled her to seek refuge in a mystery. He knew that she assumed it was a mystery for him, too. He'd arrived too late from Baltimore—when it was all over and she was lying on the hospital bed. But he hadn't. He'd arrived early enough to see their baby, and to hold him before they cremated him. At first he had recoiled at the suggestion, but the doctor said holding the baby might help him with the process of grieving. Shoba was asleep. The baby had been cleaned off, his bulbous lids shut tight to the world.

"Our baby was a boy," he said. "His skin was more red than brown. He had black hair on his head. He weighed almost five pounds. His fingers were curled shut, just like yours in the night."

Shoba looked at him now, her face contorted with sorrow. He had cheated on a college exam, ripped a picture of a woman out of a magazine. He had returned a sweater and got drunk in the middle of the day instead. These were the things he had told her. He had held his son, who had known life only within her, against his chest in a darkened room in an unknown wing of the hospital. He had held him until a nurse knocked and took him away, and he promised himself that day that he would never tell Shoba, because he still loved her then, and it was the one thing in her life that she had wanted to be a surprise.

Shukumar stood up and stacked his plate on top of hers. He carried the plates to the sink, but instead of running the tap he looked out the window. Outside the evening was still warm, and the Bradfords were walking arm in arm. As he watched the couple the room went dark, and he spun around. Shoba had turned the lights off. She came back to the table and sat down, and after a moment Shukumar joined her. They wept together, for the things they now knew.

Alice McDermott

༉

Enough

BEGIN, THEN, with the ice-cream dishes, carried from the dining room into the narrow kitchen on a Sunday night, the rest of the family still sitting contented around the lace-covered table, her father's cigarette smoke just beginning to drift into the air that was still rich from the smell of the roast, and the roasted potatoes, the turnips and carrots and green beans, the biscuits and the Sunday-only perfume of her mother and sisters. Carried just two dishes at a time because this was the good set, cabbage roses with gold trim. Two bowls at a time, silver spoons inside, carried carefully and carefully placed on the drainboard beside the soapy water where the dinner plates were already soaking, her mother being a great believer in soaking, whether children or dishes or clothes, or souls. Let it soak: the stained blouse, the bruised knee, the sin—sending them into their rooms with a whole rosary to pray, on their knees, and a full hour in which to do it.

She was the youngest child, the third girl with three brothers, and since the boys were excused and the kitchen too small, their mother said, to hold a pair of sisters in it together, this final task, the clearing of the ice-cream dishes, was hers alone. Two at a time, she gathered the plates while the others sat, contented, limp, stupe-fied with food, while she herself felt her stomach straining against the now tight waist of her good dress, felt her legs grown heavy from all she had eaten. Sunday dinner was the only meal they had with their father, who worked two jobs to keep them all fed (that was the way it was put by mother and father both, without variance), and the bounty of the spread seemed to be their parents' defiant proof of the man's long week of labor. They always ate too much at Sunday dinner and they always had dessert. Pie on the first Sunday of the month, then cake, ice cream, stewed fruit—one Sunday after the other and always in that same rotation. Ice cream being the pinnacle for her, stewed fruit the depths from which she would have to rise, through pie (if mincemeat, hardly a step in the right direction, if blueberry, more encouraging), then cake— always yellow with eggs and dusted with powdered sugar—and then at last, again, ice cream, store-bought or homemade, it hardly made a difference to she who was told once a month that a lady takes a small spoonful, swallows it, and then takes another. She does *not* load the spoon up and then run the stuff in and out of her mouth, studying each time the shape her lips have made ("Look how cross-eyed she gets when she's gazing at it"). A lady doesn't want to show her tongue at the dinner table.

Carefully, she collected the bowls and carried them two by two into the narrow kitchen. She placed one on the drainboard and then lifted the spoon out of the other and, always, with a glance over her shoulder, licked the spoon, front and back, and then raised the delicate bowl to her chin and licked that, too, licked the cabbage roses and the pale spaces in between, long strokes of the tongue from gold-edged rim to gold-edged rim and then another tour around the middle. Place it down softly and pick up the next. The creamy dregs spotting her nose and her cheeks, vanilla or chocolate, peach or strawberry—strawberry the best because her brothers and a sister always left behind any big pieces of the fruit. Heel of her hand to the sticky tip of her nose (lick that, too) and then back into the dining room again for the next two bowls. Oh, it was good, as good as the whole heaping bowl that had been filled by her father at the head of the table, passed hand to hand by her sisters and brothers, and set before her.

EXTRAPOLATE, THEN, from the girlhood ritual (not to say, of course, that it ended with her girlhood) to what came to be known as her trouble with the couch. Trouble *on* the couch would have been more accurate, she understood later, when she had a sense of humor about these things that at the time had no humor in them at all. But such precision was the last thing her family would have sought, not in these matters. Her trouble with the couch, it was called. Mother walking into what should have been the empty apartment except that the boiler at the school had broken and the pastor had sent them all home and here she was with the boy from upstairs, side by side on the couch, her two cheeks flushed fever pink and her mouth a bleary, full-blown rose, and her mother would have her know (once the boy had slipped out the door) that she wasn't born yesterday and Glory Be to God fourteen years old was a fine age to be starting this nonsense and wasn't it a good thing that tomorrow was Saturday and the confessionals at church would be fully manned. She'd had a good soaking in recriminations all that evening and well into Saturday afternoon when she finished the rosary the priest himself had prescribed, the end coming only after she returned from the Communion rail on Sunday morning and her mother caught and held her eye. A stewed-fruit Sunday no doubt.

Her oldest sister found her next, on the couch with her high-school sweetheart, midafternoon once again—their mother, widowed now, off working in an office—and the first four buttons of her dress undone, the lace bodice of her pale-pink slip all exposed. And then not a month or two later that same sister found her there with another boy, his head in her lap and his hand brushing up and down from her ankle to her knees.

Then there was that Saturday night during the war when her oldest brother, too drunk to go home to his new wife on the next block, let himself in and found her stretched out on the couch in the embrace of some midshipman who, it was clear, despite their quick rearranging of clothes, had his fingers tangled up in her garter. There were buttons undone that time, too, and yet again when she was spied on by the second sister, who never did marry herself but who had an eyeful, let me tell you—a marine, this time, his mouth, to put it delicately, where her corsage should have been and her own hands twisted into his hair as if to hold him there— which led to such a harangue about her trouble with the couch that, finally, even her old mother was moved to say that there was a war on, after all.

Later, her best girlfriend joked that maybe she would want to bring that couch along with her on her wedding night. And joked again, nine months to the week later, when her first son was born, that she didn't seem to need that old couch after all.

There were seven children born altogether, the first followed and each of the others preceded by a miscarriage, so that there were thirteen pregnancies in all, every loss mourned so ferociously that both her husband and her mother advised, each time, not to try again, each birth celebrated with a christening party that packed the small house—made smaller by the oversized floral couch and high-backed chairs and elaborate lamps she had chosen—and spilled out into the narrow yard and breezeway, where there would be dancing, if the weather allowed. A phono-graph placed behind the screen in the kitchen window and the records going all through the long afternoon, and on into the evening. You'd see her there after the last guest had gone, the baby on her shoulder and maybe another child on her hip, dancing to something slow and reluctant and melancholy ("One for my baby, and one more for the road"). Lipstick and face powder on the white christening gown that night, as well as the scent of the party itself, cigarette smoke and perfume and the cocktails on her breath.

She was a mother forever rubbing a licked finger to her chil-dren's cheeks, scrubbing at the pink traces of her own kisses, forever swelling up again with the next birth. Kids in her lap and her arms wrapped around them even after their limbs had grown longer than her own. The boys, before she knew it, lifting her off her feet when she took them in her arms.

SHE WAS forty-six when she gave birth to the last, and he was eighteen and on a weekend home from college when he recognized, for the first time in his life, what the sighs and the stirrings coming from his parents' bedroom on that Saturday morning actually signified. (He did a quick calculation of their ages, just to be sure he had it right and then thought, Still?, amazed and a little daunted.) For the rest of the weekend, he imagined ways he might rib them about it, although he couldn't bring himself to come out with anything, knowing full well that even the most good-natured mention of what went on behind their bedroom door could get him the back of his father's hand—or, worse yet, cause a blush to rise from his own cheeks well before he'd managed to raise any kind of glow in theirs.

And there was the Christmas, some years later, when one of them had given their parents a nostalgic collection of forties music and, listening to Bing Crosby sing in his slow, sleepy way, "Kiss me once and kiss me twice (and kiss me once again)," hadn't their mother said, for all assembled to hear, "If you don't turn this off, I'm going to have to find a place to be alone with your father." And hadn't he and his siblings, every one of them well versed by then in matters of love and sex, sat dumbfounded, calculating, no doubt . . . seventy-one, seventy-two . . . still?

Shades of the trouble with the couch, she took her husband's hand in his last days and unbuttoned her blouse and didn't seem to care a bit who saw her, doctor or nurse, son or daughter or grandchild—or older sister who'd never married herself and couldn't help but say, out in the waiting room, "Now, really." She leaned forward, now and again, to whisper to him, even after he was well past hearing, her open lips brushing both the surgical tape that secured the respirator in his mouth and the stubbly gray beard of his cheek.

Growing plump in her widowhood, though she was the first to admit she'd never been what you would call thin, she travelled in busloads of retirees—mostly widows, although there was the occasional man or two—only missing a museum trip or a foliage tour or a luncheon (with a cocktail) at this or that historic site or country inn if a grandchild was in need of minding. What she could do best—her own daughters marvelled at it, who else would have the patience—was sit for hours and hours at a time with a colicky baby over her shoulder or a worn-out toddler on her knee and talk or sing. She told nonsense stories, more sound than substance, or sang every tune in her lifetime repertoire, from Beatles songs to ancient hymns, hypnotizing the children somehow (her sons and daughters were sure of it) into sleep, or sometimes just a dazed contentedness, tucked under her arm or under her chin, seconds, minutes, then hours ticking by, the bars of summer or winter, late-afternoon or early-morning sunlight moving across them, across the length of a room, and neither of them, adult or child, seeming to mark the time gone by.

BUT TAKE A LOOK in your freezer after she's gone, the daughters reported to one another and to the better-liked sisters-in-law as well. Nearly a full gallon eaten—or all but a final spoonful so she didn't have to put the carton in the trash and give herself away. She's welcome to it, of course, but at her age it's a weight thing. She needs to watch her weight. It's the deceptiveness, too, don't you see. What does she eat when she's alone?

Alone, in an apartment now, ever since the night a stranger crept up the breezeway, broke the kitchen window, and made off with her purse, the portable TV, and the boxed silver in the dining room which had been her mother's, she licked chocolate pudding from the back of a spoon, sherbet, gelato, sorbet, ice cream, of course. She scraped the sides of the carton, ran a finger around the rim.

On visits to her out-of-state children she'd get up in the night, stand by the light of the refrigerator, take a few tablespoons from the gallon, or a single ice-cream bar, but always end up going back for more. A daughter-in-law found her one morning, 2 a.m., with the last chocolate/vanilla ice-cream cup and a tiny wooden spoon—leftovers from the grandchild's birthday party she had made the trip specifically to attend—and gave her such a lecture, as she put it when she got home, that you'd think she'd been shooting heroin.

It was the weight that concerned them, said her children, conferring. They were afraid it was the weight that was keeping her these days from those senior trips she used to love, from the winter vacations in Florida she'd once looked forward to. Now that the grandchildren were grown out of the need for a sitter, she should be doing more of those things, not fewer. They solicited a talking-to for their mother from her doctor, who instead reminded them all that she was past eighty and healthy enough and free to do, or not do, what she liked.

They took to stopping by to see her, on lunch hours, or before going to the grocery store, keeping their car keys in their hands, and urging her to turn off the television, to plan something, to do something. Her grandchildren, driving cars now, asked her out to their kinds of places, treated her to frothy lattes topped with whipped cream that would repeat on her the rest of the afternoon and on into the evening, despite bicarbs and antacids, until she brought herself to tell them when they called, "Thank you, dear, but I'm quite content at home."

Peach, strawberry, and reliable vanilla. Rocky road and butter pecan and mint chocolate chip. Looking at ninety and still, still, the last thing she feels at the end of each day is that longing to wrap her legs around him, around someone. The pleasure of the taste, of

loading up a spoon and finishing it bit by bit, and then taking another spoonful and another—one kind of pleasure, enhanced by
stealth and guilt, when it is someone else's carton, someone else's
home in the middle of the night, another kind when it's her own
and she carries her bowl, in full light, to the couch before the television in the living room. Forbidden youthful passion and domestic
married love, something like that, anyway, if you want to extrapolate. If you want to begin with the ice-cream dishes licked clean by
a girl who is now the old woman past all usefulness, closing her
eyes at the first taste. If you want to make a metaphor out of her
lifelong cravings, something she is not inclined to do. Pleasure is
pleasure. A remnant of strawberries, a young man's hands, a newborn in your arms, or your own child's changing face. Your lips to
the familiar stubble of your husband's cheek. Your tongue to the
last vein of fudge in the empty carton. Pleasure is pleasure. If you
have an appetite for it, you'll find there's plenty. Plenty to satisfy
you—lick the back of the spoon. Take another, and another.
Plenty. Never enough.

Alice Munro

꒰

Floating Bridge

ONE TIME, she had left him. The immediate reason was fairly trivial. He had joined a couple of the Young Offenders ("Yo-yos" was what he called them) in gobbling up a gingerbread cake she had just made, and had been intending to serve after a meeting that evening. Unobserved—at least by Neal and the Yo-yos—she had left the house and gone to sit in a three-sided shelter on the main street, where the city bus stopped twice a day. She had never been in there before, and she had a couple of hours to wait. She sat and read everything that had been written on or cut into those wooden walls. Various initials loved each other 4 ever. Laurie G. sucked cock. Dunk Cultis was a fag. So was Mr. Garner (Math).

Eat Shit. H.W. Gange rules. God hates filth. Kevin S. Is Dead meat. Amanda W is beautiful and sweet and I wish they did not put her in jail because I miss her with all my heart. I want to fuck V.P. Ladies have to sit here and read this disgusting dirty things what you write. Fuck them.

Looking at this barrage of human messages—and puzzling in particular over the heartfelt, very neatly written sentence concerning Amanda W—Jinny wondered if people were alone when they wrote such things. And she went on to imagine herself sitting here or in some similar place, waiting for a bus, alone as she would surely be if she went ahead with the plan she was set on now. Would she be compelled to make statements on public walls?

She felt herself connected at present to those people who had had to write certain things down—connected by her feelings of anger and petty outrage (perhaps it was petty?), and by her excitement at what she was doing to Neal, to pay him back. It occurred to her that the life she was carrying herself into might not give her anybody to be effectively angry at, or anybody who owed her anything, who could possibly be rewarded or punished or truly affected by what she might do. She was not, after all, somebody people flocked to. And yet she was choosy, in her own way.

The bus was still not in sight when she got up and walked home. Neal was not there. He was returning the boys to the school, and by the time he got back, somebody had already arrived for the meeting. She told Neal what she'd done, but only when she was well over it and it could be turned into a joke. In fact, it became a joke she told in company—leaving out or just describing in a general way the things she'd read on the walls.

"Would you ever have thought to come after me?" she said to Neal.

"Of course. Given time."

THE ONCOLOGIST had a priestly demeanor and even wore a black turtleneck shirt under a white smock—an outfit that suggested he had just come from some ceremonial mixing and dosing. His skin was young and smooth—it looked like butterscotch. On the dome of his head, there was just a faint black growth of hair, a delicate sprouting, very like the fuzz Jinny was sporting herself, though hers was brownish-gray, like mouse fur. At first, Jinny had wondered if he could possibly be a patient as well as a doctor. Then, whether he had adopted this style to make the patients more comfortable.

More likely it was a transplant. Or just the way he liked to wear his hair.

You couldn't ask him. He came from Syria or Jordan—someplace where doctors kept their dignity. His courtesies were frigid.

"Now," he said, "I do not wish to give a wrong impression."

She went out of the air-conditioned building into the stunning glare of a late afternoon, in August, in Ontario. Sometimes the sun burned through, sometimes it stayed behind thin clouds—it was just as hot either way. She saw the car detach itself from its place at the curb and make its way down the street to pick her up. It was a light-blue, shimmery, sickening color. Lighter blue where the rust spots had been painted over. Its stickers said, "I Know I Drive a Wreck But You Should See My House," and "Honor Thy Mother—Earth," and (this was more recent) "Use Pesticide—Kill Weeds, Promote Cancer."

Neal came around to help her.

"She's in the car," he said. There was an eager note in his voice which registered vaguely as a warning or a plea. A buzz around him, a tension, that told Jinny it wasn't time to give him her news, if "news" was what you'd call it. When Neal was around other people, even one person other than Jinny, his behavior changed, becoming more animated, enthusiastic, ingratiating. Jinny was not bothered by that anymore—they had been together for twenty-one years. And she herself changed—as a reaction, she used to think—becoming more reserved and slightly ironic. Some masquerades were necessary, or just too habitual to be dropped. Like Neal's antique appearance—the bandanna headband, the rough gray ponytail, the little gold earring that caught the light like the gold rims around his teeth, and his shaggy outlaw clothes.

While Jinny had been seeing the doctor, Neal had been picking up the girl who was going to help them with their life now. He knew her from the Correctional Institute for Young Offenders, where he was a teacher and she had worked in the kitchen. The

Correctional Institute was just outside the town where they lived, about thirty miles away. The girl had quit her kitchen job a few months ago and taken a job looking after a farm household where the mother was sick. Luckily she was now free.

"What happened to the woman?" Jinny had said. "Did she die?"

Neal said, "She went into the hospital."

"Same deal."

NEAL HAD SPENT nearly all his spare time, in the years Jinny had been with him, organizing and carrying out campaigns. Not just political campaigns (those, too) but efforts to preserve historic buildings and bridges and cemeteries, to keep trees from being cut down both along the town streets and in isolated patches of old forest, to save rivers from poisonous runoff and choice land from developers and the local population from casinos. Letters and petitions were always being written, government departments lobbied, posters distributed, protests organized. The front room of their house had been the scene of rages of indignation (which gave people a lot of satisfaction, Jinny thought) and of confused propositions and arguments, and Neal's nervy buoyancy. Now it was suddenly emptied. The front room would become the sickroom. It made her think of when she first walked into the house, straight from her parents' split-level with the swag curtains, and imagined all those shelves filled with books, wooden shutters on the windows, and those beautiful Middle Eastern rugs she always forgot the name of, on the varnished floor. On the one bare wall, the Canaletto print she had bought for her room at college—Lord Mayor's Day on the Thames. She had actually put that up, though she never noticed it anymore.

They rented a hospital bed—they didn't really need it yet, but it was better to get one while you could, because they were often in short supply. Neal thought of everything. He hung up some heavy curtains that were discards from a friend's family room. Jinny thought them very ugly, but she knew now that there comes a time when ugly and beautiful serve pretty much the same purpose, when anything you look at is just a peg to hang the unruly sensations of your body on.

Jinny was forty-two, and until recently she had looked younger than her age. Neal was sixteen years older than she was. So she had thought that in the natural course of things she would be in the position he was in now, and she had sometimes worried about how she would manage it. Once, when she was holding his hand in bed before they went to sleep, his warm and present hand, she had thought that she would hold or touch this hand, at least once, when he was dead. And no matter how long she had foreseen this, she would not be able to credit it. To think of his not having some knowledge of this moment and of her brought on a kind of emotional vertigo, the sense of a horrid drop.

And yet—an excitement. The unspeakable excitement you feel when a galloping disaster promises to release you from all responsibility for your own life. Then from shame you must compose yourself, and stay very quiet.

"Where are you going?" he had said, when she withdrew her hand.

"No place. Just turning over."

She didn't know if Neal had any such feeling, now that it had turned out to be her. She had asked him if he was used to the idea yet. He shook his head.

She said, "Me neither."

Then she said, "Just don't let the Grief Counsellors in. They could be hanging around already. Wanting to make a preemptive strike."

"Don't harrow me," he said, in a voice of rare anger.

"Sorry."

"You don't always have to take the lighter view."

"I know," she said. But the fact was that, with so much going on and present events grabbing so much of her attention, she found it hard to take any view at all.

"THIS IS HELEN," Neal said. "This is who is going to look after us from now on. She won't stand for any nonsense, either."

"Good for her," said Jinny. She put out her hand, once she was settled in the car. But the girl might not have seen it, low down between the two front seats.

Or she might not have known what to do. Neal had said that she came from an unbelievable situation, an absolutely barbaric family. Things had gone on that you could not imagine going on in this day and age. An isolated farm, a widower—a tyrannical, deranged, incestuous old man—with a mentally deficient daughter and the two girl children. Helen, the older one, who had run away at the age of fourteen after beating up on the old man, had been sheltered by a neighbor, who phoned the police. And then the police had come and got the younger sister and made both children wards of the Children's Aid. The old man and his daughter—that is, the children's father and their mother—were both placed in a psychiatric hospital. Foster parents took Helen and her sister, who were mentally and physically normal. They were sent to school and had a miserable time there, having to start first grade in their teens. But they both learned enough to be employable.

When Neal had started the car up, the girl decided to speak.

"You picked a hot enough day to be out in," she said. It was the sort of thing she might have heard people say, to start a conversation. She spoke in a hard, flat tone of antagonism and distrust, but even that, Jinny knew by now, should not be taken personally. It was just the way some people sounded—particularly country people—in this part of the world.

"If you're hot, you can turn the air-conditioner on," Neal said.

"We've got the old-fashioned kind—just roll down all the windows."

The turn they made at the next corner was one Jinny had not expected. "We have to go to the hospital," Neal said. Helen's sister works there, and she's got something Helen wants to pick up. Isn't that right, Helen?"

Helen said, "Yeah. My good shoes."

"Helen's good shoes." Neal looked up at the mirror. "Miss Helen Rosie's good shoes."

"My name's not Helen Rosie," said Helen. It seemed as if it was not the first time she had said this.

"I just call you that because you have such a rosy face," Neal said.

"I have not."

"You do. Doesn't she, Jinny? Jinny agrees with me—you've got a rosy face. Miss Helen Rosie-Face."

The girl did have tender pink skin. Jinny had also noticed her nearly white lashes and eyebrows, her blond baby-wool hair, and her mouth, which had an oddly naked look, not just the normal look of a mouth without lipstick. A fresh-out-of-the-egg look was what she had, as if one layer of skin were still missing, one final growth of coarser, grown-up hair. She must be susceptible to rashes and infections, quick to show scrapes and bruises, to get sores around the mouth and sties between her white lashes, Jinny thought. Yet she didn't look frail. Her shoulders were broad, she was lean but big-boned. She didn't look stupid, either, though she had a head-on expression like a calf's or a deer's. Everything must be right on the surface with her, her attention and the whole of her personality coming straight at you, with an innocent and—to Jinny—a disagreeable power.

They drove up to the main doors of the hospital, then, following Helen's directions, swung around to the back. People in hospital dressing gowns, some trailing their I.V.s, had come outside to smoke.

"Helen's sister works in the laundry," Neal said. "What's her name, Helen? What's your sister's name?"

"Muriel," said Helen. "Stop here. O.K. Here."

They were in a parking lot at the back of a wing of the hospital. There were no doors on the ground floor except a loading door, shut tight. Helen was getting out of the car.

"You know how to find your way in?" Neal said.

"Easy."

The fire escape stopped four or five feet above the ground, but she was able to grab hold of the railing and swing herself up, maybe wedging a foot against a loose brick, in a matter of seconds. Neal was laughing.

"Go get 'em, girl!" he said.

"Isn't there any other way?" said Jinny.

Helen had run up to the third floor and disappeared.

"If there is, she ain't a-gonna use it," Neal said.

"Full of gumption," said Jinny, with an effort.

"Otherwise she'd never have broken out," he said. "She needed all the gumption she could get."

Jinny was wearing a wide-brimmed straw hat. She took it off and began to fan herself.

Neal said, "Sorry. There doesn't seem to be any shade to park in."

"Do I look too startling?" Jinny said. He was used to her asking that.

"You're fine. There's nobody around here anyway."

"The doctor I saw today wasn't the same one I'd seen before. I think this one was more important. The funny thing was he had a scalp that looked about like mine. Maybe he does it to put the patients at ease."

She meant to go on and tell him what the doctor had said, but the fanning took up most of her energy. He watched the building.

"I hope to Christ they didn't haul her up for getting in the wrong way," he said. "She is just not a gal for whom the rules were made."

After several minutes, he let out a whistle.

"Here she comes now. Here-she-comes. Headin' down the homestretch. Will she, will she, will she have enough sense to stop before she jumps? Look before she leaps? Will she, will she—nope. Nope. Unh-*unh*."

Helen had no shoes in her hands. She got into the car and banged the door shut and said, "Stupid idiots. First I get up there and this asshole gets in my way. Where's your tag? You gotta have a tag. I seen you come in off the fire escape, you can't do that. O.K., O.K., I gotta see my sister. You can't see her now, she's not on her break. I know that. That's why I come in off the fire escape. I just need to pick something up. I don't want to talk to her. I'm not goin' to take up her time. I just gotta pick something up. Well, you can't. Well, I can. Well, you can't. And then I start to holler *Muriel, Muriel*. All their machines goin'. It's two hundred degrees in there. I don't know where she is, can she hear me or not. But she comes tearing out and as soon as she sees me—Oh, shit. Oh, shit, she says, I went and forgot. She forgot. I phoned her up last night and reminded her, but there she is. Shit, she forgot. I could've beat her up. Now you get out, he says. Go downstairs and out. Not by the fire escape, because it's illegal. Piss on him."

Neal was laughing and laughing and shaking his head.

Jinny said, "Could we just start driving now and get some air? I don't think fanning is doing a lot of good."

"Fine," said Neal, and started the car and backed and turned around, and once more they were passing the familiar front of the hospital, with the same or different smokers parading by in their dreary hospital clothes with their I.V.s. "Helen will just have to tell us where to go."

He called into the back seat, "Helen."

"What?"

"Which way do we turn now to get to where your sister lives? Where your shoes are."

"We're not goin' to their place, so I'm not telling you. You done me one favor and that's enough." Helen sat as far forward as she could, pushing her head between Neal's seat and Jinny's.

They slowed down, turned into a side street. "That's silly," Neal said. "You're going thirty miles away, and you might not get back here for a while. You might need those shoes." No answer. He tried again. "Or don't you know the way? Don't you know the way from here?"

"I know it, but I'm not telling."

"So we're just going to have to drive around and around till you get ready to tell us."

They were driving through a part of town that Jinny had not seen before. They drove very slowly and made frequent turns, so that hardly any breeze went through the car. A boarded-up factory, discount stores, pawnshops. "Cash, Cash, Cash," said a flashing sign above barred windows. But there were houses, disreputable-looking old duplexes, and the sort of single wooden houses that were put up quickly, during the Second World War. In front of a corner store, some children were sucking on Popsicles.

Helen spoke to Neal. "You're just wasting your gas."

"North of town?" Neal said. "South of town? North, south, east, west, Helen, tell us which is best." On Neal's face there was an expression of conscious, helpless silliness. His whole being was invaded. He was brimming with foolish bliss.

"You're just stubborn," Helen said.

"You'll see how stubborn."

"I am, too. I'm just as stubborn as what you are."

It seemed to Jinny that she could feel the blaze of Helen's cheek, which was so close to hers. And she could certainly hear the girl's breathing, hoarse and thick with excitement and showing some trace of asthma.

The sun had burned through the clouds again. It was still high and brassy in the sky. Neal swung the car onto a street lined with heavy old trees, and somewhat more respectable houses.

"Better here?" he said to Jinny. "More shade for you?" He spoke in a lowered, confidential tone, as if what was going on in the car could be set aside for a moment. It was all nonsense.

"Taking the scenic route," he said, pitching his voice again toward the back seat. "Taking the scenic route today, courtesy of Miss Helen Rosie-Face."

"Maybe we ought to just go on," Jinny said. "Maybe we ought to just go on home."

Helen broke in, almost shouting. "I don't want to stop nobody from getting home."

"Then you can just give me some directions," Neal said. He was trying hard to get his voice under control, to get some ordinary sobriety into it. And to banish the smile, which kept slipping back in place no matter how often he swallowed it.

Half a slow block more, and Helen groaned. "If I got to, I guess I got to," she said.

It was not very far that they had to go. They passed a subdivision, and Neal, speaking again to Jinny, said, "No creek that I can see. No estates either."

Jinny said, "What?"

"Amber Creek Estates. On the sign. They don't care what they say anymore. Nobody even expects them to explain it."

"Turn," said Helen.

"Left or right?"

"At the wrecker's."

They went past a wrecking yard, with the car bodies only partly hidden by a sagging tin fence. Then up a hill, and past the gates to a gravel pit, which was a great cavity in the center of the hill.

"That's them. That's their mailbox up ahead," Helen called out with some importance, and when they got close enough, she read out the name. "Matt and June Bergson. That's them."

A couple of dogs came barking down the short drive. One was

large and black and one small and tan-colored, puppy-like. They bumbled around at the wheels and Neal sounded the horn. Then another dog—this one more sly and purposeful, with a slick coat and bluish spots—slid out of the long grass.

Helen called to them to shut up, to lie down, to piss off. "You don't need to bother about any of them but Pinto," she said. "Them other two's just cowards."

They stopped in a wide, ill-defined space, where some gravel had been laid down. On one side was a barn or implement shed, tin covered, and over to one side of it, on the edge of a cornfield, an abandoned farmhouse. The house inhabited nowadays was a trailer, nicely fixed up with a deck and an awning, and a flower garden behind what looked like a toy fence. The trailer and its garden looked proper and tidy, while the rest of the property was littered with things that might have a purpose or might just have been left around to rust or rot.

Helen had jumped out and was cuffing the dogs. But they kept on running past her, and jumping and barking at the car, until a man came out of the shed and called to them. The threats and names he called were not intelligible to Jinny, but the dogs quieted down.

Jinny put on her hat. All this time, she had been holding it in her hand.

"They just got to show off," said Helen. Neal had got out, too, and was negotiating with the dogs in a resolute way. The man from the shed came toward them. He wore a purple T-shirt that was wet with sweat, clinging to his chest and stomach. He was fat enough to have breasts, and you could see his navel pushing out like a pregnant woman's.

Neal went to meet him with his hand out. The man slapped his own hand on his work pants, laughed, and shook Neal's. Jinny could not hear what they said. A woman came out of the trailer and opened the toy gate and latched it behind her.

"Muriel went and forgot she was supposed to bring my shoes," Helen called to her. "I phoned her up and everything, but she went and forgot anyway, so Mr. Lockley brought me out to get them."

The woman was fat, too, though not as fat as her husband. She wore a pink muumuu with Aztec suns on it, and her hair was streaked with gold. She moved across the gravel with a composed and hospitable air. Neal turned and introduced himself, then brought her to the car and introduced Jinny.

"Glad to meet you," the woman said. "You're the lady that isn't very well?"

"I'm O.K.," said Jinny.

"Well, now you're here, you better come inside. Come in out of this heat."

The man had come closer. "We got the air-conditioning in there," he said. He was inspecting the car, and his expression was genial but disparaging.

"We just came to pick up the shoes," Jinny said.

"You got to do more than that, now you're here," said the woman, June, laughing as if the idea of their not coming in was a scandalous joke. "You come in and rest yourselves."

"We wouldn't like to disturb your supper," Neal said.

"We had it already," said Matt. "We eat early."

"But there's all kinds of chili left," said June. "You have to come in and help clean up that chili."

Jinny said, "Oh, thank you. But I don't think I could eat anything. I don't feel like eating anything when it's this hot."

"Then you better drink something, instead," June said. "We got ginger ale, Coke. We got peach schnapps."

"Beer," Matt said to Neal. "You like a Blue?"

Jinny waved at Neal, asking him to come close to her window. "I can't do it," she said. "Just tell them I can't."

"You know you'll hurt their feelings," he whispered. "They're trying to be nice."

"But I can't."

He bent closer. "You know what it looks like if you don't."

"You go."

"You'd be O.K. once you got inside. The air-conditioning really would do you good."

Jinny just shook her head.

Neal straightened up.

"Jinny thinks she better just stay in the car and rest here in the shade," Neal said. "But I wouldn't mind a Blue, actually."

He turned back to Jinny with a hard smile. He seemed to her desolate and angry. "You sure you'll be O.K.?" he said for the others to hear. "Sure? You don't mind if I go in for a little while?"

"I'll be fine," said Jinny.

He put one hand on Helen's shoulder and one on June's shoulder, walking them companionably toward the trailer. Matt smiled at Jinny curiously, and followed. This time, when he called the dogs to come after him, Jinny could make out their names.

Goober. Sally. Pinto.

THE CAR WAS PARKED under a row of willow trees. These trees were big and old, but their leaves were thin and gave a wavering shade. Still, to be alone was a great relief.

Earlier today, driving along the highway from the town where they lived, they had stopped at a roadside stand and bought some early apples. Jinny got one out of the bag at her feet and took a small bite—more or less to see if she could taste and swallow it and hold it in her stomach. It was all right The apple was firm and tart, but not too tart, and if she took small bites and chewed seriously she could manage it.

She'd seen Neal like this—or something like this—a few times before. It would be over some boy at the school. A mention of the name in an offhand, even belittling way. A mushy look, an apologetic yet somehow defiant bit of giggling. But that was never anybody she had to have around the house, and it could never come to anything. The boy's time would be up, he'd go away.

So would this time be up. It shouldn't matter. She had to wonder if it would have mattered less yesterday than it did today.

She got out of the car, leaving the door open so that she could hang on to the inside handle. Anything on the outside was too hot to hang on to for any length of time. She had to see if she was steady. Then she walked a little, in the shade. Some of the willow leaves were already going yellow. Some were already lying on the ground. She looked out from the shade at all the things in the yard.

A dented delivery van with both headlights gone and the name on the side painted out. A baby's stroller that the dogs had chewed the seat out of, a load of firewood dumped but not stacked, a pile of huge tires, a great number of plastic jugs and some oil cans and pieces of old lumber and a couple of orange plastic tarpaulins crumpled up by the wall of the shed. What a lot of things people could find themselves in charge of. As Jinny had been in charge of all those photographs, official letters, minutes of meetings, newspaper clippings, a thousand categories that she had devised and had been putting on disk when she had to go into chemo and everything got taken away. All those things might end up being thrown out. As all this might, if Matt died.

The cornfield was the place she wanted to get to. The corn was higher than her head now, maybe higher than Neal's head—she wanted to get into the shade of it. She made her way across the yard with this one thought in mind. The dogs, thank God, must have been taken inside.

There was no fence. The cornfield just petered out into the yard. She walked straight ahead into it, onto the narrow path between two rows. The leaves flapped in her face and against her arms like streamers of oilcloth. She had to remove her hat, so they would not knock it off. Each stalk had its cob, like a baby in a shroud. There was a strong, almost sickening smell of vegetable growth, of green starch and hot sap.

What she had intended to do, once she got in there, was lie down. Lie down in the shade of these large, coarse leaves and not come out till she heard Neal calling her. Perhaps not even then. But the rows were too close together to permit that, and she was too busy thinking to take the trouble. She was too angry.

It was not about anything that had happened recently. She was remembering how a group of people had been sitting around one evening on the floor of her living room—or meeting room— playing one of those serious psychological games. One of those games that were supposed to make a person more honest and resilient. You had to say just what came into your mind as you looked at each of the others. And a white-haired woman named Addie Norton, a friend of Neal's, had said, "I hate to tell you this, Jinny, but whenever I look at you, all I can think of is—Nice Nelly."

Other people had said kinder things to her. "Flower child" or "Madonna of the Springs." She happened to know that whoever said that meant "Manon of the Springs," but she offered no correction. She was outraged at having to sit there and listen to people's opinions of her.

Everyone was wrong. She was not timid or acquiescent or natural or pure. When you died, of course, these wrong opinions were all that was left.

While this was going through her mind, she had done the easiest thing you can do in a cornfield—got lost. She had stepped over one row and then another, and probably got turned around. She tried going back the way she had come, but it obviously wasn't the right way. There were clouds over the sun again, so she couldn't tell where west was. And she had not checked which direction she was going when she entered the field, anyway, so that would not have helped. She stood still and heard nothing but the corn whispering away, and some distant traffic.

Her heart was pounding just like any heart that had years and years of life ahead of it.

Then a door opened, she heard the dogs barking and Matt yelling, and the door slammed shut. She pushed her way through stalks and leaves, in the direction of that noise. It turned out that she had not gone far at all. She had been stumbling around in one small corner of the field, the whole time.

Matt waved at her and warned off the dogs.

"Don't be scairt of them, don't be scairt," he called. He was going toward the car just as she was, though from another direction. As they got closer to each other, he spoke in a lower, perhaps more intimate, voice.

"You shoulda come and knocked on the door." He thought that she had gone into the corn to have a pee. "I just told your husband I'd come out and make sure you're O.K."

Jinny said, "I'm fine. Thank you." She got into the car but left the door open. He might be insulted if she closed it. Also, she felt too weak.

"He was sure hungry for that chili."

Who was he talking about?

Neal.

She was trembling and sweating and there was a hum in her head, as if a wire were strung between her ears.

"I could bring you some out if you'd like it."

She shook her head, smiling. He lifted up the bottle of beer in his hand—he seemed to be saluting her.

"Drink?"

She shook her head again, still smiling.

"Not even a drink of water? We got good water here."

"No, thanks." If she turned her head and looked at his purple navel, she would gag.

"You hear about this fellow going out the door with a jar of horseradish in his hand?" he said in a changed voice. "And his dad says to him, 'Where you goin' with that horseradish?'

" 'Going to get a horse,' he says.

"Dad says, 'You're not goin' to catch a horse with no horse-radish.'

"Fellow comes back next morning. Nice big horse on a halter. Puts it in the barn.

"Next day Dad sees him goin' out, bunch of branches in his hand.

" 'What's them branches in your hand?'

" 'Them's pussy willows—' "

"What are you telling me this for?" Jinny said, almost shaking. "I don't want to hear it. It's too much."

"What's the matter now?" Matt said. "All it is is a joke."

Jinny was shaking her head, squeezing her hand over her mouth.

"Never mind," he said. "I won't take no more of your time."

He turned his back on her, not even bothering to call to the dogs.

"I DO NOT wish to give the wrong impression or get carried away with optimism." The doctor had spoken in a studious, almost mechanical way. "But it looks as if we have a significant shrinkage. What we hoped for, of course. But frankly, we did not expect it. I do not mean that the battle is over. But we can be to a certain extent optimistic and proceed with the next course of chemo and see how things look then."

What are you telling me this for? I don't want to hear it. It's too much.

Jinny had not said anything like that to the doctor. Why should she? Why should she behave in such an unsatisfactory and ungrateful way, turning his news on its head? Nothing was his fault. But it was true that what he had said made everything harder. It made her have to go back and start this year all over again. It removed a certain low-grade freedom. A dull, protecting membrane that she had not even known was there had been pulled away and left her raw.

. . .

MATT'S THINKING she had gone into the cornfield to pee had made her realize that she actually wanted to. Jinny got out of the car, stood cautiously, and spread her legs and lifted her wide cotton skirt. She had taken to wearing big skirts and no panties this summer, because her bladder was no longer under perfect control.

A dark stream trickled away from her through the gravel. The sun was down now. Evening was coming on, and there was a clear sky overhead. The clouds were gone.

One of the dogs barked halfheartedly, to say that somebody was coming but somebody they knew. They had not come over to bother her when she got out of the car—they were used to her now. They went running out to meet whoever it was, without any alarm or excitement.

It was a boy, or young man, riding a bicycle. He swerved toward the car and Jinny went round to meet him, a hand on the warm fender to support herself. When he spoke to her, she did not want it to be across her puddle. And maybe to distract him from even looking on the ground for such a thing, she spoke first. She said, "Hello. Are you delivering something?"

He laughed, springing off the bike and dropping it to the ground, all in one motion.

"I live here," he said. "I'm just getting home from work."

She thought that she should explain who she was, tell him how she came to be here and for how long. But all this was too difficult. Hanging on to the car like this, she must look like somebody who had just come out of a wreck.

"Yeah, I live here," he said. "But I work in a restaurant in town. I work at Sammy's."

A waiter. The bright-white shirt and black pants were waiters' clothes. And he had a waiter's air of patience and alertness.

"I'm Jinny Lockley," she said. "Helen. Helen is—"

"O.K., I know," he said. "You're who Helen's going to work for. Where's Helen?"

"In the house."

"Didn't nobody ask you in, then?"

He was about Helen's age, she thought. Seventeen or eighteen. Slim and graceful and cocky, with an ingenuous enthusiasm that would probably not get him as far as he hoped. Jinny had seen a few like that who ended up as Young Offenders. He seemed to understand things, though. He seemed to understand that she was exhausted and in some kind of muddle.

"June in there, too?" he said. "June's my mom."

His hair was colored like June's, gold streaks over dark. He wore it rather long, and parted in the middle, flopping off to either side.

"Matt, too?" he said.

"And my husband. Yes."

"That's a shame."

"Oh, no," she said. "They asked me. I said I'd rather wait out here."

Neal used sometimes to bring home a couple of his Yo-yos, to be supervised doing lawn work or painting or basic carpentry. He thought it was good for them, to be accepted into somebody's home. Jinny had flirted with them occasionally, in a way that she could never be blamed for. Just a gentle tone, a way of making them aware of her soft skirts and her scent of apple soap. That wasn't why Neal had stopped bringing them. He had been told it was out of order.

"So how long have you been waiting?"

"I don't know," Jinny said. "I don't wear a watch."

"Is that right?" he said. "I don't, either. I don't hardly ever meet another person that doesn't wear a watch. Did you never wear one?"

She said, "No. Never."

"Me neither. Never, ever. I just never wanted to. I don't know why. Never, ever wanted to. Like, I always just seem to know what time it is anyway. Within a couple minutes. Five minutes at the most. Sometimes one of the diners asks me, 'Do you know the time,' and I just tell them. They don't even notice I'm not wearing a watch. I go and check as soon as I can, clock in the kitchen. But I never once had to go in there and tell them any different."

"I've been able to do that, too, once in a while," Jinny said. "I guess you do develop a sense, if you never wear a watch."

"Yeah, you really do."

"So what time do you think it is now?"

He laughed. He looked at the sky.

"Getting close to eight. Six, seven minutes to eight? I got an advantage, though. I know when I got off of work, and then I went to get some cigarettes at the 7-Eleven, and then I talked to some guys a couple of minutes, and then I biked home. You don't live in town, do you?"

Jinny said no.

"So, where do you live?"

She told him.

"You getting tired? You want to go home? You want me to go in and tell your husband you want to go home?"

"No. Don't do that," she said.

"O.K. O.K. I won't. June's probably telling their fortunes in there anyway. She can read hands."

"Can she?"

"Sure. She goes in the restaurant a couple of times a week. Tea, too. Tea leaves."

He picked up his bike and wheeled it out of the way of the car. Then he looked in, through the driver's window.

"Keys in the car," he said. "So—you want me to drive you home or what? Your husband can get Matt to drive him and Helen when they get ready. And he can bring me back from your place. Or if it don't look like Matt can, June can. June's my mom, but Matt's not my dad. You don't drive, do you?"

"No," said Jinny. She had not driven for months.

"No. I didn't think so. O.K. then? You want me to? O.K.?"

. . .

"THIS IS just a road I know. It'll get you there as soon as the highway."

They had not driven past the subdivision. In fact, they had headed the other way, taking a road that seemed to circle the gravel pit. At least they were going west now, toward the brightest part of the sky. Ricky—that was what he'd told her his name was—had not yet turned the car lights on.

"No danger meeting anybody," he said. "I don't think I ever met a single car on this road, ever. See—not so many people even know this road is here. And if I was to turn the lights on, then the sky would go dark, and everything would go dark, and you wouldn't be able to see where you were. We just give it a little while more, so then when it gets dark, we can see the stars, that's when we turn the lights on."

The sky was like very faintly colored glass—red or yellow or green or blue glass, depending on which part of it you looked at. The bushes and trees would turn black, once the lights were on. There would just be black clumps along the road and the black mass of trees crowding in behind them, instead of, as now, the individual, still identifiable, spruce and cedar and feathery tamarack, and the jewelweed with its flowers like winking bits of fire. It seemed close enough to touch, and they were going slowly. She put her hand out.

Not quite. But close. The road seemed hardly wider than the car.

She thought she saw the gleam of a full ditch ahead. "Is there water down there?" she said.

"Down there?" said Ricky. "Down there and everywhere. There's water to both sides of us and lots of places, water underneath us. Want to see?"

He slowed the car down and stopped. "Look down your side," he said. "Open the door and look down."

When she did that, she saw that they were on a bridge. A little bridge, no more than ten feet long, of crosswise-laid planks. No railings. And motionless water.

"Bridges all along here," he said. "And where it's not bridges it's culverts. 'Cause it's always flowing back and forth under the road. Or just laying there and not flowing."

"How deep?" she said.

"Not deep. Not this time of year. Not till we get to the big pond—it's deeper. And then, in spring, it's all over the road, you can't drive here, it's deep then. This road goes flat for miles and miles, and it goes from one end to the other. There isn't even any road that cuts across it. This is the only road I know of through the Borneo Swamp."

Jinny said, "Borneo Swamp? There is an island called Borneo. It's halfway round the world."

"I don't know about that. All I ever heard of was just the Borneo Swamp."

There was a strip of dark grass now, growing down the middle of the road.

"Time for the lights," he said. He switched them on, and they were in a tunnel in the sudden night. "Once I turned the lights on like that, and there was this porcupine. It was just sitting there in the middle of the road, sitting up on its hind legs, and looking right at me. Like some little tiny old man. It was scared to death and it couldn't move. I could see its little old teeth chattering."

Jinny thought, This is where he brings his girls.

"So what do I do? I tried beeping the horn, and it still didn't do nothing. I didn't feel like getting out and chasing it. He was scared, but he still was a porcupine and he could let fly. So I just parked there. I had time. When I turned the lights on again, he was gone." Now the branches really did reach the car and brush against the door, but if there were flowers she could not see them.

"I am going to show you something," he said. "I'm going to show you something like I bet you never seen before."

If this had been happening back in her old, normal life, it's possible that she might now have begun to be frightened. If she were back in her old, normal life she would not be here at all.

"You're going to show me a porcupine," she said.

"Nope. Not that."

A few miles farther on, he turned off the lights. "See the stars?" he said. He stopped the car. Everywhere, there was at first a deep silence. Then this silence was filled in, at the edges, by some kind of humming that could have been faraway traffic, and little noises that passed before you properly heard them, that could have been made by birds or bats or night-feeding animals.

"Come in here in the springtime," he said, "you wouldn't hear nothing but the frogs. You'd think you were going deaf with the frogs." He opened the door on his side.

"Now. Get out and walk a ways with me."

She did as she was told. She walked in one of the wheel tracks, he in the other. The sky seemed to be lighter ahead, and there was a different sound—something like mild and rhythmical conversation. The road turned to wood and the trees on either side were gone.

"Walk out on it," he said. "Go on."

He came close and touched her waist, guiding her. Then he took his hand away, left her to walk on these planks, which were like the deck of a boat. Like the deck of a boat, they rose and fell. But it wasn't a movement of waves, it was their footsteps, his and hers, that caused this rising and falling of the boards beneath them. "Now do you know where you are?" he said.

"On a dock?" she said.

"On a bridge. This is a floating bridge."

Now she could make it out—the plank roadway just a few inches above the still water. He drew her over to the side, and they looked down. There were stars riding on the water.

"It's dark all the time," he said proudly. "That's because it's a swamp. It's got the same stuff in it tea has got, and it looks like black tea."

She could see the shoreline, and the reed beds. Water in the reeds, lapping water, was what was making that sound.

"Tannin," she said.

The slight movement of the bridge made her imagine that all the trees and the reed beds were set on saucers of earth and the road was a floating ribbon of earth and underneath it all was water.

It was at this moment that she realized she didn't have her hat. She not only didn't have it on, she hadn't had it with her in the car. She had not been wearing it when she got out of the car to pee and when she began to talk to Ricky. She had not been wearing it when she sat in the car with her head back against the seat and her eyes closed, when Matt was telling his joke. She must have dropped it in the cornfield, and in her panic left it there.

While she had been scared of seeing the mound of Matt's navel with the purple shirt plastered over it, he had been looking at her bleak knob.

"It's too bad the moon isn't up yet," Ricky said. "It's really nice here when the moon is up."

"It's nice now, too."

He slipped his arms around her as if there were no question at all about what he was doing and he could take all the time he wanted to do it. He kissed her mouth. It seemed to her that this was the first time that she had ever participated in a kiss that was an event in itself. The whole story, all by itself. A tender prologue, an efficient pressure, a whole-hearted probing and receiving, a lingering thanks, and a drawing away satisfied.

"Oh," he said. "Oh."

He turned her around, and they walked back the way they had come.

. . .

"So was that the first you ever been on a floating bridge?"

She said yes, it was.

He took her hand and swung it as if he would like to toss it.

"And that's the first time I ever kissed a married woman."

"You'll probably kiss a lot more of them," she said. "Before you're done."

He sighed. "Yeah," he said. "Yeah, I probably will."

Amazed, sobered, by the thought of his future.

She had a sudden thought of Neal, back on dry land. Neal also startled by the thought of the future, giddy and besotted and disbelieving, as he opened his hand to the gaze of the woman with bright streaks in her hair.

Jinny felt a rain of compassion, almost like laughter. A swish of tender hilarity, getting the better of her sores and hollows, for the time given.

ZZ Packer

୬

Drinking Coffee Elsewhere

ORIENTATION GAMES BEGAN the day I arrived at Yale from Baltimore. In my group we played heady, frustrating games for smart people. One game appeared to be charades reinterpreted by existentialists; another involved listening to rocks. Then a freshman counsellor made everyone play Trust. The idea was that if you had the faith to fall backward and wait for four scrawny former high-school geniuses to catch you, just before your head cracked on the slate sidewalk, then you might learn to trust your fellow-students. Russian roulette sounded like a better game.

"No way," I said. The white boys were waiting for me to fall, holding their arms out for me, sincerely, gallantly. "No fucking way."

"It's all cool, it's all cool," the counsellor said. Her hair was a shade of blond I'd seen only on *Playboy* covers, and she raised her hands as though backing away from a growling dog. "Sister," she said, in an I'm-down-with-the-struggle voice, "you don't have to play this game. As a person of color, you shouldn't have to fit into any white, patriarchal system."

I said, "It's a bit too late for that."

In the next game, all I had to do was wait in a circle until it was my turn to say what inanimate object I wanted to be. One guy said he'd like to be a gadfly, like Socrates. "Stop me if I wax Platonic," he said. The girl next to him was eating a rice cake. She wanted to be the Earth, she said. Earth with a capital "E."

There was one other black person in the circle. He wore an Exeter T-shirt and his overly elastic expressions resembled a series of facial exercises. At the end of each person's turn, he smiled and bobbed his head with unfettered enthusiasm. "Oh, that was good," he said, as if the game were an experiment he'd set up and the results were turning out better than he'd expected. "Good, good, good!"

When it was my turn I said, "My name is Dina, and if I had to be any object, I guess I'd be a revolver." The sunlight dulled as if on cue. Clouds passed rapidly overhead, presaging rain. I don't know why I said it. Until that moment I'd been good in all the ways that were meant to matter. I was an honor-roll student—though I'd learned long ago not to mention it in the part of Baltimore where I lived. Suddenly I was hard-bitten and recalcitrant, the kind of kid who took pleasure in sticking pins into cats; the kind who chased down smart kids to spray them with mace.

"A revolver," a counsellor said, stroking his chin, as if it had grown a rabbinical beard. "Could you please elaborate?"

The black guy cocked his head and frowned, as if the beakers and Erlenmeyer flasks of his experiment had grown legs and scurried off.

"YOU WERE just kidding," the dean said, "about wiping out all of mankind. That, I suppose, was a joke." She squinted at me. One of her hands curved atop the other to form a pink, freckled molehill on her desk.

"Well," I said, "maybe I meant it at the time." I quickly saw that that was not the answer she wanted. "I don't know. I think it's the architecture."

Through the dimming light of the dean's-office window, I

could see the fortress of the old campus. On my ride from the bus station to the campus, I'd barely glimpsed New Haven—a flash of crumpled building here, a trio of straggly kids there. A lot like Baltimore. But everything had changed when we reached those streets hooded by the Gothic buildings. I imagined how the college must have looked when it was founded, when most of the students owned slaves. I pictured men wearing tights and knickers, smoking pipes.

"The architecture," the dean repeated. She bit her lip and seemed to be making a calculation of some sort. I noticed that she blinked less often than most people. I sat there, waiting to see how long it would be before she blinked again.

MY REVOLVER comment won me a year's worth of psychiatric counselling, weekly meetings with Dean Guest, and—since the parents of the roommate I'd never met weren't too hip on the idea of their Amy sharing a bunk bed with a budding homicidal loony—my very own room.

Shortly after getting my first D, I also received the first knock on my door. The female counsellors never knocked. The dean had spoken to them; I was a priority. Every other day, right before dinnertime, they'd look in on me, unannounced. "Just checking up," a counsellor would say. It was the voice of a suburban mother in training. By the second week, I had made a point of sitting in a chair in front of the door, just when I expected a counsellor to pop her head around. This was intended to startle them. I also made a point of being naked. The unannounced visits ended.

The knocking persisted. Through the peephole I saw a white face, distorted and balloonish.

"Let me in." The person looked like a boy but sounded like a girl. "Let me in," the voice repeated.

"Not a chance," I said.

Then the person began to sob, and I heard a back slump against the door. If I hadn't known the person was white from the peep-hole, I'd have known it from a display like this. Black people didn't knock on strangers' doors, crying. Not that I understood the black people at Yale. There was something pitiful in how cool they were. Occasionally one would reach out to me with missionary zeal, but I'd rebuff that person with haughty silence.

"I don't have anyone to talk to!" the person on the other side of the door cried.

"That is correct."

"When I was a child," the person said, "I played by myself in a corner of the schoolyard all alone. I hated dolls and I hated games, animals were not friendly and birds flew away. If anyone was look-ing for me I hid behind a tree and cried out 'I am an orphan—' "

I opened the door. It was a she.

"Plagiarist!" I yelled. She had just recited a Frank O'Hara poem as though she'd thought it up herself. I knew the poem because it was one of the few things I'd been forced to read that I wished I'd written myself.

The girl turned to face me, smiling weakly, as though her tri-umph were not in getting me to open the door but in the fact that she was able to smile at all when she was so accustomed to crying. She was large but not obese, and crying had turned her face the color of raw chicken. She blew her nose into the waist end of her T-shirt, revealing a pale belly.

"How do you know that poem?"

She sniffed. "I'm in your Contemporary Poetry class."

She was Canadian and her name was Heidi, although she said she wanted people to call her Henrik. "That's a guy's name," I said. "What do you want? A sex change?"

She looked at me with so little surprise that I suspected she hadn't discounted this as an option. Then her story came out in teary, hiccup-like bursts. She had sucked some "cute guy's dick" and he'd told everybody and now people thought she was "a slut."

"Why'd you suck his dick? Aren't you a lesbian?"

She fit the bill. Short hair, hard, roach-stomping shoes. Dressed like an aspiring plumber. The lesbians I'd seen on TV were wiry, thin strips of muscle, but Heidi was round and soft and had a moonlike face. Drab mud-colored hair. And lesbians had cats. "Do you have a cat?" I asked.

Her eyes turned glossy with new tears. "No," she said, her voice wavering, "and I'm not a lesbian. Are you?"

"Do I look like one?" I said.

She didn't answer.

"O.K.," I said. "I could suck a guy's dick, too, if I wanted. But I don't. The human penis is one of the most germ-ridden objects there is." Heidi looked at me, unconvinced. "What I meant to say," I began again, "is that I don't like anybody. Period. Guys or girls. I'm a misanthrope."

"I am, too."

"No," I said, guiding her back through my door and out into the hallway. "You're not."

"Have you had dinner?" she asked. "Let's go to Commons."

I pointed to a pyramid of ramen noodle packages on my windowsill. "See that? That means I never have to go to Commons. Aside from class, I have contact with no one."

"I hate it here, too," she said. "I should have gone to McGill, eh."

"The way to feel better," I said, "is to get some ramen and lock yourself in your room. Everyone will forget about you and that guy's dick and you won't have to see anyone ever again. If anyone looks for you—"

"I'll hide behind a tree."

"A REVOLVER?" Dr. Raeburn said, flipping through a manila folder. He looked up at me as if to ask another question, but he didn't.

Dr. Raeburn was the psychiatrist. He had the gray hair and

whiskers of a Civil War general. He was also a chain smoker with beige teeth and a navy wool jacket smeared with ash. He asked about the revolver at the beginning of my first visit. When I was unable to explain myself he smiled, as if this were perfectly respectable.

"Tell me about your parents."

I wondered what he already had on file. The folder was thick, though I hadn't said a thing of significance since Day One.

"My father was a dick and my mother seemed to like him."

He patted his pockets for his cigarettes. "That's some heavy stuff," he said. "How do you feel about Dad?" The man couldn't say the word "father." "Is Dad someone you see often?"

"I hate my father almost as much as I hate the word 'Dad.'"

He started tapping his cigarette.

"You can't smoke in here."

"That's right," he said, and slipped the cigarette back into the packet. He smiled, widening his eyes brightly. "Don't ever start."

I THOUGHT that that first encounter would be the last of Heidi, but then her head appeared in a window of Linsly-Chit during my Chaucer class. Next, she swooped down a flight of stairs in Harkness. She hailed me from across Elm Street and found me in the Sterling Library stacks. After one of my meetings with Dr. Raeburn, she was waiting for me outside Health Services, legs crossed, cleaning her fingernails.

"You know," she said, as we walked through Old Campus, "you've got to stop eating ramen. Not only does it lack a single nutrient but it's full of MSG."

"I like eating chemicals," I said. "It keeps the skin radiant."

"There's also hepatitis." She already knew how to get my attention—mention a disease.

"You get hepatitis from unwashed lettuce," I said. "If there's anything safe from the perils of the food chain, it's ramen."

"But you refrigerate what you don't eat. Each time you reheat it, you're killing good bacteria, which then can't keep the bad bacteria in check. A guy got sick from reheating Chinese noodles, and his son died from it. I read it in the *Times*." With this, she put a jovial arm around my neck. I continued walking, a little stunned. Then, just as quickly, she dropped her arm and stopped walking. I stopped, too.

"Did you notice that I put my arm around you?"

"Yes," I said. "Next time, I'll have to chop it off."

"I don't want you to get sick," she said. "Let's eat at Commons."

In the cold air, her arm had felt good.

THE PROBLEM with Commons was that it was too big; its ceiling was as high as a cathedral's, but below it there were no awestruck worshippers, only eighteen-year-olds at heavy wooden tables, chatting over veal patties and Jell-O.

We got our food, tacos stuffed with meat substitute, and made our way through the maze of tables. The Koreans had a table. Each singing group had a table. The crew team sat at a long table of its own. We passed the black table. The sheer quantity of Heidi's flesh accentuated just how white she was.

"How you doing, sista?" a guy asked, his voice full of accusation, eyeballing me as though I were clad in a Klansman's sheet and hood. "I guess we won't see you till graduation."

"If," I said, "you graduate."

The remark was not well received. As I walked past, I heard protests, angry and loud, as if they'd discovered a cheat at their poker game. Heidi and I found an unoccupied table along the periphery, which was isolated and dark. We sat down. Heidi prayed over her tacos.

"I thought you didn't believe in God," I said.

"Not in the God depicted in the Judeo-Christian Bible, but I do believe that nature's essence is a spirit that—"

"All right," I said. I had begun to eat, and cubes of diced tomato fell from my mouth when I spoke. "Stop right there. Tacos and spirits don't mix."

"You've always got to be so flip," she said. "I'm going to apply for another friend."

"There's always Mr. Dick," I said. "Slurp, slurp."

"You are so lame. So unbelievably lame. I'm going out with Mr. Dick. Thursday night at Atticus. His name is Keith."

Heidi hadn't mentioned Mr. Dick since the day I'd met her. That was more than a month ago and we'd spent a lot of that time together. I checked for signs that she was lying, her habit of smiling too much, her eyes bright and cheeks full, so that she looked like a chipmunk. But she looked normal. Pleased, even, to see me so flustered.

"You're insane! What are you going to do this time?" I asked. "Sleep with him? Then when he makes fun of you, what? Come pound your head on my door reciting the 'Collected Poems of Sylvia Plath'?"

"He's going to apologize for before. And don't call me insane. You're the one going to the psychiatrist."

'Well, I'm not going to suck his dick, that's for sure."

She put her arm around me in mock comfort, but I pushed it off, and ignored her. She touched my shoulder again, and I turned, annoyed, but it wasn't Heidi after all; a sepia-toned boy dressed in khakis and a crisp plaid shirt was standing behind me. He handed me a hot-pink square of paper without a word, then briskly made his way toward the other end of Commons, where the crowds blossomed. Heidi leaned over and read it: "Wear Black Leather— the Less, the Better."

"It's a gay party," I said, crumpling the card. "He thinks we're fucking gay."

· · ·

HEIDI AND I signed on to work at the Saybrook Dining Hall as dishwashers. The job consisted of dumping food from plates and trays into a vat of rushing water. It seemed straightforward, but then I learned better. You wouldn't believe what people could do with food until you worked in a dish room. Lettuce and crackers and soup would be bullied into a pulp in the bowl of some bored anorexic; ziti would be mixed with honey and granola; trays would appear heaped with mashed-potato snow women with melted chocolate ice cream for hair. Frat boys arrived at the dish-room window, en masse. They liked to fill glasses with food, then seal them, airtight, onto their trays. If you tried to prize them off, milk, Worcestershire sauce, peas, chunks of bread vomited onto your dish-room uniform.

When this happened one day in the middle of the lunch rush, for what seemed like the hundredth time, I tipped the tray toward one of the frat boys, popping the glasses off so that the mess spurted onto his Shetland sweater.

He looked down at his sweater. "Lesbo bitch!"

"No," I said, "that would be your mother."

Heidi, next to me, clenched my arm in support, but I remained motionless, waiting to see what the frat boy would do. He glared at me for a minute, then walked away.

"Let's take a smoke break," Heidi said.

I didn't smoke, but Heidi had begun to, because she thought it would help her lose weight. As I hefted a stack of glasses through the steamer, she lit up.

"Soft packs remind me of you," she said. "Just when you've smoked them all and you think there's none left, there's always one more, hiding in that little crushed corner." Before I could respond she said, "Oh, God. Not another mouse. You know whose job that is."

By the end of the rush, the floor mats got full and slippery with food. This was when mice tended to appear, scurrying over our shoes; more often than not, a mouse got caught in the grating that covered the drains in the floor. Sometimes the mouse was already dead by the time we noticed it. This one was alive.

"No way," I said. "This time you're going to help. Get some gloves and a trash bag."

"That's all I'm getting. I'm not getting that mouse out of there."

"Put on the gloves," I ordered. She winced, but put them on. "Reach down," I said. "At an angle, so you get at its middle. Otherwise, if you try to get it by its tail, the tail will break off."

"This is filthy, eh."

"That's why we're here," I said. "To clean up filth. Eh."

She reached down, but would not touch the mouse. I put my hand around her arm and pushed it till her hand made contact. The cries from the mouse were soft, songlike. "Oh, my God," she said. Oh, my God, ohmigod." She wrestled it out of the grating and turned her head away.

"Don't you let it go," I said.

"Where's the food bag? It'll smother itself if I drop it in the food bag. Quick," she said, her head still turned away, her eyes closed. "Lead me to it."

"No. We are not going to smother this mouse. We've got to break its neck."

"You're one heartless bitch."

I wondered how to explain that if death is unavoidable it should be quick and painless. My mother had died slowly. At the hospital, they'd said it was kidney failure, but I knew that, in the end, it was my father. He made her scared to live in her own home, until she was finally driven away from it in an ambulance.

"Breaking its neck will save it the pain of smothering," I said. "Breaking its neck is more humane. Take the trash bag and cover it so you won't get any blood on you, then crush."

The loud jets of the steamer had shut off automatically and the dish room grew quiet. Heidi breathed in deeply, then crushed the mouse. She shuddered, disgusted. "Now what?"

"What do you mean, 'Now what?' Throw the little bastard in the trash."

AT OUR THIRD SESSION, I told Dr. Raeburn I didn't mind if he smoked. He sat on the sill of his open window, smoking behind a jungle screen of office plants.

We spent the first ten minutes discussing the Iliad, and whether or not the text actually states that Achilles had been dipped in the River Styx. He said it did, and I said it didn't. After we'd finished with the Iliad, and with my new job in what he called "the scullery," he asked more questions about my parents. I told him nothing. It was none of his business. Instead, I talked about Heidi. I told him about that day in Commons, Heidi's plan to go on a date with Mr. Dick, and the invitation we'd been given to the gay party.

"You seem preoccupied by this soirée." He arched his eyebrows at the word "soirée."

"Wouldn't you be?"

"Dina," he said slowly, in a way that made my name seem like a song title, "have you ever had a romantic interest?"

"You want to know if I've ever had a boyfriend?" I said. "Just go ahead and ask if I've ever fucked anybody."

This appeared to surprise him. "I think that you are having a crisis of identity," he said.

"Oh, is that what this is?"

His profession had taught him not to roll his eyes. Instead, his exasperation revealed itself with a tiny pursing of his lips, as though he'd just tasted something awful and were trying very hard not to offend the cook.

"It doesn't have to be, as you say, someone you've fucked, it doesn't have to be a boyfriend," he said.

"Well, what are you trying to say? If it's not a boy, then you're saying it's a girl—"

"Calm down. It could be a crush, Dina." He lit one cigarette off another. "A crush on a male teacher, a crush on a dog, for heaven's sake. An interest. Not necessarily a relationship."

It was sacrifice time. If I could spend the next half hour talking about some boy, then I'd have given him what he wanted.

So I told him about the boy with the nice shoes.

I was sixteen and had spent the last few coins in my pocket on bus fare to buy groceries. I didn't like going to the Super Fresh two blocks away from my house, plunking government food stamps into the hands of the cashiers.

"There she go reading," one of them once said, even though I was only carrying a book. "Don't your eyes get tired?"

On Greenmount Avenue you could read schoolbooks—that was understandable. The government and your teachers forced you to read them. But anything else was anti-social. It meant you'd rather submit to the words of some white dude than shoot the breeze with your neighbors.

I hated those cashiers, and I hated them seeing me with food stamps, so I took the bus and shopped elsewhere. That day, I got off the bus at Govans, and though the neighborhood was black like my own—hair salon after hair salon of airbrushed signs promising arabesque hair styles and inch-long fingernails—the houses were neat and orderly, nothing at all like Greenmount, where every other house had at least one shattered window. The store was well swept, and people quietly checked long grocery lists—no screaming kids, no loud cashier-customer altercations. I got the groceries and left the store.

I decided to walk back. It was a fall day, and I walked for blocks. Then I sensed someone following me. I walked more quickly, my arms around the sack, the leafy lettuce tickling my nose. I didn't want to hold the sack so close that it would break the eggs or squash the hamburger buns, but it was slipping, and as I looked behind a boy my age, maybe older, rushed toward me.

"Let me help you," he said.

"That's all right." I set the bag on the sidewalk. Maybe I saw his face, maybe it was handsome enough, but what I noticed first, splayed on either side of the bag, were his shoes. They were nice shoes, real leather, a stitched design like a widow's peak on each one, or like birds' wings, and for the first time in my life I understood what people meant when they said "wing-tip shoes."

"I watched you carry them groceries out that store, then you look around, like you're lost, but like you liked being lost, then you walk down the sidewalk for blocks and blocks. Rearranging that bag, it almost gone to slip, then hefting it back up again."

"Huh, huh," I said.

"And then I passed my own house and was still following you. And then your bag really look like it was gone crash and everything. So I just thought I'd help." He sucked in his bottom lip, as if to keep it from making a smile. "What's your name?" When I told him, he said, "Dina, my name is Cecil." Then he said, " 'D' comes right after 'C.' "

"Yes," I said, "it does, doesn't it."

Then, half question, half statement, he said, "I could carry your groceries for you? And walk you home?"

I stopped the story there. Dr. Raeburn kept looking at me. "Then what happened?"

I couldn't tell him the rest: that I had not wanted the boy to walk me home, that I didn't want someone with such nice shoes to see where I lived.

Dr. Raeburn would only have pitied me if I'd told him that I ran down the sidewalk after I told the boy no, that I fell, the bag slipped, and the eggs cracked, their yolks running all over the lettuce. Clear amniotic fluid coated the can of cinnamon rolls. I left the bag there on the sidewalk, the groceries spilled out randomly like cards loosed from a deck. When I returned home, I told my mother that I'd lost the food stamps.

"Lost?" she said. I'd expected her to get angry, I'd wanted her to get angry, but she hadn't. "Lost?" she repeated. Why had I been so clumsy and nervous around a harmless boy? I could have brought the groceries home and washed off the egg yolk, but, instead, I'd just left them there. "Come on," Mama said, snuffing her tears, pulling my arm, trying to get me to join her and start yanking cushions off the couch. "We'll find enough change here. We got to get something for dinner before your father gets back."

We'd already searched the couch for money the previous week, and I knew there'd be nothing now, but I began to push my fingers into the couch's boniest corners, pretending that it was only a matter of time before I'd find some change or a lost watch or an earring. Something pawnable, perhaps.

"What happened next?" Dr. Raeburn asked again. "Did you let the boy walk you home?"

"My house was far, so we went to his house instead." Though I was sure Dr. Raeburn knew that I was making this part up, I continued. "We made out on his sofa. He kissed me."

Dr. Raeburn lit his next cigarette like a detective. Cool, suspicious. "How did it feel?"

"You know," I said. "Like a kiss feels. It felt nice. The kiss felt very, very nice."

Raeburn smiled gently, though he seemed unconvinced. When he called time on our session his cigarette had become one long pole of ash. I left his office, walking quickly down the corridor, afraid to look back. It would be like him to trot after me, his navy blazer flapping, just to eke the truth out of me. *You never kissed anyone.* The words slid from my brain, and knotted in my stomach.

When I reached my dorm, I found an old record player blocking my door and a Charles Mingus LP propped beside it. I carried them inside and then, lying on the floor, I played the Mingus over and over again until I fell asleep. I slept feeling as though Dr. Raeburn had attached electrodes to my head, willing into my mind a dream about my mother. I saw the lemon meringue of her skin, the long bone of her arm as she reached down to clip her toenails. I'd come home from a school trip to an aquarium, and I was explaining the differences between baleen and sperm whales according to the size of their heads, the range of their habitats, their feeding patterns.

I awoke remembering the expression on her face after I'd finished my dizzying whale lecture. She looked like a tourist who'd asked for directions to a place she thought was simple enough to get to only to hear a series of hypothetical turns, alleys, one-way streets. Her response was to nod politely at the perilous elaborateness of it all; to nod in the knowledge that she would never be able to get where she wanted to go.

THE DISHWASHERS always closed down the dining hall. One night, after everyone else had punched out, Heidi and I took a break, and though I wasn't a smoker, we set two milk crates upside down on the floor and smoked cigarettes.

The dishwashing machines were off, but steam still rose from them like a jungle mist. Outside in the winter air, students were singing carols in their groomed and tailored singing-group voices. The Whiffenpoofs were back in New Haven after a tour around the world, and I guess their return was a huge deal. Heidi and I craned our necks to watch the year's first snow through an open window.

"What are you going to do when you're finished?" Heidi asked. Sexy question marks of smoke drifted up to the windows before vanishing.

"Take a bath."

She swatted me with her free hand. "No, silly. Three years from now. When you leave Yale."

"I don't know. Open up a library. Somewhere where no one comes in for books. A library in a desert."

She looked at me as though she'd expected this sort of answer and didn't know why she'd asked in the first place.

"What are you going to do?" I asked her.

"Open up a psych clinic. In a desert. And my only patient will be some wacko who runs a library."

"Ha," I said. "Whatever you do, don't work in a dish room ever again. You're no good." I got up from the crate. "C'mon. Let's hose the place down."

We put out our cigarettes on the floor, since it was our job to clean it, anyway. We held squirt guns in one hand and used the other to douse the floors with the standard-issue, eye-burning cleaning solution. We hosed the dish room, the kitchen, the serving line, sending the water and crud and suds into the drains. Then we hosed them again so the solution wouldn't eat holes in our shoes as we left. Then I had an idea. I unbuckled my belt.

"What the hell are you doing?" Heidi said.

"Listen, it's too cold to go outside with our uniforms all wet. We could just take a shower right here. There's nobody but us."

"What the fuck, eh?"

I let my pants drop, then took off my shirt and panties. I didn't wear a bra, since I didn't have much to fill one. I took off my shoes and hung my clothes on the stepladder.

"You've flipped," Heidi said. "I mean, really, psych-ward flipped."

I soaped up with the liquid hand soap until I felt as glazed as a ham. "Stand back and spray me."

"Oh, my God," she said. I didn't know whether she was confused or delighted, but she picked up the squirt gun and sprayed me. She was laughing. Then she got too close and the water started to sting.

"God damn it!" I said. "That hurt!"

"I was wondering what it would take to make you say that."

When all the soap had been rinsed off, I put on my regular clothes and said, "O.K. You're up next."

"No way," she said.

"Yes way."

She started to take off her uniform shirt, then stopped.

"What?"

"I'm too fat."

"You goddam right." She always said she was fat. One time, I'd told her that she should shut up about it, that large black women wore their fat like mink coats. "You're big as a house," I said now. "Frozen yogurt may be low in calories but not if you eat five tubs of it. Take your clothes off. I want to get out of here."

She began taking off her uniform, then stood there, hands cupped over her breasts, crouching at the pubic bone.

"Open up," I said, "or we'll never get done."

Her hands remained where they were. I threw the bottle of liquid soap at her, and she had to catch it, revealing herself as she did.

I turned on the squirt gun, and she stood there, stiff, arms at her sides, eyes closed, as though awaiting mummification. I began with the water on low, and she turned around in a full circle, hesitantly, letting the droplets from the spray fall on her as if she were submitting to a death by stoning.

When I increased the water pressure, she slipped and fell on the sudsy floor. She stood up and then slipped again. This time she laughed and remained on the floor, rolling around on it as I sprayed.

I think I began to love Heidi that night in the dish room, but who is to say that I hadn't begun to love her the first time I met her? I sprayed her and sprayed her, and she turned over and over like a large beautiful dolphin, lolling about in the sun.

HEIDI STARTED sleeping at my place. Sometimes she slept on the floor; sometimes we slept sardinelike, my feet at her head, until she complained that my feet were "taunting" her. When we finally slept head to head, she said, "Much better." She was so close I could smell her toothpaste. "I like your hair," she told me, touching it through the darkness. "You should wear it out more often."

282 / MORE STORIES WE TELL

"White people always say that about black people's hair. The worse it looks, the more they say they like it."

I'd expected her to disagree, but she kept touching my hair, her hands passing through it till my scalp tingled. When she began to touch the hair around the edge of my face, I felt myself quake. Her fingertips stopped for a moment, as if checking my pulse, then resumed.

"I like how it feels right here. See, mine just starts with the same old texture as the rest of my hair." She found my hand under the blanket and brought it to her hairline. "See," she said.

It was dark. As I touched her hair, it seemed as though I could smell it, too. Not a shampoo smell. Something richer, murkier. A bit dead, but sweet, like the decaying wood of a ship. She guided my hand.

"I see," I said. The record she'd given me was playing in my mind, and I kept trying to shut it off. I could also hear my mother saying that this is what happens when you've been around white people: things get weird. So weird I could hear the stylus etching its way into the flat vinyl of the record. "Listen," I said finally, when the bass and saxes started up. I heard Heidi breathe deeply, but she said nothing.

WE SPENT the winter and some of the spring in my room—never hers—missing tests, listening to music, looking out my window to comment on people who wouldn't have given us a second thought. We read books related to none of our classes. I got riled up by "The Autobiography of Malcolm X" and "The Chomsky Reader"; Heidi read aloud passages from "The Anxiety of Influence." We guiltily read mysteries and "Clan of the Cave Bear," then immediately threw them away. Once, we looked up from our books at exactly the same moment, as though trapped at a dinner table with nothing to say. A pleasant trap of silence.

Then one weekend I went back to Baltimore. When I returned, to a sleepy, tree-scented spring, a group of students were holding what was called "Coming Out Day." I watched it from my room.

The m.c. was the sepia boy who'd invited us to that party months back. His speech was strident but still smooth, and peppered with jokes. There was a speech about AIDS, with lots of statistics: nothing that seemed to make "coming out" worth it. Then the women spoke. One girl pronounced herself "out" as casually as if she'd announced the time. Another said nothing at all: she appeared at the microphone accompanied by a woman who began cutting off her waist-length, bleached-blond hair. The woman doing the cutting tossed the shorn hair in every direction as she cut. People were clapping and cheering and catching the locks of hair.

And then there was Heidi. She was proud that she liked girls, she said when she reached the microphone. She loved them, wanted to sleep with them. She was a dyke, she said repeatedly, stabbing her finger to her chest in case anyone was unsure to whom she was referring. She could not have seen me. I was across the street, three stories up. And yet, when everyone clapped for her, she seemed to be looking straight at me.

HEIDI KNOCKED. "Let me in."

It was like the first time I met her. The tears, the raw pink of her face.

We hadn't spoken in weeks. Outside, pink-and-white blossoms hung from the Old Campus trees. Students played hackeysack in T-shirts and shorts. Though I was the one who'd broken away after she went up to that podium, I still half expected her to poke her head out a window in Linsly-Chit, or tap on my back in Harkness, or even join me in the Commons dining hall, where I'd asked for my dish-room shift to be transferred. She did none of these.

"Well," I said, "what is it?"

She looked at me. "My mother," she said.

She continued to cry, but it seemed to have grown so silent in my room I wondered if I could hear the numbers change on my digital clock.

"When my parents were getting divorced," she said, "my mother bought a car. A used one. An El Dorado. It was filthy. It looked like a huge crushed can coming up the street. She kept trying to clean it out. I mean—"

I nodded and tried to think what to say in the pause she left behind. Finally I said, "We had one of those," though I was sure ours was an Impala.

She looked at me, eyes steely from trying not to cry. "Anyway, she'd drive me around in it and although she didn't like me to eat in it, I always did. One day, I was eating cantaloupe slices, spitting the seeds on the floor. Maybe a month later, I saw this little sprout, growing right up from the car floor. I just started laughing and she kept saying what, what? I was laughing and then I saw she was so—"

She didn't finish. So what? So sad? So awful? Heidi looked at me with what seemed to be a renewed vigor. "We could have gotten a better car, eh?"

"It's all right. It's not a big deal," I said.

Of course, that was the wrong thing to say. And I really didn't mean it to sound the way it had come out.

I TOLD Dr. Raeburn about Heidi's mother having cancer and how I'd said it wasn't a big deal, though I'd wanted to say exactly the opposite. I meant that I knew what it was like to have a parent die. My mother had died. I knew how eventually one accustoms oneself to the physical world's lack of sympathy: the buses that still run on time, the kids who still play in the street, the clocks that won't stop ticking for the person who's gone.

"You're pretending," Dr. Raeburn said, not sage or professional but a little shocked by the discovery, as if I'd been trying to hide a pack of his cigarettes behind my back.

"I'm pretending?" I shook my head. "All those years of psych grad," I said. "And to tell me *that?*"

"You construct stories about yourself and dish them out—one for you, one for you—" Here he reenacted the process, showing me handing out lies as if they were apples.

"Pretending. I believe the professional name for it might be denial," I said. "Are you calling me gay?"

He pursed his lips noncommittally. "No, Dina. I don't think you're gay."

I checked his eyes. I couldn't read them.

"No. Not at all," he said, sounding as if he were telling a subtle joke. "But maybe you'll finally understand."

"Understand what?"

"That constantly saying what one doesn't mean accustoms the mouth to meaningless phrases." His eyes narrowed. "Maybe you'll understand that when you need to express something truly significant, your mouth will revert to the insignificant nonsense it knows so well." He looked at me, his hands sputtering in the air in a gesture of defeat. "Who knows?" he asked, with a glib, psychiatric smile I'd never seen before. "Maybe it's your survival mechanism. Black living in a white world."

I heard him, but only vaguely. I'd hooked on to that one word, pretending. What Dr. Raeburn would never understand was that pretending was what had got me this far. I remembered the morning of my mother's funeral. I'd been given milk to settle my stomach; I'd pretended it was coffee. I imagined I was drinking coffee elsewhere. Some Arabic-speaking country where the thick coffee served in little cups was so strong it could keep you awake for days. Some Arabic country where I'd sit in a tented café and be more than happy to don a veil.

. . .

HEIDI WANTED me to go with her to the funeral. She'd sent this message through the dean. "We'll pay for your ticket to Vancouver," the dean said.

"What about my ticket back?" I asked. "Maybe the shrink will pay for that."

The dean looked at me as though I were an insect she'd like to squash. "We'll pay for the whole thing. We might even pay for some lessons in manners."

So I packed my suitcase and walked from my suicide-single dorm to Heidi's room. A thin wispy girl in ragged cutoffs and a shirt that read "LSBN!" answered the door. A group of short-haired girls in thick black leather jackets, bundled up despite the summer heat, encircled Heidi in a protective fairy ring. They looked at me critically, clearly wondering if Heidi was too fragile for my company.

"You've got our numbers," one said, holding onto Heidi's shoulder. "And Vancouver's got a great gay community."

"Oh God," I said. "She's going to a funeral, not a 'Save the Dykes' rally."

One of the girls stepped in front of me.

"It's O.K., Cynthia," Heidi said. Then she ushered me into her bedroom and closed the door. A suitcase was on her bed, half packed. She folded a polka-dotted T-shirt that was wrong for any occasion. "Why haven't you talked to me?" she said. "Why haven't you talked to me in two months?"

"I don't know," I said.

"You don't know," she said, each syllable seeped in sarcasm. "You don't know. Well, I know. You thought I was going to try to sleep with you."

"Try to? We slept together all winter!"

"Smelling your feet is not 'sleeping together.' You've got a lot to learn." She seemed thinner and meaner.

"So tell me," I said. "What can you show me that I need to learn?" But as soon as I said it I somehow knew that she still hadn't slept with anyone.

"Am I supposed to come over there and sweep your enraged self into my arms?" I said. "Like in the movies? Is this the part where we're both so mad we kiss each other?"

She shook her head and smiled weakly. "You don't get it," she said. "My mother is dead." She closed her suitcase, clicking shut the old-fashioned locks. "My mother is dead," she said again, this time reminding herself. She set the suitcase upright on the floor and sat on it. She looked like someone waiting for a train.

"Fine," I said. "And she's going to be dead for a long time." Though it sounded stupid, I felt good saying it. As though I had my own locks to click shut.

HEIDI WENT to Vancouver for her mother's funeral. I didn't go. Instead, I went back to Baltimore and moved in with an aunt I barely knew. Every day was the same: I read and smoked outside my aunt's apartment, studying the row of hair salons across the street, where girls in denim cut-offs and tank tops would troop in and come out hours later, a flash of neon nails, coifs the color and sheen of patent leather. And every day I imagined visiting Heidi in Vancouver. Her house would not be large, but it would be clean. Flowery shrubs would line the walks. The Canadian wind would whip us about like pennants. I'd be visiting her at some vague time in the future, deliberately vague, for people like me, who realign past events to suit themselves. In that future time, you always have a chance to catch the groceries before they fall, your words can always be rewound and erased, rewritten and revised.

But once I imagined Heidi visiting me. There would be no psychiatrists or deans. No boys with nice shoes or flip cashiers. Just me in my single room. She would knock on the door and say, "Open up."

Marisa Silver

ᴕ

The Passenger

I HAVE A RING in my nose and a ring in my navel, and people make assumptions about me. None of them are true. I'm not a punk or a slave, a biker chick or a fashion hag.

I drive a limo. I take people where they want to go—to parties and airports, to score drugs at a ranch house or a piece of ass at a hotel bar. On any given night, I'll be taking the curves on Mulholland, hitting a prom in Northridge, or, if I'm lucky, flying the straight shot out the highway to Malibu. People think Los Angeles is the same everywhere—all palm trees and swimming pools. But some nights you need a passport and a two-way dictionary just to get from Hancock Park to Koreatown.

Ruthanne's my dispatcher. I've never met her but she's probably the person I talk to most. Once I saw her red jacket hanging off a chair at the office. It had a dog appliquéd across the back. Normally someone who would wear that jacket would have nothing to say to me, and so, in a sense, not meeting has brought us closer. Right now, her voice crackles over my car radio.

"EX-LAX," she says, using her helium balloon voice. "Who wants to shit or get off the pot?"

EX-LAX is her shorthand for saying there's a pickup at LAX,

the airport. She says "re-lax" when you have to make your second airport trip. Ha, ha, ha, right? But I'm smiling.

I pick up my handset. "Twenty-two. I'm all over it." We're required to use our call number, but Ruthie never does. She calls me by my name, Babe.

"Okay, Babe," she says. "You're picking up two Chins outside international baggage."

"No way."

"Yes way," she says. "You'll have to circle the drain."

I click off. The usual airport routine is that I park the limo and wait at the arrivals gate, holding a piece of cardboard with a stranger's name on it. Finally, a passenger comes off the plane. He'll smile when he sees his name, delighted that he's the same guy he was before he took off. Sometimes he'll be so relieved that he'll shake my hand, like I care one way or another. It's moments like these that kill me.

But meeting someone outside baggage is an ordeal. Security is tight, and you can't wait by the curb for more than twenty seconds before some uniform appears, telling you to scram. So you have to drive around and around until you actually see the pickup.

I click on my radio again. "It could take an hour," I complain.

"You vant I should give it to someone else, *daah-link*?" Ruthie answers, doing her Gabor sisters impersonation.

"No," I say quickly. International is promising in other ways—people are often confused by the exchange rate. I once got a hundred-dollar tip from an Indian family that had fastened their suitcases together with electrical tape. I felt bad about taking it, but not so bad about having it.

I'M TWENTY-THREE. I live alone in a second-story box on Lincoln Boulevard. I had a boyfriend for a while. I liked him, then I didn't. I have a few friends left over from high school, and we go drinking sometimes, but lately I'm not sure why. We get together and moan about rent, or we get worked up telling stories we've told before. We end up staring into our drinks because facing each other is like looking into a mirror in bad lighting.

A few years ago, my mother left L.A. to join a spiritual community in the desert. This makes it sound like she's living in a collection of gassy, glowing matter; in fact, it's a bunch of trailers on a scrubby piece of land near a Marine base.

After she left, I worked as a waitress, a copy-shop clerk, a messenger—all those jobs you get when you have nothing but a couple of community college credits in highly useless things like world literature. The difference between me and the other employees was that I didn't want to be something else. With all the other people it was, "I work in a copy shop, but I really want to act." Or, "I sell subscriptions over the phone, but I have this great idea for an Internet company." Not that I want to drive a car for the rest of my life, but I'm willing to say that driving is what I do for now.

The fifth time I circle international baggage, people begin to pour out the doors. Most of the passengers wear wrinkled nylon track suits and baseball caps with American logos—walking advertisements for a place they're seeing for the first time. These people look dazed. All but a few are Asian and I have no idea how I'm going to find my fare. Then I see a man and a woman standing at the curb with a very large black suitcase between them, and for some reason I know that they are my Chins. She's wearing a neatly cut jacket and a matching skirt. Her black high heels are so polished they reflect the lights overhead. He wears a double-breasted suit that hangs loosely over his thin body. His hair is swooped back into a gentle pompadour, and it's shiny with whatever goop he put into it. You'd never guess that these two had just spent the day on an airplane.

"Mr. and Mrs. Chin?" I call out of the passenger-side window. They don't respond for a moment, but then they nod enthusiastically. I pop the trunk and hop out of the car. I reach for their suitcase, but Mr. Chin waves me away and points towards the back seat.

"It's safer to put it in the trunk," I explain. "If the car stops suddenly, the case could fly into your face."

They both smile, as if I've said something amusing but not exactly funny, and I realize that they don't understand a word I'm saying. I go for the suitcase again, but Mr. Chin steps in front of me, shaking his head. Mrs. Chin slides into the back seat like a swan, her legs pressed together, and holds out her hands to take the suitcase, which Mr. Chin pushes inside. Finally, he tucks himself neatly into the space left over and waits for me to shut the door. I think for a minute about pressing the point: it's company policy to put luggage in the trunk. If the Chins got hit with that hard plastic bag, they could sue and I'd be out of a job in the blink of an eye. But I let it go. People do things a million different ways. It's when you interfere that guns are drawn.

I get into the driver's seat, and Mr. Chin hands me a piece of paper through the privacy window. They want to go to Tarzana. I'm surprised. I would have thought they were visiting relatives in Monterey Park or staying in one of the downtown hotels. I call my destination in to Ruthanne.

"Tarzana," she repeats after me, and she gives her trademark jungle yodel.

I start the car and head towards the 405. It's still early and I have eight hours of road ahead.

THE FIRST TIME my mother tried to off herself, I was nineteen, already living alone, working shifts at an industrial laundry on Highland. So she called me to tell me.

"Babe," she said. "I'm leaving now."

"You're calling me to tell me you're leaving the house?"

"I'm leaving," she said. "In the final sense of the word."

"Delia," I said, the way I did when I wanted to get her attention, "what the hell are you talking about?"

She said she had taken an entire bottle of Xanax. She was getting yawny and slurry as we were talking, and I couldn't get her to tell me how many pills had been in the bottle. But, since she usually avoided taking her pills when she needed them, I figured that "entire" might be the truth.

"Don't move," I said. "Don't do anything."

When I got to her shabby rental in Laurel Canyon, she was sitting on her couch with her legs crossed underneath her. Her orange dress, missing half its sequined flowers, covered her knees like a tent. Bubbles of spit shone on her chin and there was vomit on her dress.

"Babe!" she said, as if I were dropping in for a surprise visit.

"How many did you take?" I asked. The bottle of pills was on the coffee table.

"Just a couple," she said. "I started to gag and then everything just came up and out." She giggled and covered her mouth like a girl on a date. "Want some tea? Or I could make us some lunch?"

"I have to go back to work," I said. "They'll dock my pay."

"Okay," she said, pouting. She played with the sequins on her dress. "I'm fine, I guess."

"I'll come back later," I said. "I'll bring you dinner."

"That would be nice." Her voice was drifting away, like some balloon a kid had let go of. She closed her eyes. "How's the laundry, Babe?"

"How?"

"Yeah. What's it like?"

"It's like dirty sheets getting clean."

"Um," she said. She smiled and nodded as though she were remembering some favorite childhood dessert. Her long hair had begun to make her look older and I could see age spots on her chest.

I went to work, where I unloaded soggy restaurant tablecloths and hospital sheets from the washing machines and crammed them into carriers strung from the ceiling. After eight hours, my apron was soaked and my hands were waterlogged, and I was a little high off the dryer fumes. When I walked out onto Highland, I had the feeling I was swimming. The noise of the traffic was like the rubbery sounds you hear underwater.

Later that night, I brought bad Mexican takeout up to my mother. She was asleep in her bed. Her forehead was sweaty and cool. I watched her breathe a few times, then turned on the TV so she would have company when she woke up. I put the food in the refrigerator with a note to remind her to take the burrito out of the Styrofoam container before she reheated it.

MR. CHIN has something stuck in his teeth. He's working at it, first with his forefinger, then with the nail of his pinkie. Finally, he gives up, runs his tongue across his teeth, stares out the window. The traffic is starting to get a little thick for my taste, and the radio crackles on: Ruthanne, announcing a pickup in Sherman Oaks at eight-thirty.

I reach for my handset. "Twenty-two. I'll take it."

"Goody," she says. "Recording studio. Could be a *gen-u-ine* rock star."

"Goody," I shoot back. "I'll make sure he doesn't pee in the ashtray."

I cut across two lanes and exit the freeway at Sunset. I hop onto Sepulveda to save ten minutes, so I can get to the fare in time. The Chins don't register the route change, so I don't explain it. Sepulveda dips and bends underneath the freeway's underpasses, and as we swing around the curves, the Chins sway back and forth in perfect unison. *Weebles wobble but they don't fall down!* I remember this from TV somewhere when I was a kid. St. Louis? Cleveland? Driving sometimes puts me in this dreamy place where I remember strange details from my life: in one city, a bedspread covered with pictures of Cinderella; in another, the way you had to move the kitchen table to open the refrigerator. Miles go by like this without my noticing them; sometimes I'll reach a destination and have no idea how I got there.

Orange lights are flashing somewhere in my consciousness. My attention snaps back to the road. Up ahead, I see emergency vehicles and warning lights. We slow down and soon we aren't moving at all.

Mr. Chin bends forward to look out the windshield.

"Traffic," I explain. "Probably an accident."

He leans back and says something in Chinese to his wife. From her handbag, she takes out a mirror and a lipstick, which she applies with two perfect swipes. She purses her lips together, judges the result disinterestedly.

Ten minutes later, we are sitting in the same place, boxed in on one side by a line of cars; on the other, the road gives way to a gully. News choppers hover overhead. I pick up my radio.

"This is Twenty-two. Come in, Dispatch."

"I'm coming, I'm coming, I'm—unh!" Ruthie groans.

"You're a freak, you know that?" I say.

"This is what you're hogging the frequency to tell me?"

"It's molasses out here. Better take me off the Sherman Oaks."

"Not to worry. I think it was Captain and Tenille."

"Who?"

"You're making me feel old, Babe."

"I'm gonna need a lot of quickies later to make up on my tips," I say.

"I'll take care of you," she says. "Just sit tight."

"That's all I can do."

I sign off and watch the traffic flowing easily on the southbound side of Sepulveda. You can be stuck or you can be going places. Usually it's just a matter of luck.

. . .

WHEN I WAS eleven, my mother and I lived in Cleveland. All winter, the city was the color of dirty dishwater. People wore heavy coats and boots over their shoes and worried their way across icy streets, as though the roads were covered with nails. We'd come up from Pensacola and had nothing warmer to wear than sweat-shirts, so my mother took us to the Salvation Army, where I picked out a hot-pink snow jacket and some blue boots that were a size too big. When I walked, my heels rubbed up and down inside, and after a few weeks, all my socks had matching holes.

We lived in a part of town where every house was cut up into four equal apartments, like a kid's baloney sandwich. We had the bottom left-hand quarter. At school, a girl told me I lived in the "bad" part of town. What she really meant was that it was the "black" part of town, and it was true: we were the only white people on our block. But we had just come from shitty neighbor-hoods in the South, and we knew how to get along.

The only nice thing for blocks around was a temple. It had a big gold dome and walls of polished stone, and had been built when this was still the good part of town. Now it was stuck here with no place to go, like the fat girl at the dance. After school, I often took the bus to the temple, where my mother worked as a cleaning lady. She'd make me sit quietly in the pews as she dusted the altar. The pews were covered with a rough maroon material and scratched the backs of my legs when I wore a skirt. I'd pass the time staring up at the dome, wondering whether all that gold was real or fake and whether I could climb up and scrape it off with my fingernails.

My mother hated Cleveland. She said that it was an ugly city, that the lake was so polluted it had caught on fire once, that months without sun made the people depressed and crazy. I won-dered why she'd picked Cleveland if she felt this way, but I never asked. I knew that certain questions made her nervous.

One day, after my mother was finished up at the temple, we took a bus to a part of town I'd never seen. All the buildings were one-story brick, with matching green roofs. There were no stores, there were "shoppes." Everything was very clean. We stopped in a coffee shop and sat at a booth. Usually, when we ate out, I understood that I was to order the cheapest thing on the menu or share whatever my mother had. But this time she said, "You want the steak plate? Have the steak plate. That's what I'm having."

I ordered the steak plate. We didn't talk much, and about twenty minutes later a man came in with a girl a few years older than me. The coffee shop wasn't crowded, but when he got to our booth he stopped and asked if they could sit with us. My mother said yes, if they wanted. The man sat down. The girl looked upset, but he told her to sit, and she did.

The waitress came with our plates, and the man ordered a BLT for him and a grilled cheese for the girl. I felt embarrassed about my steak and I stopped eating.

"Eat your food," my mother ordered, so I did.

The man had a wide face with two strong lines that cut down each cheek like the biggest dimples I'd ever seen. He didn't take off his coat and hat, and he drank his glass of ice water with his gloves on. He caught me looking at him and he smiled. My mother didn't talk to him and he didn't talk to her. We just ate, and when the waitress brought their food the man and the girl ate too. The girl had long hair and it kept getting in her way. At one point, she found a hair in the melted cheese of her sandwich and started to pull. She pulled and pulled for what seemed a long time, concentrating as though she were playing a game with herself.

"It's mine," she determined when it finally came out, and continued to eat.

"You have long hair," my mother said. "You have to take care of that hair."

This seemed to stop everything. The man stopped chewing and put his sandwich down. The girl looked at him as if she weren't sure what she was supposed to do.

"Answer the lady," he said.

"I brush it a hundred strokes in the morning and at night."

"Somebody must have taught you that," my mother said. I wasn't sure whether she was asking or telling. The girl didn't say anything.

We finished our steaks, and my mother washed hers down with coffee, then reached behind her and inched herself back into her coat. She slid out of the booth and turned to me.

"All right, Babe," she said. "We're done."

I was confused. We hadn't asked for a check and we hadn't left any money. But I put on my pink parka and followed my mother out the door and onto the street.

"I think we forgot to pay," I said once we were headed into the freezing wind towards the bus stop.

"We paid, all right," she said.

ANOTHER TWENTY MINUTES, and the traffic on Sepulveda hasn't moved a foot. I turn to talk to the Chins.

"Don't worry about the time. It's a flat rate."

They both smile, having no idea what I just said.

Ten minutes later, the Chins start to argue. He thinks one thing, she thinks another. That's all I can make out. She gestures once or twice towards the suitcase. Their voices yo-yo up and down like a twelve-year-old boy's.

I see a cop about fifty feet in front of us. He's moving down the line of cars.

"Look!" I say. "Policeman here! He tell us!" I'm talking like a racist pig, but it seems like they might understand me if I skip some words.

Mr. Chin makes a low, deep rumble in his throat. I open my window and call out to the cop. He comes up to the car.

"What's up?" I ask.

"Accident," he says. He has a narrow face and a nose that bends to the right.

"Just when I decide to take the fast route, right?"

"Happened over two hours ago."

"Oh," I say, realizing it doesn't take two hours to clean up a fender bender. "Somebody die?"

The cop nods. "Kids." There's a sad disgust in his voice. "My daughter wants one of those," he says, looking at my nose ring. "I told her it looks like you have a piece of dirt on your nose, or worse. No offense or anything."

"She's not doing it for you," I say. "No offense or anything."

For a second, he looks like he's going to get mad, but then he smiles.

"Ain't that the truth," he says.

He looks back at the Chins, who have gotten very quiet. I don't blame them. They've probably heard about the L.A.P.D. That Rodney King video was shown something like five hundred times a day all over the world.

The cop nods towards the Chins. "Airport?"

"Don't speak a word of English either."

"Welcome to L.A.," he says. I can't tell if he's talking about the Chins or to them. Then I hear a sound, like a muffled moan, coming from the back seat. I look in the rearview. Is Mrs. Chin getting sick in my car?

"Are you all right back there?" I say.

Mr. Chin looks up. His face has come alive, as though someone flipped a switch.

"Okay," he says. "Everything okay here."

"You speak English?" I say, amazed and a little pissed.

The cop leans into the car to get a closer look at the Chins.

"There's been a bad accident," he says. "Car crash." He mimes driving, then slaps his hands together, looking pleased with his little bit of community service.

"Yes, absolutely," Mr. Chin says. He nods his head, trying to look like he understands what's going on. Suddenly I feel a little sorry for him.

"Well, that's all she wrote," the cop says, slapping his palms down on my door. "You'll see it all on the ten o'clock news." He motions with his chin towards the sky where the choppers circle, their tails dangling above their bodies like wasps.

Just as he leaves, I hear the sound again. It's coming from the suitcase. The Chins start arguing loudly.

"Jesus," I say to nobody in particular. "What the hell is going on back there?"

Mrs. Chin cries out as if she'd been stabbed, and Mr. Chin screams at her. The car in front of me inches forward, the first movement in about an hour. In the rearview, I see the cop turn around and start to jog back to the scene of the accident.

"Here we go," I say as I put my foot on the gas. But just then Mr. Chin opens his door.

"Shut the car door," I yell. "We're moving!"

But Mr. Chin is already out on the side of the road, gesturing back at Mrs. Chin to hand him the suitcase. Before she has a chance to, he reaches in and yanks it from the car. Mrs. Chin follows, her skirt sliding up her thighs. The car in front of me has moved at least twenty feet and the ones behind me are honking.

"Are you crazy?" I scream at the Chins. "Get back in the fucking car!"

By now, every car on Sepulveda is honking at me. A police cruiser moving in the opposite direction flashes its lights.

"Move the limo now!" a voice commands over the loudspeaker. "Move the limo now!" Suddenly the Chins throw the suitcase back into the car, slam the door, and take off, scrambling awkwardly down the embankment and disappearing under the freeway underpass.

I pull forward and grab my radio.

"Goddamn it, Ruthie. They bolted on me."

"Who? The little green men in your head?"

"My fare. My fucking Chins. They just dumped out of the car."

"Did they pay?"

"No, they did not pay!" I scream. Company policy: if a driver fails to collect a fare, the driver is responsible for said fare.

Another sound comes from the suitcase. It's louder now, like the wail of a feral cat.

"Something's in their goddamn suitcase, Ruthie."

But Ruthie's moved on to other things. She's calling out a pickup in Malibu. It's a big fare, and two drivers start in on who's the closest.

At the next red light, I turn around and look at the suitcase lying on the back seat. I reach back and rap on it. No sound. Okay. Batteries dead. Fine. But then I hear another muffled cry.

I pull a hard right off Sepulveda, cross over the freeway, and start to thread my way into the dark hills on Mulholland. I find a small outcropping on the side of the road, some unofficial scenic stop. I head towards the edge of the cliff, braking when I see the grid of lights down in the Valley below me. With the car lights on and the motor running, I pull the suitcase from the back seat and lay it carefully on the ground. It's an old-style suitcase and I have to push the metal tabs apart so that the clasp flips up. My heart feels as heavy as a basketball, and after I finally get up the nerve to pull the tabs, I jump back in the car and slam the door. The suitcase doesn't open. Whatever is in there hasn't moved. I turn off the ignition and get out of the car. I find a stick in the bushes, hook it through the suitcase's lid, and lift it open. I hear somebody scream "Oh, my God! Oh, my God!" but then I realize that the sound is coming from me. I look down. Inside the suitcase is a baby.

The baby is almost new, maybe one or two months old. It's lying on a soiled yellowish cloth, making weird stuttery noises that don't exactly sound like breathing. A small tank lies next to it, and an oxygen mask that must have once covered its nose and mouth hangs down around its chin. A rank, rotten smell reaches me, and I see that the baby's legs are caked with mustardy shit. I run over to the trees and puke.

After I pull myself together, I grab the jacket I keep stashed in my trunk for cold nights and go back to the suitcase. The baby stares up at me with eyes as dark as black beans. I must be a monster to this kid. I pull the mask off over its sweaty head, lift the baby up, and cover it with my jacket. It weighs no more than a chicken and goes all limp and floppy in my hands. I have to keep it close to my chest so that it doesn't slip.

When I finally get the jacket tucked around the baby, I hold it out and take another look. It's awake, but its eyes wander off to the right as if they're tracking some lazy fly. Then its face seizes up in a look of pain and, just as quickly, relaxes. Its eyes close.

I get this hot tingling sensation all over my body, the way you do when your gut realizes something before your head does: the baby's dead, I think. I hear myself moan out loud. I hold its body up to me again, its stink clouding my nostrils, my tears wetting its face. Then I feel air against my cheek. The baby is not dead, but it's as close to it as I am to its reeking stench. In a second, I have the baby in the car, strap it as best I can into the front seat, and I'm flying down the hill.

At the emergency room, the doctors treat me as if I were a criminal. They grab the baby and disappear behind a wall of green curtains. A nurse looks at me the way some of the teachers in high school did. She probably thinks I'm the one who did this to the kid. I look around. The room is full of people slumped in yellow plastic chairs, staring off into corners. One man is pressing a bloody rag to his arm. I find a seat, but another nurse comes to tell me that I have to wait in a different room. I can come on my own, she says, or security can escort me. Two guards in uniforms stand behind her, their hands casually crossed in front of their stomachs.

. . .

THE SECOND TIME my mother tried to kill herself, she used a razor blade to cut her wrists fifteen minutes before I was scheduled to go over for dinner—which gave me some idea of how serious she was. When I got to the house, she was standing at the bathroom sink, running water over her wounds.

"You'd think there would be a lot of blood," she said. Pink liquid ran over her forearms and into the cracked porcelain basin.

"You missed the vein," I said, lifting her arms out of the water and wrapping a towel tightly around the one she'd managed to cut into.

"I'm just a chickenshit, I guess," she said.

I led her over to the bed, and she sat quietly for a long time as I held her arms, putting pressure on the cuts.

"You know," she said finally, "when it comes down to it, it's very difficult to kill yourself. The whole time you're doing it, your body is going 'No! No!' and you're going 'Yes! Yes!' "

"If you really mean it, you use a gun."

"Oh," she said, shuddering, as if the idea made her think of snakes or spiders. "I could never fire a gun."

"Then we're in luck."

I took off the towel. We watched a pearl of blood bubble up from the wound.

"I'm going to have a scar. I'll have to wear long sleeves from now on."

"You should have thought of that first."

"I'm not very good at thinking ahead."

I felt a fissure open up inside of me like one of those cracks in the sink. "You get by," I said. "You do okay."

"I lose things," she said. "Then I regret it but there's nothing I can do."

I had no idea what she was talking about. "You worry too much," I said. "And about all the wrong things."

Louise Erdrich

⟡

The Shawl

AMONG THE ANISHINAABEG on the road where I live, it is told how a woman loved a man other than her husband and went off into the bush and bore his child. Her name was Aanakwad, which means cloud, and like a cloud she was changeable. She was moody and sullen one moment, her lower lip jutting and her eyes flashing, filled with storms. The next, she would shake her hair over her face and blow it straight out in front of her to make her children scream with laughter. For she also had two children by her husband, one a yearning boy of five years and the other a capable daughter of nine.

When Aanakwad brought the new baby out of the trees that autumn, the older girl was like a second mother, even waking in the night to clean the baby and nudge it to her mother's breast. Aanakwad slept through its cries, hardly woke. It wasn't that she didn't love her baby; no, it was the opposite—she loved it too much, the way she loved its father, and not her husband. This passion ate away at her, and her feelings were unbearable. If she could have thrown off that wronghearted love, she would have, but the thought of the other man, who lived across the lake, was with her always. She became a gray sky, stared monotonously at the walls, sometimes wept into her hands for hours at a time. Soon, she couldn't rise to cook or keep the cabin neat, and it was too much for the girl, who curled up each night exhausted in her red-and-brown plaid shawl, and slept and slept, until the husband had to wake her to awaken her mother, for he was afraid of his wife's bad temper, and it was he who roused Aanakwad into anger by the sheer fact that he was himself and not the other.

At last, even though he loved Aanakwad, the husband had to admit that their life together was no good anymore. And it was he who sent for the other man's uncle. In those days, our people lived widely scattered, along the shores and in the islands, even out on the plains. There were no roads then, just trails, though we had horses and wagons and, for the winter, sleds. When the uncle came around to fetch Aanakwad, in his wagon fitted out with sled runners, it was very hard, for she and her husband had argued right up to the last about the children, argued fiercely until the husband had finally given in. He turned his face to the wall, and did not move to see the daughter, whom he treasured, sit down beside her mother, wrapped in her plaid robe in the wagon bed. They left right away, with their bundles and sacks, not bothering to heat up the stones to warm their feet. The father had stopped his ears, so he did not hear his son cry out when he suddenly understood that he would be left behind.

As the uncle slapped the reins and the horse lurched forward, the boy tried to jump into the wagon, but his mother pried his hands off the boards, crying, *Gego, gego,* and he fell down hard. But there was something in him that would not let her leave. He jumped up and, although he was wearing only light clothing, he ran behind the wagon over the packed drifts. The horses picked up speed. His chest was scorched with pain, and yet he pushed himself on. He'd never run so fast, so hard and furiously, but he was determined, and he refused to believe that the increasing distance between him and the wagon was real. He kept going until his throat closed, he saw red, and in the ice of the air his lungs shut. Then, as he fell onto the board-hard snow, he raised his head. He watched the back of the wagon and the tiny figures of his mother and sister disappear, and something failed in him. Something broke. At that moment he truly did not care if he was alive or dead. So when he saw the gray shapes, the shadows, bounding lightly from the trees to either side of the trail, far ahead, he was not afraid.

THE NEXT the boy knew, his father had him wrapped in a blanket and was carrying him home. His father's chest was broad and, although he already spat the tubercular blood that would write the end of his story, he was still a strong man. It would take him many years to die. In those years, the father would tell the boy, who had forgotten this part entirely, that at first when he talked about the shadows the father thought he'd been visited by *manidoog*. But then, as the boy described the shapes, his father had understood that they were not spirits. Uneasy, he had decided to take his gun back along the trail. He had built up the fire in the cabin, and settled his boy near it, and gone back out into the snow. Perhaps the story spread through our settlements because the father had to tell what he saw, again and again, in order to get rid of it. Perhaps as with all frightful dreams, *amaniso,* he had to talk about it to destroy its power—though in this case nothing could stop the dream from being real.

The shadows' tracks were the tracks of wolves, and in those days, when our guns had taken all their food for furs and hides to sell, the wolves were bold and had abandoned the old agreement between them and the first humans. For a time, until we understood and let the game increase, the wolves hunted us. The father bounded forward when he saw the tracks. He could see where the pack, desperate, had tried to slash the tendons of the horses' legs. Next, where they'd leaped for the back of the wagon. He hurried on to where the trail gave out at the broad empty ice of the lake. There, he saw what he saw, scattered, and the ravens, attending to the bitter small leavings of the wolves.

For a time, the boy had no understanding of what had happened. His father kept what he knew to himself, at least that first year, and when his son asked about his sister's torn plaid shawl, and why it was kept in the house, his father said nothing. But he wept when the boy asked if his sister was cold. It was only after his father had been weakened by the disease that he began to tell the story, far too often and always the same way: he told how when the wolves closed in Aanakwad had thrown her daughter to them.

When his father said those words, the boy went still. What had his sister felt? What had thrust through her heart? Had something broken inside her, too, as it had in him? Even then, he knew that this broken place inside him would not be mended, except by some terrible means. For he kept seeing his mother put the baby down and grip his sister around the waist. He saw Aanakwad swing the girl lightly out over the side of the wagon. He saw the brown shawl with its red lines flying open. He saw the shadows, the wolves, rush together, quick and avid, as the wagon with sled runners disappeared into the distance—forever, for neither he nor his father saw Aanakwad again.

WHEN I WAS little, my own father terrified us with his drinking. This was after we lost our mother, because before that the only time I was aware that he touched the *ishkode waaboo* was on an occasional weekend when they got home late, or sometimes during berry-picking gatherings when we went out to the bush and camped with others. Not until she died did he start the heavy sort of drinking, the continuous drinking, where we were left alone in the house for days. The kind where, when he came home, we'd jump out the window and hide in the woods while he barged around, shouting for us. We'd go back only after he had fallen dead asleep.

There were three of us: me, the oldest at ten, and my little sister and brother, twins, and only six years old. I was surprisingly good at taking care of them, I think, and because we learned to survive together during those drinking years we have always been close. Their names are Doris and Raymond, and they married a brother and sister. When we get together, which is often, for we live on the same road, there come times in the talking and card-playing, and maybe even in the light beer now and then, when we will bring up those days. Most people understand how it was. Our story isn't uncommon. But for us it helps to compare our points of view.

How else would I know, for instance, that Raymond saw me the first time I hid my father's belt? I pulled it from around his waist while he was passed out, and then I buried it in the woods. I kept doing it after that. Our father couldn't understand why his belt was always stolen when he went to town drinking. He even accused his *shkwebii* buddies of the theft. But I had good reasons. Not only was he embarrassed, afterward, to go out with his pants held up by rope, but he couldn't snake his belt out in anger and snap the hooked buckle end in the air. He couldn't hit us with it. Of course, being resourceful, he used other things. There was a board. A willow wand. And there was himself—his hands and fists and boots— and things he could throw. But eventually it became easy to evade him, and after a while we rarely suffered a bruise or a scratch. We had our own place in the woods, even a little campfire for the cold nights. And we'd take money from him every chance we got, slip it from his shoe, where he thought it well hidden. He became, for us, a thing to be avoided, outsmarted, and exploited. We survived off him as if he were a capricious and dangerous line of work. I suppose we stopped thinking of him as a human being, certainly as a father.

I got my growth earlier than some boys, and, one night when I was thirteen and Doris and Raymond and I were sitting around wishing for something besides the oatmeal and commodity canned milk I'd stashed so he couldn't sell them, I heard him coming down the road. He was shouting and making noise all the way to the house, and Doris and Raymond looked at me and headed for the back window. When they saw that I wasn't coming, they stopped. C'mon, *ondaas,* get with it—they tried to pull me along. I shook them off and told them to get out quickly—I was staying. I think I can take him now is what I said.

He was big; he hadn't yet wasted away from the alcohol. His nose had been pushed to one side in a fight, then slammed back to the other side, so now it was straight. His teeth were half gone, and he smelled the way he had to smell, being five days drunk. When he came in the door, he paused for a moment, his eyes red and swollen, tiny slits. Then he saw that I was waiting for him, and he smiled in a bad way. My first punch surprised him. I had been practicing on a hay-stuffed bag, then on a padded board, toughening my fists, and I'd got so quick I flickered like fire. I still wasn't as strong as he was, and he had a good twenty pounds on me. Yet I'd do some damage, I was sure of it. I'd teach him not to mess with me. What I didn't foresee was how the fight itself would get right into me.

There is something terrible about fighting your father. It came on suddenly, with the second blow—a frightful kind of joy. A power surged up from the center of me, and I danced at him, light and giddy, full of a heady rightness. Here is the thing: I wanted to waste him, waste him good. I wanted to smack the living shit out of him. Kill him, if I must. A punch for Doris, a kick for Raymond. And all the while I was silent, then screaming, then silent again, in this rage of happiness that filled me with a simultaneous despair so that, I guess you could say, I stood apart from myself.

He came at me, crashed over a chair that was already broken, then threw the pieces. I grabbed one of the legs and whacked him on the ear so that his head spun and turned back to me, bloody. I watched myself striking him again and again. I knew what I was doing, but not really, not in the ordinary sense. It was as if I were standing calm, against the wall with my arms folded, pitying us both. I saw the boy, the chair leg, the man fold and fall, his hands held up in begging fashion. Then I also saw that, for a while now, the bigger man had not even bothered to fight back.

Suddenly, he was my father again. And when I knelt down next to him, I was his son. I reached for the closest rag, and picked up this piece of blanket that my father always kept with him for some reason. And as I picked it up and wiped the blood off his face, I said to him, Your nose is crooked again. He looked at me, steady and quizzical, as though he had never had a drink in his life, and I wiped his face again with that frayed piece of blanket. Well, it was a shawl, really, a kind of old-fashioned woman's blanket-shawl. Once, maybe, it had been plaid. You could still see lines, some red, the background a faded brown. He watched intently as my hand brought the rag to his face. I was pretty sure, then, that I'd clocked him too hard, that he'd really lost it now. Gently, though, he clasped one hand around my wrist. With the other hand he took the shawl. He crumpled it and held it to the middle of his forehead. It was as if he were praying, as if he were having thoughts he wanted to collect in that piece of cloth. For a while he lay like that, and I, crouched over, let him be, hardly breathing. Something told me to sit there, still. And then at last he said to me, in the sober new voice I would hear from then on, *Did you know I had a sister once?*

THERE WAS a time when the government moved everybody off the farthest reaches of the reservation, onto roads, into towns, into housing. It looked good at first, and then it all went sour. Shortly afterward, it seemed that anyone who was someone was either drunk, killed, near suicide, or had just dusted himself. None of the old sort were left, it seemed—the old kind of people, the Gete-anishinaabeg, who are kind beyond kindness and would do anything for others. It was during that time that my mother died and my father hurt us, as I have said.

Now, gradually, that term of despair has lifted somewhat and yielded up its survivors. But we still have sorrows that are passed to us from early generations, sorrows to handle in addition to our own, and cruelties lodged where we cannot forget them. We have the need to forget. We are always walking on oblivion's edge.

Some get away, like my brother and sister, married now and living quietly down the road. And me, to some degree, though I prefer to live alone. And even my father, who recently found a woman. Once, when he brought up the old days, and we went over the story again, I told him at last the two things I had been thinking.

First, I told him that keeping his sister's shawl was wrong, because we never keep the clothing of the dead. Now's the time to burn it, I said. Send it off to cloak her spirit. And he agreed.

The other thing I said to him was in the form of a question. Have you ever considered, I asked him, given how tenderhearted your sister was, and how brave, that she looked at the whole situation? She saw that the wolves were only hungry. She knew that their need was only need. She knew that you were back there, alone in the snow. She understood that the baby she loved would not live without a mother, and that only the uncle knew the way. She saw clearly that one person on the wagon had to be offered up, or they all would die. And in that moment of knowledge, don't you think, being who she was, of the old sort of Anishinaabeg, who thinks of the good of the people first, she jumped, my father, *n'dede,* brother to that little girl? Don't you think she lifted her shawl and flew?

Andrea Lee

✤

The Birthday Present

A CELLULAR PHONE is ringing, somewhere in Milan. Ariel knows that much. Or does she? The phone could be trilling its electronic morsel of Mozart or Bacharach in a big vulgar villa with guard dogs and closed-circuit cameras on the bosky shores of Lake Como. Or in an overpriced hotel suite in Portofino. Or why not in the Aeolian Islands, or on Ischia, or Sardinia? It's late September, and all over the Mediterranean the yachts of politicians and arms manufacturers and pan-Slavic gangsters are still snuggled side by side in the indulgent golden light of harbors where the calendars of the toiling masses mean nothing. The truth is that the phone could be ringing anywhere in the world where there are rich men.

But Ariel prefers to envision Milan, which is the city nearest the Brianza countryside, where she lives with her family in a restored farmhouse. And she tries hard to imagine the tiny phone lying on a table in an apartment not unlike the one she shared fifteen years ago in Washington with a couple of other girls who were seniors at Georgetown. The next step up from a dorm, that is—like a set for a sitcom about young professionals whose sex lives, though kinky, have an endearing adolescent gaucheness. It would be too disturbing to think that she is telephoning a bastion of contemporary Milanese luxury, like the apartments of some of her nouveau-riche friends: gleaming marble, bespoke mosaics, boiserie stripped from defunct châteaux, a dispiriting sense of fresh money spread around like butter on toast.

Hmmm—and if it *were* a place like that? There would be, she supposes, professional modifications. Mirrors: that went without saying, as did a bed the size of a handball court, with a nutria cover and conveniently installed handcuffs. Perhaps a small dungeon off the dressing room? At any rate, a bathroom with Moroccan hammam fixtures and a bidet made from an antique baptismal font. Acres of closets, with garter belts and crotchless panties folded and stacked with fetishistic perfection. And boxes of specialty condoms, divided, perhaps, by design and flavor. Are they ordered by the gross? From a catalogue? But now Ariel retrieves her thoughts, because someone picks up the phone.

"Pronto?" The voice is young and friendly and hasty.

"Is this Beba?" Ariel asks in her correct but heavy Italian, from which she has never attempted to erase the American accent.

"Yes," says the voice, with a merry air of haste.

"I'm a friend of Flavio Costaldo's and he told me that you and your friend—your colleague—might be interested in spending an evening with my husband. It's a birthday present."

WHEN A MARRIAGE lingers at a certain stage—the not uncommon plateau where the two people involved have nothing to say to each other—it is sometimes still possible for them to live well together. To perform generous acts that do not, exactly, signal desperation. Flavio hadn't meant to inspire action when he suggested that Ariel give her husband Roberto *"una fanciulla"*—a young girl—for his fifty-fifth birthday. He'd meant only to irritate, as usual. Flavio is Roberto's best friend, a sixty-year-old Calabrian film producer who five or six years ago gave up trying to seduce Ariel, and settled for the alternative intimacy of tormenting her subtly whenever they meet. Ariel is a tall, fresh-faced woman of thirty-seven, an officer's child who grew up on Army bases around the world, and whose classic American beauty has an air of crisp serviceability that—she is well aware—is a major flaw: in airports, she is sometimes accosted by travellers who are convinced that she is there in a professional capacity. She is always patient at parties when the inevitable pedant expounds on how unsuitable it is for a tall, rather slow-moving beauty to bear the name of the most volatile of sprites. Her own opinion—resolutely unvoiced, like so many of her thoughts—is that, besides being ethereal, Shakespeare's Ariel was mainly competent and faithful. As she herself is by nature: a rarity anywhere in the world, but particularly in Italy. She is the ideal wife—second wife—for Roberto, who is an old-fashioned domestic tyrant. And she is the perfect victim for Flavio. When he made the suggestion, they were sitting in the garden of his fourth wife's sprawling modern villa in a gated community near Como, and both of their spouses were off at the other end of the terrace, looking at samples of glass brick But Ariel threw him handily off balance by laughing and taking up the idea. As she did so, she thought of how much affection she'd come to feel for good old Flavio since her early days in Italy, when she'd reserved for him the ritual loathing of a new wife for her husband's best friend. Nowadays she was a compassionate observer of his dawning old age and its accoutrements, the karmic doom of any superannuated playboy: tinted aviator bifocals, and reptilian complexion; a rich, tyrannical wife who imposed a strict diet of fidelity and bland foods; a little brown address book full of famous pals who no longer phoned. That afternoon, Ariel for the first time had the satisfaction of watching his composure crumble when she asked him sweetly to get her the number of the best call girl in Milan.

"You're not serious," he sputtered. "Ariel, *cara,* you've known me long enough to know I was joking. You aren't—"

"Don't go into that nice-girl, bad-girl Latin thing, please, Flavio. It's a little dated, even for you."

"I was going to say only that you aren't an Italian wife, and there are nuances you'll never understand, even if you live here for a hundred years."

"Oh, please, spare me the anthropology," said Ariel. It was pleasant to have rattled Flavio to this extent. The idea of the *fanciulla,* to which she had agreed on a mischievous impulse unusual for her, suddenly grew more concrete. "Just get me the number."

Flavio was silent for a few minutes, his fat, sun-speckled hands wreathing his glass of *limoncello.* "You're still sleeping together?" he asked suddenly. "Is it all right?"

"Yes. And yes."

"*Allora, che diavolo stai facendo?* What the hell are you doing? He's faithful to you, you know. It's an incredible thing for such a womanizer; you know about his first marriage. With you there have been a few little lapses, but nothing important."

Ariel nodded, not even the slightest bit offended. She knew about those lapses, had long before factored them in to her expectations about the perpetual foreign life she had chosen. Nothing he said, however, could distract her from her purpose.

Flavio sighed and cast his eyes heavenward. "*Va bene;* O.K. But you have to be very careful," he said, shooting a glance down the terrace at his ever-vigilant wife, with her gold sandals and anorexic body. After a minute, he added cryptically, "Well, at least you're Catholic. That's something."

So, THANKS to Flavio's little brown book, Ariel is now talking to Beba. Beba—a toddler's nickname. Ex-model in her twenties. Brazilian, but not a transsexual. Tall. Dark. Works in tandem with a Russian blonde. "The two of them are so gorgeous that when you see them it's as if you have entered another sphere, a paradise where everything is simple and divine," said Flavio, waxing lyrical during the series of planning phone calls he and Ariel shared, cozy conversations that made his wife suspicious and gave him the renewed pleasure of annoying Ariel. "The real danger is that Roberto might fall in love with one of them," he remarked airily, during one of their chats. "No, probably not—he's too stingy."

In contrast, it is easy talking to Beba. "How many men?" Beba asks, as matter-of-factly as a caterer. There is a secret happiness in her voice that tempts Ariel to investigate, to talk more than she normally would. It is an impulse she struggles to control. She knows from magazine articles that, like everyone else, prostitutes simply want to get their work done without a fuss.

"Just my husband," Ariel says, feeling a calm boldness settle over her.

"And you?"

Flavio has said that Beba is a favorite among rich Milanese ladies who are fond of extracurricular romps. Like the unlisted addresses where they buy their cashmere and have their abortions, she is top-of-the-line and highly private. Flavio urged Ariel to participate and gave a knowing chuckle when she refused. The chuckle meant that, like everyone else, he thinks Ariel is a prude. She isn't—though the fact is obscured by her fatal air of efficiency, by her skill at writing out place cards, making homemade tagliatelle better than her Italian mother-in-law, and raising bilingual daughters. But no one realizes that over the years she has also invested that efficiency in a great many amorous games with the experienced and demanding Roberto. On their honeymoon, in Bangkok, they'd spent one night with two polite teen-agers selected from a numbered lineup behind a large glass window. But that was twelve years ago, and although Ariel is not clear about her motives for giving this birthday present, she sees with perfect feminine good sense that she is not meant to be onstage with a pair of young whores who look like angels.

The plan is that Ariel will make a date with Roberto for a dinner in town, and that instead of Ariel, Beba and her colleague will meet him. After dinner the three of them will go to the minuscule apartment near Corso Venezia that Flavio keeps as his sole gesture of independence from his wife. Ariel has insisted on dinner, though Flavio was against it, and Beba has told her, with a tinge of amusement, that it will cost a lot more. Most clients, she says, don't request dinner. Why Ariel should insist that her husband sit around chummily with two hookers, ordering antipasto, first and second courses, and dessert is a mystery, even to Ariel. Yet she feels that it is the proper thing to do. That's the way she wants it, and she can please herself, can't she?

As they finish making the arrangements, Ariel is embarrassed to hear herself say, "I do hope you two girls will make things very nice. My husband is a wonderful man."

And Beba, who is clearly used to talking to wives, assures her, with phenomenal patience, that she understands.

As ARIEL PUTS down the phone, it rings again, and of course it is her mother, calling from the States. "Well, you're finally free," says her mother, who seems to be chewing something, probably a low-calorie bagel, since it is 8 a.m. in Bethesda. "Who on earth were you talking to for so long?"

"I was planning Roberto's birthday party," Ariel says glibly. "We're inviting some people to dinner at the golf club."

"Golf! I've never understood how you can live in Italy and be so suburban. Golf in the hills of Giotto!"

"The hills of Giotto are in Umbria, Mom. This is Lombardy, so we're allowed to play golf."

Ariel can envision her mother, unlike Beba, with perfect clarity: tiny; wiry, as if the muscles under her porcelain skin were steel guitar strings. Sitting bolt upright in her condominium kitchen, dressed in the chic, funky uniform of black jeans and cashmere T-shirt she wears to run the business she dreamed up: an improbably successful fleet of suburban messengers on Vespas which she claims was inspired by her favorite film, "Roman Holiday." Coffee and soy milk in front of her, quartz-and-silver earrings quivering, one glazed fingernail tapping the counter as her eyes probe the distance over land and ocean toward her only daughter.

What would she say if she knew of the previous call? Almost certainly, Ariel thinks, she would be pleased with an act indicative of the gumption she finds constitutionally lacking in her child, whose lamentable conventionality has been a byword since Ariel was small. She herself is living out a green widowhood with notable style, and dating a much younger lobbyist, whose sexual tastes she would be glad to discuss, girl to girl, with her daughter. But she is loath to shock Ariel.

With her Italian son-in-law, Ariel's mother flirts shamelessly, the established joke being that she should have got there first. It's a joke that never fails to pull a grudging smile from Roberto, and it goes over well with *his* mother, too: another glamorous widow, an intellectual from Padua who regards her daughter-in-law with the condescending solicitude one might reserve for a prize broodmare. For years, Ariel has lived in the dust stirred up by these two dynamos, and it looks as if her daughters, as they grow older—they are eight and ten—are beginning to side with their grandmothers. Not one of these females, it seems, can forgive Ariel for being herself. So Ariel keeps quiet about her new acquaintance with Beba, not from any prudishness but as a powerful amulet. The way, at fourteen, she hugged close the knowledge that she was no longer a virgin.

"Is anything the matter?" asks her mother. "Your voice sounds strange. You and Roberto aren't fighting, are you?" She sighs. "I have told you a hundred times that these spoiled Italian men are naturally promiscuous, so they need a woman who commands interest. You need to be effervescent, on your toes, a little bit slutty, too, if you'll pardon me, darling. Otherwise, they just go elsewhere."

.   .   .

INSPIRED BY HER own lie, Ariel actually gives a dinner at the golf club, two days before Roberto's birthday. The clubhouse is a refurbished nineteenth-century castle built by an industrialist, and the terrace where the party is held overlooks the pool and an artificial lake. Three dozen of their friends gather in the late-September chill to eat a faux-rustic seasonal feast, consisting of polenta and *Fassone* beefsteaks, and the pungent yellow mushrooms called *funghi reali,* all covered with layers of shaved Alba truffles. Ariel is proud of the meal, planned with the club chef in less time than she spent talking to Beba on the phone.

Roberto is a lawyer, chief counsel for a centrist political party that is moderately honest as Italian political parties go, and his friends all have the same gloss of material success and moderate honesty. Though the group is an international one—many of the men have indulged in American wives as they have in German cars—the humor is typically bourgeois Italian. That is: gossipy, casually cruel, and—in honor of Roberto—all about sex and potency. Somebody passes around an article from *L'Espresso* which celebrates men over fifty with third and fourth wives in their twenties, and everyone glances slyly at Ariel. And Roberto's two oldest friends, Flavio and Michele, appear, bearing a large gift-wrapped box. It turns out to hold not a midget stripper, as someone guesses, but a smaller box, and a third, and a fourth and fifth, until, to cheers, Roberto unwraps a tiny package of Viagra.

Standing over fifty-five smoking candles in a huge pear-and-chocolate torte, he thanks his friends with truculent grace. Everyone laughs and claps—Roberto Furioso, as his nickname goes, is famous for his ornery disposition. He doesn't look at Ariel, who is leading the applause in her role as popular second wife and good sport. She doesn't have to look at him to feel his presence, as always, burned into her consciousness. He is a small, charismatic man with a large Greek head, thick brush-cut black hair turning a uniform steel gray, thin lips hooking downward in an ingrained frown like those of his grandfather, a Sicilian baron. When Ariel met him, a dozen years ago, at the wedding of a distant cousin of hers outside Florence, she immediately recognized the overriding will she had always dreamed of, a force capable of conferring a shape on her own personality. He, prisoner of his desire as surely as she was, looked at this preposterously tall, absurdly placid American beauty as they danced for the third time. And blurted out— a magical phrase that fixed forever the parameters of Ariel's private mythology—"*Tu sai che ti sposerò*. You know I'm going to marry you."

Nowadays Roberto is still *furioso,* but it is at himself for getting old, and at her for witnessing it. So he bullies her, and feels quite justified in doing so. Like all second wives, Ariel was supposed to be a solution, and now she has simply enlarged the problem.

ROBERTO'S BIRTHDAY begins with blinding sunlight, announcing the brilliant fall weather that arrives when transalpine winds bundle the smog out to sea. The view from Ariel's house on the hill is suddenly endless, as if a curtain had been yanked aside. The steel-blue Alps are the first thing she sees through the window at seven-thirty, when her daughters, according to family custom, burst into their parents' bedroom pushing a battered baby carriage with balloons tied to it, and presents inside. Elisa and Cristina, giggling, singing "Happy Birthday," tossing their pretty blunt-cut hair, serene in the knowledge that their irascible father, who loathes sudden awakenings, is putty in their hands. Squeals, kisses, tumbling in the bed, so that Ariel can feel how their cherished small limbs are growing polished, sleeker, more muscular with weekly horseback riding and gymnastics. Bilingual, thanks to their summers in Maryland, they are still more Italian than American; at odd detached moments in her genuinely blissful hours of maternal bustling, Ariel has noticed how, like all other young Italian girls, they exude a precocious maturity. And though they are at times suffocatingly attached to her, there has never been a question about which parent takes precedence. For their father's presents, they have clubbed together to buy from the Body Shop some soap and eye gel and face cream that are made with royal jelly. "To make you look younger, Papa," says Elisa, arriving, as usual, at the painful crux of the matter.

"Are we really going to spend the night at Nonna Silvana's?" Cristina asks Ariel.

"Yes," Ariel replies, feeling a blush rising from under her nightgown. "Yes, because Papa and I are going to dinner in the city."

The girls cheer. They love staying with their Italian grandmother, who stuffs them with marrons glacés and Kit Kat bars and lets them try on all her Pucci outfits from the sixties.

When breakfast—a birthday breakfast, with chocolate brioche—is finished, and the girls are waiting in the car for her to take them to school, Ariel hands Roberto a small gift-wrapped package. He is on the way out the door, his jovial paternal mask back in its secret compartment. "A surprise," she says. "Don't open it before this evening." He looks it over and shakes it suspiciously. "I hope you didn't go and spend money on something else I don't need," he says. "That party—"

"Oh, you'll find a use for this," says Ariel in the seamlessly cheerful voice she has perfected over the years. Inside the package is a million lire in large bills, and the key to Flavio's apartment, as well as a gorgeous pair of silk-and-lace underpants that Ariel has purchased in a size smaller than she usually wears. There is also a note suggesting that Roberto, like a prince in a fairy tale, should search for the best fit in the company in which he finds himself. The note is witty and slightly obscene, the kind of thing Roberto likes. An elegant, wifely touch for a husband who, like all Italian men, is fussy about small things.

. . .

DROPPING OFF the girls at the International School, Ariel runs through the usual catechism about when and where they will be picked up, reminders about gym clothes, a note to a geography teacher. She restrains herself from kissing them with febrile intensity, as if she were about to depart on a long journey. Instead she watches as they disappear into a thicket of coltish legs, quilted navy-blue jackets, giggles and secrets. She waves to other mothers, Italian, American, Swiss: well-groomed women with tragic morning expressions, looking small inside huge Land Cruisers that could carry them, if necessary, through Lapland or across the Zambezi.

Ariel doesn't want to talk to anyone this morning, but her rambunctious English friend Carinth nabs her and insists on coffee. The two women sit in the small *pasticceria* where all the mothers buy their pastries and chocolates, and Ariel sips barley cappuccino and listens to Carinth go on about her cystitis. Although Ariel is deeply distracted, she is damned if she is going to let anything slip, not even to her loyal friend with the milkmaid's complexion and the lascivious eyes. Damned if she will turn Roberto's birthday into just another easily retailed feminine secret. Avoiding temptation, she looks defiantly around the shop at shelves of meringues, marzipan, candied violets, chocolate chests filled with gilded chocolate cigars, glazed almonds for weddings and first communions, birthday cakes like Palm Beach mansions. The smell of sugar is overpowering. And, for just a second, for the only time all day, her eyes sting with tears.

At home, there are hours to get through. First, she e-mails an article on a Milanese packaging designer to one of the American magazines for which she does freelance translations. Then she telephones to cancel her lesson in the neighboring village with an old artisan who is teaching her to restore antique *papiers peints,* a craft she loves and at which her large hands are surprisingly skillful. Then she goes outside to talk to the garden contractors—three illegal Romanian immigrants who are rebuilding an eroded slope on the east side of the property. She has to haggle with them, and as she does, the leader, an outrageously handsome boy of twenty, looks her over with insolent admiration. Pretty boys don't go unnoticed by Ariel, who sometimes imagines complicated sex with strangers in uncomfortable public places. But they don't really exist for her, just as the men who flirt with her at parties don't count. Only Roberto exists, which is how it has been since that long-ago third dance, when she drew a circle between the two of them and the rest of the world. This is knowledge that she keeps even from Roberto, because she thinks that it would bore him, along with everyone else. Yet is it really so dull to want only one man, the man one already has?

After the gardeners leave, there is nothing to do—no children to pick up at school and ferry to activities; no homework to help with, no dinner to fix. The dogs are at the vet for a wash and a checkup. Unthinkable to invite Carinth or another friend for lunch; unthinkable, too, to return to work, to go shopping, to watch a video or read a book. No, there is nothing but to accept the fact that for an afternoon she has to be the loneliest woman in the world.

AROUND THREE o'clock, she gets in the car and heads along the state highway toward Lake Como, where over the years she has taken so many visiting relatives. She has a sudden desire to see the lovely decaying villas sleeping in the trees, the ten-kilometre expanse of lake stretching to the mountains like a predictable future. But as she drives from Greggio to San Giovanni Canavese, past yellowing cornfields, provincial factories, rural discothèques, and ancient village churches, she understands why she is out here. At roadside clearings strewn with refuse, she sees the usual highway prostitutes waiting for afternoon customers.

Ariel has driven past them for years, on her way to her mother-in-law's house or chauffeuring her daughters to riding lessons. Like everyone else, she has first deplored and then come to terms with the fact that the roadside girls are part of a criminal world so successful and accepted that their slavery has routines like those of factory workers: they are transported to and from their ten-hour shifts by a neat fleet of minivans. They are as much a part of the landscape as toll booths.

First, she sees a brown-haired Albanian girl who doesn't look much older than Elisa, wearing black hot pants and a loose white shirt that she lifts like an ungainly wing and flaps slowly at passing drivers. A Fiat Uno cruising in front of Ariel slows down, makes a sudden U-turn, and heads back toward the girl. A kilometre further on are two Nigerians, one dressed in an electric-pink playsuit, sitting waggling her knees on an upended crate, while the other, in a pair of stilt-like platform shoes, stands chatting into a cellular phone. Both are tall, with masses of fake braids, and disconcertingly beautiful. Dark seraphim whose presence at the filthy roadside is a kind of miracle.

Ariel slows down to take a better look at the girl in pink, who offers her a noncommittal stare, with eyes opaque as coffee beans. The two-lane road is deserted, and Ariel actually stops the car for a minute, because she feels attracted by those eyes, suddenly mesmerized by something that recalls the secret she heard in Beba's voice. The secret that seemed to be happiness, but, she realizes now, was something different: a mysterious certitude that draws her like a magnet. She feels absurdly moved—out of control, in fact. As her heart pounds, she realizes that if she let herself go, she would open the car door and crawl toward that flat dark gaze. The girl in pink says something to her companion with the phone, who swivels on the three-inch soles of her shoes to look at Ariel. And Ariel puts her foot on the gas pedal. Ten kilometres down the road, she stops again and yanks out a Kleenex to wipe the film of sweat from her face. The only observation she allows herself as she drives home, recovering her composure, is the thought of how curious it is that all of them are foreigners—herself, Beba, and the girls on the road.

. . .

SIX O'CLOCK. As she walks into the house, the phone rings, and it is Flavio, who asks how the plot is progressing. Ariel can't conceal her impatience.

"Listen, do you think those girls are going to be on time?"

"As far as I know, they are always punctual," he says. "But I have to go. I'm calling from the car here in the garage, and it's starting to look suspicious."

He hangs up, but Ariel stands with the receiver in her hand, struck by the fact that besides worrying about whether dinner guests, upholsterers, babysitters, restorers of wrought iron, and electricians will arrive on schedule, she now has to concern herself with whether Beba will keep her husband waiting.

SEVEN-THIRTY. The thing now is not to answer the phone. If he thinks of her, which is unlikely, Roberto must assume that she is in the car, dressed in one of the discreetly sexy short black suits or dresses she wears for special occasions, her feet in spike heels pressing the accelerator as she speeds diligently to their eight-o'clock appointment. He is still in the office, firing off the last frantic fax to Rome, pausing for a bit of ritual abuse aimed at his harassed assistant, Amedeo. Next, he will dash for a pee in his grim brown-marble bathroom: how well she can envision the last, impatient shake of his cock, which is up for an unexpected adventure tonight. He will grab a handful of the chocolates that the doctor has forbidden, and gulp down a paper cup of sugary espresso from the office machine. Then into the shiny late-model Mercedes— a monument, he calls it, with an unusual flash of self-mockery, to the male climacteric. After which, becalmed in the Milan evening traffic, he may call her. Just to make sure she is going to be on time.

. . .

EIGHT-FIFTEEN. She sits at the kitchen table and eats a frugal meal: a plate of rice with cheese and olive oil, a sliced tomato, a glass of water.

The phone rings again. She hesitates, then picks it up.

It is Roberto. *"Allora, sei rimasta a casa,"* he says softly. "So you stayed home."

"Yes, of course," she replies, keeping her tone light. "It's your birthday, not mine. How do you like your present? Are they gorgeous?"

He laughs, and she feels weak with relief. "They're impressive. They're not exactly dressed for a restaurant, though. Why on earth did you think I needed to eat dinner with them? I keep hoping I won't run into anybody I know."

In the background, she hears the muted roar of an eating house, the uniform evening hubbub of voices, glasses, silver, plates.

"Where are you calling from?" Ariel asks.

"Beside the cashier's desk. I have to go. I can't be rude. I'll call you later."

"Good luck," she says. She is shocked to find a streak of malice in her tone, and still more shocked at the sense of power she feels as she puts down the phone. Leaving him trapped in a restaurant, forced to make conversation with two whores, while the other diners stare and the waiters shoot him roguish grins. Was that panic she heard in Roberto's voice? And what could that naughty Beba and her friend be wearing? Not cheap hot pants like the roadside girls, she hopes. For the price, one would expect at least Versace.

AFTER THAT, there is nothing for Ariel to do but kick off her shoes and wander through her house, her bare feet unexpectedly warm on the waxed surface of the old terra-cotta tiles she spent months collecting from junk yards and wrecked villas. She locks the doors and puts on the alarm, but turns on only the hall and stairway lights. And then walks like a night watchman from room to darkened room, feeling flashes of uxorious pride at the sight of furnishings she knows as well as her own body. "Uxorious"—the incongruous word actually floats through her head as her glance passes over the flourishes of a Piedmontese Baroque cabinet in the dining room, a watchful congregation of Barbies in the girls' playroom, a chubby Athena in a Mantuan painting in the upstairs hall. When has Ariel ever moved through the house in such freedom? It is exhilarating, and slightly appalling. And she receives the strange impression that this is the real reason she has staged this birthday stunt: to be alone and in conscious possession of the solitude she has accumulated over the years. To contemplate, for as long as she likes, the darkness in her own house. At the top of the stairs she stops for a minute and then slowly begins to take off her clothes, letting them fall softly at her feet. Then, naked, she sits down on the top step, the cold stone numbing her bare backside. Her earlier loneliness has evaporated: the shadows she is studying seem to be friendly presences jostling to keep her company. She relaxes back on her elbows, and playfully bobs her knees, like the roadside girl on the crate.

TEN O'CLOCK. Bedtime. What she has wanted it to be since this afternoon. A couple of melatonin, a glass of dark Danish stout whose bitter concentrated taste of hops makes her sleepy. A careful shower, cleaning of teeth, application of face and body creams, a gray cotton nightdress. She could, she thinks, compose a specialized etiquette guide for women in her situation. One's goal is to exude an air of extreme cleanliness and artless beauty. One washes and dries one's hair, but does not apply perfume or put on any garment that could be construed as seductive. The subtle enchantment to be cast is that of a homespun Elysium, the appeal of Penelope after Calypso.

By ten-thirty, she is sitting up in bed with the *Herald Tribune*, reading a history of the F.B.I.'s Most Wanted list. Every few seconds, she attempts quite coolly to think of what Roberto is inevitably doing by now, but she determines that it is actually impossible to do so. Those two pages in her imagination are stuck together.

She does, however, recall the evening in Bangkok that she and Roberto spent with the pair of massage girls. How the four of them walked in silence to a fluorescent-lit room with a huge plastic bathtub, and how the two terrifyingly polite, terrifyingly young girls, slick with soapsuds, massaging her with their small plump breasts and shaven pubes, reminded her of nothing so much as chickens washed and trussed for the oven. And how the whole event threatened to become a theatre of disaster, until Ariel saw that she would have to manage things. How she indicated to the girls by a number of discreet signs that the three of them were together in acting out a private performance for the man in the room. How the girls understood and even seemed relieved, and how much pleasure her husband took in what, under her covert direction, they all contrived. How she felt less like an erotic performer than a social director setting out to save an awkward party. And how silent she was afterward—not the silence of shocked schoolgirl sensibilities, as Roberto, no doubt, assumed, but the silence of amazement at a world where she always had to be a hostess.

She turns out the light and dreams that she is flying with other people in a plane precariously tacked together from wooden crates and old car parts. They land in the Andes, and she sees that all the others are women and that they are naked, as she is. They are all sizes and colors, and she is far from being the prettiest, but is not the ugliest, either. They are there to film an educational television special, BBC or PBS, and the script says to improvise a dance, which they all do earnestly and clumsily: Scottish reels, belly dancing, and then Ariel suggests ring-around-the-rosy, which turns out to be more fun than anyone had bargained for, as they all flop down, giggling at the end. The odd thing about this dream is how completely happy it is.

. . .

SHE WAKES to noise in the room, and Roberto climbing into bed and embracing her. "Dutiful," she thinks, as he kisses her and reaches for her breasts, but then she lets the thought go. He smells alarmingly clean, but it is a soap she knows. As they make love, he offers her a series of verbal sketches from the evening he has just passed, a bit like a child listing his new toys. What he says is not exciting, but it is exciting to hear him trying, for her benefit, to sound scornful and detached. And the familiar geography of his body has acquired a passing air of mystery, simply because she knows that other women—no matter how resolutely transient and hasty—have been examining it. For the first time in as long as she can remember, she is curious about Roberto.

"Were they really so beautiful?" she asks, when, lying in the dark, they resume coherent conversation. "Flavio said that seeing them was like entering paradise."

Roberto gives an arrogant, joyful laugh that sounds as young as a teenage boy's.

"Only for an old idiot like Flavio. They were flashy, let's put it that way. The dark one, Beba, had an amazing body, but her friend had a better face. The worst thing was having to eat with them—and in that horrendous restaurant. Whose idea was that, yours or Flavio's?" His voice grows comically aggrieved. "It was the kind of tourist place where they wheel a cart of mints and chewing gum to your table after the coffee. And those girls asked for doggie bags, can you imagine? They filled them with Chiclets!"

The two of them are lying in each other's arms, shaking with laughter as they haven't done for months, even years. And Ariel is swept for an instant by a heady sense of accomplishment. "Which of them won the underpants?" she asks.

"What? Oh, I didn't give them away. They were handmade, silk. Expensive stuff—too nice for a hooker. I kept them for you."

"But they're too small for me," protests Ariel.

"Well, exchange them. You did save the receipt, I hope." Roberto's voice, which has been affectionate, indulgent, as in their best times together, takes on a shade of its normal domineering impatience. But it is clear that he is still abundantly pleased, both with himself and with her. Yawning, he announces that he has to get some sleep, that he's out of training for this kind of marathon. That he didn't even fortify himself with his birthday Viagra. He alludes to an old private joke of theirs by remarking that Ariel's present proves conclusively that his mother was right in warning him against immoral American women; and he gives her a final kiss. Adding a possessive, an uxorious, squeeze of her bottom. Then he settles down and lies so still that she thinks he is already asleep. Until, out of a long silence, he whispers, "Thank you."

IN A FEW minutes he is snoring. But Ariel lies still and relaxed, with her arms at her sides and her eyes wide open. She has always rationed her illusions, and has been married too long to be shocked by the swiftness with which her carefully perverse entertainment has dissolved into the fathomless triviality of domestic life. In a certain way that swiftness is Ariel's triumph—a measure of the strength of the quite ordinary bondage that, years ago, she chose for herself. So it doesn't displease her to know that she will wake up tomorrow, make plans to retrieve her daughters, and find that nothing has changed.

But no, she thinks, turning on her side, something is different. A sense of loss is creeping over her, and she realizes it is because she misses Beba. Beba who for two weeks has lent a penumbral glamour to Ariel's days. Beba, who, in the best of fantasies, might have sent a comradely message home to her through Roberto. But, of course, there is no message, and it is clear that the party is over. The angels have flown, leaving Ariel—good wife and faithful spirit— awake in the dark with considerable consolations: a sleeping man, a silent house, and the knowledge that, with her usual practicality, she has kept Beba's number.

Grace Paley

〜

My Father Addresses Me on the Facts of Old Age

MY FATHER had decided to teach me how to grow old. I said O.K. My children didn't think it was such a great idea. If I knew how, they thought, I might do so too easily. No, no, I said, it's for later, years from now. And, besides, if I get it right it might be helpful to you kids in time to come.

They said, Really?

My father wanted to begin as soon as possible. For God's sake, he said, you can talk to the kids later. Now, listen to me, send them out to play. You are so distractable.

We should probably begin at the beginning, he said. Change. First there is change, which nobody likes—even men. You'd be surprised. You can do little things—putting cream on the corners of your mouth, also the heels of your feet. But here is the main thing. Oh, I wish your mother was alive—not that she had time—

But Pa, I said, Mama never knew anything about cream. I did not say she was famous for not taking care.

Forget it, he said sadly. But I must mention squinting. DON'T SQUINT. Wear your glasses. Look at your aunt, so beautiful once. I know someone has said men don't make passes at girls who wear

glasses, but that's an idea for a foolish person. There are many handsome women who are not exactly twenty-twenty.

Please sit down, he said. Be patient. The main thing is this—
when you get up in the morning you must take your heart in your
two hands. You must do this every morning.

That's a metaphor, right?

Metaphor? No, no, you can do this. In the morning, do a few
little exercises for the joints, not too much. Then put your hands
like a cup over and under the heart. Under the breast, he said tact-
fully. It's probably easier for a man. Then talk softly, don't yell.
Under your ribs, push a little. When you wake up, you must do this
massage. I mean pat, stroke a little, don't be ashamed. Very likely no
one will be watching. Then you must talk to your heart.

Talk? What?

Say anything, but be respectful. Say—maybe say, Heart, little
heart, beat softly but never forget your job, the blood. You can
whisper also, Remember, remember. For instance, I said to it yesterday, Heart, heart, do you remember my brother, Grisha, how he
made work for you that day when he came to the store and he said,
Your boss's money, Zenya, right now? How he put a gun in my
face and I said, Grisha, are you crazy? Why don't you ask me at
home? I would give you. We were in this America not more than
two years. He was only a kid. And he said, he said, Who needs your
worker's money? For the movement—only from your boss. O little
heart, you worked like a bastard, like a dog, like a crazy slave, bang,
bang, bang that day, remember? That's the story I told my heart
yesterday, my father said. What a racket it made to answer me, I remember, I remember, till I was dizzy with the thumping.

Why'd you do that, Pa? I don't get it.

Don't you see? This is good for the old heart—to get excited—
just as good as for the person. Some people go running till late in
life—for the muscles, they say, but the heart knows the real purpose. The purpose is the expansion of the arteries, a river of blood,
it cleans off the banks, carries junk out of the system. I myself

would rather remind the heart how frightened I was by my brother than go running in a strange neighborhood miles and miles, with the city so dangerous these days.

I said, Oh, but then I said, Well, thanks.

I don't think you listened, he said. As usual—probably worried about the kids. They're not babies, you know. If you were better organized you wouldn't have so many worries.

I STOPPED by a couple of weeks later. This time he was annoyed.

Why did you leave the kids home? If you keep doing this, they'll forget who I am. Children are like old people in that respect.

They won't forget you, Pa, never in a million years.

You think so? God has not been so good about a million years. His main interest in us began—actually, he put it down in writing fifty-six, fifty-seven hundred years ago. In the Book. You know our Book, I suppose.

O.K. Yes.

Probably a million years is too close to his lifetime, if you could call it life, what he goes through. I believe he said several times— when he was still in contact with us—I am a jealous God. Here and there he makes an exception. I read there are three-thousand-year-old trees somewhere in some godforsaken place. Of course, that's how come they're still alive. We should all be so godforsaken.

But no more joking around. I have been thinking what to tell you now. First of all, soon, maybe in twenty, thirty years, you'll begin to get up in the morning—4, 5 a.m. In a farmer that's O.K., but for us—you'll remember everything you did, didn't, what you omitted, whom you insulted, betrayed—betrayed, that is the worst. Do you remember, you didn't go see your aunt, she was dying? That will be on your mind like a stone. Of course I myself did not behave so well. Still, I was so busy those days, long office hours, re-member it was usual in those days for doctors to make house calls.

No elevators, fourth floor, fifth floor, even in a nice Bronx tenement. But this morning, I mean *this* morning, a few hours ago, my mother, your babushka, came into my mind, looked at me.

Have I told you I was arrested? Of course I did. I was arrested a few times, but this time for some reason the policeman walked me past the office of the local jail. My mama was there. I saw her through the window. She was bringing me a bundle of clean clothes. She put it on the officer's table. She turned. She saw me. She looked at me through the glass with such a face, eye-to-eye. Despair. No hope. This morning, 4 a.m., I saw once more how she sat there, very straight. Her eyes. Because of that look, I did my term, my sentence, the best I could. I finished up six months in Arkhangel'sk, where they finally sent me. Then no more, no more, I said to myself, no more saving Imperial Russia, the great pogrom-maker, from itself.

Oh, Pa.

Don't make too much out of everything. Well, anyway, I want to tell you also how the body is your enemy. I must warn you it is not your friend the way it was when you were a youngster. For example. Greens—believe me—are overrated. Some people believe they will cure cancer. It's the style. My experience with maybe a hundred patients proves otherwise. Greens are helpful to God. That fellow Sandburg, the poet—I believe from Chicago—explained it. Grass tiptoes over the whole world, holds it in place—except the desert, of course, everything there is loose, flying around.

How come you bring up God so much? When I was a kid you were a strict atheist, you even spit on the steps of the synagogue.

Well, God is very good for conversation, he said. By the way, I believe I have to tell you a few words about the stock market. Your brother-in-law is always talking about how brilliant he is, investing, investing. My advice to you: Stay out of it.

But people *are* making money. A lot. Read the paper. Even kids are becoming millionaires.

But what of tomorrow? he asked.

Tomorrow, I said, they'll make another million.

No, no, no, I mean TOMORROW. I was there when TO-MORROW came in 1929. So I say to them and their millions, HA HA HA, TOMORROW will come. Go home now, I have a great deal more to tell you. Somehow, I'm always tired.

I'll go in a minute—but I have to tell you something, Pa. I had to tell him that my husband and I were separating. Maybe even divorce, the first in the family.

What? What? Are you crazy? I don't understand you people nowadays. I married your mother when I was a boy. It's true I had a first-class mustache, but I was a kid, and you know I stayed married till the end. Once or twice, she wanted to part company, but not me. The reason, of course, she was inclined to be jealous.

He then gave me the example I'd heard five or six times before. What it was, one time two couples went to the movies. Arzemich and his wife, you remember. Well, I sat next to his wife, the lady of the couple, by the way a very attractive woman, and during the show, which wasn't so great, we talked about this and that, laughed a couple times. When we got home, your mother said, O.K. Anytime you want, right now, I'll give you a divorce. We will go our separate ways. Naturally, I said, What? Are you ridiculous?

My advice to you—stick it out. It's true your husband, he's a peculiar fellow, but think it over. Go home. Maybe you can manage at least till old age. Then, if you still don't get along, you can go to separate old-age homes.

Pa, it's no joke. It's my life.

It is a joke. A joke is necessary at this time. But I'm tired.

You'll see, in thirty, forty years from now, you'll get tired often. It doesn't mean you're sick. This is something important that I'm telling you. Listen. To live a long time, long years, you've got to sleep a certain extra percentage away. It's a shame.

. . .

IT WAS at least three weeks before I saw him again. He was drinking tea, eating a baked apple, one of twelve my sister baked for him every ten days. I took another one out of the refrigerator. "Fathers and Sons" was on the kitchen table. Most of the time he read history. He kept Gibbon and Prescott on the lamp stand next to his resting chair. But this time, thinking about Russia for some reason in a kindly way, he was reading Turgenev.

You were probably pretty busy, he said. Where are the kids? With the father? He looked at me hopefully.

No hope, Pa.

By the way, you know, this fellow Turgenev? He wasn't a showoff. He wrote a certain book, and he became famous right away. One day he went to Paris, and in the evening he went to the opera. He stepped into his box, and just as he was sitting down the people began to applaud. The whole opera house was clapping. He was known. Everybody knew his book. He said, I see Russia is known in France.

You're a lucky girl that these books are in the living room, more on the table than on the shelf.

Yes.

Excuse me, also about Turgenev, I don't believe he was an anti-Semite. Of course, most of them were, even if they had brains. I don't think Gorky was, Gogol probably. Tolstoy, no, Tolstoy had an opinion about the Mexican-American War. Did you know? Of course, most were anti-Semites. Dostoyevsky. It was natural, it seems. Ach, why is it we read them with such interest and they don't return the favor?

That's what women writers say about men writers.

Please don't start in. I'm in the middle of telling you some things you don't know. Well, I suppose you do know a number of Gentiles, you're more in the American world. I know very few. Still, I was telling you—Jews were not allowed to travel in Russia. I told you that. But a Jewish girl if she was a prostitute could go anywhere throughout all Russia. Also a Jew if he was a merchant first class. Even people with big stores were only second class. Who else? A soldier who had a medal, I think St. George. Do you know nobody could arrest him? Even if he was a Jew. If he killed someone a policeman could not arrest him. He wore a certain hat. Why am I telling you all this?

Well, it is interesting.

Yes, but I'm supposed to tell you a few things, give advice, a few last words. Of course, the fact is I am obliged because you are always getting yourself mixed up in politics. Because your mother and I were such radical kids—socialists—in constant trouble with the police—it was 1904, 5. You have the idea it's O.K. for you and it is not O.K. in this country, which is a democracy. And you're running in the street like a fool. Your cousin saw you a few years ago in school, suspended. Sitting with other children in the auditorium, not allowed to go to class. You thought Mama and I didn't know.

Pa, that was thirty-five years ago, in high school. Anyway, what *about* Mama? You mentioned the Arzemich family. She was a dentist, wasn't she?

Right, a very capable woman.

Well, Mama probably felt bad about not getting to school and, you know, becoming something, having a profession like Mrs. What's-Her-Name. I mean, she did run the whole house and family and the office and people coming to live with us, but she was sad about that, surely.

He was quiet. Then he said, You're right. It was a shame, everything went into me, so I should go to school, I should graduate, I should be the doctor, I should have the profession. Poor woman, she was extremely smart. At least as smart as me. In Russia, in the movement, you know, when we were youngsters, she was considered the more valuable person. Very steady, honest. Made first-class contact with the workers, a real organizer. I could be only an intellectual. But maybe if life didn't pass so quick, speedy, like a winter day—short. You know, also, she was very musical, she had perfect pitch. A few years ago your sister made similar remarks to me about Mama. Questioning me, like history is my fault. Your brother only looked at me the way he does—not with complete approval.

THEN ONE DAY my father surprised me. He said he wanted to talk a little, but not too much, about love or sex or whatever it's called—its troubling persistence. He said that might happen to me, too, eventually. It should not be such a surprise. Then, a little accusingly, After all, I have been a man alone for many years. Did you ever think about that? Maybe I suffered. Did it even enter your mind? You're a grownup woman, after all.

But Pa, I wouldn't ever have thought of bringing up anything like that—you and Mama were so damn puritanical. I never heard you say the word "sex" till this day—either of you.

We were serious Socialists, he said. So? He looked at me, raising one nice thick eyebrow. You don't understand politics too well, do you?

Actually, I had thought of it now and then, his sexual aloneness. I was a grownup woman. But I turned it into a tactful question: Aren't you sometimes lonely, Pa?

I have a nice apartment.

Then he closed his eyes. He rested his talking self. I decided to water the plants. He opened one eye. Take it easy. Don't overwater.

Anyway, he said, only your mother, a person like her, could put up with me. Her patience—you know, I was always losing my temper. But finally with us everything was all right, ALL right, accomplished. Do you understand? Your brother and sister finished college, married. We had a beautiful grandchild. I was working very hard, like a dog. We were only fifty years old then, but, look, we bought the place in the country. Your sister and brother came often. You yourself were running around with a dozen kids in bathing suits all day. Your mama was planting all kinds of flowers every minute. Trees were growing. Your grandma, your babushka, sat on a good chair on the lawn. In back of her were birch trees. I put in a nice row of spruce. Then one day in the morning she comes to me, my wife. She shows me a spot over her left breast. I know right away. I don't touch it. I see it. In my mind I turn it this way and that. But I know in that minute, in one minute, everything is finished, finished—happiness, pleasure, finished, years ahead black.

No. That minute had been told to me a couple of years ago, maybe twice in ten years. Each time it nearly stopped my heart. No.

He recovered from the telling. Now, listen, this means, of course, that you should take care of yourself. I don't mean eat vegetables. I mean go to the doctor on time. Nowadays a woman as sick as your mama could live many years. Your sister, for example, after terrible operations—heart bypass, colon cancer—more she probably hides from me. She is running around to theatre, concerts, probably supports Lincoln Center. Ballet, chamber, symphony— three, four times a week. But you must pay attention. One good thing, don't laugh, is bananas. Really. Potassium. I myself eat one every day.

But, seriously, I'm running out of advice. It's too late to beg you to finish school, get a couple of degrees, a decent profession, be a little more strict with the children. They should be prepared for the future. Maybe they won't be as lucky as you. Well, no more advice. I restrain myself.

Now I'm changing the whole subject. I will ask you a favor. You have many friends—teachers, writers, intelligent people. Jews, non-Jews. These days I think often, especially after telling you the story a couple of months ago, about my brother Grisha. I want to know what happened to him.

I guess we know he was deported around 1922, right?

Yes, yes, but why did they go after him? The last ten years before that, he calmed down quite a bit, had a nice job, I think. But that's what they did—did you know? Even after the Palmer raids—

that was maybe 1919—they kept deporting people. They picked them up at home, at the Russian Artists' Club, at meetings. Of course, you weren't even around yet, maybe just born. They thought that these kids had in mind a big revolution—like in Russia. Some joke. Ignorance. Grisha and his friends didn't like Lenin from the beginning. More Bakunin. Emma Goldman, her boyfriend, I forgot his name.

Berkman.

Right. They were shipped, I believe, to Vladivostok. There must be a file somewhere. Archives salted away. Why did they go after him? Maybe they were mostly Jews. Anti-Semitism in the American blood from Europe—a little thinner, I suppose. But why didn't we talk? All the years not talking. Me seeing sick people day and night. Strangers. And not talking to my brother till all of a sudden he's on a ship. Gone.

Go home now. I don't have much more to tell you. Anyway, it's late. I have to prepare now all of my courage, not for sleep, for waking in the early morning, maybe 3 or 4 a.m. I have to be ready for them, my morning visitors—your babushka, your mama, most of all, to tell the truth, it's for your aunt, my sister, the youngest. She said to me, that day in the hospital, Don't leave me here, take me home to die. And I didn't. And her face looked at me that day and many, many mornings looks at me still.

I stood near the door holding my coat. A space at last for me to say something. My mouth open.

Enough, already, he said. I had the job to tell you how to take care of yourself, what to expect. About the heart—you know it was not a metaphor. But in the end a great thing, a really interesting thing, would be to find out what happened to our Grisha. You're smart. You can do it. Also, you'll see, you'll be lucky in this life to have something you must do to take your mind off all the things you didn't do.

Then he said, I suppose that is something like a joke. But, my dear girl, very serious.

About the Authors

Margaret Atwood

MARGARET ATWOOD was born in 1939 and raised in Ottawa, Ontario. She published her first book of poems, *Double Persephone*, in 1962, the same year she graduated from the University of Toronto. After receiving her master's degree from Radcliffe, she took a series of positions in English departments at various Canadian universities. In the fall of 1972, she achieved prominence with *Surfacing*, a novel popular in women's studies courses, and *Survival*, a thematic study of Canadian literature that helped disengage Canada's cultural identity from both English and American influences. In 1985 Atwood was given the Governor General's Award for her novel *The Handmaid's Tale*. Internationally one of the best-known Canadian writers, Atwood is the author of more than twenty books, including poetry, fiction, and nonfiction. Her works of fiction include *The Edible Woman* (1969), *Surfacing* (1972), *Lady Oracle* (1976), *Dancing Girls and Other Stories* (1977), *Life Before Man* (1978), *Bodily Harm* (1982), *Bluebeard's Egg* (1983) and *Murder in the Dark* (1983), both collections of short stories, *The Handmaid's Tale* (1986), *Cat's Eye* (1988), *Good Bones* (1992), *The Robber Bride* (1993), *Alias Grace* (1996), *The Blind Assassin* (2000), and *Oryx and Crake* (2003). Atwood currently lives and writes in Toronto.

Toni Cade Bambara

TONI CADE BAMBARA was born in 1939 and grew up in Harlem and Bedford-Stuyvestant, New York. In 1959, she graduated from

Queens College with a B.A. in theater arts and literature; she received an M.A. in American literature from City College of New York in 1963. Trained as a dancer and actress, Bambara worked with Katherine Dunham at the Etienne Decroux School of Mime in New York and Paris. She was a founding member of the Southern Collective of African-American Writers and edited the anthologies *The Black Woman* (1970) and *Tales and Short Stories for Black Folks* (1971). Bambara worked as an assistant professor at Rutgers University and a visiting professor at Duke University, where she frequently conducted writers' workshops. Her two collections of short stories, *Gorilla, My Love* (1972) and *The Sea Birds Are Still Alive and Other Stories* (1971), have received acclaim for their critique of stereotypes of black women. Her documentary *The Bombing of Osage* (1986) won the Best Documentary Award from the Pennsylvania Association of Broadcasters and the Documentary Award from the National Black Programming Consortium. In 1990, she received an Honorary Doctorate of Letters from the State University of New York–Albany. Diagnosed with colon cancer in 1993, Bambara died on December 9, 1995. Her works include *The Salt Eaters* (1980), which won the American Book Award, *If Blessing Comes* (1987), and *Raymond's Run* (1989), as well as several posthumous publications: *Deep Sightings and Rescue Missions: Fictions, Essays, and Conversations* (1996), *Those Bones Are Not My Child* (1999), and the documentary *W. E. B. DuBois: A Biography in Four Voices* (1996).

Andrea Barrett

ANDREA BARRETT was born on Cape Cod, Massachusetts, in 1954. She began her studies in the sciences, and her writing conveys her enthusiasm for history, science, and literature. Barrett had written four novels, *Lucid Stars* (1988), *Secret Harmonies* (1989), *The Middle Kingdom* (1991), and *The Forms of Water* (1993), before receiving the National Book Award for her first collection of short stories, *Ship Fever*, in 1996. Since then, she has published a novel,

The Voyage of the Narwhal (1998), and more short fiction in *Servants of the Map* (2002). Her body of work has taken on a life of its own as readers discover intertextual connections among her many characters. Barrett researches extensively while she writes, recently as a Fellow at the New York Public Library. She lives in Rochester, New York, and teaches writing at Warren Wilson College in North Carolina.

Ann Beattie

ANN BEATTIE was born in Washington, D.C., in 1947. She graduated from American University with a B.A. in English in 1969. During her graduate school days at the University of Connecticut, she began to take her writing seriously. She published her first short story, "A Rose for Judy Garland's Casket," in 1972. The recipient of a Guggenheim Grant (1977) and an Excellence Award from the National Academy and Institute of Arts and Letters (1980), Beattie taught briefly at the University of Virginia and at Harvard as the Briggs Copeland Lecturer in English. Beattie's works include *Distortions* (1976), *Chilly Scenes of Winter* (1976), *Secrets and Surprises* (1979), *Falling in Place* (1980), *Jacklighting* (1981), *The Burning House* (1982), *Love, Always* (1985), *Spectacles* (1985), *Where You'll Find Me, and Other Stories* (1986), *Picturing Will* (1989), *What Was Mine* (1991), *Another You* (1995), *My Life, Starring Dara Falcon* (1997), *Park City: New and Selected Stories* (1998), *Perfect Recall* (2001), and *The Doctor's House* (2002).

Amy Bloom

AMY BLOOM was born in New York City in 1953 and attended Wesleyan University, graduating in 1975. In 1978, she received her M.A. in social work from Smith College and opened a private psychotherapy practice in Middletown, Connecticut. Bloom's first book, *Come to Me* (1993), a collection of short stories, was a finalist for the National Book Award. Her work often involves the keen observation of relationships and people, an aspect that reflects her work in psychotherapy. When asked about the problems faced by her characters, Bloom responded, "The truth is I don't know anybody over thirty who has not had to encounter illness, change or loss, or love that did not work out the way they wanted it to . . . If you are paying attention at all, that's pretty much the way life develops. With all sorts of great things in it but also things that are difficult." Bloom is also the author of *Love Invents Us* (1996), *A Blind Man Can See How Much I Love You* (2000), and a book about the transsexual community entitled *Normal: Transsexual CEOs, Cross-dressing Cops, and Hermaphrodites with Attitude* (2002). She is divorced and now lives in Connecticut with her female partner.

Sandra Cisneros

SANDRA CISNEROS was born in Chicago in 1954. As an undergraduate, she studied at Loyola University of Chicago. She received a B.A. in English in 1976 and an M.F.A. in creative writing from the University of Iowa Writers' Workshop in 1978. Cisneros was awarded two National Endowment for the Arts Fellowships for fiction and poetry (1982, 1988), and a MacArthur Foundation Fellowship (1995). She has taught creative writing at many levels and has been a guest professor at several universities. Her writing is very personal and based on real people and real encounters: "If I were asked what it is I write about, I would have to say I write about those ghosts inside that haunt me, that will not let me sleep, of that which even memory does not like to mention." Her works include *Bad Boys* (1980), *The House on Mango Street* (1984), *My Wicked Wicked Ways* (1987), *Woman Hollering Creek and Other Stories* (1991), *Loose Woman: Poems* (1994), and *Caramelo* (2002). She lives in the American Southwest.

Louise Erdrich

LOUISE ERDRICH, a member of the Turtle Mountain Band of Chippewa, was born in 1954 in Little Falls, Minnesota, to a French Ojibwe mother and a German American father. Erdrich's mixed cultural heritage inspires her to explore the meaning of cultural identity in America through her fiction. She has said of her work, "My fondest hope is that people will be reading me in ten or twenty years from now as someone who has written about the American experience in all of its diversity." Erdrich received her undergraduate degree at Dartmouth College and attended the John Hopkins creative writing program. She has won the Pushcart Prize in Poetry, the O. Henry Prize for short fiction, and the National Book Critics Circle Award for *Love Medicine* (1984). She lives in Minneapolis, Minnesota, with her three youngest children. Her other works include *The Beet Queen* (1986), *The Bingo Palace* (1994), *Tales of Burning Love* (1996), *Tracks* (1998), *The Antelope Wife* (1998), *The Last Report on the Miracles at Little No Horse* (2001), and *The Master Butchers Singing Club* (2003).

Lynn Freed

LYNN FREED was born in South Africa and came to the United States as a graduate student, receiving her M.A. and Ph.D. from Columbia University. Her novels and short stories depict the complexities of South African life and the meanings of travel. She comments, "I am a natural foreigner. I find home all over the place, and not always where I expect to. I suppose travel, for me, is a sort of search for home." Her stories have been published in *The New Yorker, Harper's,* and *The Atlantic Monthly,* among many other periodicals, and her novels include *Heart Change* (1982), *Home Ground* (1986), *The Bungalow* (1993), *The Mirror* (1997), and *House of Women* (2002). Freed is currently Professor of English at the University of California, Davis.

Mary Gaitskill

MARY GAITSKILL was born in 1954 in Lexington, Kentucky. The daughter of a teacher and a social worker, she ran away from home at age sixteen and performed as a stripper in Toronto for two years. She received her B.A. at the University of Michigan in 1981, earning an award for her first story collection, *The Woman Who Knew Judo and Other Stories*. In her fiction she explores sex, isolation, obsession, and fear in American life. Gaitskill has said of her writing, "I usually start with just an image, or a conversation that haunts me, or an experience I had that's really striking to me. I work with superficial detail first . . . I just start with some small thing and dig into it that way." Gaitskill's other works include two collections of stories, *Bad Behavior* (1988) and *Because They Wanted To* (1997), and a novel, *Two Girls, Fat and Thin* (1991). Her writing has also appeared in the O. Henry Prize collections and *Best American Short Stories*.

Ellen Gilchrist

ELLEN GILCHRIST was born in Vicksburg, Mississippi, in 1935 and attended Vanderbilt University in Tennessee, where she received a B.A. in philosophy. After marrying at the age of nineteen and having three children, Gilchrist divorced her husband. She enrolled in a creative writing course at Millsaps College in Jackson, studying under Eudora Welty. She published her first book when she was forty-six, and since then has written over twenty novels and story collections. Gilchrist is best known for her regional short stories about the South. She has said, "I was a poet before I was a fiction writer, and one reason I like stories so much is because I feel they are so close to poetry." Her works include *Victory over Japan*, a winner of the National Book Award (1984), *Light Can Be Both Wave and Particle* (1989), *Rhoda: A Life in Stories* (1995), *The Courts of Love* (1996), *Sara Conley: A Novel* (1997), *Flights of Angels: Stories* (1998), and *I, Rhoda Manning, Go Hunting with My Daddy, & Other Stories* (2002).

Amy Hempel

AMY HEMPEL was born in Chicago in 1951. She attended Whittier College and San Francisco State College. Hempel has written three collections of short fiction: *Reasons to Live* (1985), *At the*

Gates of the Animal Kingdom (1995), and *Tumble Home: A Novella and Short Stories* (1997). In addition, Hempel has coauthored *Pit Bull: Lessons from Wall Street's Champion Day Trader* (1999) and coedited *Unleashed: Poems by Writers' Dogs* (1999). Hempel eloquently describes the inventiveness of her own writing: "I have stood a story on its head and started at the end. . . . I have dressed a delicate subject in hard, tough prose. And the reverse: described in lyrical language something ugly, something bad. Used a genteel voice to describe violence, an angry voice to take on the harmless." Hempel teaches at Bennington College and New School University and is a contributing editor for *Bomb Magazine*.

Gish Jen

GISH JEN was born in New York in 1956. A second-generation Chinese American, Jen grew up in the large Jewish community of Scarsdale, New York, and received her undergraduate degree from Harvard in 1986. In her short stories, Jen frequently returns to the theme of the mythology of the American Dream. She has commented, "It's a long way from Horatio Alger. I wanted to make the reader reconsider what a 'typical American' really is." Jen uses her characters to explore the conundrum of the complexity of ethnic and cultural identity in the United States. Her writing has appeared in *The New Yorker, The Atlantic Monthly,* and *The Best American Short Stories of the Century.* Her works include *In the American Society* (1986), *Typical American* (1991), *Mona in the Promised Land* (1996), and *Who's Irish?* (1999). She currently lives in Cambridge, Massachusetts, with her family.

Jamaica Kincaid

JAMAICA KINCAID was born Elaine Potter Richardson in St. John's, Antigua, in 1949. In 1966, at age seventeen, she left Antigua for the United States to work as an au pair in New York. Between 1966 and 1973 she earned her high school diploma, attended community college, studied photography at the New School, and attended Franconia College in New Hampshire for one year. In 1973, she changed her name to Jamaica Kincaid and began writing for *The Village Voice* and *Ingénue* magazine. In 1976, she became a staff writer for *The New Yorker,* where she worked for nine years. Kincaid's work is often characterized as angry. She responds, "I really do believe that whatever is a source of shame—if you are not responsible for it, such as the color of your skin or your sexuality— you should just wear it as a badge." Her works include *Annie John* (1985), *A Small Place* (1988), *Lucy* (1990), *At the Bottom of the River* (1992), *The Autobiography of My Mother* (1996), *My Brother* (1997), *My Garden* (1999), *Talk Stories* (2001), *Seed Gathering Atop the World* (2002), and *Mr. Potter* (2002). Kincaid teaches creative writing at Bennington College and Harvard University.

Jhumpa Lahiri

JHUMPA LAHIRI was born in London in 1967. Her family moved to Rhode Island while she was still an infant but often vacationed in Calcutta during her youth. She received her B.A. from Barnard College and went on to attain a Master's degree in English, a Master's in creative writing, and a Master's in comparative studies in literature and the arts, as well as a Ph.D. in Renaissance Studies, all from Boston University. Her first book was a collection of stories, *The Interpreter of Maladies* (1999), for which she won the Pulitzer Prize; her novel *The Namesake* was published in 2003. Lahiri's work is deeply influenced by her own multicultural heritage, and she incorporates Indian traditions in her stories as well as American culture. She says of her writing, "The characters I'm drawn to all face some barrier of communication. I like to write about people who think in a way they can't fully express." Lahiri currently lives near Greenwich Village in New York City.

Andrea Lee

ANDREA LEE was born in Philadelphia and received her Bachelor's and Master's degrees from Harvard University. Lee was a journalist for the *The New Yorker,* and her fiction and nonfiction have appeared in the *New York Times Magazine,* the *New York Times Book Review, The New Yorker,* and *Vogue.* Her first book, *Russian Journal* (1981), was nominated for a National Book Award and won the Jean Stein Award from the National Academy of Arts and Letters. Just three years later, she completed a novel, *Sarah Phillips* (1984). Lee delights in the short story, however, which she says "can offer a sharp concentrated insight like a stiletto thrust." Her first collection of stories, *Interesting Women,* was published in 2002. Lee married an Italian baron and lives with her husband and two children in a villa in Turin, Italy. She has commented, "In Italy, though I feel completely at home in my family and my household, I feel like a mindful sojourner—someone with deep knowledge of and few illusions about the country around me. Affectionate, but always slightly detached, always foreign." Many of her stories address these very issues, depicting American women living abroad. She is currently at work on another novel.

Bobbie Ann Mason

BOBBIE ANN MASON was born in 1940 in rural Mayfield, Kentucky, into a family of dairy farmers. Living in a small town, Mason found escape from her rural life in rock-and-roll, the local drive-in, and detective novels. She received her B.A. in 1962 from the University of Kentucky and her M.A. in 1966 from the State University of New York at Binghamton, and in 1972 she received her Ph.D. from the University of Connecticut. Mason has written extensively for magazines and has taught English as an assistant professor at Mansfield State College in Pennsylvania. Her earliest writings were two works of literary criticism, *Nabokov's Garden: A Nature Guide to "Ada"* (1974) and *The Girl Sleuth: A Feminist Guide to the Bobbsey Twins, Nancy Drew, and Their Sisters* (1975). Mason's subsequent works include *Shiloh and Other Stories* (1982), for which she was nominated for a P.E.N. Faulkner Award for fiction and was awarded the Ernest Hemingway Foundation Award, as well as

Spence + Lila (1988), *Love Life* (1989), *Feather Crown* (1993), *Midnight Magic* (1998) and *Zigzagging Down a Wild Trail* (2001). Her novel *In Country* (1985), about a girl whose father was killed in Vietnam, was developed into a feature film.

Alice McDermott

ALICE MCDERMOTT grew up in an Irish-American family on Long Island and attended the State University College at Oswego and the University of New Hampshire. All of her five novels draw on themes of storytelling, art, and memory. After publishing three works to great acclaim, *A Bigamist's Daughter* (1982), *That Night* (1987), and *At Weddings and Wakes* (1992), McDermott won the National Book Award for *Charming Billy* in 1998. Her most recent novel, *Child of My Heart* (2002), was written "quickly, almost in a single breath" after the events of September 11. McDermott works on more than one novel at a time, moving back and forth between projects, and writing while her children are in school. She comments, "I wouldn't want to spend energy just telling a story. I've got to hear the rhythm of the sentences; I want the music of the prose. I want to see ordinary things transformed not by the circumstances in which I see them but by the language with which they're described. That's what I love when I read."

Lorrie Moore

LORRIE MOORE grew up in Glen Falls, New York, and attended St. Lawrence University and Cornell University. Known for their sharp-witted characters, her stories convey both humor and tragedy. She has said, "I do feel that when you look out into the world, the world is funny. And people are funny. And that people always try to make each other laugh." Her stories explore topics such as music, birds, the significance of place, and children. Her works include *Self-Help* (1985), *Anagrams* (1986), *The Forgotten Helper* (1987), *Like Life* (1990), *Who Will Run the Frog Hospital* (1994), and *Birds of America* (1998). She also has edited *I Know Some Things: Stories About*

Childhood by Contemporary Writers (1992). Moore currently teaches creative writing at the University of Wisconsin.

Alice Munro

ALICE MUNRO was born in 1931 in Wingham, Ontario, to a farming family. She received a scholarship to the University of Western Ontario but left school to get married. Most of her stories have a regional focus, enlivened by characters with rural idiosyncrasies. Munro says of her writing, "I want to tell a story, in the old-fashioned way—what happens to somebody—but I want that 'what happens' to be delivered with quite a bit of interruption, turnarounds, and strangeness. I want the reader to feel something is astonishing—not the 'what happens' but the way everything happens." She is a three-time winner of the Governor General's Literary Award, Canada's highest literary honor. In addition, she has received the Lannan Literary Award and the W. H. Smith Award for the best book published in the United Kingdom in 1995. Her stories have appeared in *The New Yorker, The Atlantic Monthly, The Paris Review,* and other publications. Her works include *Dance of the Happy Shades* (1968), *The Beggar Maid* (1978), *The Progress of Love* (1986), *Friend of My Youth* (1990), *The Love of a Good Woman* (1998), and *Hateship, Friendship, Courtship, Loveship, Marriage* (2001).

Joyce Carol Oates

JOYCE CAROL OATES was born in 1938 in the countryside outside of Lockport, New York. She received her B.A. at Syracuse in 1960 and her M.A. at the University of Wisconsin in 1961. In 1962, she settled in Detroit with her husband. Describing her Detroit experience, Oates remarks, "Enduring the extraordinary racial tension of that city, and indeed, living only a few blocks from some of the looting and burning of the summer of 1967, made me want to write directly about the serious social concerns of our time." Between 1968 and 1978, Oates taught at the University of Windsor in Canada. In 1978, she moved to New Jersey to teach creative writing at Princeton University, where she is now the Roger S. Berlind Distinguished Professor of Humanities. Her novel *Blonde* was a finalist for both the 2001 National Book Award and the 2001 Pulitzer Prize. Her other works include *Them* (1969), *Wonderland* (1971), *Bellefleur* (1980), *You Must Remember This* (1987), *Because It Is Bitter, and Because It Is My Heart* (1990), *Where Is Here?: Stories* (1992), *Where Are You Going, Where Have You Been?: Selected Early Stories* (1993), *Haunted: Tales of the Grotesque* (1994), *Will You Always Love Me? And Other Stories* (1996), *We Were the Mulvaneys* (1996), *My Heart Laid Bare* (1999), *Blonde* (2001), and *I'll Take You There* (2002). Oates has also written under the pseudonym Rosamond Smith.

ZZ Packer

ZZ PACKER'S work has appeared in *The New Yorker*, *Harper's*, *Ploughshares*, *Story*, and in several anthologies, including *The Best American Short Stories 2000*. Packer recently received a Whiting Writer's Award and a Rona Jaffe Foundation Writer's Award. Her first short story collection, *Drinking Coffee Elsewhere*, was published in 2003. Packer's stories tell of characters caught between multiple worlds, not always able to see the truths of their lives. She comments, "Most writers would agree that fiction illuminates the greater truths of life in a way that living life does not." Packer currently lectures at Stanford University and is at work on her first novel, based on the "Buffalo Soldiers" who served in the army after the American Civil War.

Grace Paley

GRACE PALEY was born in 1922 in the Bronx, New York, to a family of Socialist Russian Jews. She studied at Hunter College and New York University. Paley received a Guggenheim Fellowship in 1961, a grant from the National Endowment for the Arts in 1966, and an award from the National Institute of Arts and Letters in

1970. She has taught at Columbia and Syracuse Universities and currently teaches at City College of New York, where she is writer-in-residence, and Sarah Lawrence College, where she has taught creative writing and literature for eighteen years. Paley draws from her experiences in New York to capture the everyday situations of people living in the city. Her works include *The Little Disturbances of Man* (1959), *Enormous Changes at the Last Minute* (1973), *Later the Same Day* (1985), *Collected Stories* (1994), and *Just as I Thought* (1998). She currently lives with her family in New York City and Thetford, Vermont.

Marisa Silver

MARISA SILVER worked in the film industry for ten years, directing such well-known motion pictures as *Indecency, Vital Signs,* and *He Said, She Said.* After enrolling in a creative writing program, however, she turned all of her attention to writing fiction and published a collection of stories, *Babe in Paradise,* in 2001. Her film background gives her a unique perspective on writing: "I think the concerns in film about where you place the camera are related to the concerns in fiction about where your point of view comes from. Are you close up to a person, looking right into their eyes? Or do you stand back far enough to see them in a landscape?" Her stories, set in Los Angeles, depict complex characters whose lives are deeply influenced by their surroundings. Although she plans to write a novel, Silver is at home with the short story: "It feels good to believe that this isn't just a stepping-stone for me but a craft I can continue to develop."

Stephanie Vaughn

STEPHANIE VAUGHN was born in Millersburg, Ohio, in 1943. She spent her childhood moving with her family to various military bases in Ohio, New York, Oklahoma, Texas, the Philippine Islands, and Italy. She received her B.A. from Ohio State University, her M.F.A. from the University of Iowa, and was awarded a Wallace Stegner Creative Writing Fellowship at Stanford University. Vaughn's stories have appeared in *Antaeus, The New Yorker, Redbook,* and the O. Henry and Pushcart Prize collections. Her collection of short stories, *Sweet Talk,* was published in 1990. Vaughn currently teaches creative writing and literature at Cornell University.

Permissions Acknowledgments

Grateful acknowledgment is made to the following for permission to reprint previously published material:

Alfred A. Knopf: "Beg, Sl Tog, Inc, Cont, Rep," from *Reasons to Live* by Amy Hempel. Copyright © 1985 by Amy Hempel. Reprinted by permission of Alfred A. Knopf, a division of Random House, Inc.

Alfred A. Knopf and Faber and Faber Ltd.: "Dancing in America," From *Birds of America* by Lorrie Moore. Copyright © 1998 by Lorrie Moore. Reprinted by permission of Alfred A. Knopf, a division of Random House, Inc., and Faber and Faber Ltd.

Alfred A. Knopf, McClelland & Stewart Ltd., and The Random House Group Limited: "The Floating Bridge," from *Hateship, Courtship, Loveship, Marriage* by Alice Munro. Copyright © 2001 by Alice Munro. Reprinted by permission of Alfred A. Knopf, a division of Random House, Inc., McClelland & Stewart Ltd., *The Canadian Publishers* and The Random House Group Limited.

Don Congdon Associates, Inc.: "Light Can Be Both Wave and Particle," from *Light Can Be Both Wave and Particle* by Ellen Gilchrist. Copyright © 1989 by Ellen Gilchrist. Reprinted by permission of Don Congdon Associates, Inc.

Doubleday, McClelland & Stewart Ltd. and Bloomsbury Publishing plc.: "Hairball," from *Wilderness Tips* by Margaret Atwood. Copyright © 1991 by O. W. Toad Limited. Reprinted by permission of Doubleday, a division of Random House, Inc., McClelland & Stewart Ltd., *The Canadian Publishers,* and Bloomsbury Publishing plc.

Elaine Markson Literary Agency: "My Father Addresses Me on the Facts of Old Age," first appeared in *The New Yorker* 2002. Copyright © by Grace Paley. Reprinted by permission of the Elaine Markson Literary Agency.

Georges Borchardt, Inc.: "Able, Baker, Charlie, Dog," by Stephanie Vaughn. Copyright © 1990 by Stephanie Vaughn. Reprinted by permission of Georges Borchardt, Inc.

Harcourt, Inc. and William Morris Agency, Inc.: "Ma, a Memoir," first appeared in *The New Yorker* on September 30, 1996. Copyright © 1996 by Lynn Freed, and subsequently in *The Curse of the Appropriate Man*. Copyright © 1999 by Lynn Freed. Reprinted by permission of Harcourt, Inc. and the William Morris Agency, Inc. on behalf of the author.

HarperCollins Publishers Inc. and Rosenstone/Wender: "Silver Water," from *Come to Me* by Amy Bloom. Copyright © 1993 by Amy Bloom. No part of this material may be reproduced in any way in whole or in part without the express written permission of the author. Reprinted by permission of HarperCollins Publishers Inc. and Rosenstone/Wender.

HarperCollins Publishers Inc. and Joyce Carol Oates on behalf of The Ontario Review, Inc.:" "Love Forever," from *Where Is Here? Stories* by Joyce Carol Oates. Copyright © 1992 by The Ontario Review, Inc. Reprinted by permission of HarperCollins Publishers Inc. and Joyce Carol Oates on behalf of The Ontario Review, Inc.

The Harriet Wasserman Literary Agency, Inc.: "Enough," originally published in *The New Yorker* (April 10, 2002). Copyright © 2002 Alice McDermott. Reprinted by permission of the Harriet Wasserman Literary Agency, Inc.

Houghton Mifflin Company and HarperCollins Publishers Ltd.: "A Temporary Matter," from *The Interpreter of Maladies* by Jhumpa Lahiri. Copyright © 1999 by Jhumpa Lahiri. All rights reserved. Reprinted by permission of Houghton Mifflin Company and HarperCollins Publishers Ltd.

International Creative Management, Inc.: "Big Bertha Stories." Copyright © 1982 by Bobbie Ann Mason. Reprinted by permission of International Creative Management, Inc.

ABOUT THE EDITOR

WENDY MARTIN is Chair of the Department of English at Claremont Graduate University, where she has been Professor of American Literature and American Studies since 1987; previously she was on the faculty at Queens College, CUNY. She has been a visiting professor at Stanford University, the University of North Carolina, and the University of California at Los Angeles. The author of numerous articles and reviews on American women writers and early American literature and culture, she is the founding editor of *Women's Studies: An Interdisciplinary Journal,* which she has edited since 1972. She is the author of *An American Triptych: The Lives and Work of Anne Bradstreet, Emily Dickinson, and Adrienne Rich* (1984) and the editor of *The American Sisterhood: Feminist Writing from Colonial Times to the Present* (1972); *New Essays on The "Awakening"* (1988); *We Are the Stories We Tell: The Best Short Stories by North American Women Since 1945* (1990); *Colonial American Travel Narratives* (1994); *The Beacon Book of Essays by Contemporary American Women* (1997); and *The Cambridge Companion to Emily Dickinson* (2002). She is also a member of the editorial board of *The Heath Anthology of American Literature.*